IMOGEN ROBERTSON

Theft of Life

headline
review

First published in 2014 by HEADLINE REVIEW
An imprint of HEADLINE PUBLISHING GROUP

First published in paperback in 2015 by HEADLINE REVIEW
An imprint of HEADLINE PUBLISHING GROUP

1

Cataloguing in Publication Data is available from the British Library

ISBN 978 0 7553 9017 5

Typeset in Poliphilus and Blado by Palimpsest Book Production Limited,
Falkirk, Stirlingshire

Printed and bound in Great Britain by
Clays Ltd, St Ives plc

HEADLINE PUBLISHING GROUP
An Hachette UK Company
338 Euston Road
London NW1 3BH

www.headline.co.uk
www.hachette.co.uk

To Flora

ACKNOWLEDGEMENTS

As always, grateful thanks to my brilliant editor, Flora Rees, everyone at Headline and to my agent Annette Green. I really have no idea what I'd do without them. Well, I do – I'd starve in a gutter in a pile of my own spelling mistakes and throttled by dangling narrative threads.

My particular thanks to Kayo Chingonyi for his generous and thoughtful reading of the manuscript.

More than thanks to my husband, Ned Palmer, for dragging me out of every hole I fell into while writing this book.

I'd also like to thank Peter Fryer, a man I've never met but whose brilliant history of black people in Britain, *Staying Power*, introduced me to the works of Ignatius Sancho, 1729–80, Olaudah Equiano 1745–97 and Quobna Ottobah Cugoano, 1757 –?. It is my sincere hope that their voices echo somewhere in these pages.

I own I am shock'd at the purchase of slaves
And fear those who buy them and sell them are knaves;
What I hear of their hardships, their tortures and groans,
Is almost enough to drive pity from stones.

I pity them greatly, but I must be mum
For how could we do without sugar and rum?

William Cowper 'Pity for Poor Africans'
Northampton Mercury, 9 August 1788

*Look round upon the miserable fate of almost all of our unfortunate colour
— superadded to ignorance, — see slavery, and the contempt of those very
wretches who roll in affluence from our labours [. . .] hear the ill-bred and
heart-racking abuse of the foolish vulgar. — You, S[oubis]e, tread as
cautiously as the strictest rectitude can guide ye — yet must you suffer
from this —*

Letter from Ignatius Sancho to Mr Soubise
Richmond, 11 October 1772

PART I

I.1

Saturday, 7 May 1785

T HE BODY WAS STAKED out in the north-east corner of the church-yard. The first light of a warm spring morning glanced off the pale stone of St Paul's Cathedral, and shone in full blank surprise on the corpse. A driver taking barrels of coriander seed north first noticed the body face down in the dew. It was, or had been, a man, and the shift covering him, though yellow with age, still showed up strongly against the fresh-mown grass. The driver shouted down from his perch high on the wagon to a pair of men walking towards the docks, pointed over the railings with his whip, then urged his horses on. The men shrugged at each other and went to investigate, peering through the metal bars into the shadow of the Cathedral, then seeing what the driver had seen, they climbed over. The corpse had lengths of rope tied to his wrists and ankles, and the rope on his right ankle was attached to a stake half-driven into the ground. They approached cautiously. One knelt down by the corpse's head and lifted it slightly from the shoulder. What they saw frightened them. They began to call out. The younger man swung himself back over the railings and, yelling as he went, ran to the door of the Chapter House and started beating on it with his fist.

William Geddings should have seen nothing of this. In the general way of things he would have woken in Berkeley Square, put on his footman's livery in his attic bedroom then joined the rest of the upper servants for breakfast before beginning his duties in the house. The previous evening, however, he had gone to hear the music at the Elephant in Fenchurch Street, and by chance met an old shipmate. They had drunk too much in celebration of their deliverance, and he had slept in his friend's room in Honey Lane Market.

By the time he left, the air was already warm. Only a month ago, back home in Sussex, there had been snow on the ground, but now the air was dry and heavy. William's head throbbed and the morning light seemed tinged with orange and red. Whenever the family he served came to London he would ask permission to go, once or twice, to the places where other Africans gathered, and there listen to the music and songs of his childhood and those he had heard first as a slave in Jamaica. Rich, dancing, talking tunes they were, and some had already worked their way through the hands of curious English and German composers into the drawing rooms of the city. He would hear them from time to time as he passed trays of champagne glasses among the guests at Berkeley Square – strange, half-strangled translations of his own heritage. He did not completely understand his compulsion to seek out the originals; for the music brought back memories painful as well as sweet. His own language returned to his tongue, and remade him into the boy he had been. In the pulse of the music and talk around him he caught glimpses of his lost family, his father's laugh and the feel of the black soil of the fields outside his village between his fingers. When his shipmate saw him and they embraced, under the joy of seeing him alive and safe in London, William's body flickered with remembered pain: the weight of iron on his ankles, the sores on his side, the stench. No wonder they drank deeply. Now, his blood thickened by the memories, he prepared to return to the world of the

English family he served, to the dramas and pleasures of the servants' hall, to his responsibilities.

He had set out at a good pace, happy he would be back in Berkeley Square before the house was fully awake. Then he saw the crowd gathering close to St Paul's Cathedral's northern flank, inside the railings. He hesitated, but curiosity drove off the pain in his head; he crossed the roadway and clambered up on the stone wall, clinging onto the railings to look down at whatever the crowd was circling.

A constable was trying to shoo the people back, but what they saw excited them too much and they continued to move past and about him like water round a rock. It was an early-morning crowd all dressed in labouring clothes; the ragged who had been turfed out of their tuppenny beds at first light; the porters on their way to the riverside and markets; servants and housewives ready to lose sleep for the best bargains. London's broad base in all its colours and conditions. Then, as the constable harried and begged them to move away, William caught his first sight of the body. A man, dressed only in his undershirt, face down in the dirt. A drunk? A lunatic? But the people seemed disturbed – shocked, not amused. William lifted himself a little higher and craned his neck. He saw the loops of rope. The skin on the body's thin and naked calves looked a greyish-blue. William began to sweat under his linen shirt. A clergyman was kneeling by the man's head, hiding it from William's view. As he lifted his eyes and looked around the crowd, William saw desperate tears running down his pink, round face.

'I cannot get it off!' he cried out. 'There's a padlock! Is there a key?'

William saw the iron and leather bands around the body's skull, and his heart began to thud, leap and pitch but he could not look away. A man in a soft-brimmed hat pushed to the front of the crowd and knelt by the priest. He swung his satchel off his shoulder and pulled out a chisel and hammer. William's mouth was dry. The hammer came down and the echo of it was lost in the sudden clang of the bell of St Paul's striking the half-hour. The priest pulled away the broken padlock and threw it aside, then, as the man with the tools stood back, he turned the body over gently, onto his knee.

The heavy metal mask which still hid the corpse's face was a rough bit of work. It was a rude clamp, with a plate welded under the chin to hold the jaw closed. Almond-shaped eye-holes, a riveted pyramid open at the base for the nose, and a blank where a mouth should be so that whoever wore it could breathe and go about their work, but could neither eat, drink nor speak. William had never seen such a thing on the head of a white man. The priest lifted it carefully away and William saw the face underneath, the high cheekbones, long nose and sharp chin, a heavy white stubble. The skin was slightly purplish, bruised. So many years older, but it was him. Unmistakably him. It seemed to William as if he had come crashing and floundering down to the dust, though he still could not move. Suddenly he smelled the heat of the docks, tar and rope; the sweet scent of white orange blossom . . .

The priest looked around the crowd. 'Does anyone know this man? His name?'

William managed to release his grip on the railings and, slowly and painfully, slid down to the roadway, then began to walk away while the priest was still calling for a name. He reached the relative privacy of Swan Yard before his stomach gave a final heave and he threw up, resting his forearm against the crumbling Tudor bricks among the chemical stink coming from the workshops and the sharp rot of old piss. He rested there a minute till the colours of London, the rattle of carriages and the fading clap of the bells returned him the five thousand miles and fifteen years from the harbour of Kingston, Jamaica. Then he began, a little more unsteadily now, his walk home to the London residence of the Earl of Sussex and his family in Berkeley Square where his employer, Mrs Harriet Westerman, was staying for some weeks; and where, even now, she would be stirring in her bed and ringing her bell for her maid and her coffee.

Cutter, the clerk of Hinckley's Bookseller, Stationer & Printer in Ivy Lane, brought word of the body in on his first breath. He was delighted to have the chance to tell the news. Ivy Lane was close by St Paul's, off Paternoster Row, so in the heart of the book-printing and bookselling district of the capital. He thought the others would all have heard about it by now, but it seemed they had stumbled from their lodgings to their place of employment at first light, before the body was found. The presses were already at work upstairs; the more hours of light in the day there were, the more pages could be printed. Cutter, however, who served, bowed and totted up the accounts in the shop, did not come in until the later hour of eight. The respectable clientele who bought their stock of novels, histories, prints, music and more novels never thought to attend before nine. He rattled through a description of the body and its discovery with great excitement.

The shop's senior salesman and de facto manager, Mr Francis Glass, looked up sharply at the mention of the mask but made no comment.

'Perhaps they'll never know who he is,' Cutter said cheerfully, looking about the shop for something to neaten or straighten or dust with the edge of his coat-sleeve. 'I dare say they'll have to keep his head in a jar of spirits. All the abandoned ladies of London can go and see if it's their husband come back.'

Mr Francis Glass began writing in the account book again and spoke without looking up. 'Was he white, this man in the churchyard?'

Cutter had found a mark visible only to himself on the edge of a bookshelf, seldom disturbed, holding a run of Histories of the Anglican Church. He scrubbed at it furiously. 'What? Oh yes. He was white. Why do you ask?'

Mr Glass returned his pen to its stand and carefully blotted the page.

'Because in that case it will not be long before he is identified, I am sure. All the West Indian slavers and traders know each other.' Puzzled, Cutter frowned and opened his mouth. Francis closed the book. 'What you describe is a punishment mask for slaves, Cutter. The dead man must have connections with the West Indian community in London, don't you think?' His voice was as calm as ever.

Cutter suddenly became aware that the conversation was moving into a dangerous area, but was not quite sure why. He was about to ask something further, but at that moment Francis looked up at him. Mr Glass had large eyes, very dark, and the smooth ebony glow of his skin made Cutter very conscious of the red veins becoming visible in his own cheeks as he reached middle age. 'Oh, was it? Do they? No head in a jar then. Understood.' He returned to his invisible mark with renewed concentration.

I.2

MRS MARTIN WAS HOUSEKEEPER to the family of the Earl of Sussex, a role which gave her both standing and satisfaction. She had grown used to the great ancestral hall in Hartswood, but since she was by birth, habit and choice a Londoner, she had an especial love of the family's Town residence at 24, Berkeley Square and took pride in its smooth running. The senior servants of the other great families of England thought Mrs Martin very young for her responsibilities but, they admitted grudgingly, she acquitted herself well – particularly given the circumstances.

Jonathan Thornleigh, Earl of Sussex, nominal head of the family and inheritor of its vast wealth, was eleven; his elder sister, Lady Susan, was fourteen. The pair were orphans. They were not the first children of blood to find themselves parentless, but their situation was complicated by the fact that they had been raised in ignorance of their heritage, growing up above a music shop in Soho; furthermore, their murdered father had at his death entrusted the children to the care of a young writer and lover of music named Owen Graves.

The great families of England had been disturbed. Most of the dukes in the country could claim some sort of kinship with the Thornleigh family, and it was suggested to young Graves – a good fellow, but of no family at all – that it might be more fitting to bring up the children in one of their established, aristocratic households. Graves, uncertain of his capacity, also thought it might be for the best, but Jonathan and Susan would not leave him. So Mr Graves took on his shoulders the management of the young Earl's great wealth, and to help him brought into the household an elderly, impoverished widow named Mrs Service, who had known the children since their birth. Graves also took on the care of the Honorable Eustache Thornleigh, half-uncle to the newly orphaned Jonathan and Susan, though a little younger than them both. Various dukes had offered the child a home also, but were secretly relieved when he refused them. Eustache reminded them too much of his horrendous parents and their disgrace.

Graves saw Thornleigh Hall rebuilt after a terrible fire, and bought the lease of a handsome building in Berkeley Square. He seemed to be discharging his responsibilities well enough and had since married himself and purchased with his wife's dowry the little music shop where the Earl had been born. In the face of such 'circumstances', the housekeeper Mrs Martin managed very well indeed.

Mrs Martin had arrived in London three months ago, in the middle of February, and opened up the house in Berkeley Square. She set about airing the nursery rooms for Lord Sussex, Lady Susan and Master Eustache, hired two girls as undermaids, a kitchen boy and, after a lengthy correspondence with Mrs Service, an excellent cook.

The idea was that now Lady Susan was fourteen years old, it was time she acquired a little town polish. Graves wrote to the Duke of Devonshire for advice and he suggested that Susan attend as a day pupil one of the fashionable schools for young ladies in the capital; he recommended one based in Golden Square. His Grace also gave a hint that perhaps the young Earl should attend one of the better schools close to London. It was time the children got to know their peers and the world in which they operated.

Mr Graves took His Grace's advice very seriously, and after talking it over with Mrs Service and Verity, his wife, the plan was made. They would spend at least two months in London. Jonathan and Eustache would take lessons in the morning to prepare them for the curriculum at Harrow or Eton. Susan would go to school and learn how to behave in a manner fitting to her rank. Graves would deal in person with the bankers, investors, creditors and lawyers who swarmed round Jonathan's money, and Verity would accompany him, to make sure he didn't mind it all too much.

The plan had gone terribly wrong. First of all, Graves's wife had discovered she was in a delicate condition and began to feel the exhaustion that often troubles young mothers-to-be. Her physician advised her to remain in the country, but she insisted that Graves go up to London without her. Mrs Service would be mistress of the London house in her place and she would have peace in the country. Graves reluctantly agreed and the family came to town. Then, after only a fortnight had passed, their Sussex neighbour, Mrs Harriet Westerman, descended on them for a visit of unknown duration with her own two children, several servants and only half a day's notice. Her sudden arrival shook up the whole household. She also seemed to be in a high temper. Her personal servants were discreet, but there were hints that Mrs Westerman had been arguing with her younger sister, Rachel. To crown it all, two days ago, Lady Susan had come home with a letter from the Headmistress of the Respectable Establishment. It covered a great many pages with complaints relating to Susan's character and behaviour, and an assertion that unless she undertook to behave better in future she would no longer be welcome at the school. Mr Graves had spoken to the girl at length about the letter and Susan had refused absolutely to apologise for anything or return to Golden Square. Mrs Martin herself had heard the end of the interview, when the young lady had sworn that if Graves expected her to go back there, they would have to tie her up and deliver her like a parcel. The elegant furniture of Berkeley Square shuddered as she ran from her guardian's office and slammed every intervening door between there and her own chamber at the top of the house.

Now, despite all of Mrs Martin's best efforts on this Saturday morning, the general bad temper and confusion had made its way down into the servants' hall. William, Mrs Westerman's senior footman who had travelled with her, should have been helping to serve breakfast, but instead he was having a rather tense interview with Mrs Westerman's maid, Dido, in one corner of the kitchen. He hadn't been home last night, and he and the maid were sweethearts. Not so sweet this morning though. Mrs Martin would never have allowed similar relations between the servants under her authority, but these two served Mrs Westerman, so she could do nothing but hope they would not quarrel too loudly. The cook's boy, in trying to eavesdrop, had left the sausages to burn, which led to a great deal of smoke and raised voices. Cook was trying to pack a hamper while asking everyone in earshot if they wanted kippers this morning upstairs and whether the children liked raisin bread, and Mrs Westerman's coachman was arguing with the groom about their mistress's abilities as a judge of horseflesh. Into the middle of this turmoil Philip, senior footman at Berkeley Square and Mrs Martin's right hand, came charging into the room, his face red and coffee spilled over the front of his waistcoat.

'Philip, what on earth have you done?' Mrs Martin felt her voice had come uncomfortably close to a wail.

'Those damned children! Young Master Westerman always gets My Lord playing the goat,' Philip said, pulling off his jacket and throwing it over the back of a wooden chair. Mrs Westerman's coachman and groom turned slowly towards him and glowered. Any suggestion of an insult to young Stephen was an insult to them. Philip didn't notice.

'Simon, go and fetch a clean waistcoat from my room.' He began to undo his buttons as the kitchen boy scampered out and up the back stairs, thudding all the way, and Mrs Martin took over the watch on the next batch of sausages. 'Master Stephen teased My Lord into chasing him round the table while I was serving Mr Graves his coffee, then I swear Master Eustache just put out his foot to trip him as he came by. He goes falling into me and the pot goes flying.' The groom and coachman turned back to their discussion. They felt no obligation to defend Master Eustache.

'Onto Mr Graves too?' Mrs Martin asked.

'Oh yes. He shouted at them to sit still and went up to change.'

Mr Graves's valet sprang to his feet. 'You should have told me at once!'

'I'm telling you now, aren't I?' Philip said. 'Where is that damn boy with my waistcoat?'

Mrs Martin took a deep breath. 'And the table linens?'

'Covered in coffee.' The boy came back, waistcoat over his arm and red in the face. Philip grabbed it from him.

'I shall take up fresh linen,' Mrs Martin said. 'William, perhaps you could go and serve. Philip, stay here until you have recovered your temper. Dido, is your mistress come down yet?'

'She is dressed and will be down as soon as she has finished reading her sister's letter.' There was a collective groan.

'Enough!' Mrs Martin said. 'Do the work you are paid for. Behave as if you work in the chophouse and you may go and earn your living there. Cook, if those sausages burn too, I shall take their purchase price from your wages.' She found the key to the linen cupboard on the ring at her waist and strode out of the room.

By the time Mrs Martin reached it, the Breakfast Room was surprisingly quiet. Master Eustache was reading a book, but as Mrs Martin deftly removed and replaced the soiled cloth at the head of the table she thought she saw him look across at Lord Sussex from under his long dark eyelashes and grin. Jonathan, who would one day control a fortune to make him the envy of kings, was slightly flushed and staring hard at the table in front of him. He was a sensitive boy, eager to please, and hated it when Graves shouted at him. Stephen Westerman was chewing toast and sitting sideways in his seat to stare out into the Square behind him. Mrs Martin thought, not for the first time, that it was very sensible of Mrs Service to take her own modest breakfast in her room.

The door opened and Lady Susan entered, her back ramrod straight. She was shaping up to be a very pretty young woman, fair like her brother and with large blue eyes and clear skin, but quick and lively as a monkey. She had a talent for play-acting and loved to make the servants laugh with her impressions of their friends and neighbours. They were horribly accurate, but Mrs Martin had begun to try and persuade the staff not to encourage her. Susan would soon be entering the world of drawing rooms and assemblies, and her talents for mimicry would earn her no friends there. As soon as she saw that her guardian was not present, the girl seemed to relax a little and even smiled at William when he put down a plate in front of her and poured her tea. He winked at her, which Mrs Martin pretended not to notice.

'Is there a kipper, Mrs Martin?' Stephen asked.

'I shall ask Cook to make you one, Master Stephen,' she said, smoothing down the cloth.

'Oh, may I have one too, Mrs Martin?' Jonathan said.

'Certainly, My Lord.' The child blushed a deeper pink. They had

11

been asked to address the children more formally now, and no one much liked the change, least of all the little aristocrats. Graves came back into the room, no stains of coffee visible.

'And for me please,' he said.

Mrs Martin nodded to William and took his station by the buffet as he left the room with the order.

'I'm sorry I fell over, Graves,' Jonathan said quietly.

'I seem to have survived, Jon,' he answered with a smile, then looked at Stephen Westerman and raised his eyebrows. Jonathan nudged him.

'What? Oh, I'm sorry for running, Graves,' the boy said quickly.

Graves leaned back while Mrs Martin shook out a napkin and placed it over his lap. 'Good, the servants have enough to do without you two creating more work. Thank you, Mrs Martin.' He looked at Susan. 'And may I expect any apology from *you* this morning, Susan?'

The girl said nothing. Mrs Martin wanted to shake her. Any fool could see the girl was upset. Her eyes were damp and Anne Westerman's nurse said Susan had been weeping since the letter from her headmistress had arrived, but she was proud as the devil himself.

'I see. Jonathan, Stephen, we shall go to the balloon-raising as promised.' The boys let out whoops, then sat very straight and quiet when Graves's eye rested on them again. 'Susan, I have spoken to Mrs Service. She goes to see an acquaintance of hers this morning who knows a great deal about female education. You shall go with her, not to Barbican.'

The girl turned towards him, her eyes wide. 'Graves, no! It is Monsieur Blanchard! It is the same machine with which he crossed the Channel! I so want to go!'

Mr Graves only shook his head. 'I want an apology and an explanation from you, Susan. There will be no more treats and excursions until I receive both. How can I take you into the civilised world until you know how to behave in it?'

It broke Mrs Martin's heart. The girl stared back at her plate, breathing hard against her stays. Go steady, my dear, Mrs Martin thought, or you shall faint. After a few moments Susan spoke very quietly. 'I have had all I wish to eat, Graves. May I leave the table?' A bite of bread and butter was no breakfast for a growing girl, Mrs Martin thought, but it was not her place to speak.

'You may.'

Susan left with an attempt at dignity, nodding to Mrs Martin as she did, but they all heard the choking noise she made as she began to cry the moment she was through the door, and her steps as she raced back upstairs to her room.

She must have passed Mrs Westerman on her way, for the latter came into the room looking rather distracted, and it was only William's quick reactions that saved the kippers from being knocked to the floor as he entered with them on a tray behind her.

'No balloons for Susan, I assume,' she said as she sat down and Mrs Martin served her coffee from the fresh pot.

'Good morning, Mrs Westerman,' Graves replied. 'No, not today. But Anne is still welcome to join us if you think she would enjoy it.'

Harriet Westerman smiled. 'She is singing her new balloon song already. Her nurse will go with you, of course.'

'She was singing it all last evening too,' Stephen said, and rolled his eyes before beginning on his kipper. 'I'm not sure it really is a song, Mama, when all she does is chant *baallooon!* in a silly voice.'

'It amused you yesterday,' she replied.

Her son grinned and swallowed whatever was in his mouth with a great sucking gulp, then waved his fork about as he answered. 'Well, it is a bit funny, and then when we laughed she started doing it more and more. Even Susan laughed till she could hardly breathe in her frock.'

The mention of her name made everyone quiet. The fork was reapplied to the kipper. Graves cleared his throat. 'Eustache, would you like to come and see the balloon?'

The boy looked around at them all from under his lashes without lowering his book, then sighed. 'No, thank you, Graves.'

'But Eustache, it's a *balloon*!' Stephen said in amazement, a forkful of kipper forgotten halfway to his mouth. 'You can't just want to stay here and *read*! We don't even have lessons today.' The bit of kipper fell back onto his plate and he huffed unhappily at it.

'I can and I do, as it happens, Stephen.' There was something about the way he spoke that made any phrase sound vaguely insulting. Clever enough to confuse his tutors at times, Eustache spoke like a boy three times his age. It could be unnerving, and such a way of watching people. Mrs Martin thought of what she had heard of his mother — beautiful, corrupted, mad — then found she could not look at Eustache any more. 'I don't have to go, do I, Graves?'

His guardian looked slightly uncomfortable. 'No, Eustache, but you cannot stay in the house all day. If you do not wish to come with us, perhaps you might go with Mrs Service and Susan. At least you'll get some air that way.'

Eustache looked back to his book and turned a page with a noisy sigh. 'I will.'

Harriet finished her coffee and held the cup up to Mrs Martin. She went to refill it, glad to stop thinking about Eustache. Mrs Westerman had a lovely smile. It came from her eyes and made you realise she was a young woman still. Mrs Martin felt guilty about her less than charitable feelings for the young widow. The house was big enough for them all and she was a dear friend and neighbour in Sussex, so she should always be made welcome, even if she descended on them at a moment's notice. Hadn't Mrs Westerman saved the lives of Jonathan and Susan? Hadn't she saved her brother-in-law from the executioner's axe only last year? Yet here she was, polite and genteel as any woman. Let people call her wild or unfeeling. Let the booksellers and printmakers spread their sensational versions of her adventures. Let the Sussex gentry tut and fuss at her behaviour. It was jealousy. It was only natural that she could be a little eccentric, a little impulsive after all her travels and troubles. They all had cause to be grateful she was such good friends with Mr Gabriel Crowther – and Mrs Martin had never seen anything improper in their relationship. Anyone saying otherwise was a mean-spirited gossip! Mrs Westerman was a good woman who helped people. She had two handsome, kind-hearted children, an estate that produced some of the best potted fruits Mrs Martin had ever tasted, and she knew how to conduct herself with ease and charm in the best houses in the country . . . when she wanted to. Why, the King himself had bowed over her hand and called her a good woman.

Mrs Martin went back to her post by the sideboard. The morning was under her control again. The kippers were being eaten with apparent delight and William was handing round sausages, not burned, to those that wanted them. Philip would have calmed down by now, and with most of the family out for the day Mrs Martin would be free to make all those necessary adjustments in the household to keep it running as well as it should.

Mrs Westerman patted her napkin to her lips. 'William, Dido said you needed to speak to me. Perhaps you can come to my room after breakfast. Something about a body?'

It is a testament to Mrs Martin's character that the coffee pot was not dropped a second time.

I.3

BREAKFAST DONE, HARRIET WESTERMAN returned to her private sitting room on the first floor and picked up her sister's letter again. It could be read as an apology for interfering, for telling Harriet her business, but as she restated all her arguments and insisted on the fact that her actions were justified, it did not read as a very *sincere* apology. Harriet loved her sister, but she irritated her deeply on occasion. Since Rachel had given birth to a daughter and bloomed into motherhood so completely, the irritations had increased, for she seemed to believe that the event had conferred on her some ultimate wisdom. Every time she wished to criticise Harriet or her behaviour, she began her little homilies with, 'as the mother of a daughter . . .' and this drove Harriet to screaming point. She had been the mother of a daughter for many years more than Rachel – not a particularly good one perhaps, but nevertheless . . . She put the letter down and stared miserably out into the Square below. There was the guilt again. Harriet loved her children, fiercely, absolutely, but her world consisted of more than her son, her daughter and their interests. She sometimes thought that made her an unnatural parent in Rachel's eyes. Perhaps charging off to London had been a mistake. She had no pressing need to be here and at least in Hartswood she had plenty to do in running the estate.

A light rap on the door and William entered and gave his slight, formal bow. He looked grim and unhappy. Harriet asked him why they needed to speak and he replied that as far as he was concerned, they did not need to speak at all. He apologised, but it was all some foolishness of Dido's.

'Some foolishness of Dido's? A body?' Harriet's voice was sharp. 'Come, William. Simply tell me what happened and let me judge for myself. You were out of the house last night, I think?'

He did not look up but she heard him draw in a deep breath. 'I was. And on my way back here this morning I saw the corpse of a Jamaican plantation-owner in St Paul's churchyard, ma'am. Naked, apart from his undershirt, rope on his ankles and wrists as if he was being staked out for a whipping and with a punishment mask clamped round his head. I confess, Mrs Westerman, I don't see what business that is of Dido's, or of yours.'

There was a pause while Harriet let the words settle in her mind and controlled the shock of them. 'I am minded to agree with you, William.' She turned in her chair to look at him more directly, Rachel's letter still loose between her fingers. 'How did you know him if he was wearing a mask?'

'They struck it off while I was watching.'

'Was he stabbed? Throttled?'

William put his hands behind his back, spoke evenly. 'I cannot say for certain, but I did not see much blood, and after a whipping of that kind there is normally a great deal.'

'But there is something more in this. Dido would not want me to know about dead bodies as a matter of course; she fears I'll tear my lace running after them. Why would she risk that by sending you to me?'

He did not smile. 'No one knew him in the crowd. His name was Trimnell, Mrs Westerman. He owned a small estate in Clarendon, Jamaica. He only arrived back in London six weeks ago. I said all of this to Dido as I came into breakfast. She thinks I should return to St Paul's and give the authorities his name, but I would rather let things alone.'

Harriet did not normally believe in letting things alone, but neither did she want to place her servant into a position he found uncomfortable. She put her elbow on the curved arm of her chair and rested her chin in her hand. 'How do you know that he was only recently arrived in town?'

'I read it in the paper, ma'am. Can't help my eyes drifting to the West Indies news. Mrs Martin says any mention of the place should be cut out of the page before it's handed to me.' He smiled briefly. 'I admit it darkens my temper. Still, I told the story and Dido said I should go back to St Paul's – but I do not wish to, and I said so. I believe Dido wishes you to order me to do my Christian and civic duty.'

Harriet turned back to her desk for a moment, and glanced out of the window. Two carriages were drawn up in front of the house and the complicated business of putting some of the family into one, and the rest into the second was in progress. Harriet could see her youngest child, Anne, her hand held firmly by her nurse, watching the developing circus with her usual air of happy enthusiasm until it was her turn to be lifted inside. Harriet would never understand how she had managed to bear such cheerful children. Her temper was more like Susan's, darkening and brightening suddenly like a sky driven by a high wind. She watched Stephen and Jonathan clambering into the first coach, followed by Graves. Her daughter and the nurse followed them and Philip passed up a hamper to the coachman then clambered up behind. Susan and Eustache were getting more slowly into the second carriage with Mrs Service.

'What exactly is a punishment mask, William?' she asked.

He swept his hand in front of his face and spoke quickly. 'Normally made of iron. It holds the jaw shut. It prevents a slave from eating the cane as they work. Sometimes a cook is made to wear one to stop them stealing food, sometimes others if they are caught eating dirt. It is fastened with a padlock.'

'Eating dirt? I am not sure I understand you.'

He seemed impatient. 'Some slaves eat the soil. Some brought the habit from Africa, some do it hoping to die. Whatever their reasons, the owners do not like it, and take steps.'

William had arrived at Caveley in 1779, bearing a letter from Harriet's husband recommending him for a position in the household. She remembered now seeing him for the first time as he walked up the carriage drive, his skin chalky with the dust of the summer roads, the slightest limp that suggested a wound badly healed. An hour afterwards, he stood before her in the Long Salon while she read the letter. Her housekeeper had brushed his coat and he had washed the dust from his hands and face. She had liked him at once and had never since had cause to regret taking him into her household. Within a month she had discovered he understood the workings of the account books rather better than she did, and often asked him to check over her work. He was patient about it and she admired his tact, managing to instruct her without ever appearing to forget the fact that she was his employer. For the first six months at Caveley, he was referred to as 'Mrs Westerman's black', but as the inhabitants of the area got to know and like him, he became known by his given name. Any strangers who remarked wonderingly on the colour of his skin found their reception grew chilly.

Outside, she heard the carriages start away. 'It must be many years since you last saw this Trimnell,' she said. 'Six, at the very least. Are you quite sure it was the same man? Were you . . . ?' She did not know the words to use. 'Intimately acquainted?'

There was a brief spark of amusement in his eyes. 'He did not own me, Mrs Westerman, if that is what you mean.' She blushed and his voice became more serious again. 'But I am quite certain. I watched him kill a slave, some fifteen years ago, a man I made the crossing with, and roll his body into the harbour for the sharks. It was my first day in Jamaica. Trimnell beat him to death there on the docks for not having the strength to walk. He realised he'd got a bad bargain at the scramble and lost his temper. You don't forget a face or a name when you've seen that.'

There were times when Harriet wished she could not see in her mind's eye the things she heard spoken of. 'I would imagine not,' she said. The house seemed very quiet. The sun was shining full into the room now. The branches on the chinoiserie wallpaper seemed to shiver, and the porcelain in its alcoves glinted. She felt more ignorant now than when she was confronted with sheets of numbers. 'What is a scramble?'

'It is a way of selling slaves, Mrs Westerman.' William passed a hand over his eyes again. 'As the ship gets in, slaves are rubbed in oil and gunpowder, to make their skins glossy, and any who can still walk are paraded about. Then all who can stand are put in a yard. Buyers come in, try to grab the healthiest, bind 'em together. The price per head is set. It's a rush.' He stopped for a moment and cleared his throat. 'The traders can often get full price for some soul almost dead from the flux by standing him near men with work still left in them.'

Outside in Berkeley Square, a fruit-seller was calling her wares. Oranges and limes, fresh off the docks.

'Were you . . . ?'

'First time I was sold, yes. We thought the buyers were demons coming to rip us apart and eat us.'

The clock on the mantelpiece chimed.

'I shall go, William.'

He looked up at her. 'You, Mrs Westerman?'

'I shall visit St Paul's to admire the architecture. I shall make enquiries as I am passing by, and if they have not found out this man's name for themselves, I shall give it to them. You need not involve yourself further, and Dido can stop worrying at you.'

'If you think that is best, Mrs Westerman.'

She did not know quite how to judge what was best and what was not in these circumstances. Still, it would give her something other to think of than Rachel's latest outpouring of advice. William still looked doubtful; she felt a rush of affectionate understanding for him.

'I am sorry indeed you had to see such a thing,' she told him. 'The memories it must have brought back to you are no doubt very disturbing. I am not surprised that Dido was concerned.'

'The memories are there every day,' he said, so quickly she was startled. 'And I dream of those times one night in three. Dido knows that.' For a moment she saw him as an exotic object imported into the room to decorate it like the porcelain. People as objects. She had once overheard a titled lady offer one of her black servants to a friend. She said that she knew her friend, 'had one already and thought they would make a charming pair'.

20

'But I thank you for your concern, Mrs Westerman, and again for taking the trouble on yourself.'

Had there been something about William having his own room in the attic at Caveley? Mrs Heathcote, her housekeeper, had mentioned it. He was a senior servant so it was perfectly proper, but had there not also been some reference to his being a bad sleeper? Harriet had never in her life met a sailor who could not fall asleep before his head hit a pillow – some trick the body learned after years of watches. She started to look for her reticule. 'How long did you live in Jamaica, William?'

'Seven years – though I am not sure you could call it living. I was eight years old when I was sold to the slavers. Fifteen when I joined Captain Westerman's ship.'

She found the little beaded bag under Rachel's letter. Hat and gloves were laid out on a sofa table for her.

'How did you gain your freedom?' she asked. 'You were so young. Did your master die? I have heard that often slaves are given their freedom in that way.' There was an attempt at casualness in her tone.

'Captain Westerman bought me, Mrs Westerman,' he said. Harriet became very still, staring at her kid gloves lying waiting for her on the polished tabletop. William was still speaking. 'I served him at table when he visited my master's house and he took a liking to me. He bought me from him – for thirty-five pounds. He said if I worked hard, he'd let me keep a quarter of the prize money due to me. We had a fat couple of years. Then he let me buy my freedom with the proceeds.'

She understood the words as they were spoken, but they seemed to fly away from the surface of her mind, like a stone skimming. 'I do not understand,' she said at last, but without turning round. 'Are you telling me you were Captain Westerman's slave?'

'Yes, Mrs Westerman. For two years.'

'And did my husband own any *other* slaves?'

'Not to my knowledge, ma'am.'

It was impossible. It was simply impossible. James had said nothing to her of buying a man. He knew she objected to the idea of slavery, as any decent person did. He would not, against her wishes. Even so far away. Something whispered to her that she had taken advantage of James serving overseas to act as she saw fit, even though she knew her husband might not approve of what she did. But that was not the same. That was simply not the same.

'And my husband kept three-quarters of the prize money due to you during that period?'

'He did, though he could have kept it all.' William sounded cautious. 'He let me learn mathematics, navigation and reading with the midshipmen too, ma'am. Not many take the time to educate their slaves and in the West Indies it is frowned upon to teach a slave navigation in case of mutiny – yet he let me learn.' The word 'slave' beat against the flow of her blood every time he said it. 'Once I'd bought my freedom I'd have got my full share of prize money, only I fell and broke my leg before we had had much luck. It didn't heal quite right, and I lost my nerve for climbing. Captain Westerman could have put me on shore there in the Indies, but he asked if I fancied service in England. I did, so he got me passage here with a friend of his. I was glad of it, Mrs Westerman. Free or not, the West Indies are a dangerous place to be a black man with no friends. Providence has served many of my countrymen worse.'

'Providence?' The word sprang from between her lips, bitter and fast. She controlled herself. 'I shall go to St Paul's as soon as I might. Tell Dido so, if you please, and have Peters bring round the chaise. I shall drive myself.'

'Yes, Mrs Westerman.' She heard him leave, but she could not look at him.

I.4

T HE PORTER TOLD HER there was still no word as to the identity of the body, and when she intimated that she might have a name, he left his booth to lead her to a pink-faced young canon who was pointing out the glories of Wren's dome to a pair of very well-dressed Frenchmen. He excused himself at once and grasped Harriet's hands. 'You might know him? Oh thank the Lord indeed! You are the answer to my most fervent prayer, dear madam.' Harriet managed to remove her hands gently from his as he spoke, but her attempts to explain that she did *not* know the man herself were lost in his rush to show her the body. 'He is laid out in the Chapter House. Just this way, madam, please – a few steps.'

He was an enthusiastic servant of the Lord, chivving her through the traffic that circled the Cathedral. Harriet, not wishing to distract him from the carts and carriages processing by, held her tongue and found herself following the young man up the steps of the Chapter House, by now feeling somewhat out of breath. He showed her into a long, high chamber, apparently some manner of meeting hall. It would be well-lit by the windows that looked out onto St Paul's itself, but these were still shuttered and gave only a partial and broken light. There was indeed what appeared to be a body, draped in linen on a trestle against the far wall. What left Mrs Westerman speechless, however, was the sight of her friend, the anatomist Gabriel Crowther, standing in the centre of the room. She knew he was in London, of course. He had already been in town some weeks and they saw each other almost every day, but she had certainly not expected to see him here. There was something almost mythic about him, posed there in the half-light; tall, thin and leaning slightly on his silver-headed cane. The unreal flavour of the scene was added to by the fact that at his feet, another gentleman – in the costume of a verger – lay prone, his arms reaching high above his head and slightly spread.

Harriet's curate came to an abrupt halt and Crowther looked up at them.

'There you are, Mrs Westerman. You have taken your time getting here. I arrived almost a quarter hour ago and must have left Berkeley Square a good ten minutes after you.'

'Crowther!'

'Did you walk?'

She flushed. 'I did not walk. I took the chaise.' And she had made good time, but before looking for some official of the church she had spent a little time in prayer, thinking over what William had told her. She had not found the calm she had been looking for, and now here was Crowther to make her feel a fool. 'You spoke to Dido, I suppose?' she said.

'Yes, I met her in the square on my way to call on you and she told me where you were and why. And I have sent a boy to the Jamaica Coffee House to find some acquaintance of Mr Trimnell's who may positively identify him.' She found his evident satisfaction irritating.

'I am delighted to hear you acted so quickly, but there was no need for you to come charging across town, Crowther. I did not leave any message asking you to meet me here.' She was aware that this might sound pettish, but she could not help herself.

'I thought Mr Trimnell was invitation enough,' Crowther said innocently glancing at the body then back towards her. 'It sounded interesting. This young man has kindly been showing me the manner in which the corpse was lying when it was found.' He turned his attention to the body at his feet. 'You may get up now.'

The verger struggled quickly into a low crouch and scuttled away from Crowther till he was slightly hidden behind the clergyman who had accompanied Harriet. Crowther watched his progress with amusement.

The canon was now looking between them with a look of alarm and dawning recognition. 'You are Mrs Westerman. You are Mr Crowther.'

Crowther was eyeing the body on the table. He leaned his slight weight on his silver-headed cane. 'We are. Where is the coroner? I would like his permission to examine the corpse.'

Before the man could reply, there was a knock at the outer door, but the gentleman ushered in was not the coroner, rather the owner of the Jamaica Coffee House himself. His dress was somewhat old-fashioned – a full wig and wide sleeves on his coat. He introduced himself as Mr Sanden, and Harriet had the impression that the duties of the day weighed on him. He was much the same age as Crowther, though shorter and broader; his eyes bulged large from their sockets and his chin, mouth and nose seemed to hang close to each other on his face. He reminded Harriet of a tree frog from the East Indies, only dressed for town. He chewed his lip. Crowther asked him if he would indeed know Mr Trimnell well enough to identify the body.

'Aye, aye, I'd say so.' He shot suspicious glances at the body in the corner. 'There are others might know him better, but he did not have many good friends at my establishment.'

'I understand he had not been back in London long,' Harriet said, smiling at him encouragingly.

Sanden looked at her, a little confused and his eyebrows climbing his wide expanse of forehead. He coughed into his fist. 'As you say. Not long.' He chewed at his bottom lip again, leaving it damp and pink. 'But if it is Trimnell, I'll know him. His father-in-law, Sawbridge, is a financial partner in my house and lives above the shop. So I've seen him.'

'Why did Mr Sawbridge not accompany you here this morning?' Harriet asked.

'Balloon. Barbican. Party of Sir Charles Jennings. He's gone out already for the day.' Sanden added, 'But, as I said, I can tell you if it's him.'

The verger had helpfully moved to the trestle table, a corner of the linen sheet laid over the body clamped in his small fist. Sanden went towards him, sighing and rubbing his hands, and Harriet and Crowther followed. The verger folded the sheet back to the chin.

A thin face was revealed, the jaw covered in a heavy white stubble. The eyes were sunk deep in the sockets. It was more skull than human head. Harriet looked at the corpse steadily and thought of what William had told her, of watching this man beat another to death on the quayside under the blistering sun.

'Aye. That's him.' Sanden sighed. 'Jacob Trimnell. Married and living across from the Bow Church on Cheapside.'

'How old was he?' Harriet asked.

'Lord knows. Fifty and a few?'

'He seems much older.'

'Well, he'd been ill, ma'am. That's why he came home. Sold his estate for not much, which didn't please Mr Sawbridge, but what was he to do about it? Then he hopped on a boat with his lady wife.' He looked around them. 'Found on the street, was he? Died on his way home? Some sort of seizure, I dare say.'

The verger placed the cloth back over the shrunken face and in as few words as possible told Sanden the circumstances in which Trimnell had been found. Sanden opened his bulging eyes wide.

'What? One of the free blacks got him, did they?'

Crowther raised an eyebrow. 'Why do you say that?'

'Clear enough, isn't it?' Sanden said, going a little pink. 'Him weak and alone, they took their chance. Treacherous dogs, the lot of them — and they'll bear a grudge. What, you think I'm wrong? Not me. I lived among them for too many years.' He shuddered, then half-lowered his lids. The action seemed to force the globes of his eyes back into his head. 'Well, that's Trimnell. And now I must be away. Even with the hours Londoners keep we are all up and doing now, so goodbye to you.' He turned and left, his shoulders hunched.

The clericals began to discuss who should go to Mrs Trimnell to give her the news and Harriet, feeling that she was performing an act of charity, offered to accompany one of them. The pink-faced young canon who had thought her an answer to his prayers now looked at her in horror. He murmured his thanks in a polite and halting style and said he would go alone, but his feelings were clear enough. Harriet turned away. Crowther offered her his arm and suggested they walk around the Cathedral until the coroner arrived, then carried her from the room before she was required to say anything further.

I.5

THE CLAMOUR OF THE city burst around them as they left the Chapter House. Harriet did not know this part of the capital well and its character was very different to that of the fine houses and obvious elegances of the streets and avenues near Berkeley Square. The city stank of blood and tallow, and the smoke coming from the close-packed chimneys turned the air so thick, the Cathedral itself appeared smudged and indistinct. The pavements were busy; people of every condition in life from beggars to dandies pushed or dawdled past the book- and print-sellers that lined the Yard. Satires and squibs plastered the windows of one shop and in others were displayed scenes of heroes from history, exotic animals, botanical prints of great beauty, and adventurers and villains from the late war with America and France. In one, the weight of books seemed to press its ancient bowed windows outwards.

Porters and chairmen jogged past them, variously laden. One could catch occasional notes of their wares on the sickly breeze – spice, a blast of citrus. The riders and drivers in the road shouted greetings or threats to each other or those passing by. A blind ballad singer leaned against his patch of soot-stained wall, his one-sheet songs laid out around him for sale, and sung an air about England's green pastures in a high, wavering voice. A pair of lascar sailors were watching him, swaying from side to side in time to his song, their faces mottled with gin and an early-morning sentimentality. A woman with a maid trotting behind her examined them out of the corner of her eye as she passed.

Harriet looked up at her companion. Gabriel Crowther looked rather younger now than he had when they first met five years ago. While she sometimes felt tired and ancient as the hills, Crowther over those same years had begun to flourish. He had been a recluse, preoccupied with the marks left by violence on the body, and pursuing his interests in isolation, eaten up by old demons. Harriet had dragged him out into the light, and eventually his demons had been forced to loosen their grip. He now had an acknowledged heir to his fortune, a nephew of whom he was beginning to become fond, and he had begun to make his knowledge more available to his peers in a growing correspondence. His world seemed to expand while Harriet's continued to contract. She had felt it. Then he had announced on the day that Graves left their village for the house in Berkeley Square that he would also be spending some weeks in London as he was on the point of publishing a book about his forensic researches and wished to discuss the printing and illustration with his publisher. It was the first mention he had made of having written a book. Harriet had been surprised and a little hurt, and Crowther seemed to think her surprise odd. He said the weather was warming, making his dissection work more difficult, and so there was no good reason to remain in Hartswood. Harriet could not help resenting it.

'What are you thinking of, Mrs Westerman?' he asked now, seeing her expression. 'Not of that pink-faced crow? You should not take his reaction to heart. He is quite obviously an idiot, and I have tried to persuade you never to listen to idiots.' This was part of his transformation. He could still absent himself for weeks when he was working, happily snub his neighbours or insult them when he found their conversation dull, but then there were these moments, just as she was becoming angry with him, when he showed an understanding of her feelings and said or did something kind. It was very irritating.

'I am thinking that you look very pleased with yourself this morning, Crowther,' she said as he led her into the lee of the great Cathedral. 'Why do I have the impression you have a particular delight in ruffling my nerves before the morning is over?'

'Years of observation, I should imagine,' he replied, escorting her round to the eastern end of the building and letting the unfairness of her remark wash by them both with the shouts and the smoke of the city reaching its peak of business. 'I punish you for your habit of talking at the breakfast table. You heard how the body was laid out? The mask?'

'I did,' she said. 'Crowther, do not think I am saying this because of that ridiculous priest, but though I understand why you are curious to see the body, I am not sure that I wish to help find who might have killed this man.'

He looked down at her with surprise. 'But it is interesting.'

She only shook her head. 'William recognised him because he saw this Mr Trimnell murder a slave fifteen years ago in Jamaica.'

Crowther paused. 'That, Dido did *not* tell me.'

She sighed. 'Then William told me James *bought* him, Crowther. James never told me he owned a slave!' Crowther did not reply. 'I cannot believe it. We never much spoke of the subject, but I am sure he disapproved of slavery. There must be some mistake.'

'Whatever the truth of it,' he said at last, 'William is a slave no longer and he stays in your household out of choice. It cannot come as a revelation to you, Mrs Westerman, that slavery exists and we all profit by it. Sugar brings a great deal of wealth into this country. The planters say they cannot grow it without slaves. It is unfortunate, but it is what they say. And whatever this Trimnell was, surely you do not approve of his being murdered in the streets.' He stopped and looked down at her. 'Do you think William may have killed him?'

She had wondered for a moment, listening to him in her sitting room in Berkeley Square, even if she had not admitted it to herself until now. She stared up at the bright green of the young plane trees planted around them and struggling to grow in the Cathedral's shade, the London smoke. William had been out all night. Dido had told her he had gone to meet some of his fellow Africans in London and she had imagined him, a little drunk, on his way to his friend's house seeing a murderer wandering free and taking this chance to punish him, but she shook her head and spoke firmly. 'No. Even if he were foolish enough to tell Dido of having seen the body and recognised him having had a hand in the killing, his attitude this morning was of disgust, rage . . . not guilt.'

He released her arm and leaned on his cane. 'But when you see a slave-owner murdered, you believe an African might well be guilty.'

'Murdered in such a manner? And wearing a punishment mask? Of course I do.'

'And you sympathise?'

Sometimes his coldness, his unfeeling habit of putting her under examination like one of his samples was unbearable. 'Perhaps, Crowther, it is simply that we find ourselves in London where there are magistrates, constables and thief-takers enough! Our help is not required, and no friend of ours is in danger. Or perhaps I have had enough of death.'

'Perhaps you have, but you have a talent for it.'

She turned her back on him completely. 'You are too kind.'

'Mrs Westerman,' his voice showed traces of irritation now too. 'You are here, and on the external evidence to be found on a murder victim, you are as expert as I am. The coroner must have roused himself out of bed now. Stay an hour.' She said nothing. 'We have been recognised. If you run away, perhaps the coroner will, quite reasonably, ask why you do so. Perhaps their enquiries will lead them to William. How could you forgive yourself if suspicion alighted on his head because of *your* actions? Given your husband's history with that young man and his importance in your household, surely you owe him that?'

She turned back towards him, feeling the blood rush into her face. 'You were doing better when you were praising my talents, Crowther, rather than taking the chance to insult my husband and my intelligence. I told you, as a friend, what William said about my husband. Please do not use it to try and play on me like a cheap fiddle!'

He must have realised he had gone too far. He said awkwardly, 'I apologise, Mrs Westerman. And I ask your assistance, in so far as you feel able to give it.'

She let the frustration rise and fall away again within her before she spoke. However unfeelingly he had put it, there was some truth in what he had said. 'Shall we see if we can find exactly where Mr Trimnell was found?'

Much of the grass in the churchyard had been flattened by the crowd which had gathered around the body, so it was difficult at first to find exactly the spot. Still, the minutes of silence as they searched gave them both a chance to let their tempers cool a little.

Harriet found herself speaking before she remembered she was angry with him. 'There is another reason I believe William to be blameless. The body was staked out, and wearing the mask. Do you think William carries such things with him on the off-chance of meeting a murderer? This was planned.'

Crowther looked up, and she was almost surprised by the ice blue of his eyes.

'True. Yes, I suppose it probably was – though there are many men in London who have made their wealth through the slave trade. No doubt you could expect one to cross your path if you waited here in the shadows and were willing to be patient. So an attack *was* planned, but we do not know if Mr Trimnell was the specific target of the attack, or just one of many who might have sufficed.'

Crowther continued turning the grass at his feet with the tip of his cane and testing the ground to see if he could find the places where a stake might have been driven in. Perhaps he had found something – there seemed to be a hole in the turf that would fit a peg. Harriet came to his side, and borrowed his cane to feel the depth of the hole herself. It seemed very shallow and they could find no others, yet this was certainly the area in which he was found.

'Why here?' Harriet said, looking up at the towering white walls of the church. 'Could it have been for practical reasons? Mr Trimnell was known at the Jamaica Coffee House, and he lived in Cheapside. Is this the nearest open ground where a man might be staked out? But the Coffee House and Trimnell's rooms are both further to the east. He would not pass this way going between the two.'

Crowther crouched down and felt the turf. The hole did seem to be the right size and shape for a stake driven partway into the ground, but where were the other three? 'If you are right and this *is* the work of a former slave out for revenge, perhaps he means to insult the Church as well as Mr Trimnell.'

'I do not understand you.'

'The Church of England, Mrs Westerman. The Church has holdings in Barbados, and the West Indies are under the authority of the Bishop of London: this is the Bishop's church.' He looked up at the buildings on the other side of the railings and the roadway. They were quite high enough to peer down on the place, but the trees would obscure the view, and of course in darkness . . . 'Or it might be that this was the nearest place to stake a man out. Overlooked to a degree, but not directly under the noses of the neighbours as most things are in London.'

He walked away from her to the edge of the churchyard with a vague idea of looking through the borders, where there were still long patches of grass, for some remnant of the attack on Mr Trimnell. He was not sure what he was looking for and swiped his cane almost at random, bending back the stalks and letting them spring back. On feeling that uncanny sensation of being watched, he stopped and looked up: a small boy was peering at him through the railings. He looked rather healthier than many of the specimens Crowther saw roaming the streets. Someone had got him to wash his face within the last few days at any rate, and he did not have the pinched, starving look Crowther associated with unaccompanied children in the capital.

'Lost something, guv? Funny what people drop when they're staring up at the Cathedral.'

'Do you know about the man who was killed here last night?'

The boy clambered up onto the stone wall and hung onto the railings so he could look Crowther in the eye.

'Do I ever! I was one of the first here.' He nodded over his shoulder. 'Me and my ma live in Queen's Head Alley. I was out fetching breakfast and saw him laid out while Jo was hammering for the priest to come along.'

Crowther fished a shilling from his pocket and turned it between his fingers so it caught the sun. He heard a step behind him and realised Mrs Westerman had come to join them. The boy watched the coin and licked his lips.

'Tell me what you saw. All of it,' Crowther said slowly.

'Bloke laid out there.' He thrust his arm through the railings to point at the patch of ground. 'Simon crouched down next to him.'

'What else?'

The boy shrugged. 'There was a mallet on the ground by his foot. I fought Fred Moore for it, but he's bigger than me and got off with it before the constable turned up.'

'What sort of mallet was it?'

'Ordinary. He got sixpence for it from Mother Brown. He'd have got more from Old Beattie, but Mother don't ask questions or tell tales. There were a couple of short sticks too, like the one his ankle was tied to. People took 'em as keepsakes.'

'Did you see his clothes?' Harriet asked.

The boy thought hard, then shook his head decisively. 'No. Nothing like that. He just had his shift on, and that was torn at the back.' Crowther flipped the coin and it sailed over the railings. The boy reached out and caught it with such grace that Crowther smiled.

'Thank you, young man.' The boy nodded then sprang off into the crowd, disappearing as neatly as the coin had done. 'Well, Mrs Westerman?'

'I am thinking of ordering a man to strip, Crowther, though I would not confess it to anyone other than yourself. Coat, waistcoat, breeches, shoes and hat. They must have bundled them away while Trimnell was still alive, or something would have been left behind with the mallet. I wonder how many pawnshops there are in London?'

He looked up at the broad flank of the Cathedral, the weight of its stone, the tumbling heights of it frowsting in the London smoke. A movement caught his attention and he saw the verger who had played the corpse for him bustling towards them. 'I suspect the coroner has finally arrived, Mrs Westerman.'

I.6

FRANCIS GLASS WAS TYING a parcel for one of their provincial customers when the young people dashed into the shop. He was trying to ignore the conversation passing between Cutter the clerk and Francis's friend, the engraver, Walter Sharp. Walter was a fine artist and Francis valued his friendship, but wished he would spend a little more time at his work rather than guessing at the identities of the aristocrats and notables whose scandals were hinted at in the latest *Town and Country Magazine*. Still, the shop was relatively thin of customers, it being early in the day, so he swallowed his irritation and tried to focus on his knots.

The two small figures darted into the shadows on the far side of the main staircase. Francis finished tying up the parcel and addressed the label in his perfect copperplate handwriting; then, as the children did not leave, he came round the edge of the counter and crossed to the corner whence the suppressed giggles were coming. His arms were folded and he was prepared to be stern, but the children surprised him. He had expected to see some of the pinch-faced and dirty specimens that travelled singly or in packs through the streets, rummaging through the waste piles or holding out their hands with tears trembling in their eyes while their friends dipped in your pockets for your valuables, but these two, it was obvious from their dress, were gentry. The girl could not even be properly called a child – being, he guessed, some fourteen years or so of age. The boy was perhaps a few years younger, nearer ten, and though he was rather slender and thin about the face, there was no mistaking these children for vagrants.

'Oh, sir, do not give us away!' the girl said in an urgent whisper. There was no fear in her voice, only mischief. 'We have only just slipped the leash.'

Francis narrowed his eyes. Even though there were more Africans in London since the end of the war with America, he found that white children still tended to fear him. They saw him frown, thought of the stories of cannibals they had heard, and became quiet and willing in case he ate them. This young girl showed no sign of fright, however. She continued to look up at him with a confident, trusting smile. He found he had to speak.

'Miss, you cannot dash about the place like this. Even with your brother.'

She was peering past him into the street. 'Oh, he's not my brother, he's my uncle. Ha! Eustache, I told you, no one follows. No more studying improving volumes while they prose on about female education over their tea. Liberty! Now we may run up to Barbican and see the balloon after all.'

Francis raised an eyebrow. He knew now exactly where they had fled from. Eliza Smith's shop was a minute's walk away. There she sold any number of volumes on the proper way to educate children, both boys and girls. Her shelves groaned under the weight of moral tales adapted for the improvement of young minds, as well as dictionaries and books on geography, mathematics and music. Her walls were decorated with prints, created in her house, of children personifying Christian virtue, and her rooms were always full of well-dressed and enthusiastic mothers with slightly downcast children following in their wake.

'You have abandoned your guardian at Mrs Smith's establishment, I understand.'

The girl's face fell. It was difficult not to smile, so sudden and complete was the transformation from exaltation to despair, but Francis remained impassive. 'How did you know? Oh, do not carry tales, sir! I've had nothing but lectures all morning and I just wanted a moment to breathe. Mrs Smith is very nice, but she looked so disappointed at me, then led Mrs Service away upstairs to "discuss my behaviour". Then Mrs Smith's maid said she hoped I was not a bad girl and gave me such a look, and she made us sit in a corner with a prayer book while we waited. And I could *not*.'

Francis knew Mrs Smith's maid, Penny, and knew how the girl had made her money before Mrs Smith had taken her in. He felt a little burst of sympathy for the young woman in front of him.

The boy did not seem to completely share her delight in his freedom. 'I don't want to see the balloon. If you didn't want to be lectured and looked at, you shouldn't have got sent home from Miss Eliot's, Susan.'

'I'd like to see you or Jonathan or Stephen stand half an hour in that place, Eustache,' she replied. 'Those stupid girls! I did very well not to tear all their hair out on the first afternoon.' She looked up at Francis with wide blue eyes like a cat begging for scraps. 'I tried, sir! But Miss Eliot was shocked, *shocked* at everything from morning till night. "A lady should never say this, a lady should never do that . . ."' The girl had transformed herself in a moment into a female three times her age, rigid with disapproval. Francis could not help enjoying the performance, though he was careful not to show it. 'Seems to me Miss Eliot thinks a lady should not do any damn thing at all.'

'Susan!' the uncle said. 'You must not swear.'

'Bah! I'm sure this gentleman doesn't mind.' She looked up with absolute confidence into Francis's face, but obviously did not find the confirmation she expected. Her voice faltered. 'Oh! You do mind.'

He nodded. 'I do not like bad language, that is true. I think words are too important to be used carelessly.'

She recovered herself well enough, though Francis was glad to see she had the decency to blush. 'Then, my apologies.' She straightened her shoulders and lifted her chin in a very passable impression of a grand lady speaking to her inferiors. 'Do you sell music here, sir? I would be very happy to see your selection if you have any before I leave.'

'We do, and you are free to examine it,' Francis said, 'but I shall not pass over this "slipping of your leash" so quickly, so stop giving yourself airs.' The uncle snorted and the girl pouted. 'Who have you left worrying for you at Mrs Smith's? Come, tell me and be quick about it if you wish us to be friends, miss.'

A deep, weary sigh. 'Mrs Service. She has charge of us today and I do love her, but she has been so cross with me all morning. And yesterday. And the day before. I wanted to go to the balloon-raising but am not allowed to do anything until I apologise, and I won't! It was a stupid school. I don't know what the Duke was thinking, because he is usually quite a nice and sensible man.'

Francis decided he did not need to understand completely everything the young lady said at this moment and turned towards the boy. 'And you, sir? What harm did Mrs Service do to you that you should abandon the poor lady so?'

He rolled his eyes. 'I couldn't just let Susan run off on her *own*.'

'It would have been better not to let her run off at all.'

The boy became indignant. 'That's not fair! If I keep quiet, then Graves and Verity and Mrs Service all lecture me, and if I don't, then Susan and Jonathan say I am a tattle-tale. I wish everyone would just leave me *alone*.' He looked very angry and the girl saw it.

'Crybaby,' she muttered. Francis held up his hand.

'That is an unpleasant thing to say, miss, after he followed you.' He spoke sharply enough to shock her, and the boy looked surprised and pleased. Francis spoke on while the girl was still at a disadvantage. 'I suppose matters could be worse. I am certainly glad you didn't tumble into Mrs Humphrey's gallery across the way.' The girl's face lit with sudden curiosity and she tried to look past him into the street. He raised his eyebrows and she gazed down at her hands, a model of polite submission. 'I am afraid I cannot allow you to leave unaccompanied. There are scoundrels enough to eat children like you alive between here and there.' He looked over his shoulder. The engraver was grinning at him. 'Walter, would you be so kind as to go to Mrs Smith's and tell Mrs Service that Miss . . .' He looked back at the girl.

'Thornleigh,' the girl mumbled.

'. . . Thornleigh has just stepped in to see what music we have, and she and her uncle will wait for her here.' The girl looked as if she would cry now. Francis smiled at her. 'We have a clavichord under the window, Miss Thornleigh. No balloons, but it is better than prayer books, is it not?' She nodded.

The man behind the desk wrinkled his nose, however. 'I'd do anything to oblige you, Mr Glass, but I still owe Mrs Smith work. Daren't show my face there. Every time I try and draw one of her examples of angelic children, they go cross-eyed.' The girl giggled damply and Walter winked at her. Francis sighed and retreated behind the counter again to fetch his coat.

'I'll remember this,' he murmured to Walter, who only grinned, then he said to the children, 'I'll return in a little while.'

In truth Francis did not greatly mind having an excuse to leave the shop for a moment. It made a pleasant change from the bills, appeals for credit, advances against copyright and negotiations with ink- and papermakers that made for the bulk of his life as a printer and seller of books. He touched his hat to his neighbours and received their greetings in turn. Respectable people going about their respectable business in a respectable corner of town, and he, by good luck and hard work, was one of them. His employer, whose name was inscribed above the door of the bookshop, had spent thirty years in the London booktrade and had prospered. Francis had been his lieutenant for the last five, and while Mr Hinckley now lived in quiet retirement in Hampstead, giving good dinners to his favourite and most impoverished authors, Francis managed his business with great success. He commissioned works, he supervised their printing, placed adverts in the papers and cultivated friendly relationships with the reviewers and gentlemen of letters. When he read something he liked, he suggested that Mr Hinckley ask the author to dine. The authors always accepted and came back bursting with that gentleman's praises. Francis suspected they would have felt a little differently if they knew they had been invited on the recommendation of Mr Hinckley's African clerk, but there was no need to mention the fact.

He turned the corner at the end of Ivy Lane into Paternoster Row. The maid, Penny, who served in the shop when needed, was standing on the doorstep looking up and down the street. Francis made her a shallow bow. 'Miss Weeks, if you are looking for a young lady and gentleman who just dashed out of here, they have taken refuge at Mr Hinckley's. I have come to inform their guardian.'

The girl puffed out her cheeks, relieved. 'Little devils. I only turned my back a moment to serve Mrs Rule.' She looked at Francis for a long moment then stepped aside to allow him into the shop. 'Mrs Smith is upstairs with Mrs Service in her private parlour. You know where that is, of course.' She winked and Francis passed her with the barest nod and climbed the stairs to the first floor two at a time.

Mrs Smith was serving tea and bread and butter to a far older lady. Mrs Smith rose as soon as he entered and took his hand. She was a good-looking woman of not more than thirty, plumper than most Englishwomen, and with a pale, heart-shaped face. She was soberly dressed and her chestnut hair, as always, a little untidy. She smiled a great deal and there was something in her walk that suggested she might be about to start dancing at any moment. She was in truth a spinster, but like other ladies who went into business, she took the title 'Mrs' as a sign of her independence. Her guest was a thin, gentle-looking female with a friendly smile. The introductions were made, and when Francis explained his mission, Mrs Service looked more sorrowful than angry and put down her cup.

'Thank you, Mr Glass, for coming to fetch me. I am very sorry that the young people have been a trouble to you.'

He bowed, enjoying the sound of her neat clipped vowels and the evenness of tone. 'Not at all, madam. Their company is . . . enlivening. And please do not cut your visit to Mrs Smith short on my account. I am happy to keep watch over the young people until you are ready to collect them.' Mrs Service looked uncertain, then grateful and gave him her thanks. He was ready to leave again with the satisfaction of a Good Samaritan, but in the doorway Mrs Smith stopped him.

'Francis, dear . . .' She was blushing furiously, spots of red showing through the thin pale weave of her skin in a way Francis thought charming. 'I have something here I wish you to read. It was given to me by an acquaintance and is not at all in my usual line, but I would be most grateful to have the authority of your opinion.'

Francis gave her a slightly weary look. 'Eliza . . .'

'Please, Francis! I hardly ever ask you . . .'

He lowered his voice. 'Eliza Smith, you know that is not true. What of that novel of Mrs Bentley's you gave me? You told *her* you thought it very good, though again more in my line than yours, when you knew very well that it was terrible.'

She blushed again, but her eyes sparkled. 'Oh, Francis, that was at least a year ago!'

'And she has only just stopped calling on me every week.'

'Oh dear, and I can imagine how polite you were to her every time she visited! I know it was a *little* naughty of me, but she is one of my best customers. And such a good charitable lady. I couldn't risk offending her, poor dear. And this is quite a different matter.' She became more serious. 'Quite different. I wasn't sure whether I could ask you to read it, but God sent you to me today, Francis.'

'Eliza, we see each other three times a week.' He spoke even more quietly, looking up quickly to be certain Mrs Service could not hear him. 'And it was not God, but a pair of rather ill-behaved children.'

'He moves in mysterious ways!' She smiled then looked at him with a sort of silent pleading that had never failed in all the years they had known each other.

'Very well.'

Mrs Smith wrinkled her nose at him, and he waited as she went to her desk and returned with a manuscript gathered together in a dark brown leather portfolio. 'Thank you,' she whispered. 'Will you come tomorrow after you have seen Mr Hinckley as usual?'

'You know I shall.'

She shook her head. 'I wish I could persuade you to come to church instead.'

'I am in the shop six days a week; the last I divide between Mr Hinckley and yourself. I am certain God approves of my plan.'

She tried not to smile back at him, but patted the sleeve of his coat and he felt his skin glow there with her touch.

Francis tucked the manuscript under his arm, bowed to Mrs Service and returned to the shop. The boy was reading and the girl was playing through various sheets of music on the little clavichord. As far as Francis could judge, she was doing so with taste and accuracy. Walter was making her laugh. Francis put the manuscript on the pile of other such documents in his office and returned to his work.

I.7

THE BODY WAS REMOVED to a cramped outhouse before Crowther was allowed to start his examination. The gentlemen of the cloth knew enough of dissection to realise the work would leave unpleasant traces. They formed a little funeral procession for the executed planter. One of the vergers took the lead, a lantern in his hand and clutching a bundle of moulded candles which had been made to light the Cathedral itself, scurrying ahead to fill the shabby little building to the side of the Chapter House with light. The corpse of Mr Trimnell, shrouded in fresh white linen from the household store, rested on a plank, carried by two of the servants. Crowther came behind them carrying a leather case which Harriet knew contained the scalpels and saws, scissors and tweezers, all neatly packed in velvet, which he used for his work. He must have collected it from his own house in Grosvenor Street on the way to St Paul's. Harriet followed him, walking slowly at the coroner's side like a mourner.

The body was set down on a long oak dining table too ancient and crooked for the clergy to eat off and now used – it seemed by the tools and wood-shavings around the place – as a work-bench. The candles and lantern were placed at Crowther's direction and the servants left to fetch water and spare linens. The coroner, a Mr Bartholomew, remained in the doorway, his broad shoulders blocking out half the light, and shifted his weight from side to side. Feeling in the way, he made the decision to leave and turned away, but Crowther called him back.

'One moment, Mr Bartholomew,' he said, carefully folding the linen back from the body and setting it aside. Harriet watched as the man was uncovered once more. Someone had folded his hands across his chest, and the ropes William had mentioned around his wrists had been removed. Mr Trimnell looked like a divine who had died peacefully in his bed, dreaming of salvation. The skin showing round the open neck of his shift was livid. Harriet knew enough now about the process of death to know this was probably the result of the blood beginning to settle in his tissues as he lay prone in the churchyard. There was no obvious sign of violence.

Crowther bent over the corpse and sniffed, then looked up at Bartholomew. 'The body has been washed,' he said.

Mr Bartholomew looked down at the earth floor. 'Ah.'

Crowther felt the fabric of the shift between his hands. 'And I very much doubt this is his shift. It seems to have been plucked from the washing line an hour ago.' He turned to Mrs Westerman. 'Madam, if I am unfortunate enough to suffer a violent death, will you kindly make certain the clergy of St Paul's do not conspire to destroy all the evidence before some competent individual appears to examine it?'

'I shall, Crowther,' she said sweetly.

'I apologise, Mr Crowther,' Bartholomew said. 'The ignorance of the population in general has made my work difficult on many occasions. I understand you are to publish a book?' Crowther nodded. 'I am glad. It will be of great use to me and men like me. We are mostly lawyers, you know, and the medical evidence offered to us is often imperfect.'

Crowther turned aside and picked up his knife and Bartholomew started but Crowther merely turned the blade and slit the thin material of the shift from neck to hem. He then folded it back to show the naked body below.

There were some bruises around Trimnell's belly – they looked to Harriet as if they had been delivered with a fist. The body was thin almost to emaciation. It seemed impossible to believe such a fragile-looking creature could have been walking and talking yesterday, taking his coffee with his West Indian cronies.

'Mr Bartholomew,' Harriet said, 'the owner of the coffee house mentioned that this man lived on Cheapside. That is an unusual address for a rich man, is it not?'

The coroner looked surprised. 'From what I've heard, Trimnell was not a particularly rich man, Mrs Westerman. Not everyone who lives in Jamaica makes his fortune. The wars, the exhaustion of the soil . . . Many of our friends in the West Indies are suffering a great deal.'

She looked into his face for some sign of irony, but there was nothing but well-mannered concern.

'Do you know anything else of the man?'

Bartholomew ran his hand over his chin. 'I have heard of him, and met his wife. She was at a gathering at the home of Sir Charles Jennings in Portman Square two evenings ago. A private concert.'

'Mrs Westerman?' Crowther had no interest in Mr Bartholomew and his social connections. She approached the body and watched carefully as Crowther turned the wrists and hands. Mr Trimnell had long fingers and hands which showed no sign of injury, nor the calluses of physical labour. His ankles, like his wrists, were unmarked. Strange. Crowther ran his fingers across the man's scalp, then gently pulled open the jaw and felt inside the mouth for any hidden injury. He caught Harriet's eye and shook his head.

'I wish to turn the body. Your assistance please, Mr Bartholomew,' he said, wiping his fingers on a corner of Mr Trimnell's shroud.

The coroner stepped forward and between them the two turned the corpse onto its front. Crowther pulled the shift free from Trimnell's shoulders and threw it into the corner of the room. Harriet felt a hiss on her lips; across Trimnell's back, from the top of the right shoulder-blade and reaching diagonally down to the spine, was a single raw wound. The skin was not torn away completely, but its path was clear by the areas that were scourged and bloody.

'A whip-strike,' she said. 'But not a nine-tails – a single strap and narrow.'

'They tied him up like an animal and whipped him,' Bartholomew said in a whisper.

'Like a slave,' Harriet said, her voice neutral. 'Or a vagrant. How many whippings are ordered every day in this city?'

'Enough,' Bartholomew said after a pause. His tone remained polite. 'But not in a churchyard, not in darkness, and only after due process of law.' Harriet nodded, conceding the point.

'I am not certain that is quite what happened, Mr Bartholomew. Mrs Westerman,' Crowther said, 'what do you think?'

She considered for a while. She had served long enough with her husband to see men flogged, tied upright to the grating while the drum beat and the company looked on. Part of the theatre of discipline. She remembered too the curate laid out at Crowther's feet, arms above his head. She imagined Crowther with a whip in his hand rather than the familiar cane.

'No, I think not.'

'How can you know?' Bartholomew asked, and stopped pulling on his buttons for a moment.

'The angle and placing of the strike.' And when he continued to look puzzled, she went on: 'Turn your back to me,' and warily, he did so. 'If you were struck now from behind, by someone making use of a whip in their right hand, the blow would catch your shoulder here,' she placed her hand on his right shoulder and he flinched, 'then come down on this slope.' With the side of her hand she pressed against his back showing the angle she meant, the angle that matched the wound on Trimnell's back. 'If you were to lie face down on the ground, Mr Bartholomew, I would have to stand on the small of your back to deliver that blow. Wounds struck from the side would be longer, marked more across the body, their focus most likely on the centre of the back. Any higher wound would probably start in the middle of the shoulder-blade rather than across the shoulder.'

The coroner turned to look at her, intrigued but slightly repulsed. She smiled tightly at him.

Crowther was moving the lamp up and down the body again. He examined the scalp and the base of the neck, the inner thighs – then stepped back and set the lamp down with a sigh. 'Well, I can give you my thoughts at this stage, Bartholomew. If Mrs Westerman disagrees, she may contradict me. Trimnell was hit by a fist several times in the belly. The bruises developed. Then he was hit with a whip once, when standing. His assailant began to stake him out as if for a more concerted attack, but abandoned the attempt and did not use the whip again.'

The coroner cleared his throat. 'What is your conclusion?'

'That it seems a rather curious way to behave,' Crowther said, looking up at him blankly.

'But a whip-strike is not fatal. How did he die?'

'I cannot say as yet.'

Mr Bartholomew looked frustrated. There was a sound and they turned to see the pink-faced canon hovering in the doorway. He was trying not to stare at the naked corpse. 'Mr Bartholomew, a word.'

Bartholomew bowed and followed him out into the daylight.

The mask had been left for them in a neat linen parcel by the corpse's feet, like the grave goods of a warrior. Harriet unwrapped it and held it in her gloved hands, looking into the empty eyes. The metal reflected the lamplight. It was the lack of a mouth, she thought, that made it so unnerving. Such a complete silence was implied. *You shall be voiceless.* Whoever put this on another man did so because he could rip out another man's vocal cords without killing him. The mask had held the cold of the night and she felt it suck away the heat of her fingers as she turned it over. The shadows pooled and flowed from it like water. The piece under the chin was rather jagged, unfinished. Was that part of its purpose? To struggle in it would push the soft parts of the throat against those sharp edges. She felt disgust sweep through her bones like a spring tide.

While Crowther continued his examination of the body, she placed the mask over her own face, felt it push her mouth closed with the uncomfortable pressure of the plate under her chin. The world narrowed, she could see only what was directly in front of her – the candles, Crowther and the body. She felt her heart beginning to kick and her breathing deepen. Crowther paused in his examination of the body for a moment to look at her, and she lifted the mask away from her face and set it down again, feeling shamed.

His expression changed. He walked up to her and with one hand lifted her chin while he raised the lantern in the other. She felt his dry fingers push her head back a little way. 'Don't move, my dear,' he said, then set the lantern down and pulled his handkerchief from his pocket and with it wiped the place at the top of her throat where the mask had pressed. He released her and put the handkerchief into her hand. She looked down at it. A rusty red stain was worked into the fabric. She felt a lurch of shock, turned the fabric to a clean space and rubbed hard at her throat while Crowther picked up the mask.

'Certainly blood, I think, and in some quantity,' he said, 'though the skin on Mr Trimnell's neck is unbroken. Interesting.' He ran his finger high under the corpse's throat. 'Perhaps whoever attached it to him was unaware it had that extra bite to it and injured themselves. There is something here though, but the lividity makes it difficult to see.' He looked up at her to ensure that she followed and sighed. 'The blood is quite gone, Mrs Westerman. Do stop that or you will bruise yourself, and all and sundry will start to believe I have been throttling you.' He put his hand out and reluctantly she returned his handkerchief to him. 'The cut must have been quite deep to have bled so much. Whoever the mask bit, we should be able to see the wound.'

She swallowed and tried to speak again. 'Might he have been throttled, Crowther?'

He opened one of the corpse's eyes. Harriet could not help noticing it had the same greenish tint as her own, but this one was as dead as glass. 'The eyes are clear. In cases of suffocation or strangulation, one normally expects to see the blood vessels damaged.' He stepped back slightly. 'Now, Mrs Westerman, what of the mystery of his hands and wrists?'

She took one of Trimnell's hands in her own and turned it as much as the slow stiffening of the body would allow. 'They *are* a mystery. Clean and unmarked. He did not bruise his knuckles while fighting back; did not pull against the ties around his wrists and ankles. Crowther, are you quite *sure* there is no serious head wound?' He did not reply, but she felt the weight of his look. 'My apologies. If he were held, perhaps?' She thought of the bodies she had seen. 'Might he have been drugged?'

Crowther was now leaning against one of the wooden supports. 'It is a possibility,' he agreed. 'We know there are such drugs in existence, but we also know that their traces are hard to find.'

She nodded. 'But fists and a whip . . . they suggest a brute rage to me. A man who uses a drug is, I think, more controlled.'

'Perhaps. I am troubled still that there are no signs that he put up a defence. We fight death as far as we are able. It is our animal nature.

He was standing when he was struck in the belly, just as he was for the whip-strike, and I cannot see how he could have been securely held without some marks being left.'

Harriet had withdrawn a little way and crossed her arms, an attitude of protection. 'But it is possible. He *could* have been held by the arms as the blows were struck. A mob?'

Crowther had once seen a man set on by a mob, and remembered quite clearly the sounds of fists hitting flesh. 'I doubt it. They would have hit everywhere around the body, I would think, and once begun they would not have stopped before he was dead. This is one man, punching right and left like a boxer, a fighting man. And no, if he were held upright while those blows were delivered, there should be bruises on the upper arm. Think on that wound again, Mrs Westerman. He must have been standing still when it was delivered, and anyone holding him would have been caught by the whip-strike also.' He shook his head. 'I do not understand it.'

Mr Bartholomew reappeared in the doorway. 'Mrs Trimnell was collected from her rooms early this morning by her father, Mr Sawbridge. The maid had no information as to where she might have gone.'

'Mr Sawbridge, who lives above the Jamaica Coffee House?' Harriet asked.

'Yes, that is her father.'

'Mr Sanden told us he had gone to the balloon-raising at the Barbican with Sir Charles Jennings. No doubt Mrs Trimnell is one of the party.'

Bartholomew put his hand to his cravat. 'She is with Sir Charles? Then I should go myself to inform him – that is to say, to inform Mrs Trimnell.'

'I shall drive you there if you wish it. My groom and chaise are waiting for me,' Harriet said and Mr Bartholomew bowed.

Crowther was still examining the corpse. 'It is a warm day. It would be best if I begin my examination at once – with your permission, Mr Bartholomew.'

'Yes – that is . . .'

'Do not fear. The body will be in a proper state to be viewed by the jury or the widow when I am done.'

Harriet smoothed her gloves. 'You do not wish to take the chance to see the balloon being raised, Crowther? You should applaud the pursuit of knowledge. Were you not very impressed when Mr Blanchard managed to cross the Channel in it, in January? It is his machine that is being raised this morning.'

'As for knowledge, I already had reliable information as to where France is, and I was more impressed by his luck than his skill.'

Harriet laughed softly, then caught the look of shock in Mr Bartholomew's eye.

'Come, sir. Let us leave Mr Crowther to his work.'

I.8

FRANCIS FOUND HE COULD not settle to his work. He had caught a glimpse of St Paul's on his way back from Mrs Smith's establishment in Paternoster Row, the great white heft of it dominating the city and making them all low. The thought of the man in the mask troubled him. Francis had not spent long in Jamaica, not quite a year, so it was unlikely he would know the dead man; however, his ghost still seemed to hover close by. Today, Francis seemed to notice more black faces in the crowd, seemed to feel them noticing him. It was as if they were all asking each other, who among them might have done this? His position as a respectable man of business in London felt obscurely threatened. He was in need of distraction. Walter was still flirting in a suitably avuncular fashion with Miss Thornleigh. The boy, Eustache, was reading a novel he had taken down from the shelves. Francis noticed he was stroking the page as he read as if to comfort it. He put a hand on the boy's shoulder and the child looked up as if afraid he had done something wrong. 'You like books, do you?' Francis asked, and when the boy nodded, 'Would you like to see one being made?'

The boy looked a little wary. 'May I? Yes, I would find that interesting.' His face was not unattractive when he stopped looking sulky, and now pleasure made it almost handsome.

'Come with me.' Francis nodded to Cutter and took the boy into the back of the shop and up to the first floor where the other inhabitants of Mr Hinckley's empire were at work.

However refined their authors and their audience, the making of books was a messy, stinking, sweating sort of business. The compositor, Ferguson, worked where the light was best, rattling the type, the individual letters, into the composing stick held in his left hand. He plucked them from the cases in front of him, his gaze never leaving the page of manuscript pinned up at eye level. The metal clicked into words, the sentences and arguments growing in his hands. He glanced up as they climbed the stairs and nodded to them. Francis quietly explained to Eustache what Ferguson was about; that the upper case of type held the capitals, that the largest box on the lower case held the 'e', that spaces were shanks shorter than those that held the letters so that the ink would not catch on them. The boy was fascinated, and in his interest Francis remembered his own. The business of creating books had become so familiar to him, he had almost ceased to wonder at it.

'Can you do that, Mr Glass?' the boy said, gesturing at Mr Ferguson. 'I was trained to it,' Francis replied, 'but I was never as good at it as Mr Ferguson. And it requires constant practice to be as fast and accurate as he.'

Ferguson, a white-haired, long-necked man with a slight stoop, snorted as he crossed to the form to empty out his composing stick onto the lengthening page. 'You used to be reading the lines all the time, Mr Glass, when you should have been setting them. You'd stop moving when you got to a bit you liked and we'd have to clap our hands at your ears to wake you to what you were supposed to be doing.' He said it with a smile and returned to the cases of type.

Francis leaned towards Eustache and said in an undertone, 'That's quite right. Enthusiasts such as we are, are better off downstairs among the completed books, I fear.' The boy looked up at him and then smiled, the first quick natural smile Francis had seen from him.

Behind Ferguson, two others inked and pressed the forms, the second man pulling free the damp sheets and hanging them to dry over the racks that ran the whole length of the room. There was a rhythm to it that Francis appreciated. It was a pleasure to him to see things being done well.

'My guardian has a shop where he prints music,' the boy said. Francis was surprised; the children were far better dressed than he would expect the wards of a printer to be. 'But it is not like this. Mr Crumley works on copper plates. I've seen them.'

Francis realised finally who the boy and girl were. Thornleigh . . . of course. 'That is more like engraving. I have seen Crumley's work. He is a fine artist. You must be one of Mr Graves's wards then? I have not met him, though I know something of him, of course. Are you the Earl of Sussex? I apologise – should I have been calling you My Lord all this time?'

The boy gave a windy sigh. 'No. I'm only an Honourable.' He became still, staring at Ferguson as he transferred another half-dozen lines of type to the form. 'Graves started looking after me after my mother killed herself and tried to kill me. She set fire to the Hall and she had Jonathan and Susan's father murdered. They don't really blame me, but I know they think about it sometimes. Especially Susan when people try and make her a lady and she wishes she still lived over the music shop.' He said it simply. 'I remember she was beautiful.'

'Your mother? Have you not seen her picture?' Francis asked.

The boy shook his head and reached out to touch the damp sheets. The breeze from the window stirred them, and they seemed to sigh and whisper. 'I am not supposed to talk about what happened. It upsets people.'

'It must,' Francis answered, then hesitated. Perhaps the boy's guardian had his reasons, but Francis had last seen his own mother when he was six years old; her face had become clouded in his memory as if it were sinking away. He wondered what he would give to see her portrait. 'Come with me, Eustache.'

He led him downstairs, picked a volume off the shelves as he passed, and took the child to a quiet corner. Susan had begun to sing as she played, one of the dozen tunes that appeared each month about flowers and sweet maidens. She had a pleasant voice. Francis opened the book he held to one of the illustrations sewed in with the text and showed it to the boy. It was an engraving of Eustache's mother, copied from the Gainsborough portrait. The engraver had added a frame, and an inscription of her name, *Jemima, Countess of Sussex*. She was indeed very beautiful, and her large, dark eyes were the mirror of Eustache's own. The boy took the volume in his hands and stared. Francis put his hand on his shoulder and felt him tremble. He would happily have made him a present of the book, but he could not. It was a volume of family romances, and contained an account of Jemima that Francis felt Eustache should never read.

The street door opened behind them and the music came to an abrupt halt. Francis heard Mrs Service's voice; her tone was a little sharp, and he turned away from the boy so he could greet his latest guest.

I.9

THE DRIVE FROM ST Paul's to the Barbican was painfully slow, and though Mrs Westerman was an excellent horsewoman, she had to concentrate to manoeuvre the little vehicle through the carts and carriages along St Martins Le Grand. Once or twice her groom hissed as she came rather close to a vehicle travelling in the opposite direction. She managed to ignore him. Mr Bartholomew was either well used to the London traffic, or had developed a quick and absolute faith in her skills. He supplied the conversation himself and it seemed to centre more on Sir Charles Jennings than on Mr Trimnell or his widow.

'He is a remarkable man, of course. So many men who inherited wealth in the West Indies remained in England and left their estates to be run by lesser men and adventurers, which did them no good in the end. Sir Charles, however, only returned to England permanently five years ago. Before then he spent a great deal of time on his property in Jamaica. Now he is such an ornament of the city. Tireless as an Alderman, and he served as Lord Mayor two years ago.'

'A paragon,' Harriet said dryly. 'I wonder what his slaves think of him.' There was a dray unloading barrels outside the King's Head and the shire horse in harness seemed nervous. Harriet kept an eye on him as she went by. Her own horse was fresh from the country and inclined to be skittish.

'Oh, I believe they are all very fond of him,' Bartholomew said comfortably. 'They are better off with him than among the savages of Africa. He seldom has to buy new stock, as those born on the estate itself supply his needs for labour. It is a testament to his care of them and the generosity of his treatment. He is the model of what an owner should be.'

The roadway narrowed as they passed by the spot where the gate in London Wall had once stood, and Harriet had no opportunity to reply. As they found themselves in Aldersgate itself and the roadway widened, she could loosen her grip on the reins. Harriet had heard of Sir Charles. He had become a model member of London society too, gracious and gregarious; friends with every man of influence, but though he had money and leisure, his address was modest, his reputation unsullied by talk of opera singers or married women, his clothing elegant but restrained. A paragon indeed, and now Harriet learned he was also very good to his slaves.

'How is Sir Charles acquainted with Mrs Trimnell and her father?' she asked.

'Mr Trimnell owned a neighbouring plantation, and Mr Sawbridge was Sir Charles's overseer for many years,' Bartholomew said with a sort of lazy satisfaction. 'And Sir Charles is most generous to his friends. He provides entertainments for them, such as the concert which I attended on Thursday evening, for instance. Such hospitality, and the best musicians, naturally. Mr Paxton was there and several others of similar distinction.'

Harriet had met Mr Paxton at Graves's house and thought him a very pleasant man, but was not musical enough to fully understand why he was a celebrity. Both Graves and Susan had simply told her he was of the first rank in his profession, and she believed them.

'Today as well,' the coroner went on, 'I am sure all his guests will have the very best spot from which to view the balloon.'

'Mr Trimnell was not at the entertainment on Thursday, however?'

'Perhaps he is not a lover of music.'

'Nor of balloons, I suppose. His wife attends: if he had been invited, would he not have been looked for and missed before this time?'

Bartholomew shifted his position and folded his arms. 'I could not say. As I told you, I have never met Mr Trimnell.'

They drove on in silence a little further. The traffic had become very dense once more, and looking ahead Harriet thought it was probably the balloon-raising causing the crowd. There was some altercation on the corner of Aldersgate and Barbican itself. A large coach with coronets on the doors had become entangled with a hackney carriage and the drivers appeared to be in dispute. Harriet pulled up where she still might have a little room to manage an escape.

'You know Sir Charles through your work as a coroner, I suppose, Mr Bartholomew?'

He beamed. 'No. Rather, Mrs Westerman, I owe my position as coroner to the patronage of Sir Charles. I was born on his estate, the son of a carpenter. Sir Charles took notice of me in my youth on his visits home, and paid for my schooling and saw me established in the law. I am deeply grateful to him. He has helped several men like me from humble backgrounds to better themselves.'

Harriet resisted the impulse to remark that the coroner was lucky not to have been born to one of Sir Charles's workers in Jamaica. The altercation that was blocking the corner showing no sign of abating, she turned to her groom. 'Peters, you had better drive the chaise home. Mr Bartholomew, I think we must walk from here.' She swung herself lightly from her perch and handed her whip to her groom.

Langhorne's repository was built off Barbican and was of sufficient size to allow the gentlemen who came to buy their carriage horses there to see the animals trot at a decent pace. For today's event, however, the carriages and horses had been cleared from the arena, and replaced by the great balloon.

Harriet was amazed by the crush and despairing of finding anyone in the crowd, but almost as soon as they had pushed their way into the throng, Mr Bartholomew touched her arm and pointed up towards the galleries. In the middle of an upper balcony a long table had been laid. Even at this distance Harriet could see the gleam of white table-cloths and silverware, and the sun touched the gold on the livery of the footmen serving a dozen or so ladies and gentlemen. Harriet was preparing to plunge through the crowd towards the building's entrance when she heard herself being hailed. Behind her, perched on the top of a coach, squeezed by some miracle against the southern wall of the yard, was the party from Berkeley Square. The horses had been led away, but the coach remained to give the party a platform from which to observe the wonders of M. Blanchard. Graves was waving a chicken leg at her. Little Anne was clasped firmly on her nurse's lap and seemed absorbed in licking her fingers. Jonathan and Stephen were too engaged in staring at the swelling body of the gold and green balloon to give her more than a distracted wave. Harriet returned the salutes and managed to mime both her love and her intention to go elsewhere, then return later.

Bartholomew was at her elbow. 'Isn't that the shopkeeper who lives off the Thornleigh family? Who is he waving at?'

Harriet gave him a look that had made many an Admiral nervous when her late husband was in the Navy. 'That young man has devoted himself to the children and their welfare for five years. He is one of the best men I have ever met in my life.'

Bartholomew, to his credit, blushed violently. 'Of course, my apologies. I misunderstood the situation.'

'You did.'

'It is simply I was told, when he . . .' Wisely, Mr Bartholomew gave up the attempt to excuse himself further. He became instead vigorous and effective in clearing a way for her through the crowd until they could reach the building where Sir Charles was feasting. They passed under the high carriage arch then into the lower, darker interior and climbed the stairs. Partway through their ascent, Mr Bartholomew hesitated and turned to her. 'Mrs Westerman, may I apologise again for that careless remark? I am sure any young man thrust into such a position of respon, sibility must occasionally make decisions that appear to older men, more experienced in business, as strange or foolish.'

She looked at him coldly. 'Perhaps. I have lived as a neighbour to Thornleigh Hall for many years and I can assure you the estate is a great deal better managed now than it was before Jonathan inherited. Do *you* have any first,hand knowledge of his business?'

He admitted he did not, bowed, and they climbed the remaining stairs. He did seem genuinely contrite. The door to the private parlours that led onto the balcony was open, but guarded by a pair of immaculate footmen, facing outwards towards the stairs. Harriet suspected that her own servants would be craning their necks for a view of the balloon. Bartholomew spoke to one, who disappeared for a moment out into the air of the balcony while his fellow stood aside and invited them with an elegant sweep of his white-gloved hand to come into the parlour he guarded. It was a pleasant room, timbered and low; the paint on the plaster smelled fresh and a good run of windows gave out onto the arena outside. The glass was old and thick, but Harriet could see the first footman bend discreetly over the shoulder of one of the party and in a moment the latter had stood, handed off his napkin and appeared in the doorway. He was a handsome man, not more than fifty and dressed in a buff, close-fitting coat and fawn breeches. His only jewellery other than the signet ring on his left hand was a garnet or ruby on a pin in his snow-white cravat. He approached with a quick firm tread, and as Bartholomew made a low bow, put out his hand and placed his other on Bartholomew's shoulder.

'Fletcher Bartholomew, my dear boy! A pleasure to see you. I had no idea you were interested in these aeronauts. Come, we can shift to make space for you and your companion at our table. I think the show is about to begin.'

Mr Bartholomew looked very pleased by the warmth of his reception. 'Forgive me, Sir Charles. May I present Mrs Harriet Westerman.'

Sir Charles gave no sign of recognising the name, but smiled and bowed low over her hand. 'Delighted, madam.'

'My warmest thanks for the invitation, Sir Charles, but I fear we cannot join you. Our mission is less pleasant.' Sir Charles's expression became one of friendly concern. Harriet thought Mr Bartholomew would ask to speak to Mrs Trimnell at once, but instead the coroner gave Sir

Charles all the details of the discovery of Mr Trimnell's body. Sir Charles did not interrupt or exclaim, but looked only sad and sorry.

'Grim news indeed, my boy.' Then as Bartholomew described the initial examination of the body and the wounds found, his grey eyes turned to Harriet.

'You took part in the examination of Trimnell, Mrs Westerman?'

She hoped she did not blush. 'I have assisted Mr Crowther on numerous occasions, Sir Charles.'

He smiled politely. 'Of course. I know Mr Crowther a little from the meetings of the Royal Society. Come to think of it, I am certain he mentioned your name.' Harriet was surprised to find that something in his manner of saying this made her feel she had been insulted by Crowther and saved by Sir Charles. 'I hope he may discover more when he opens the body. You gave him leave to do so, Bartholomew?'

'I did, Sir Charles.'

'Very good. James, would you fetch Mrs Trimnell?' The footman disappeared out onto the balcony again. Through the distortion of the glass and in the narrow view available between the heads of Sir Charles's guests and the balcony roof, Harriet could see the bulk of the balloon lifting and shifting slightly in the wind. There were cheers coming from the arena now and smatterings of applause that sounded like a rain squall against the windows.

Mrs Trimnell appeared in the doorway with a young man on her arm and approached with a wide smile. She was a great deal younger than Harriet had expected, not more than a year or two past thirty at the most. Her dress was extraordinary. Wide crimon skirts, gathered high over a petticoat of emerald silk, the bodice cut very low and only just saved from indecency by folds of sheer lace. Her neck and wrists were garlanded with matching strings of garnets, all cut and set in patterns of stars or flowers. She looked like a bird of paradise. Her hair was very dark, piled high, and the ostrich blooms on her hat added to the impression of the expensive and exotic. The young man on her arm was handsome, younger than she, and looked at her with a sort of hungry admiration. Sir Charles frowned when he saw him.

'Randolph, there is no necessity for you to be here. Please return to our guests. Perhaps though, you might ask Mr Sawbridge and Dr Drax to step in.'

The youth bowed. 'Yes, Father.'

Mrs Trimnell looked up at her squire and smiled at him in such a frankly sensual way, Harriet was shocked. She squeezed his arm as she released him, then turned to Harriet and Bartholomew. To the latter she nodded, and made a curtsey to Harriet.

'Happy to know you, I'm sure.' There was a lilt in her voice.

Sir Charles offered Mrs Trimnell his hand and guided her to a chair. She allowed it and her movements were fluid and graceful. How could that thin and unshaven body in the Chapter House be her husband? As Sir Charles took a chair beside her, two more gentlemen appeared in the doorway. One was in plain costume, his hooked nose and hooded eyes giving him the look of a watchful hawk. The other man was younger, wore a plum-coloured coat and as he sauntered across the threshold was feeding a grape to a little monkey that sat on his shoulder. It wore a gold collar attached by a chain to his waistcoat. When it finished its grape it rubbed its paws together as if to clean them.

Sir Charles ignored them as he took Mrs Trimnell's hand. 'My dear, he began. 'My dear . . .'

Outside, the crowd was growing more excited. Harriet could still see the balloon straining against the tight rope mesh around it. Bartholomew took the arm of the hawk-faced man and walked him a few steps away. In the arena there was a moment of silence. A distant voice shouted, '*Allez! Coupez les lignes!*' and the sound of a half-dozen axes brought down at once rang through the sudden still. The cheers became deafening and Harriet saw through the narrow window available the balloon lifting away from the ground. For a moment she glimpsed Monsieur Blanchard waving hard with his pocket handkerchief from the basket, and the frightened face of a woman by his side. It seemed they were being lifted on the shouts of the crowd. Mrs Trimnell gasped and fell back in her chair – and at the same moment the hawk-faced man shook Bartholomew off, strode across the room and dropped to his knees beside her. That must be her father, Mr Sawbridge.

Harriet felt a sting under her ribs and moved away, embarrassed to be watching at that moment. She glanced out of the doorway onto the balcony. The arena was packed; men and women of the better class, the shopkeepers and tradesmen of London, the gentlemen and scholars, their womenfolk watching progress take form in the shape of the balloon. They followed its movements, shifted by those same breezes that brought into their shops and homes their porcelains and spices, their Indian muslin, their wines, their sugar and rum. Their mouths were slightly agape, and from where Harriet watched as she tried not to hear the weeping behind her, all she could see were their white, exposed throats.

I.10

HARRIET JOINED GRAVES AND the children as the arena emptied, and travelled back with them to Berkeley Square. She told him briefly of Mr Trimnell's death and her reason for appearing at the raising. Jonathan and Stephen competed with each other talking of the balloon, how far it might have gone and how high. Anne fell asleep on the nurse's lap. While the boys chattered, Harriet thought about the handsome Mrs Trimnell and the men around her. Her clothes were dramatic, but not necessarily expensive. Those jewels though looked to Harriet as well beyond the means of anyone living in rented rooms in a house on Cheapside.

The day rolled steadily on towards evening. In the shadows of the outhouse near St Paul's, Crowther lifted Mr Trimnell's heart out of his chest, and by the light of an oil lamp examined the aortic valves, trying to fit his long thin finger into the vessel, and failing. The pink-faced canon Crowther had requested as an assistant went grey and gagged. Not far away, Francis Glass wrote up his notes for his weekly meeting with Mr Hinckley in Hampstead on Sunday, making his guesses as to what the public appetite might be in the weeks to come, and thought about the strange children who had invaded his shop. The story of the body in the churchyard ran through the streets with the crowds. Several gentlemen near Paternoster Row set pen to paper and handed their paragraphs, outraged, disturbed and horrified, to the printers to be set into morning papers on Monday, then shrugged into their coats and set off comfortably for their homes or their clubs in the gloom. The streets began to empty and a fog crawled up from the river, dampening the echoes and folding each household up in its cold arms.

The coffee house on the corner of King Street and Charles Street, Westminster, was always relatively quiet at this time of the evening. There were a number of tables occupied and a low hum of conversation, but those who did public business near Parliament went in general to more fashionable places to see and be seen. That said, anyone might stop in there for a moment and fall into conversation without it being remarked upon. It was known to the more influential people in the capital that a Mr Palmer was to be found in this place every evening for an hour or two with the newspapers, his favourite table being one that gave him a view of the door, yet remained in the half-shadows. Various people spoke to him during the course of an evening and the regular patrons and waiting staff found it was more profitable not to notice who they were, nor what their demeanour was on entering or leaving. This evening, as Mr Palmer folded the *Gazette* with a sigh and opened the *Advertiser*, he noticed a man in a plum-coloured coat just coming in at the door. He made some enquiry of the waiter and then turned in Palmer's direction. It was only then that Mr Palmer noticed the monkey sitting on his shoulder. Palmer shifted slightly in his chair and seemed somehow with that subtle movement to make himself visible. The man with the monkey saw him, approached and was invited to take a seat.

Mr Palmer was a valued man at the Admiralty though his duties were somewhat obscure, and his wage, and the expenses of his office, were paid from certain confidential funds controlled by His Majesty's Government. For that Government he traded in confidential information, favours, rumours and secrets, followed threads and ideas across the oceans without leaving the streets around Whitehall, and by so doing guarded the interests of Britain against the squalls caused by disruption in foreign courts. Politicians from all parties sought him out, and it was not unknown for influential citizens to do the same in this manner when the city's interest in trade became political and it was necessary to have a friend who had the ear of the First Lord. He had not been sought out by Dr Drax before, however. He knew him, of course – a physician who, without owning land, had built up a modest fortune in the West Indies. Now he had a large and fashionable practice in the city and cared for the health of the men whose money made England healthy. He was often seen in the company of Sir Charles Jennings and that nobleman's circle of bankers, merchants and the City Aldermen. Mr Palmer also knew that Drax had written to the newspapers under various names on matters of trade affecting Britain's colonies in the West Indies. He had talent as a writer, a style of apparently shaking his head in despair at the naviety of those who disagreed with him. His arguments made his enemies indignant and defensive while flattering his friends.

Drax pulled out a chair and made himself comfortable while Palmer folded his paper and set it down. The monkey clambered down from Drax's shoulder then placed one paw on his sleeve. Drax looked at the little creature and raised an eyebrow.

'Now, Cleopatra?' The monkey bobbed its head and Drax pulled out an enamelled snuffbox from his waistcoat, opened it and held it out. The monkey reached forward and took a pinch from the box, then waited until Drax had snapped the box shut again. At this signal the little creature put the pinch to its nostril and inhaled, sneezed and stretched itself upwards, pirouetting on its back legs. The chain on its collar clinked. It then sprang up Drax's arm again and buried its head in the man's neck.

'Would *you* care for any refreshment, Dr Drax?' Palmer asked.

'My thanks, but no, Mr Palmer. This is an out-of-the-way place, isn't it? How many dark corners there are in London.' Mr Palmer felt no need to answer so waited. Drax smiled swiftly.

'You have heard, I think, of this murder this morning at St Paul's?' he said, tapping on the short squashed paragraph in the evening paper. Palmer only nodded. 'I understand you are acquainted with Lord Keswick – that is, the man who calls himself Gabriel Crowther – and with the Widow Westerman.'

'Captain Westerman was much admired in the service, Dr Drax. And is still greatly missed.'

Drax seemed to be trying to read his face. Mr Palmer silently wished him luck.

'That is, some friends out of Germany hinted perhaps . . . and that business at the opera house some years ago. There was some suggestion you might . . .' Drax's eyes were almost hazel and the half-smile on his lips did not reach them. Without looking round, he put his hand up to stroke the monkey. She gripped his fingers and rubbed her cheek against them. Palmer watched for a moment before replying.

'I am still acquainted with Mrs Westerman, and I have met Mr Crowther on occasion. He has spoken twice at the Royal Society this year and is not, I think, the recluse he once was. Does the Lord Mayor perhaps wish for their assistance? Or the Aldermen? Is that why you mention the killing?'

'I was there when Mrs Westerman and the coroner brought the news to the widow. Poor Mrs Trimnell. Deeply upsetting. Mr Crowther has already taken it upon himself to examine the body on the coroner's behalf.'

Palmer held the coffee pot in the air and as the girl came to collect it, said, 'Indeed. I understand Mr Crowther and Mrs Westerman were able to give Bartholomew the first hint as to poor Mr Trimnell's identity. Useful, since so many of his acquaintance were watching the balloon-raising. Was it edifying?'

Palmer's life was that of a gambling man, though he never sat at a table. He guessed that his information was better than Drax's or that of Sir Charles Jennings, and felt it was worth demonstrating it in this small way. If a man is about to ask you a favour, show him your strength.

'It was inspiring,' Drax replied, 'but what is the good of all this wondrous progress, this innovation and our investment in human ingenuity, if we are not safe from the savages on the street. I have, as I am sure you know, appealed to the Government on numerous occasions to stem the tide of Negroes sweeping into this country. Mr Trimnell's death was an unavoidable result of our concerns being ignored.'

Mr Palmer appeared interested. 'Was it? You have proof of that?'

'I am certain proof will be forthcoming.'

'So, a strong suspicion only.' Drax shrugged and spread his hands. Palmer continued. 'Many of the Africans recently arrived here fought with our troops in America and were promised their freedom. Would you have had us desert them?'

Drax looked amused. The monkey chattered and bobbed its head. 'Yes, and returned to their masters. It would have been better for us, better for our relations with this new "United States", better for Mr Trimnell possibly and certainly better for the Negroes. We brought them here to idle, thieve and starve on the London streets. I fear that many do not understand the Negro nature as we who have lived with them do. They are savage, brutish, and given their freedom have no notion of how to live in a civilised world. Slavery is their salvation. Free them, and their minds turn easily to mischief and revenge. Undoubtedly this is the case in this instance. We did try and warn you.' He sighed.

Palmer spoke slowly. 'Then you must be eager to see Trimnell's killer bought to justice. Mrs Westerman and Mr Crowther have had some success – you must welcome their help.'

'Indeed. Whoever made this foul mockery of a man in the Bishop of London's own churchyard must be brought to justice, but I have . . . concerns. Suppose those who would destroy our trade with Africa out of some mistaken sense of fellow feeling with the slaves, suppose they were to suggest there was some justification for the killing . . . Oh, my dear! The argument could become violent on both sides. And while I would not call Mrs Westerman foolish as such, women *are* sensitive, and prone to be swayed by passionate appeals from those who like to pretend their misfortunes are the fault of others. Did you know Mrs Westerman has a black servant who, I hear, helps her with her accounts? Whom she left in charge of her estate, and her white tenants, when she went dashing off to Maulberg last year? I understand she is a widow and so whatever help is available must be welcome – but still! There are rumours she is likely to let her black marry one of her other servants. Are there not enough tawny brats clogging up the poorhouses already? Keswick's father owned shares in some of our enterprises, but he sold them out and then, of course, Mrs Westerman is currently residing in Berkeley Square with *Mr Graves*.' He spread out his arms, inviting sympathy, and the monkey ran down one of them again and crouched on the table, staring hard at Mr Palmer, while Drax tutted more in sorrow than in anger. 'The people of this country do not understand the trade, Mr Palmer. We are accused of being monsters by people who have never left this island and step over their starving countrymen on their own doorsteps to wave their fingers at us. There are some ugly necessities, of course, but the Africans we take from that dark place are saved from the savagery of their own people. Mr Palmer, I have seen with my own eyes black traders slit the throats of men who have been rejected as unfit for sale off the coast of Guinea. Many captains risk their profits to buy such slaves out of mercy, and yes, then some die on the journey.'

'It is strange the Africans are not more grateful for their deliverance,' Palmer said innocently. 'Many go to great lengths to destroy themselves, rather than be saved by you, I am told. Must not the ships be fitted with netting to stop them throwing themselves to the sharks?'

'You make my case for me. Some people must be protected even from themselves. They are children. Now, all right-thinking subjects of His Majesty are, naturally, quite grateful to Mr Crowther and Mrs Westerman for their energy, but they do not understand the city, the trade or the Negro race. Many of us would be glad if they might be informed, tact-fully, by a friend such as yourself that they need trouble themselves no more in this particular matter. The city has its own resources.'

'Your confidence is most reassuring,' Palmer said.

Drax was waiting, hoping perhaps for an assurance that the message would be passed along. None came. He studied the air above Mr Palmer's head as the low chatter in the coffee house continued. Notes exchanged, plans made, futures plotted and pasts picked over.

'The city, Mr Palmer, our great city. It seems so robust, so vigorous, but it is in truth a delicate place. The right conditions must exist for it to flourish, like a bloom in a hot house. The air itself must be managed.' He lifted his hand as if to stimulate the breezes where they languished. 'There is no doubt Mr Crowther and Mrs Westerman have righted wrongs. I admire their industry, but . . . now what is the naval phrase? I have it. The city would not have loose cannon on its streets.'

Mr Palmer remained silent. It was not an entirely unreasonable argu-ment. Mrs Westerman and Mr Crowther did have a talent for stirring things up, but he did not like the argument, or Drax. He continued to listen while thinking on other rumours, other currents he had felt moving in the city waters.

'They might damage that delicate balance of which I speak. You would not have children throwing stones near a glasshouse? Whatever their intention, if some pane were broken, some new current allowed within, all our prize blooms might begin to sicken. Think of the waste, the expense.' He smiled again. 'A word from a good friend, Mr Palmer. I think you understand me.'

He waited, his head on one side until Palmer smiled back. 'I do.'

'Excellent.' Drax got to his feet and the monkey leaped lightly into the crook of his arm and up onto his shoulder.

'Dr Drax, did you like Trimnell?'

A slight hesitation. 'We were not well acquainted, even during my time on Jamaica.'

Palmer finally stood and bowed to him, then remained on his feet until Drax had left the room. Then he took his seat once more and picked up the newspaper article again. Without moving, he said softly, 'Did you hear that, Mr Molloy?'

There was a grumble in the shadows behind him. 'Not deaf yet, son. I've got sharper hearing than you, I'd reckon.'

'What do you think of it?'

The shadows seemed to shrug and a curl of pipe smoke lifted from them and into the light. 'I think that fellow is a slimy bugger, and I'd count my fingers after I shook hands with him for one thing.'

Palmer smiled. 'As would I. Mrs Westerman *is* staying in Berkeley Square, I take it?'

'She is. The Coroner's Court are meeting in the back parlour of the Black Swan off Little Carter Lane, Monday morning. And Mr Crowther will be giving his evidence around ten, should you happen to find yourself in the area.'

'Did you discover anything else?'

'There's a big fella owns a riding and fencing school in Soho Square, name of Christopher. It's said he helps slaves who come to England and get it into their heads they should be paid for their work.' There was a long pause and the curl of tobacco smoke curled ghostly upwards through the gloom. Palmer knew to wait. There was a sigh and a creak as the shadow stretched its legs out under the table and yawned. 'Talked to a couple of boys. One says, "You want to know about Trimnell, ask Christopher." Other fellow then cuffs him over the back of the head. I took that as a confirmation, you might say, that the information was good.'

Palmer stared blindly at the table in front of him. The relationship between the merchants of London and the Royal Navy was of vital importance. The Merchant Navy trained and employed the sailors the Navy needed in time of war, and the revenue the Government managed to chivvy out of them fitted out the Navy's ships with guns and powder. In return, the Navy protected trade. Businessmen, bankers, admirals and politicians in easy concord. It was, in general, a situation that Palmer applauded and he exerted his considerable influence to keep these relationships easy and friendly, but the slave trade – the trade which gathered such great armfuls of revenue into the country, which paid its servants and filled its ships with tobacco, rum and sugar – made Mr Palmer uneasy.

Those captains and sailors who spent years buying slaves on the African coast then shipping them to Barbados or Jamaica had, in his experience, something broken about them. It was as if some cord between them and their fellow men had been severed. The gossip he heard in the dockyards unsettled him. Any captain might order a whipping; it was part of the code of discipline, but the punishments some of these slave-ship captains handed out to their sailors were of such severity, they suggested the actions of madmen. Ordinary seamen deserted before they were paid rather than risk being pressed into service in their crews again. Suicide was not uncommon and the general rates of mortality among the sailors were appalling. He had read accounts of the trade and had found them disturbing, even when they were written to reassure the reading populace that the trade was of benefit to all men, savages included.

There were more of these accounts appearing every year. A strange, narrow-faced man from a family of musicians — a self-taught master of the law named Granville Sharp — had taken up the Negro cause twenty years ago. He had been dismissed at first, but slowly and surely his prosecutions of slave-owners, his writs of *habeus corpus* and petitions had attracted notice. The man subsisted happily on the charity of his family and no one could find any subtle way of making him stop. Poems were being written against the trade. The Quakers published against it, then last year the Reverend James Ramsay's book had been widely read. It did not condemn slavery absolutely, but it shone a light on the practices that had shocked many. His character had been attacked with such ferocity by the planters and their friends, that Mr Palmer had begun to think there must be a great deal of truth in what he had written.

Indeed, Mr Palmer thought it possible the public mood might change, and it would be wise of the Government to reconsider its closeness to the West Indies. But then they had such a great deal of money and, one way or another, had paid for half the Members of Parliament currently in the Chamber.

'Do you know the Jamaica Coffee House, Mr Molloy?' Mr Palmer said at last.

'Well enough to spend the rest of my evening hours of leisure in that part of town. You'll be at your lodgings tonight?'

'Sleeping the sleep of the pious and righteous, as always.'

The shadows gave a low sound that might have been a laugh. Mr Palmer took a small purse from his pocket and passed it over his shoulder into the shadows. There was a soft chink of coin and a low grunt which

Palmer chose to interpret as satisfaction. He stood and dusted off his hat. 'Always a pleasure, Molloy.'

'Likewise, I'm sure,' the shadows rasped and Mr Palmer went to pay his bill.

I.11

IT WAS LATE IN the evening when Crowther was shown into the Library at Berkeley Square. He found Mrs Westerman writing at the large desk under the north window. She put her pen aside.

'Crowther! I thought you had seen enough of your fellow beings today. You are become such friends with the world, I hardly know you. Do we go to the Opera? The Pleasure Gardens?'

'You are satirical.' He sat down on one of the armchairs near the fire and half-closed his eyes. 'Are you writing to your sister?'

'Yes,' she admitted and leaned back in her own chair. 'We argued before I came away. Rather badly, I'm afraid. She feels I should marry again. Her little hints I could ignore, but she has taken it upon herself to find a number of suitable candidates.'

Crowther put his long fingers together. 'So I understand.'

Harriet sat up rather sharply. 'And how, may I ask, do you know anything of it?'

He reached into the pocket of his coat and removed a letter. 'She wrote to me.' He turned the pages over in his hand while Harriet gaped at him. 'She has some concern that you may have fled to London because of your passion for me.' Harriet was speechless. Crowther kept his voice as even as he could manage. 'Why else could you object to the charming Mr Babington, after all, as Rachel so reasonably asks, were it not for some other guilty passion?'

'She *wrote* to you?'

71

'She begs me to be kind.' Crowther looked up at the ceiling. 'She rightly suspects that I do not wish to be anything other than a bachelor, and hints that although we are good friends, we might not be compatible as husband and wife.'

There was a silence and a log cracked in the fireplace before Harriet spoke. 'I shall return to Hartswood at once and murder her in her bed.'

Crowther's laughter was rare and sounded like dry leaves turning in the breeze more than anything else, but it made his eyes gleam. 'Your sister is usually a sensible woman, Mrs Westerman. I can only think the sleeplessness that must follow nursing her child herself has softened her brain a little. You might be pleased to know that within hours I had a letter from her husband telling me to ignore whatever his wife had said. I think he must have been in a passion when he wrote it. Mr Clode's handwriting is normally far more legible.'

Harriet did not speak and he turned to look at her. The light of the fire and candles brought out the most vivid runs of red in her hair, and he noticed for the first time that the lace on her sleeves and bodice was worked with silver threads, which shifted and shimmered as the flames breathed around her. He felt a pang in his chest in the region he knew from his studies was occupied by his heart.

'Are you quite certain you do not wish to marry again, Harriet? Are you certain you do not wish to marry me?'

'Good God, quite certain. We would deal terribly with each other.' He returned his gaze to the modest fire in the grate and heard her stand and move across the room. She went on: 'Though I did feel a little abandoned when you left. I believe I thought you could play the dragon at the gate, scaring off anyone who dared come pressing his suit.' He felt her hand resting on his shoulder and without looking away from the fire reached up to take hold of it in his own and briefly turned to kiss the knuckles by the mourning ring she wore for her dead husband.

'I deserted you, my dear. I apologise.'

She squeezed his fingers and he released her then watched as she crossed the room to take the chair opposite him. 'No matter, Crowther. I escaped the Tower.' She too stared into the fire, her chin in her hand. 'No, worse than Rachel was Verity Graves. I went to her, full of indignation about Rachel's machinations, and Verity told me she thought I should marry as well. For the good of the estate.' She looked thoroughly miserable. 'My instructions and wishes are unclear. Apparently I pay too much to some of the tradespeople and forget the kindnesses of others. Added to which, William made various arrangements while we were on the continent, and I, not knowing he had done so, set about countermanding him as soon as we came home. I did not realise how much he had been doing on our behalf. I felt a very great fool listening to her, Crowther.'

'Mrs Graves is a sensible woman, but I do not understand why she thinks marrying you off to that idiot Babington would be of benefit to the estate.'

She looked at him. 'I thought you rather liked Babington.'

'Certainly not. I simply disliked him a little less than most of our neighbours.'

She laughed at that, and the sound cheered him. He leaned forward to give her the letter he had received from Rachel. 'Do not read it, Mrs Westerman. Burn it and forget it.'

She held it between her thin fingers for a moment. 'What Verity said about the estate hurt me deeply. Am I really so incapable?'

'Burn it, Harriet.'

She threw it on the fire then stood again and began to walk back and forth along the hearth rug. Mrs Westerman was never able to stay still very long. He watched her with an obscure sense of relief and a certain warmth in his bones that he had learned to interpret as happiness. 'Come then, Crowther. Complete your brilliance. Tell me then, what did you learn this afternoon?'

He tilted his head back and stared at the elaborate mouldings that wound their way around the ceiling and the various painted scenes and skies they framed. He was enjoying her attention and the anticipation of the effect his next words would have.

'I learned that Mr Trimnell was not murdered.'

Harriet came to a sudden halt. He examined her sideways; her expression showed a pleasing degree of wonderment. 'It seems a rather complex suicide,' she said at last.

Crowther laughed again. 'He was assaulted, certainly, but if his assailants did mean to kill him, I'm afraid they didn't have the opportunity to do so. His heart was grossly enlarged. In my opinion it was the shock of the blow across his back that killed him, but in truth he could have fallen at any time.'

Harriet began to walk again. 'So someone beat him, stripped him to his shift, attached that mask to him, dealt that first blow.'

'They had no time to do anything else. By the by, those idiots at the Cathedral had thrown his shift on the fire. I do not think they shall do such a thing again.'

'He falls to the ground and they begin to stake him out . . .'

'But before they have finished doing so, they realise he is already dead – and flee.'

'How *interesting*,' Harriet said, a light sparkle in her eye. 'The charge would be manslaughter then. They may not have meant to kill him at all, merely humiliate or punish him. I wonder what they thought when they found they were binding a corpse?' She frowned suddenly. 'I still want no part of it, Crowther. Not even if you share your guinea fee with me.'

Crowther sighed and picked up the evening paper. 'I give my evidence on Monday at the Black Swan at ten, Mrs Westerman. Perhaps you might come along and frown at me if I use too much Latin in my answers to the jury.'

PART II

II.1

Sunday 8 May 1785

EVERY FAMILY HAS ITS own rituals. In Sussex, it was expected that the entire family attend Sunday worship in the village church. In London, Mrs Service indulged her interest in theological fashions and the family never knew until breakfast was over and Mrs Service was giving her orders to the servants which church they would be attending. However, in the weeks that they had been in London she had developed a decided preference for St Mary Woolnoth in the city. It was at St Mary's she had met Mrs Eliza Smith and she felt it was only proper to see her again and make Susan apologise for running out of her shop.

The Rector at St Mary's was an attractive, energetic kind of man. Mrs Service was disappointed by most of the Church of England clergy, all decaying and, it seemed to her, careless of their duties, mouthing their way in obvious boredom through other people's sermons read from a book. Mrs Service would never be a Methodist, but she took her religion seriously so it was a pleasure to see Dr Fischer so engaged, and engaging with God and with his parishioners. She also noticed that Stephen Westerman had paid more attention during Dr Fischer's sermon than during any other. What Stephen did, the Earl of Sussex did also. Mrs Westerman did not always attend church when they were in town, but Mrs Service had asked her to, in the hopes that she might set an example for Susan.

St Mary's was a fine church. Where other, older places of worship in the city had been crushed and harried by the new buildings surrounding them, St Mary's high-columned frontage pushed everything else back from it. The interior was all light and elegance, the columns grouped like groves of silver birch – and best of all, the preaching was full of passion.

The Reverend Dr Fischer was an evangelical and a powerful rhetorician and he had gathered an impressive, wealthy congregation around him with his skills. He had enjoyed an adventurous and dissolute youth until he heard the call of God, he told them, and while caught in a week-long storm in the Pacific, he had answered Him. In the years that followed, he had studied his faith still seeking his fortune on the waves, until an illness had kept him on shore when he had wished to undertake another voyage. That illness had saved his life. A fever that started among the slaves in the hold had spread to the men who guarded them, and killed the man who had taken Fischer's place on the journey. Seeing the hand of Providence in that, he took Holy Orders. It made excellent matter from which to build his sermons. Faith to him was a storm, God's love a good sailing wind, doubt was a calm when the water supplies ran low, and salvation was a return to your own shores, your people and their love. It was no surprise then that Stephen, son of a sailor, listened to him with delight.

As Harriet and Mrs Service escorted the children into the church, Harriet was aware of being watched. It was a familiar sensation. She neither dropped her eyes to the marble floor nor lifted her chin to stare about her defiantly, but concentrated instead on appearing entirely natural. The verger showed them where they might sit, and she ushered the boys, Eustache holding Anne's plump fist, ahead of her and was preparing to follow them when she saw Mrs Service and Susan

exchanging greetings with a pleasant-looking woman with slightly
untidy chestnut hair. Susan murmured something, upon which the
woman with the chestnut hair smiled at her very warmly and put a
hand on her shoulder – then, in a gesture that surprised Mrs Westerman
– she leaned forward and kissed Susan on her cheek before moving away
to find her own place in the growing congregation. Harriet had heard
all about Susan and Eustache's escapade the previous afternoon, so was
ready to guess the identity of the pleasant-looking woman.

'What did she say to you, Susan?' Harriet asked as the girl slipped
in beside her.

'That the most important thing is to be kind,' she said quietly. 'I
thought she would be cross, but she seemed to think it was funny. She's
much nicer than her books about virtuous little children.'

Mrs Service settled and smoothed down her black skirts. 'She is wise
beyond her years and had a great many sensible things to say on your
education, Susan. I now have a new list of schools.'

Susan groaned loudly enough for a woman in front of them to turn
and look at her over her shoulder. 'Does she think I should spend an
hour every day learning to get in and out of a carriage without showing
my ankles?'

'You shall hear nothing of what she thinks until we have that apology
from you, my girl. I cannot understand where this stubbornness comes
from,' Mrs Service whispered.

'I wish someone had taught me that trick,' Harriet said gently. 'I
think I was twice your age before I managed it, Susan.' Mrs Service
gave her a grateful smile and Susan scowled at her hands.

Harriet looked around at the congregation and noticed with a slight
start that Sir Charles Jennings was seated in the front with an elderly
lady to his right.

'I did not know Sir Charles worshipped here,' she said.

'Oh yes,' Mrs Service said. 'That is his cousin, Mrs Jennings, with him; she has acted as his hostess since he came to London. He is a widower, has been for many years. He and many of the Aldermen and bankers started coming here when Dr Fischer took over the living. Are you acquainted with him?'

'A very little,' Harriet said, and continued examining the rest of the crowd. The coroner, Mr Fletcher Bartholomew, was in the centre of the congregation with a wife and two young children alongside him. She had to turn slightly to see him and when they had exchanged civilised nods, Harriet wondered if he still felt the pressure of her hand on his back showing him the way Trimnell had been whipped. As she turned back towards the front of the church, Harriet thought of the many congregations she had prayed with over the years. St James's in Piccadilly, with its scattering of titles, personages from the theatre and musicians – a living page from the gossip magazines; the country gentry of the village in Sussex, old England all itching to be at table or at sport; and here, here she tasted money in the air. In all of them there was this careful grading of the congregation; the richer you were, the closer to God. On impulse she turned again and looked behind her. There were no black faces in the crowd at all. 'Is that Dr Fischer?' she said.

A handsome man in dark robes with a full wig was standing talking to Mrs Eliza Smith. They were too far away to hear, but Harriet thought the conversation looked serious. After a few minutes, Mrs Smith turned her back rather decidedly on the priest and, a little while later, the service began.

There were places in England that were sacred to Francis Glass, and this, the library of Mr Hinckley in Hampstead, was one of them. He was an intimate of the family. The servants smiled at him and Miss Hinckley always shook his hand. Mr Hinckley and he sat by the French windows that opened out onto his lawn and talked. When Francis first began this Sunday ritual Mr Hinckley would study the account books closely; now it was a matter of form, and once Francis had asked whatever advice he particularly wished for, Mr Hinckley would sit back and tell stories from his youth, of his first victories and disasters in the book trade, of the personalities of the authors, of talents squandered or mediocrities made rich. He would apologise, 'I have reached my anecdotage, Francis!' Then laugh, but when Francis spoke of some-thing new or different he had read, a hungry light would appear in his eyes. As the younger man, Francis felt it should be Mr Hinckley's role to counsel caution, but often those roles were reversed. 'Be bold, Francis! I have no time for fools who wander into our business with no idea of the price of paper and ink, but you have earned the right to trust your instincts. You have enough politeness on the shelves, put a little mustard into it!'

Then with Mr Hinckley's mustard in his ears, Francis would stride back into London, call on Mrs Smith and ask her to marry him. Eliza would refuse, very sweetly, and Francis would be cautions, careful and polite again – until the following Sunday.

Dr Fischer's sermon was rousing. He was one of that breed of men who become something other than their everyday selves when given a pulpit and a sea of faces looking up at them, asking for their souls to be saved. He seemed to flatter and rouse his audience at the same moment. He spoke of love, kindness and bravery, spoke of the balloon lifting towards the Heavens and the winds which carried it, which carried English civilisation, English freedom across the globe. Harriet realised the priest must have been one of Sir Charles's party sitting on the balcony and admiring the balloon's manoeuvres while Mrs Trimnell learned she had become a widow. Stephen's eyes shone as he listened. Eustache, normally so withdrawn from his fellows, listened with a sort of glow on his pale skin, nodding from time to time. Even Harriet felt it, the pride pushing upwards and out of the white cube of the church. The final hymn was sung, a simple tune easy for even someone as unmusical as Harriet to hear and repeat. It fitted together very neatly, the poetry in which they all promised God to be better versions of themselves and the tune which marched along underneath it.

Sir Charles and the older woman on his arm led them all out of the church, but he paused on his way in order to reach over to Harriet, shake her hand and treat her to his fatherly smile. She smiled back at him and felt the exchange being noted by all the burgers and merchants of the city. It was as if a single ray of light had illuminated her through the church window and made her briefly beautiful to them.

He passed by, and took the light of the crowd's attention with him. Mrs Service began the process of corralling the children, finding what they had lost, put down or tucked away, and giving them coins for the retiring collection while Harriet dawdled, watching Dr Fischer from the corner of her eye. He had taken the opportunity to speak again to Mrs Smith, who was shaking her head. Another parishioner was plucking at Dr Fischer's sleeve and the woman moved away as soon as she had the opportunity to do so.

'Mrs Westerman?' Harriet found the family assembled and waiting for her.

II.2

Mrs SMITH ALWAYS RECEIVED Francis in her private parlour upstairs. It was another sacred space for him. The prints of Bible stories and churches which hung around her walls had become familiar friends, as had the blue and yellow wallpaper which she had scolded herself for buying and stared at happily, her pleasure spiced with just a little guilt, ever since. She had placed her favourite armchair where the light was best, and there he found her every Sunday with the tea things ready beside her and a book in her hand. He felt the comfort of their rituals. Her first question was always about the health of Mr Hinckley, the second about his own, but today instead she stood up from her chair rather more quickly than usual, put the book she was reading carelessly aside and asked after the manuscript she had given him the day before. He had forgotten it entirely and the surprise on his face told her so at once. 'Oh, Francis!' she said. 'I do so want you to read it.'

'I shall.' He would have read a thousand manuscripts to make her smile at him again.

She tutted. 'You were plotting how to make Mr Hinckley even richer, I know it. Well, I cannot scold you when you are working so hard. Mr Hinckley is a good man, isn't he?'

'Of course he is, Eliza.'

'He does not take advantage of you, Francis?'

He guessed that she meant something to do with the colour of his skin. Such things were seldom mentioned between them and it disturbed him. He answered seriously. 'He reminds me of your father, and everything I know about bookselling I have learned from Mr Hinckley, but what is it, Eliza? Why do you ask if he is a good man? I promise you he pays me a fair wage.'

'No, no.' She put her hand out to him again as if he had just entered the room. 'I have heard nothing against Mr Hinckley, only sometimes I think it is hard to tell who is good and who is not.'

A sudden selfish doubt. 'You think I am a good man, don't you?'

'Only too good.' Her smile was warm again, as if she had thrown off whatever pressed on her. 'Even if you are *very* slow in reading manuscripts which I give to you.'

The sun was bright again, and the room home and safety once more. 'Give me my tea, Eliza, and my answer, then I shall read the manuscript this afternoon and come back with my opinion this evening.'

She claimed it a fair bargain and they fell into their usual pattern of conversation until the sales and purchases of their rival booksellers had been discussed, and whatever they had read that week praised or damned. When the bread and butter was gone, Francis stood and picked up his hat and coat then asked her, as he did every week, if she would marry him. He then waited for her usual refusal and the smile that accompanied it, soft and regretful enough to give him hope, and kind enough to warm him for the next day or two at his duties.

Instead she looked up at him, her pale white skin with the lines just beginning to show around her eyes, and asked a question of her own. 'Francis, why do you want to marry me?'

'Because I wish you to be my wife. You know that, Eliza.'

She shook her head. 'No, Francis. I am not sure that I do, I think sometimes it is because you loved my father, and he was good to you when the rest of the world was not. I'm afraid that you wish to marry me out of gratitude. And I do not wish you to marry me for that.'

It was deeply unfair, of course it was unfair – but worse than that, it was not the usual order of things. Words would not come to him, struggling and stuttering on his lips. 'I do love what I see of him in you, Eliza. Naturally I do, but you yourself—'

She rushed on. 'And sometimes I believe it is because I am English, and by marrying me you hope to make yourself English also.' Why was that wrong? What was wrong with binding himself to his adopted country? 'You never speak of Africa, or what family you had there. When I first met you, you could hardly speak English at all. You cannot simply forget what happened to you by marrying me! And it is not fair of you to ask me to marry you just to wipe it all out.'

Francis was too shocked to look at her, and dropped his eyes to his hands, the neat tricorn of his newish felt hat held between them. He remembered suddenly when he had first come to London, met Eliza and her father and brother, how he had tried to scrub his hands white. He had thought if he could only do so, his master would not take him back to the West Indies, away from the ordinary kindness of the house where they had lodged. He concentrated. 'Does it not occur to you, Eliza, that I ask you to marry me every week, because I love you very much?'

'It does. That is what I hope, of course.' She came close to him and put her hand high on his chest. By chance she touched the place where under his clothes he was branded with the mark of the first man who had bought him. He put his hand around her fingers and lifted them to his lips, then let them lie again against his collarbone. Some part of him wondered, if she kept her hand there long enough, the brand would disappear. 'But I need to be certain of it, Francis. And I do not think I can be while you deny . . .'

'I do not deny!' He moved away from her, running his palm against the close-cut hair on his head. He felt the scars on his back burn under his clean coat. 'I do not forget! But I would have some peace from it, Eliza. Every man or woman in London sees my history in my face. I am alone with the fear or curiosity of every stranger. I have only hoped that our long friendship, my constant devotion to you and your family, might make you – you of all people – forget my colour and treat me as a man.'

She took his arm again.

'Francis, my dear, I do not wish to forget your colour, nor do I need to do so in order to see you as a man. I do not. That doubt is in *your* mind, not mine.'

'You want to hear my history? Does my tragedy appeal to you? Do you wish to make me a parable? We could end it in a church with me expressing my gratitude to God for my deliverance.'

She came closer to him again. She was speaking more slowly now, the heat in her first words gone. 'My God and I want the same thing, Francis. Your honesty. My dear, I do not think you have to choose between being a bookseller in London and an African.' He found his mind empty, an ocean in airless days. 'You will tell me of your history and I shall grieve with you, but I will not pity you.'

He lowered his head until it rested on her shoulder and felt her hand around the nape of his neck. He was a man shipwrecked. 'I had a brother,' he said at last. 'Three years younger than I am. We were taken at the same time and he died before we even reached the coast.' He pulled himself away from her and wiped his face on his handkerchief. 'There, now will you marry me?'

She laughed. 'Probably, Francis,' then, serious again: 'What was his name?'

Francis saw him suddenly, his eyes too large for his face. He was laughing at something, a strange snorting laugh that shook his small body. 'Tanimola.'

'Tanimola,' she repeated carefully. His heart hurt, ached in a way it had not done for years, hearing the name come hesitating from between her rose lips.

Her face was flushed, and her hair more disordered than usual. He put his hands around her waist and kissed her full on the mouth. A golden thread ran through him. 'Probably?'

She pushed him away, but he could feel the shake in her hand. 'Probably.'

'May I come back to see you then this evening, Eliza?' She nodded and he turned to go, but found he could not. He turned back, held her to him again, kissed her again then left, hardly knowing how he managed to put one foot in front of the other.

II.3

CROWTHER DID NOT MAKE an appearance at Berkeley Square that afternoon, and after Harriet had walked in the Square with the children for a little while, she went off in search of Mr Paxton, the celebrated cellist who was an old friend of Graves and who had played at Sir Charles's party on the Thursday evening. She took Susan with her to call at his house, but did not find him at home. His wife, however, was happy to shake Harriet's hand, kiss Susan and ask after the family in Berkeley Square, then direct her to a house in Bond Street where her husband was rehearsing that afternoon.

By four o'clock then, Harriet found herself seated beside one of the panelled walls on the first floor of a very pleasant house rented by a violinist from the Low Countries called Pieltain. There were four musicians in the room working through the slow movement of a quartet of Mr Haydn's. She was provided with the score to entertain her while they worked, and was guiltily aware that a great many people in London would have paid handsomely to trade places with her and listen to these gentlemen. She had not the ear to understand the subtleties of what they played or the skill of the performance, so she let her mind wander over the surface of the music and its elegant desires. The musicians stopped and started, questioning each other and the markings on the manuscripts in front of them. Their ability to be practical and precise at one moment, then play again with such feeling amazed Harriet, as did their apparent ability to read each other's minds. Monsieur Pieltain played a rising, dramatic figure that was then captured and held by the other players, till the movement ended in a single plucked note that seemed to Harriet somehow shocking and seductive.

She watched Susan out of the corner of her eye. The girl sat with her head slightly on one side as she listened intently. Harriet felt guilty: she had no business being here, and she certainly had no business bringing Susan with her. Poor Mrs Service had mentioned that she had had a note from Mr Babington's sister, who happened to be in town and planned to call that afternoon. Harriet immediately stated that she would be out visiting Mr Paxton, and had invited Susan to go with her out of nothing but bad temper.

'A pause before the Allegro,' Paxton suggested now. 'It will work up an old man like myself into a sweat, and I would like to talk to Mrs Westerman without puffing and panting at her.'

The violinist nodded and set down his bow on the stand in front of him. Paxton gently laid his cello on its side and patted it before he stood and shrugged on his coat so he could greet Mrs Westerman and Susan properly.

He smiled at Susan and enquired after Mrs Service and Graves and Jonathan. His voice, though he had been in the capital many years, still had a trace of his roots in the north of the country, and he had an old-fashioned courtliness about him. He told Susan he thought she looked more like her mother every day. Harriet was reminded of her own father, a man of kindness and faith who always seemed about to smile.

Harriet made some attempt to compliment the music she had just heard, and he replied, 'It does have a certain charm, doesn't it? Though I think Mr Haydn borrowed rather heavily from Gluck for that little tune.' He added conspiratorially, 'And really it is just a chance for young Monsieur Pieltain to seduce the ladies who sit in the front rows with his talents.'

Harriet noticed the violinist shake his head over his score as he heard this, though he grinned as he did so. 'Now, Mrs Westerman, what can I do for you?'

'I came to ask you about a party you played at on Thursday night, in Portman Square.' She hesitated. 'It may seem a little strange, but I wondered what your impressions were.'

The other members of the quartet all looked up with renewed interest and Paxton invited them into the conversation with a sweep of his hand. 'We were all there, my dear. And we all know better than to ask why you wish to hear what we thought.'

'Money,' said M. Pieltain, pushing back his shirt-sleeves. 'My impression was of money. There must have been ninety people there, and as many servants to hand them their wine.'

'Sir Charles has taste though,' the viola player said. He was reclining lazily in his chair, a complete contrast to his rigid stance when he played. It was as if he had unravelled when the music stopped. 'At least when it comes to music.'

'Naturally,' Paxton said. 'He hired *us*!'

'And permitted us to play something other than Handel,' Pieltain said. 'I even managed to smuggle in a couple of my own pieces. And I wish everyone would pay us as he did for the pleasure of our company.'

'Oh, have you written something new, Monsieur Pieltain?' Susan said. 'May I see it? I so enjoyed your Concerto.'

'I have the score for my latest work of genius – a quartet – here, if you wish to see it, dear lady.'

Susan skipped over to where he was standing.

Paxton raised his eyebrows, looking at Harriet. 'I doubt that you, Mrs Westerman, are much concerned with Sir Charles's musical tastes. The evening was very well organised. We, and the other musicians hired, were well treated and well paid. There was a Negro band playing in addition to ourselves.'

'Damn fine musicians, some of those black fellas,' the viola player said with a yawn. 'Seems the darker they are, the better they can blow a horn. Not that a great number of Sir Charles's lot would know quality when they heard it.' The man, Harriet noted, had the nose and red cheeks of a drinker. His bitterness has stained him, she thought.

Paxton continued. 'A great number of people ate and drank until midnight at least, which was when I took my leave, but aside from the magnificence of the occasion, I do not believe that there was anything of particular interest that occurred.'

Harriet felt foolish. The musicians were being kind to her, but she did not know what questions to ask. 'There was a woman there – a

Mrs Trimnell,' she said. 'I know a great crowd was present, but might you have seen anything of her? She is a handsome woman, something just over thirty, and dresses rather showily, if well.' She remembered the man with whom Mrs Trimnell had walked into the private parlour the previous day. 'And she may have spent much of her time flirting with Sir Charles's son, Randolph. Her husband was killed on Friday evening, though he did not attend the party.'

Mr Paxton scratched his chin, his still handsome face suddenly sad and thoughtful. 'Killed? Ah, what times we live in. Now, there was a fellow seemed to be making himself unpleasant to a woman like that at the back of the room while Miss Park was singing, do recall, Shield?'

The viola player nodded. 'I do at that. Almost told them to shut their traps. She was dressed like a peacock. Pretty gems on her too.'

'Do you recall what was said?'

He frowned. 'Couldn't hear much, though there was "husband" and "disgrace" in there.' Harriet wondered if someone had taken it upon themselves to criticise Mrs Trimnell's flirting. Shield picked up his viola and thrummed at the strings with his left hand. 'To be frank with you, Mrs Westerman, I didn't notice much of what was said. You see, I was too busy watching the fellow's monkey. I swear it was swaying in time to the song. I had a lovely time telling Miss Park about her new admirer.'

II.4

FRANCIS SPENT THE REST of the afternoon walking, moving between the crowds of Sunday idlers at a determined pace. He went down Fleet Street and along the Strand, passing the great houses, the clusters of shops – some shuttered, some not – without looking at them and thinking only of Eliza. Her 'probably' made him happy beyond belief; her questions about his past and his motivations for marriage confused and upset him. So his heart expanded and he forged his way blindly through the city until he found himself, to his great surprise, in St James's Park. The crowds were already beginning to thin. Well-dressed couples with their children and dogs still strolled down the wooded paths and he could hear the lowing of cattle in the middle distance. He was looked at with the usual mild curiosity of a crowd who still found his race a novelty, but did not wish to damage their carefully contrived air of sophistication by showing it.

He glanced up into the sky. There was a strong hint of evening in the clean air, and he turned and began to walk back towards the city again, his thoughts, like his pace, more measured now. He recalled what she had said about him being both African and a bookseller. He had loved books with a hungry passion for many years. The first man he had seen reading was the blood and thunder steward on board one of the slavers where his master had loaned him as a servant to the captain. He had asked what the man was doing, and when he was told that the thing he held contained stories, he thought there must be witchraft in it. When the steward was elsewhere, he lifted the book to his ear and asked it very politely if it would tell him a story of the Tortoise and the Elephant. It would not speak to him and he remembered that sting of disappointment and shame at its silence. Perhaps the book thought it was beneath it to tell the tales he wanted to hear.

He learned more clearly what a book was on his first visit to England. Then on the return voyage to the West Indies, one of the other boys on the ship had taken pity on him and begun to teach him to read from a book of his own. The book was *Robinson Crusoe* and slowly, painfully, Francis learned to understand it. It was his first friend and ally, and it spoke of a world he understood. He thought at first it was the Holy Book of the white men. When he discovered it was not, he made it his own. The boy made him a present of it. There were several days in his life that Francis would always remember so vividly he could relive them at will. The day of his capture, that of his trial, that of his freedom and the day he puzzled out a chapter of *Robinson Crusoe* on his own and understood it. Who better than him to sell books? Who better than him to understand what they could do for a man?

As he passed under the Temple Bar he realised that he had not read the manuscript, and that it was already dark. Lamps were lit along the road, pools of yellow light. It was a great deal later than he had thought. He hesitated, wondering whether to collect the manu-script from his office and read it overnight before returning to Eliza in the morning with his report on it like a schoolboy. He remembered the kiss; he had never held her like that before. Surely it would be better to go to her house as promised, even at this late hour, even if it was only to apologise again. She would forgive him. She must realise that their conversation would have set him racing about all afternoon. He would not try to kiss her again, he would not propose again. He would be honest with her. He would say he had thought about what she had said and intended to think more on it, then return to his bed and hope the day of walking would have worn him out sufficiently; and even if his mind still sped forwards and back into different futures, different pasts, he would sleep anyway. He did not turn up the road to his own lodgings then, but turned past the dark mass of St Paul's towards her home.

Fear crashed over him before he could make sense of what he smelled in the warm evening air. Smoke. Not the usual soot of charcoal and iron – something sharper. He looked up: the upper window of Mrs Smith's shop was open and he could just see flames, dully flickering free in the room, the plume of smoke creeping out and upwards.

'Fire.' The word struggled from his throat in a whisper. He ran the final couple of yards to the house and forced his voice into a shout. 'Fire!' This time he screamed it and began hammering at the door. 'Fire, I say! Awake!' A face or two appeared out of the gloom of the street and other voices took up the call. Panic swirled and swung through his muscles, closing his throat. He battered at the shop door again and tried to peer in through the windows. They were crowded with prints and advertisements, but beyond them he could see the dark interior – and no movement but the billowing smoke.

He felt a hand heavy on his shoulder, and twisted round. A constable stood behind him in a short cape and wide-brimmed hat that left his face in shadow. 'You know the house?' he said. 'How many here?'

'A maid and a boy sleeping downstairs at the back. The mistress of the house. We must get this door down!' He all but yelled it into the constable's face.

The man nodded and reared back, and together they barged at the lock. Once, twice, and at the third assault – the shock of it splintering through his shoulder – there was a crack as the wood around the lock gave way and they tumbled into the shop. Deep dark and thick smoke. Shadows and light from the upper floor, the parlour, a strange crack and grinding in the air like a giant's teeth snapping bones.

'Out back in the kitchen – the maid and a boy,' Francis shouted, and the smoke sank into his lungs and stung him. The constable blundered off into the darkness, his cape held over his nose and mouth, his lamp swinging wildly to right and left. Francis pulled his handkerchief out and held it over his face then sprinted up the stairs. 'Eliza!' he shouted, though it came out as a croak. The fire was loud, but he could hear the bells being rung outside. He reached the top of the stairs, stumbled blindly forward and fell; his hands went forward to save him and he was on his knees, his palms among shattered glass. There was a stink of cold gravy. He got to his feet again and the door to her parlour was also fastened against him. He turned and kicked sideways at the brass lock and it gave way on the second blow. The heat was suddenly intense. Ribbons of flame ran around the room – the curtains and soft fabrics were alight; flames ate up the prints on the walls, burning them out of their frames. The door to Eliza's bedchamber was half-open. He called again, stepped into the sitting room, his eyes now streaming. It seemed as if the flames hesitated and turned towards him, then settled into a crouch.

He saw her. She lay on the floor half-concealed by the bulk of the sofa, its fabric already alight. He dropped to his knees and crawled towards her through the smoke. Her pale round face was turned towards him, her lips slightly open as if caught in mild surprise. One of her blue eyes was open and staring, the other gone – a bloody wound. His breath left him. No. It could not be. He denied it, absolutely. He heard himself call her name, heard himself screaming out. He reached for her hand. He must get her out, he must carry her out of here. Her skin, in the middle of the heat of the room, was cold.

There was a thunder crack above, and the ceiling seemed to bulge and pulse. The fire had found him. No matter. If he could not carry her out he would stay with her in the flames. It would only take a moment to die here. He put his arms around her – then another arm grabbed him around the chest, and as the ceiling exploded and fell, he was wrestled and dragged down the stairs and half-pushed, half-carried out into the street. He fought the man who rescued him, frantic to be free, but there were other hands on him now and they would not let him leap back into the flames. He tried to call for her but the fire had scorched out his lungs and he was voiceless. His struggles died down. The men who had held him moved away. He collapsed against the wall of one of the houses opposite, blank and broken. The fire engine had appeared and was shooting great gusts of water over their heads. Someone else collapsed onto the stones next to him – the constable who had helped him break in.

'Did you drag me out?' Francis said in a whisper.

'I did.'

'I cannot thank you.'

Someone pushed a mug into the constable's hand. He drank about half of it, then passed it to Francis. 'That's your own business.' It was porter – hard and dark drinking to Francis's mind – but it did something to cool the torn ragged burning in his throat. He could see nothing in the darkness but Elizabeth.

'The maid, the boy?' he asked at last.

The constable tried to speak but his first atempt was cut off in a fit of coughing. 'Boy was sleeping in the kitchen.' He nodded towards a small figure hunched and shivering in the shadows of a doorway opposite. 'No sign of a woman. The back window was open.' He started coughing again and spat richly on the ground. 'What about Mrs Smith?'

'She was already dead,' Francis said. It seemed as if he felt the cold of her flesh again. He managed to lift his eyes. The blaze of the upper storey was retreating under the jets of water. The men worked the pumps like furies, their sweating faces visible in the lights of the lanterns and shadows of the fire. The flames lifted and sulked. Retreating rather than dying. The constable got slowly to his feet.

'I'm grieved at that. A good lady. Well, she's thanking me in Heaven for saving you.'

Francis looked up. The man's face was streaked with soot.

'I hope I did not hurt you,' he said.

The constable bent down and patted him rather awkwardly on the shoulder. 'No, lad, you did not.' He moved away into the crowd that had come to look at the show. Francis continued to watch the flames. He could not think; a strange numbness had settled over his mind and body, so if minutes or hours passed, he could not tell.

Another tankard was put in his hands. It was then he began to shake, a bone-rattling convulsion that refused to end. A woman he knew, the wife of a grocer, put a blanket round his shoulders and asked after Mrs Smith by her first name. He croaked out the news and she held him to her until he had stopped crying. Then she looked into his face. 'Lord save us, your eyes look like the devil's, Mr Glass.' He reached up to rub the soot out of them, and only when he heard her gasp of distress did he see the blood on his hands and realise his palms were a network of sharp pains. He remembered his fall outside the parlour door. 'Right, Mr Glass. Come with me. You need cleaning up before that goes bad.' He twisted round towards the boy in the doorway and she saw him. 'That's her apprentice, Joshua, isn't it?' He nodded, unable to speak through the hurt and the smoke. 'I suppose we had better fetch him too.' She looked over her shoulder at the print shop, the slackening flames. 'Ah, poor lady.'

Francis, feeling shambling and old, let her lead him away, each step discovering new hurts from his heels to his head, and all he could see was Miss Eliza's face and the bloody wound that had been her left eye.

II.5

HARRIET AND SUSAN EXTENDED their visit to the musicians long enough to hear the Allegro and, Harriet was sure, to avoid the visit of Mr Babington's sister. They were both rather quiet as the carriage trundled out of Soho and west towards Berkeley Square. M. Peltain had lent a score to Susan, who held it tightly to her chest as she stared out of the window at the streets where she had grown up in the freedom of relative poverty. Harriet felt as if she was driving the girl back to a prison cell.

'Susan, dear, what happened in that school?'

She continued to stare out into the gloom. Lights were being lit now and her face was in shadow. 'It was such nonsense. No real lessons at all, just needlework and dancing – and all the curtseys! "This is how you speak to a servant, this is how you address a duke, this is how you pour tea for a baronet".'

'These things must be learned, Susan.'

'Bah! You don't believe that, Harriet, I'm sure you don't.'

'We must go out into the world, dear.'

'I don't want to go into that world. The girls were foul beasts. Whenever I did something wrong, they would whisper "shop-girl" to each other again and again. And they were all so stupid.'

Harriet sighed. 'Dear, you have a large fortune and a high rank. If that brings certain restrictions it also brings great advantages. In a few years you will be married and have to entertain dukes and manage your servants. You must learn these skills somehow.'

The carriage turned into Berkeley Square and came to a gentle stop outside the house.

'I do not want to be married!' Susan said fiercely. 'Why should I be? You don't want to be married again, do you? I know we only went to see Mr Paxton so you wouldn't have to be at home to Mr Babington's sister.'

Philip came down the front steps to open the door for them. Susan swept out and into the house without looking at him. Harriet thanked him as she got out of the carriage and climbed the steps at a more sedate pace. She entered the hall. Graves and Mrs Martin were standing just outside his office. Susan was already halfway up the staircase.

'Susan! Lady Susan!' Graves called out. The girl stopped but did not turn round. Harriet saw the rage on Graves's face. 'When you come into this house, you will greet your guardian and the servants in a civil manner.'

She span round. 'I do not *want* to be a lady – I told you so! The night before Father was murdered, he asked me if I wanted to be a lady and have a carriage and dresses and all this,' she waved her hand at the mouldings, the paintings, the furniture and the people, 'and I said *no*. I said no, and he said I didn't have to be a lady if I didn't want to, and now you have made me. You made me do it all anyway.' She burst into tears and ran away up towards her room, still clutching the score to her narrow chest.

Graves stared after her for a moment, looking very pale, then he turned back into his office and slammed the door closed behind him.

The grocer's wife, Mrs Perkins, took quiet good care of Francis and the boy, feeding the apprentice with soup and strong tea then plucking shards of glass from Francis's shredded palms. It was long past midnight when her husband joined them and told them the fire was out.

'Glad you got there when you did, Mr Glass,' he said, taking his place in a wooden armchair by the fire. 'A fair amount in the shop itself might be saved, and the flames didn't spread to its neighbours, praise the Lord. All down that row they owe you their livelihoods. If you ask me, some of those timbers were rotted, or hurting under the weight of the press upstairs already. Why do you inky fellas put all the metalware up top?' For a moment Francis thought he was referring to his colour, but Perkins looked only comfortable and interested and he realised it was his profession he meant.

'For the light,' he said, then winced as another sliver of glass was teased out of his hand.

'Oh aye! Fair enough,' he said, and pulled on his pipe until his wife finished washing and bandaging Francis's hands. 'You're old friends with the Smith family, ain't you?'

'I am. Mr Smith was very kind to me and I've known Miss Eliza and her brother since we were children.'

The grocer rolled his shoulders. 'Good people. Poor lady. Hope she didn't suffer much. I am sorry for your grief, son. But know that everywhere it's said you almost lost your own life trying to save her. Old Smith would have been proud of you. And grateful for your efforts.' His voice became rather thick and he turned towards the fire, puffing hard at his pipe until he could control his feelings.

Francis felt his grief at the core of him. A stone that made it hard to swallow or breathe. He glanced at the apprentice in the corner of the room. He had fallen asleep as soon as he had finished feeding and slept still. 'Miss Eliza was dead before I reached her,' he said at last and slowly. 'Cold. And there was a wound . . . her eye.'

Mrs Perkins crossed herself and her husband abandoned his pipe for a moment and frowned. 'You're certain, Mr Glass?' Francis nodded. Perkins looked grave. 'The cashbox hasn't been found.' He looked towards the child in the corner. 'You don't think . . . ?'

Francis shook his head. 'He's hardly a boy yet. I can't think it. Kill his mistress, set the fire then go down to the kitchen and wait to be saved?' His chest stung and he began to cough. It felt as if the soot of Eliza's burning home would never leave his lungs. Perkins filled his mug for him and waited until he had got it down.

'It's murky,' the grocer said when Francis had recovered. 'No sign of the maid, Penny. Suppose she tired of being virtuous, fought Mrs Smith and ran off back to the brothels with the takings?'

Francis did not speak. He had wondered the same thing.

'Oh, these strays the Smith family were always spending their charity on. Had to come to bad in the end.' Perkins came to an embarrassed halt. 'Present company excepted, Mr Glass. Naturally. It was a good day when they took you in. The "on-dit" is she fell with her candle. Perhaps that's all that needs to be said.'

Her duties as a nurse done, Mrs Perkins had taken up her sewing. She snipped her thread and spoke without looking up from her work. 'Mr Glass saw it – Mr Glass has to say it. Her brother will be along in the morning. He can lend a hand there.'

'God, Mr George,' Francis said, his voice still thin and parched. 'Who carries word to him?'

Perkins lifted a hand to calm him. 'The marshal has George's direction and they said they'll have a constable travel off at first light.'

His wife was watching Francis carefully. 'Enough talk now,' she said, and gathered up Francis's coat. 'You'll stay here tonight, Mr Glass, and don't think to argue because we won't hear you. Finish your beer while my girl and I make up a bed for you and the boy.' She got up, resting her hand on his shoulder for a moment.

Francis wondered if he had even strength enough to stand. 'I'll not argue, ma'am, but I'd as lief sleep here in the kitchen as anywhere. There's no need to disturb the lad then either.'

She hesitated. Francis was a man of some standing now, but she had known him many years, and in those times when he was well-used to a hard floor to sleep on. 'If you wish it?'

'I do.'

'I'll fetch something in to make you comfortable at least.'

The grocer finished his pipe and knocked out the embers, and when he and his wife had seen to it, Francis had all he needed and they left him to get what sleep he might. He curled up on the nest of blankets and thought of Eliza, adrift somewhere beyond grief. She was in his arms again, saying his brother's name. She had never had the chance to learn his own.

PART III

III.1

WILLIAM HANDED MRS WESTERMAN her gloves and was waiting for her to pull them straight over her wrists before he opened the door onto Berkeley Square. There was the sudden sound of a raised voice upstairs. They both flinched. Harriet finished smoothing on her gloves. 'Not one of my children, I think.'

'No, ma'am,' William replied, managing not to smile.

'You know where I am going this morning, William?'

'Yes, ma'am.' He stared straight in front of him, serious again.

'I found what you told me the other morning deeply distressing. I hate to believe that my husband ever owned a slave, or that he and our family ever profited by it. I hope very much that you are mistaken, that there may have been some misunderstanding – and that is why I have asked for various accounts from that period to be sent up from Caveley. I am sure you will have heard about this, and drawn your own conclusions. I do not wish you to think I believe you to be lying. As I say, I am only hoping there might have been some error. Do you understand?'

She looked up at him; his face remained impassive. 'I understand, Mrs Westerman.'

'Thank you.' She nodded to him and he went to open the door.

The back chamber of the Swan was full when Harriet arrived. The coroner, Mr Bartholomew, sat at a table at the north of the room under a portrait of the King with the jurors seated to his right. Crowther was already giving his evidence. Most of the jurors seemed to be following him attentively. Harriet examined the faces of those seated nearest the jury. Mrs Trimnell was today dressed in black silk. Sir Charles was seated by her side, and from the careful glances she saw Mr Bartholomew casting at the front row, she assumed he was not the only one of the City Aldermen in attendance. The younger Jennings was not present, but the man with the monkey was. He seemed bored again. The older woman who had been at church with Sir Charles sat beside him, and Sawbridge, the hawk, was seated by his daughter.

When Crowther was done, he moved to take a chair on the right-hand side of the room. He noticed Harriet as he did so, and nodded. She smiled back at him ruefully.

Bartholomew thanked Crowther and asked for Mrs Trimnell. The widow stood and made her way to the chair where Crowther had sat to give his evidence. She really did have a beautiful figure. She sat down rather stiffly and folded her hands together in her lap. Her gloves were black, but fastened with large pearls like perfect tears at the wrists. She gave her name very softly. The jurors looked sympathetic. Mrs Trimnell explained that she had been at the theatre on Friday evening with Mrs Jennings, the elderly lady who sat with Sir Charles. She thought her husband intended to work in his study a while longer, then spend the evening with friends. She did not know which friends. 'Perhaps he had it in mind to go to the Jamaica Coffee House,' she said. 'And was prevented.' She turned her head away and lifted her handkerchief as she said this. The coroner enquired very gently, if Mrs Trimnell's servants might have more exact information as to where Mr Trimnell had been going and at what time. Mrs Trimnell shook her head. 'I had given my maid the evening off, and the house girl would not notice a thing.'

Harriet thought the woman did seem genuinely upset, but it was a rather elegant grief. Harriet had been capable of neither thought nor speech in the days immediately following her husband's death, but then she knew there were many species of marriage. The coroner glanced at the front row of chairs and Harriet thought she saw the man in purple give a tiny nod. 'Mrs Trimnell, do you have any particular reason to think that your husband might have intended to go to the Jamaica Coffee House at some point during the evening?'

She smiled sadly. 'We did not speak of his plans, sir. But I thought he might be going there to show the gentlemen the mask.'

Harriet felt her back straighten and there were whisperings in the crowd. Not from those in the front of the room, however. They continued looking calmly ahead.

'You refer to the mask in which Mr Trimnell was discovered, madam?' Bartholomew asked. He said it rather too smoothly. This was obviously not the shock to him that it was to Harriet.

Mrs Trimnell nodded, then turned to the jury with a sweet sad smile. 'It was his own design and it worked very well. The Negroes did not like it at all and were much better behaved after they had been made to wear it a while. Several of the other estates nearby copied the style.' She said it as calmly as if she had been discussing a new trimming for a bonnet.

There was a general shuffling in the courtroom and some of the jury members who wore the dress of tradesmen and shopkeepers shot sidelong glances at each other. The rest only regarded Mrs Trimnell with continued sympathetic interest. Mr Bartholomew straightened his papers. 'I understand such masks are occasionally used to prevent the workers damaging their internal organs by eating soil.'

Mrs Trimnell nodded. One of the jury members whispered to his neighbour, who raised his hand. 'Yes?' Bartholomew said.

'Just was wondering, please, if Mr Trimnell carried a whip and pegs with him too?'

Mrs Trimnell answered at once. 'Why on earth would he do that? There is nothing special about the design of a whip.'

The juror blushed and looked at his hands.

Harriet felt a touch on her arm which made her start, and she turned to find herself looking into the grey-green eyes of Mr Palmer of the Admiralty. She discovered after her first surprise that she was very pleased to see him and offered him her hand. He guided her to a couple of free chairs towards the back of the room. 'I had begun to think you would not come,' he said to her softly as they sat down.

'I meant not to,' she whispered back to him, 'but I grew restless in Berkeley Square and found I had ordered the chaise brought round before I even knew what I was about. Crowther offered me a shilling to come, so that may have had something to do with it.' He smiled at her. 'What have I missed?'

'A great deal of jargon from our coroner, a rather disjointed account of the finding of the body from the verger. The Aldermen have distributed handbills asking for information about Trimnell's missing clothes and personal effects.' He handed one to her as he spoke and she tucked it into her reticule.

'What do you think the jury will say, Mr Palmer?'

He considered. 'The foreman of the jury and Mr Bartholomew seem to be leading the rest a little. I suspect they will find that on his way to the coffee house, Mr Trimnell was set upon by footpads. They found the mask on him and made him wear it, then struck the blow that caused his heart to stop . . .'

'. . . Then they panicked and fled with his clothes and valuables,' she concluded thoughtfully. 'It is not an unreasonable story. But you say *on his way* to the coffee house?'

'No one saw him there that evening. Given they knew him there . . .'

She said thoughtfully, 'I have not Crowther's knowledge, but by the stiffness of his limbs when we examined him, he cannot have died before midnight.'

She heard the smile in his voice. 'Mr Crowther made that point early in his testimony. And insisted that Trimnell died immediately on the blow being struck, rather to the foreman's irritation. They have compromised on the fact that no one saw what time he left his lodgings.'

She frowned and watched the man she took to be the foreman. He glanced once at Sir Charles while she watched. Drax had shifted in his seat and was looking at Mr Palmer and herself. He did not quite stare, but Harriet had the distinct feeling she was under observation. She was about to ask Palmer some further question, but he interrupted her. 'Mrs Westerman, would you do me the kindness of frowning as if I am saying something surprising and perhaps a little unwelcome? . . . Thank you, and now if you would perhaps look down and nod a little while you absorb the force of my arguments? . . . *Excellent*. I am obviously very persuasive, but remember to keep looking displeased. Thank you. One more thing. I suspect there will be a little drama before the session closes. Please do not get caught up in it, and drag Mr Crowther away by the ear if you have to.' Her eyes narrowed and she looked up sharply at him. 'Trust me, Mrs Westerman. Now perhaps if you might sigh and nod, then I will say goodbye and we will part with reluctant politeness.'

She obeyed, but by a slight pressure on his arm prevented him from rising. 'Why are you here, Mr Palmer?'

'I wish I knew,' was all he would say. She released his arm and they shook hands. She felt him press something into her palm, but not until he had left the room and Drax had turned away again did she look to see what it was. It was Palmer's visiting card, though she noted that it gave neither address nor title. It was simply his name, with *Admiralty Office* printed below it. She knew a little of what Palmer did there; following the way the winds of war and change blew across Europe like an exquisitely sensitive weather-vane. The image amused her, and as she turned the card over she was smiling. He had written on the back only three words. *Berkeley Square, midday*. Her smile faded. It would be difficult to tell Mr Palmer she wanted none of this case. He had done Crowther and herself some expensive favours over the last few years. Also, Mr Palmer, like Crowther, had an uncomfortable habit of being able to tell what she was thinking. They would guess she was already curious. If Trimnell was going to show his cronies the mask, why then did he not arrive at the coffee shop? If he meant to spend the evening elsewhere, why carry the mask? Did the people around her really believe a footpad in London went armed with a whip, and equipment to stake out a man?

There was some movement to her left. A child was pushing his way through the crowd with an air of urgent intent. She watched his progress then lifted her eyebrows as she saw he was approaching an African man on the extreme edge of the room. The African was wearing a long riding cloak and had his hat pulled low over his face, but she was at once surprised she hadn't noticed him before. He was a head taller than the other men standing about him and the breadth of his shoulders suggested he had strength to match. He was dressed like a gentleman – it was not livery or a coachman's uniform he wore, though he stood among the poorer class of people who had come to watch proceedings. She saw him bend down as the boy tugged at his arm. At first he waved the boy off, but the child persisted and eventually with every movement suggesting deep annoyance, he followed the small figure from the room. Harriet looked out of the window to her right and saw the child leading him towards a hackney carriage. There was a short conversation between the African and the man inside, then the former climbed in and the carriage drew away. Harriet was fairly certain she recognised Mr Palmer's profile as it passed. *What are you about, Palmer?* she wondered, and tucked his card into her glove.

Mrs Trimnell concluded her evidence with an account of her father coming early to fetch her to the balloon-raising. She then returned to her chair, whereupon there was a sound of shouting in the passageway outside. All present immediately turned away from the coroner's instructions to the jury to see what was happening.

A pair of city constables were pulling a man through the chamber towards the coroner. His skin was pale brown, his coat and trousers ragged and dirty. Harriet thought he could not be more than twenty; he had the long-limbed and awkward appearance of a young man not yet fully grown. He was thin, and his eyes stared out wide and suspicious from his smooth, rounded face. His hair was cut close to his skull.

The coroner looked at the two constables with considerable irritation. 'What business do you have here? Who is this boy?'

'This is your killer, Mr Bartholomew!' the elder of the two constables said with relish. He looked around the room as if making sure everyone in the attentive crowd had the chance to see and remember his face. 'Me and Higgins here pulled him up out of the doss-house not an hour ago, acting on information given that he'd pawned a watch belonging to a slaver and got drunk on the proceeds. He was boasting as it was the first wages he'd got for his work. A concerned subject of His Majesty came to us with this information.'

Everyone began talking at once. Everyone, that is, except the boy. He remained with his head down while shouts and brays swept through the room. The monkey on Drax's shoulder danced onto its hind legs and applauded with its tiny leathery paws.

'Enough! Some quiet!' Bartholomew called, and enough of those present listened to him to allow him to be heard asking the constable if the watch had been found.

The constable lifted his chin. '*This* was found on his person!' He produced a slip of paper with the panache of a huckster unveiling his miracle pill. 'We went to the pawnbroker and he showed us the watch that was given for it.'

'Is it here?' Bartholomew said impatiently.

'Mr Thirkle!' A spindly gentleman emerged from behind the second constable and blinked at the court through thick glasses.

'Are you the pawnbroker, sir?' Bartholomew asked.

The spindly man bobbed an assent and then darted forward and put something into Bartholomew's hand. 'And is this boy the one who pledged you the watch?' It seemed the pawnbroker was not enjoying his sudden celebrity as much as the constable was. Harriet could not hear his reply, but guessed it from Bartholomew's change of expression. The coroner stood up from his chair and walked over to where Mrs Trimnell sat. She looked at what he held in his hand and nodded. Bartholomew turned away from her again and addressed the young man, still hunkered between the marshals.

'What is your name, boy?' He whispered something. 'Speak up, there's a good lad.'

'Guadeloupe.'

'And you have heard what these gentlemen are saying, Guadeloupe? Do you understand them?'

'I never killed no man,' the prisoner said with sudden fierceness. 'Not on these shores.'

The answer didn't do him any good with the crowd. There were shouts of 'monster,' and 'savage' around the room. He bared his teeth at them. Harriet was uneasy. With Bartholomew and the constables there, the boy would not come to any physical harm, and this must be the scene Mr Palmer had spoken of in which they should not intervene. She was beginning to believe, however, that removing Crowther quietly from the place might require some particular effort. She looked around her for some help. A pair of young women were lounging a little way behind her. They were finely dressed, but Harriet knew a woman of the town when she saw one. She slipped out of her seat and approached them.

Bartholomew shouted for quiet again. 'Where did you get the watch?'

'Found it.'

'Found it where?'

Guadeloupe shrugged and looked at the coroner as if he thought him rather simple, then he pointed to the world outside the windows. 'Out there.'

Bartholomew sighed. 'Have you anything else to say? Anyone to speak for you?'

'I have nothing to say. I wish to go back to my own country.'

Crowther seemed to be studying the boy with considerable interest. Harriet nodded to the two girls, one of whom immediately and with no apparent cause or embarrassment began to scream. All attention turned towards her. Harriet felt a brief spasm of sympathy for the coroner. She made her way up to Crowther's side and plucked at his sleeve. On the other side of the room and apparently out of pure sympathy, another woman began to scream as if in fear of her life. 'Come, Crowther, we have to leave.'

He looked irritated. 'Nonsense. I want to examine that boy's hands.'

'Gabriel, please.' He hesitated, but the use of his Christian name had the desired effect. He stood up, offered his arm to her, and while Bartholomew and the constables were still trying to gain control of the room, they edged their way through the crowd and out of the building.

Crowther thought he noticed the female who had started screaming and was now apparently in full hysterics on the flagstone floor look up and wink at Harriet with every sign of sense and health as they passed, but he thought it best not to remark on it.

III.2

F RANCIS WAS WOKEN BY the sounds of women moving around the room. Mrs Perkins and her servant were beginning their day. For a moment he was a boy again, ten years old and sleeping in Norfolk Street. The daily dread of his old master stirred under his ribs. Then he remembered he was a grown man with a trade, independence, freedom; his hands began to ache and his throat to burn. He remembered the fire and tasted ash. Life without Eliza, without hope of Eliza, opened out in front of him, bleak and broken.

He dragged himself up to his knees. The grocer's wife smiled at him and pointed at the pitcher and ewer set out on the table. He wiped his face on the cloth and inspected the bandages on his hands.

'Don't pick at them, Mr Glass,' she said. 'Don't want the London air getting into the cuts for a day.' She set down a tankard in front of him, and when he tried to thank her, his chest ached and he retched. 'What'll happen to the lad?' she said when he'd recovered himself a bit, nodding towards the apprentice in the corner.

'I might take him on,' Francis said. 'Or rather, recommend to Mr Hinckley that we take him on.' Mrs Perkins hid a smile. 'Miss Eliza said he was a willing boy and I think Ferguson would welcome an apprentice compositor. She got him out of the Foundling Hospital.'

It was the one thought that held any comfort for him – that he could at least look after those she had cared for. The boy was still sleeping hard, his arms flung about as if he'd been fighting flames in his sleep.

The grocer himself came in while they were still talking. He was in his coat and had the smell of the fresh air about him.

'Mrs Smith's been taken out of the house,' he said gently, taking his place at the table and picking up the knife. Francis saw him glance at the maid and he continued in a stage whisper: 'The poor woman couldn't be known. The ceiling beams collapsed right where she was lying. Smashed her skull, the constable said.'

Francis felt it first, then understood his wider meaning. Her body would not testify. The only thing that said she had not died in the fire and by an accident was his own memory of that wound in her eye and the coldness of her skin.

'And the cashbox?' he asked.

'No sign of it, or the maid,' Perkins said. 'But it's a terrible state in there, and I was thinking, perhaps Penny just got scared and ran off. Maybe it was an accident?' His voice sounded hopeful and he sighed heavily when Francis shook his head.

Within an hour, and having changed and washed the rest of the smoke off his skin at his own lodgings, Francis was back behind the counter in the shop. He did not know what else he could do. Ferguson, the two printers and the clerk had all heard about the disaster and the death of Mrs Smith. They knew her, liked her and liked Francis, so were solemn and kind. They patted him on the shoulder and welcomed young Joshua into the place. Cutter the clerk brought Francis coffee he had brewed himself in the back kitchen. He had never done so before, so Francis took it that Perkins was right and people had spoken well of what he had done in the fire. He watched Ferguson lead Joshua up to the print room, his broad hand on the boy's shoulder, and smiled briefly. He remembered being led that way himself and the hours of back-bending work that followed, undoing the dabbers every evening and soaking them in night lyme to keep them soft, the dampening of the sheets for the next day's printing. He was disposed to like the boy. Joshua had wept hard when he woke and remembered that Miss Eliza was dead, and Francis reckoned it was more out of grief for her than worry for himself. He had practically burst out dancing though, when Francis had suggested he might serve out his apprenticeship at Hinckley's.

'Real books!' he had shouted, then obviously fearing that this was some disrespect to his old mistress, looked fearful and deflated as if he had been flattened by the palm of some invisible justice. 'I do like helping to make the pictures with Mrs Smith too. But I can't draw, so I know I'd never make an engraver, sir.' Francis assured him that he understood. Walter came by very early, stinking of last night's gin but pale with worry about his friend. Francis was touched, but sent him home to sleep off the fumes.

The shutters were only just raised when a well-dressed gentleman whom Francis did not recognise entered the shop. His face was set and angry and he was marching in front of him the strange boy, Eustache, who had invaded his shop on Saturday morning.

'Stand there!' the gentleman ordered, and the boy obeyed, his chin on his chest. The man stepped forward to the desk and put out his hand. 'Mr Glass? My name is Graves. I own Adams Music Shop on Tichfield Street.'

Francis nodded. 'I am glad to know you, Mr Graves, and I would shake your hand if I could.' He lifted up his bandaged hands and Graves lost his stern expression and looked at Francis with new attention and concern.

'What on earth happened?' He peered at him. 'God, your eyes are red as Hell.'

Francis looked away. 'There was a fire last night. Mrs Smith was killed. I believe she and Mrs Service, the lady who was with the children yesterday, were friends.'

Graves rocked back on his heels. 'Oh, I am sorry to hear that indeed!

Yes, they were acquainted. Mrs Service thought very highly of her. She had the impression you were old friends?'

'We were playfellows in our youth, she, her brother and I.' Francis was glad of the smoke in his throat. It gave him a better excuse for the break in his voice.

Mr Graves spoke gently. 'My sympathies to you, sincerely. May I ask you to let us know in Berkeley Square when the funeral is arranged?' He took a visiting card from his pocket and handed it to him. Francis took it without a word. 'I am very sorry to have disturbed you.'

'Mr Graves, I have unlocked the door and taken my place on the floor. How may I be of service to you?'

Graves straightened. 'Thank you, Mr Glass. Eustache, come here and confess your sins.' The news of Mrs Smith's death had knocked the rage out of him, but his voice was still serious and low. The boy had looked surly when he first came in; now he seemed confused, nervous.

He stepped up to the counter and reached into his coat pocket to produce a board-bound volume Francis recognised with a sinking heart. The volume which held the portrait of Eustache's mother, and the tale of her scandalous youth and later, terrible crimes.

'I stole a book, sir. And I am very sorry for it.' His voice was a whisper.

'An accident?' Francis said. 'Perhaps you put it in your pocket by mistake.'

It was Graves who answered. 'Even if it was a mistake it became a crime. Look inside.' Francis picked up the book and opened it rather awkwardly. On the title page someone had written in unsteady copper-plate *Ex libris Eustache Thornleigh 1785*. It was slightly smudged.

'I am sorry for taking it, Mr Glass,' the boy said again.

Francis sighed. He would have to explain to Graves and take the blame for placing such a thing in the hands of his ward in the first

place. 'No, Eustache, I understand. Let me explain . . .' The boy's face
went white and his eyes became very wide and pleading. Francis paused.
The boy did not want his guardian to know his choice of reading
materials? Very well. He cleared his throat. 'It is one of the most exciting
volumes we sell here; there are a great many pirates in these family
romances. It was cruel of me to put it in Eustache's hands when he had
not the opportunity to finish it.' The boy's shoulders sagged with relief.

Graves replied, 'I could pay you for the book, Mr Glass, and if you
prefer it I shall, but I would be grateful if instead you let the boy earn
back its purchase. He will sweep your floors for a week. Give him the
worst jobs you can find, if you please. He must learn that what he takes,
must be earned.'

If Francis had been rested, or less sunk in his own misery, he would
have made some other answer, but as it was the words were out of his
mouth before he was aware of even thinking them. 'Since when did a
child born rich in this country have to work for what they make use of?'
Graves looked away and Francis closed his eyes for a moment. 'Forgive
me, Mr Graves. That was ill-said. Master Eustache, has your guardian
explained to you that children are transported or whipped for stealing in
this country?'

'Yes.'

'Are you willing to work?'

'Yes, sir.'

Francis could feel the wounds pulsing in his hands. He thought for
a few moments before he spoke again. 'You'll forgive me, Mr Graves,
but I would not like it to be known that a boy of Eustache's birth is
sweeping up in my shop. It might bring the wrong sort of talk, and I
am sure you do not wish every loiterer in the city to come in and stare
at him.' It was clear Graves had not thought about this. He looked more
embarrassed than Eustache. 'But I think we can find a use for him',
Francis went on. 'I cannot hold a pen, so I may need a scribe – and

Master Eustache, there is a pile of manuscripts in the back room that must be nearly as tall as you are. You will read them and tell me which of them you think Mr Hinckley and I should print and why. Would that be punishment enough?'

Eustache bit his lip. 'Yes, sir.' Graves looked doubtful for a moment, then nodded his agreement. Francis called Joshua and told him to show Eustache into the back room, but before he could be led off, Eustache turned back to him.

'Do bookshops often catch fire?' he said.

'Not often, Eustache,' Francis said, 'and never during the day.'

'Do you promise?'

'I do. Get along now.' And he let himself be taken away.

'The boy has a particular fear of fire,' Graves said awkwardly.

'Because of his mother, no doubt,' Francis said.

Graves clasped his hands behind his back. 'You know who we are, of course, and must have heard the stories . . . We make efforts not to mention it in front of the children. He in particular was so young, we doubt he remembers.'

'Eustache told me the story himself within a minute of our meeting, Mr Graves. It seems to me he remembers quite enough.' Francis thought of the fire running round the blue and yellow wallpaper, knowing that the image and sound would remain in his bones though he lived to a thousand.

Graves crumpled rather. He was a little younger than Francis, but at that moment they both looked like old men. It took him some moments to find his voice again. 'A neighbour of ours in Sussex makes the most excellent cures. I think perhaps your throat pains you?' Francis conceded that it did. 'We never come to London without a supply. I shall have some sent here. Your hands are burned also?'

'Cut by glass.'

'Something for that too then.'

'That is kind of you, Mr Graves. I thank you for it.'

Graves shook his head. 'It is a kindness to let me do some little good when it seems I manage so much else so badly,' he said.

'I liked both the children, Mr Graves. I know enough of men to trust my feelings in such matters. Whatever trouble they cause you, I think their hearts are good.'

'Is that enough, Mr Glass?'

'It has to be,' Francis replied. They exchanged polite bows and Graves left the shop obviously deep in thought. Francis watched him go and for a moment pitied him, then heard a stifled laugh from the back room. The boys had made friends already, it seemed.

'Joshua, get back upstairs to Mr Ferguson,' he said over his shoulder, then turned once more to his accounts, trying to find comfort in the unthinking numbers.

III.3

HARRIET AND CROWTHER WERE waiting for Mr Palmer in the library, but when he was announced they were surprised to find he was not alone. The tall African Harriet had noticed in the Coroner's Court came with him, and was introduced to them as Mr Tobias Christopher. Harriet was surprised to see Crowther smile and step forward with his hand out when he heard the name.

'How do you do, Mr Christopher,' he said as they shook hands. 'I had it in mind to visit you while I was in town. There are gentlemen at the Royal Society who swear you are the best swordsman in London.'

Christopher's voice was deep; his vowels were rounded and broad. Harriet found she had a sense of his words decorating the room as if he were placing polished stones in the air between them. 'They do me much honour to say so, though they are quite right. And you would be welcome indeed in my home.'

'If Mr Christopher likes you, he will teach you to fight for survival as well as elegance,' Mr Palmer said. 'What he taught me yesterday will probably save my life at some point.'

Harriet looked from Mr Christopher to Palmer with interest. She had always thought of him as confined to the offices and coffee houses near Whitehall and his wars fought largely on paper or in whispers. It was interesting to know he expected to be in bodily danger. She felt oddly forced out of communion with the gentlemen, however, by the presence of all these invisible swords.

'Mr Palmer, I thought our involvement in this business would end this morning. What do you want of us?' The men turned towards her as if they had forgotten she was there.

'You had questions at the inquest, Mrs Westerman,' Palmer said with a polite smile. He leaned against the mantelpiece while Crowther and Tobias took their seats opposite one another in front of the empty fireplace. Harriet settled herself on the cherry-striped sofa, her silks rustling.

'I was curious. But still, I have no great wish to find whoever it was that beat Mr Trimnell. Nor do I think Crowther and I are the best people to find the guilty party, even if we wished to do so. I know you have found us useful in the past, Palmer, but we would make ourselves ridiculous asking questions among those who inhabit the city at that hour of the night. Surely the constables and thief-takers are better suited for the task.'

Christopher gave her a slow and careful smile. 'You agree with the hints of the newspapers this morning, Mrs Westerman? That it was an ugly act of revenge by a savage who does not understand the English way of life? You think when they took Guadeloupe they had the right of it?'

She found his gaze unsettling. 'I do not know, Mr Christopher. The manner of the attack suggests revenge of a former slave, does it not? I suppose a decent English thief might make a man found with such a thing wear it, but the attempt to stake him out certainly implies some knowledge of slavery. And the boy did have the watch.'

'It does,' he said. 'And he did. And I like your notion of a decent English thief, madam, though I cannot say I have enjoyed the pleasure of meeting such a one.'

Harriet was not sure she had met one either, other than in the tales of Robin Hood, and she looked away.

'You think Guadeloupe is innocent, Mr Christopher?' Crowther asked. 'Palmer would not have removed you from the room if he did not fear you might protest.'

Christopher crossed his legs and sat back in the chair. 'Very few of us are innocent, and Guadeloupe is poor enough to want to rob, but I do not think he attacked Trimnell. He has been sleeping in the outbuilding behind my house for the last week while we try to find him work. He is new in England, but before then was in a field-gang in Barbados. He would not know Trimnell as a slave-owner.'

'And that is why you think him innocent?' Harriet asked. 'Suppose he aimed to rob Trimnell, then found that mask about his person – would that not enrage him?'

Christopher considered for a moment. 'It might. Would you understand me, Mrs Westerman, if I said, however, that this simply does not taste right under my tongue?' He folded his hands together under his chin and watched her expression. 'It does not taste so sweet to you either, is my thinking. That is what my friend Mr Palmer meant when he said you had questions. Good. Would you unfold them before us, madam? As a favour to myself?'

Before she could do so, William entered the room with a tray of wine glasses and a decanter. He sat it down and they watched as he poured and handed the glasses to their guests. Mr Christopher said something to him as he took what was offered and William replied. There followed a short conversation. William seemed slightly embarrassed, Mr Christopher delighted.

'Do you and William know each other, Mr Christopher?' Harriet asked, taking her own glass.

'We have not had that pleasure,' Christopher said. 'But we are both from Igbo stock. Not close relatives, that is why I am so much more handsome than he is.' His eyes shone, suddenly mischievous. 'But our language is close enough that we can exchange proper greetings.'

Crowther took his glass from the tray and noticed William's suppressed smile. 'Thank you, William.'

'Mr Crowther.'

He left the room and Harriet watched him go; he seemed another being suddenly to her, having heard that language on his tongue.

'Your questions, Mrs Westerman?' Christopher said after William had closed the door. 'What sticks and bites when we say Guadeloupe has done this thing and must be punished?'

She tried to collect her thoughts. 'The timing of the attack. The unlikelihood of a boy as slight as Guadeloupe managing Trimnell alone. And it seemed . . . elaborate – personal – his killing. I realise I only saw Guadeloupe for a moment, but nevertheless . . .'

'Your instinct is correct. A knife in the belly on a dark street would be more his fashion,' Christopher said. His voice was almost affectionate. 'And where are Mr Trimnell's clothes? Guadeloupe was not caught pawning them, I think.' He looked up at Palmer for confirmation. The man from the Admiralty nodded. Mr Christopher brought his hands together and smiled. 'But I think my new friend has brought me here to tell you something else, to feed your curiosity – and not about Guadeloupe – though I can't be certain what Mr Palmer's larger purpose is. Does our friend always have a larger purpose, do you think, Mrs Westerman?'

She studied Palmer, who remained quite calm under their combined scrutiny, neither amused nor uncomfortable. 'I believe he does, though what it is I cannot say. What do you think, Crowther?'

Crowther sipped his wine then set it down beside him. 'Sometimes I think Mr Palmer treats us like dried leaves, Mrs Westerman. He throws us up into the air just to see which way the wind is blowing.'

The corner of Palmer's mouth twitched slightly at that, but he said nothing. The African laughed, low and soft. 'Very well. This is what I told Mr Palmer yesterday, after he had flattered his way into my confidence, and what I think he wishes you to know. It is not a story I like to tell, but here in this beautiful room, with my new friends, how could I refuse to share it? I am a runaway slave, madam. It was Trimnell himself I ran from some fourteen years ago. I managed to smuggle myself on board a merchant ship, made my way here and learned my trade. I am a warrior by nature and took to the sword. Now I own a school of the defensive arts in Golden Square.'

Harriet looked again at the whiteness of his shirt collar, the cut of his coat and the gleam on his shoe buckles.

'You have done very well,' she said.

'I have. But hear this, madam: not one day in all these years have I forgotten that the shadows might hold a group of men desirous to bundle me onto a ship and back to Trimnell and his whip. Is it any wonder I studied to fight well and quickly? That mask has stopped my tongue, madam, and many times. I swore the day I escaped, it would never do so again. Never.'

'I hope you have not come to make confession, Mr Christopher,' Crowther said coolly. 'I am not sure what the rules of hospitality would suggest in such a circumstance.'

Christopher looked across at him. 'Ha! Indeed, a terrible thing it would be, to put a lady in that position. But I am not such a monster. I have English manners now.' His smile was broad and sudden, then it disappeared again. 'No. I had reason to hate Trimnell. I loathed him, I despised him – but when I heard he was in London, I was also afraid. Afraid he would know me and claim me.' The idea of this man having anything to fear from that hollowed-out corpse with its broken and failed heart seemed incredible to Harriet. 'Mrs Westerman, my family have a letter ready for a lawyer I know. If I am late coming home they have instructions to run to him quick as they might with it so he may lay a writ of habeus corpus.'

'Habeus corpus?' Harriet asked.

'It is the legal method used to prevent slaves being taken out of this country against their will,' Palmer said, an elegant chorus. 'There was a legal case in 1772, Somersett. A slave cannot be forced against his will onto a ship to the West Indies, though of course it still happens from time to time. When it does, obtaining a writ of habeus corpus has proved effective. Assuming it can be delivered in time.'

'I believed slavery illegal on English soil, after that case. I remember being proud,' Harriet said faintly. She put her hands together on her lap again and her silks sighed with her.

Palmer studied his wine 'Many do. In truth, the matter is more complex.'

The African reached into his coat pocket and produced a heavy sheet of paper, folded into thirds. 'I raised my glass on that Day of Judgement too, madam. But the legal ins and outs are not the business of today. Yes, I hated Trimnell. Trimnell was my master. Yet Mr Trimnell came alone to my house last week – and he brought me this.'

He gave the paper to Harriet. She read it and handed it to Crowther.

'Your manumission,' he said simply. 'So Trimnell relinquished all legal claim over your person and gave you this document to prove it. You have the air of a wealthy man, Mr Christopher. Did Trimnell ask you for money? I would imagine you would be worth a great deal.'

For a moment Harriet thought Mr Christopher was angry, then he smiled again. 'I am. And he so wasted and dirty a man, sir, I was ashamed to think he owned my fine blood and bones.' Christopher tutted a little, then turned his face to Crowther's, his dark eyes wide and serious. 'But no, Mr Crowther. He did not ask for my money, and here we come to why Mr Palmer has brought us together to tell stories in this handsome room. You see, Mr Trimnell asked for my forgiveness.'

III.4

THE LETTER ARRIVED A little after midday. It was brought into the shop by the same constable who had pulled Francis from the flames. Francis was glad of the chance to see him again and this time managed to thank him. The constable – Miller, he said his name was – was grateful for the offer of refreshment. It was not until they were both seated in the privacy of the back parlour that Francis broke the seal and read the letter. It was from Eliza Smith's sister-in-law, and he had to read it twice before it made much sense to him. As its meaning became clear, his heart sank. Her husband George – Francis's old friend, Eliza's brother and presumably her heir – was travelling in the north of the country. Letters were being sent to his friends there, but his itinerary was uncertain, and with the best will in the world it was likely to be a week before he could be back in London. His wife, who was still in fragile health after the birth of her fourth child, begged Francis to take charge of affairs in London until her husband returned. She wrote that she trusted in his good sense and loyal heart, and gave her authority that he should act just as he saw fit. It was all Francis could do to stifle a groan; the weight on his shoulders already felt more than he could bear. The constable was watching him.

'She sent us a note too, Mr Glass. Saying it was all put into your hands.' He cleared his throat; the smoke had got deep into his lungs too. 'There's a fair bit of stock could be saved, I think. And some of the machinery too. Printed up engravings, didn't they? Fire sort of smashed itself out when it came down on that poor lady's head. Then there's her body: she needs burying and the bloke who owns the land wants the place pulled down and cleared so he can get building again. He came around looking while I was on guard this morning. Drooling like a dog outside a butcher's, he was.'

Francis put the letter to one side. 'The ashes aren't even cold.'

'Aye well, business in the city, you know. They're not ones to stand about. My impression was he reckoned he's been underpaid for that spot for years. But you know, with Mrs Smith's reputation so high I guess he never dared put up the rent on her.'

Francis looked at the constable, frowning suspiciously, and Miller read his mind. 'No, no. He got off the Bath stage this morning – I checked. So he couldn't have had anything to do with it. Yet it does seem queer, the fire going off like that. The inquest takes place this afternoon. Three o'clock in the Black Swan.'

Through the taste of smoke in his throat, Francis told him again of what he had seen – Eliza's body, her wound and the coldness of her flesh. The constable rubbed his chin with his yellow fingers and made him describe the fire again, the way it ran around the room in waves.

'Don't like the sound of that, Mr Glass. Not at all. I've seen enough fires here in my time and they don't just dash about like that unless they're following a trail that's been set for them. You'll have to tell the coroner and he'll look down his nose at you. He'd rather have an accident than a murder. But you'll have to tell him, just the same. First things first though. If you're at liberty now, you'd best come with me and sort through what's worth saving and make some arrangements.' He set down his tankard. 'The maid's still not turned up, you know. There's talk on her.'

Francis thought of the sharp-faced girl. 'I did not wish Eliza to employ her. But Mrs Smith said she was doing well, and seemed to be growing fond of her. Perhaps Penny's evil habits did stay with her and even Eliza's kindness could not wash her clean.' He got up from his chair, his bandaged hands making him clumsy.

'I can't say that being a constable has taught me to think better of my fellow creatures, Mr Glass, but I hope you're wrong.' Miller hauled himself up and blew out a long breath. 'Girl seemed to be doing well with Mrs Smith, as you said. Still, she isn't there, and there's still no sign of the cashbox and poor Mrs Smith killed.'

Francis began to struggle into his coat, and seeing his difficulty Miller helped him, holding it so he could slide in his arms without pulling at the bandages. 'You'd best bring a purse with you,' Miller advised. 'There'll be men to be paid for gathering and carrying and guarding, and now you've got that letter looks like they'll be on your charge.'

The expense did not disturb him. He drank little and his entertainment consisted of the books he read, so he had a fund saved from his wages. However, Francis realised for the first time through his grief that he was angry. It was not an emotion with which he was very familiar and it took him a few moments to identify the feeling of cold constriction under his heart. Someone had taken Eliza away. Someone had destroyed her, broken her and left her as if she was of no account, as if no one would miss her or come for her. He put the letter into his pocket. Someone would pay. If it were the maid, then she would be found.

'All that can be done, I'll do,' he said. 'Might I ask your assistance, Mr Miller?'

'Happy to oblige, Mr Glass, in all that's lawful.'

The two men did not manage to leave at once; as they passed through the shop floor Francis stopped a moment to tell Cutter what had occurred and where his business was taking him. Cutter only nodded and scratched his ear. This he did in a manner that suggested the world was a wicked and weary-making place, and that he was happier to stay in the shop. As Francis was still speaking, a very tall gentleman in a scholar's clothing and with wide blue eyes came in. He had red hair, a sight which always stopped Francis dead even after all these years in England. He had thought the first red-headed man he had seen a demon for certain, so unnatural did the colour seem, and he still could not help suspecting them a little.

'Good day,' the demon said, smiling very widely. 'I am looking for a book.' He had got the whole sentence out before he noticed the colour of Francis's skin. His expression changed from open enquiry to surprise to a sort of fascination. The constable mumbled something about waiting for Francis outside.

'You are certainly in the right place,' Francis said with a slight bow. 'Was it a particular book you are looking for?'

The man laughed. 'Oh yes, Edward Long's *History of Jamaica*. Do you have it?'

'We do not,' Francis said evenly.

'Are you *quite* sure?' the demon asked, still beaming. 'I was told by the gentleman in Humphrey's to come here specifically to buy it.' It seemed to dawn on him that the atmosphere in the shop was become suddenly chilly. 'Have I said something wrong?' Francis wondered if any face could in truth be as innocent as this one appeared to be. 'I am writing an essay for the Cambridge Latin Prize. This year, the subject is *Anne liceat invitos in servitutem dare*. That means—'

'Is it legal to sell a man against his will. I have enough Latin to understand that, sir.'

'*Do* you? How interesting! Yes, and I am here in London to buy books and I was told . . .' He tailed off.

Francis prayed for patience; the man did not seem to be malicious. 'The clerk in the other shop means to make a joke of us both, sir,' he explained. 'The book you mention contain some unflattering commentary about people of my colour. We sell works of fiction here, music and some history. But not that book.'

The man flushed such a furious scarlet, it was as if his pale skin had been suddenly doused in red paint. 'Oh, I see. My apologies.'

Francis bowed. 'You could not know. If you require anything else, my clerk will be happy to help.'

The young man put his hand on Francis's sleeve. The blush had faded a little, leaving his skin looking mottled. Francis could not help noticing the dry skin on his lips, the thin-boned fingers. He stooped slightly, his head on one side.

'Were *you* a slave? I do hope you were. You would do me a great kindness by telling me of it. I won the Junior Latin Prize last year, and if I were to win the Senior Prize, my chances for a good career in the Church would be much enhanced. I am sure the judges would be impressed if I managed to get a first-hand testimony. You know, the winning essay is often *published*.'

Francis felt his muscles tense. 'You must forgive me, I am much occupied today.'

The man had sense enough to release his hold and take a step backwards. 'Of course, I understand. But should you have a moment over the next few days . . . My name is Clarkson and I'm staying at the White Rose until Friday.' Francis nodded and began to turn away. 'I am against it,' Clarkson said, too loudly. 'Slavery, I mean. The Bible does not support it, I think I can demonstrate that *unanswerably*. And it would aid my thesis, in that section where I argue against the assertion that Negroes are not human as such but part-monkey, to talk to some unusually intelligent examples of the sable brotherhood.' His wide blue eyes remained as innocent as ever.

It was impossible to make him understand. 'I really must leave you now, Mr Clarkson. Perhaps you might ask Cutter here to show you the verses of Miss Phillis Wheatley. She remains a slave and the book contains a number of letters from prominent people supporting her claim to be the genuine author.'

Clarkson looked delighted. 'Oh, has a Negress written a poetry book? How wonderful! Yes, that's *just* the sort of thing. I am grateful. You know, there are reports of another in America who is terribly good at mathematics!'

Cutter was already trotting towards them with the volume mentioned, and as quickly as possible. Clarkson all but clapped his hands and Francis took his chance to finally leave the shop. As he left, he saw the clerk of Humphrey's shop in his doorway. The man raised his hand and smirked. Francis resisted the temptation to cross the road and spit in the man's face, though how he did so he could not readily say.

III.5

'TRIMNELL CAME TO ASK your forgiveness?' Harriet repeated. Tobias Christopher only nodded. 'And did you give it to him?'

He took the glass in his hand and drank from it slowly before replying. 'I did not do so. I *could* not do so. Perhaps I fail as a Christian to say it, but I cannot forgive or forget what that man did, what hundreds of others such as him have done. How can I offer forgiveness for all that death? I cannot. Some sins only God can forgive, and even then . . . No. He and all his kind must stand before Heaven to answer. I heard him as far as I could. I let him speak and he left my home as he came to it. He could ask no more than that. I am not a priest to hear his confession and send him into the world clean.'

'You have no desire for revenge?' Crowther asked.

'Revenge?' His voice was soft. He stared off into the air above them for a while. Harriet wondered if he was examining the paintings on the library ceiling. There was a theme of exploration among them, ships, high seas, foreign shores – painted to inspire, Harriet supposed, the reading and dreaming of those land-locked within the house. They made her uncomfortable as she tried to see them again through Mr Christopher's eyes.

'Have you heard of a ship named the *Zong*, Mr Crowther?' Christopher said at last. Crowther shook his head, though Harriet noticed Palmer blink and look away. 'So few Englishmen have. Four years ago, that ship sailed from the coast of Africa with more than six hundred Africans packed into her hold. There was sickness on the ship, there is always sickness on the ship, and before they got near to Jamaica, there were many dead. Now the commander of that ship, Collingwood, was a bad sailor and he missed his way. There he is, out at sea watching his profit vomiting and dying in the hold, and he makes a plan. The cargo is insured. If the slaves he carries die in their own blood and filth below, it is his loss. If, however, *of necessity*, they are thrown overboard while breathing, the insurers must pay him money for each soul he destroys.' His voice still had that low and rocking tone to it, like a father telling a story to his child before he sleeps. 'Necessity. So Mr Collingwood declares there is not enough fresh water left, and orders his crew to throw the living sick into the waters. More than two hundred of the slaves he carried were cast off that ship, and even when the rain had fallen and filled up his water casks again, he sent more to the bottom of the ocean. Still fettered together. Some nights I dream of them sinking in their chains.' He looked away from the spreading sails painted above him. 'He was prosecuted by the insurers, Mr Crowther, but for fraud, not murder and Lord Mansfield – a man whose health I drank in 1772 when he freed the slave Somersett – said there was no difference in the case between the killing of slaves, or the killing of sheep. Now what would you say if Collingwood asked you to forgive him? If the sailors who obeyed him asked you? If the insurers? What of the man who toils away making the fetters that bound those slaves together? What of the man who owns shares in the enterprise? How could you forgive, and how would you take revenge for that?' Crowther said nothing. 'What I desire, Mr Crowther, is not revenge. I am a more ambitious man than that. I would have truth.' His voice grew stronger. 'I would have every person in these islands stand up, declare themselves against slavery and curse the slavers and plantation-owners for the lying, inhuman dogs they are. The insurers, the smith, the shipbuilder, the housekeeper who sweetens her tea with slave sugar, let them stand up beside me and call not for revenge or forgiveness, but for truth. Let them tell the truth.' He passed a hand over his eyes. 'They tell the world we are hardly human, fit only for whip and chains so the English will not feel for us. I have been a slave and worn that mask and I am a *man*. Just as much a man as those who sold me. That is the truth. That is what must be acknowledged.' He finished his wine then set the glass very carefully back on the table as if conscious it might break into nothing between his fingers. His voice softened again. 'The English people here, the rich, the educated, the civilised people I meet and train . . . Sometimes I am at a loss to understand. You are become so dissolute you think robbery, slavery, rape and murder no crimes?'

'That is not so, Mr Christopher. Justice . . .' Harriet said faintly.

He answered her sharply. 'It *is*, madam. If the victim is a black and if the crime takes place far enough away, you will shake hands with the man who did it.'

'I would not.' Then she remembered Sir Charles bowing over her hand, and did not protest any further.

'Justice. Another fine English word.' Christopher said slowly: 'I must believe in God, and in believing in God must think He sees and hears what I have seen, what I have heard. I must believe He hopes for the repentance of the people of Britain, that in His *infinite* mercy He offers a chance for repentance. And if the repentance comes not, I must believe He will deliver His justice, and if it does come, believe me – not one stone will stand on another in this city. That would be justice in proper measure for what has been done. *That* would be the justice. Not whipping some broken soul in a churchyard. No, there would not be one stone left on another.'

The silence in the room was that of a church. Outside in the square, a carriage passed, the sound of the horses' hooves striking the ground clean in the air. It was Christopher's voice that broke it and he spoke quietly.

'Will you enquire into the matter of Trimnell's death?'

It was Crowther who answered. 'If you wish it, Mr Christopher. But what Mrs Westerman said still holds true. We are not the people to ask questions of the itinerants of the city.'

Christopher waved his hand in the air. 'You still will not understand me, Mr Crowther.'

Mr Palmer spoke from his place by the fire. 'I cannot believe that Trimnell's change of heart is unrelated to his death. Think on it, Mr Crowther. We know only too well that the city is full of unrepentant slave-drivers. They go about in safety. One repents and is killed. Surely then the repentance is significant.'

'It must be,' Harriet said reluctantly. Her mind was full of horrors, the rush of deep water. The ghosts crowded into the room with them, desperate and cold, and she wanted only to drive them out. How else otherwise could it be borne?

'If it was an African who did this, let him be found – and with the support and cooperation of my people,' Christopher said with a deep sigh. 'At the very least I will not let the West Indians take this chance to paint we Africans as animals. Though they do, they do. Every black man in London is walking carefully today, wondering what thoughts of savages and sacrifice are dancing behind their white neighbours' eyes. But I believe you will not find a black fist around that whip. Trimnell was become a strange and broken man. He mismanaged his estate and came home poor. He sought me out in London to try and tell me his sins, as if I did not know them. Something had happened to him. Perhaps his mind broke finally under the knowing of what he had done. He spoke of God. Perhaps he knew he was dying and was racing to make amends before the devil caught him.' He smiled up at Harriet. 'This terrible divine justice with which I have only a moment ago threatened you all – maybe he heard it at his back in the shadows.'

She looked down at her hands again. 'You would make a great preacher if you were not a swordsman, Mr Christopher.'

'We Africans were born poets, ma'am, and we have had time and silence to consider what has been done to us. If Cicero had been Igbo, Rome would never have fallen.'

Palmer spoke. 'Trimnell's conversion into an abolitionist must have been an embarrassment.'

'He told me he had tried to talk to his fellow owners and traders,' Christopher said. 'He told me they threw him out of the Jamaica Coffee House and into the dirt. He seemed proud of that.'

'It does not surprise me, that they found him unsympathetic.' Harriet turned to Palmer. 'Why did you remove us from the Coroner's Court?'

'I did not want you to present yourselves in front of that audience as champions of the Africans. All the planters would shut themselves away from you at once,' Palmer said.

Harriet examined him more closely. 'But what of the pantomime you had me perform with you?'

He put down his glass, his expression not so much uncomfortable as unhappy. 'I am in a delicate position, Mrs Westerman. The West Indians have many friends in Parliament and the Admiralty.'

'So it is better for you if they believe you tried to warn us away from this killing, even while you encourage us to investigate it?'

He simply nodded.

There was a bitter taste under Harriet's tongue. 'They will slam their doors on us the moment we ask a question, and you know it, Palmer.' She straightened her skirts and would look at none of them. 'If it was another planter who did this, let them continue to murder each other with my blessing.'

It was Christopher who answered. 'If it was a white man who did this, because Trimnell repented, then let your countrymen see that. Do it at my request, madam, and with my thanks. As for my friend Mr Palmer, I hope one day he will stand up and tell the truth for the good of his soul. But he will have to find another profession when he does so.' Christopher looked round them all.

Harriet bit her lip, before saying, 'Very well, Mr Christopher. Did Trimnell explain why he felt a need for forgiveness after all these years?'

'He told me he began to read the New Testament during his illness in Jamaica. More than that I cannot say, but he was passionate when he spoke of God.'

'Had he lived in London before?' Crowther asked and Tobias shook his head.

'Not that I know. He was born in Jamaica and inherited his land and people though he bought many more as we failed and died. All the whites seemed to consider England their home, born there or not. When I lived in that particular Hell he was unmarried, sweating and rotting, and trying to squeeze money out of each inch of land he owned.'

'What of Guadeloupe?' Harriet said. 'We must find out how he came to have Trimnell's watch.'

Christopher stood and Harriet and Crowther did the same. 'I believe my work here is done: you are eager for the chase. Leave Guadeloupe to me, Mrs Westerman. I will visit him at Bridewell now, let him know he is not forgotten and see what he can tell me. He will not answer you. You will find me at home tomorrow morning and I would be happy to tell you what I have learned.'

He handed Harriet a card. *The Christopher Academy*, it said. *Soho Square*. His sign was that of crossed swords. 'Until tomorrow then, Mr Christopher,' she said.

He bowed over her hand and his fingers were dry and cool. 'I look forward to the opportunity of welcoming you to my home.'

Mr Palmer left with him and Harriet found herself alone with Crowther under those painted medallions of trade and exploration.

'Where shall we begin, Mrs Westerman?' he asked her.

She was still watching the door, thinking of Palmer, Christopher and of the many ghosts that surrounded her. 'The Jamaica Coffee House, I think.'

III.6

WHILE THE CARRIAGE WAS being fetched, Harriet went to find Graves. He was in his office, surrounded as always by untidy stacks of paper and looking worried and ill-kempt. His valet did his best to make him look like a suitable guardian to Jonathan and his wealth, but his best work could not last half an hour when Graves was in a distracted mood. He pulled at the sleeves of his coat, yanked at his cravat and ran his inky hands through his hair. It was always touching to see how he disliked being separated from his wife.

He smiled on seeing Harriet though and invited her in. She sat down beside his desk and folded her hands in her lap.

'I have come to apologise for taking Susan away yesterday, Graves. It was childish of me.'

He looked at her and sighed. 'You could at least have brought her back in a better temper.'

Harriet confessed: 'I hinted that her school might have some useful things to teach her.'

'And so instead of being her champion, you allied yourself with her oppressors. Well, at least I understand that scene on the stairs now. God knows, she is an intelligent child, too intelligent perhaps, but she will not see . . .' He looked exhausted.

Harriet told him of what had passed at the Coroner's Court, and the visit of Palmer and Mr Christopher. She waited for his response.

'You must do what you think best, Harriet.'

'You don't feel I will be a bad influence on the children?'

'No more than you usually are,' he said. 'I think they are beyond saving. Susan thrown out of her school – and I caught Eustache stealing. I will blame you as much as I can, naturally, but I do not think you can shoulder all of the fault. Did you know Eustache remembers his mother? What she did?'

'I did not. I am sorry for it.'

'As am I. Jonathan still has nightmares, Susan hates me for trying to make her into a lady. Now Verity is with child, and I am afraid the children will resent the baby, see it as more my child than they are. And I swim daily through the seas of Jonathan's money and remain poor. Whatever is to become of us all?'

Harriet thought of her own account books and the pile of correspondence on her desk at Caveley. All abandoned because she was lonely and out of temper with her sister. 'I do not know.'

'I want them to be happy, but do not know how to make them so.'

Her eyes suddenly sparkled. 'I understand a submissive nature and good works are *highly* recommended.' He grinned briefly, but then stared at the mound of paper in front of him again. 'Graves, Susan is angry because you don't want her to be one of these aristocratic milksops any more than she does, and she recognises the hypocrisy. You gave up your life to look after those children rather than leave them with the great families they are related to, because you knew they would be miserable there. Now, I understand some accommodation must be made with the world, but you have thrown her into the swamp of those overly mannered misses without explanation or guidance. Be honest with her, Graves. And perhaps we should be honest with Eustache too.'

He looked up from his papers. 'Should I be honest with you too, Harriet?'

She said cheerfully, 'As a rule I would think not – I am not your ward, after all. But tell me what you wish to say this time at least.'

'My best wishes to you and Crowther for your success. The resources of this house are at your disposal as ever, and I shall not complain when the servants are sent out at all hours helping you to pursue your enquiries.'

'But?'

'But for God's sake, Harriet, try not to bring the danger home this time. Think of the children.'

She felt her throat tighten, then nodded and left the room.

When they had arrived at the ruins of Mrs Smith's home and place of business, Francis came to a halt on the pavement opposite and stared. Miller the constable glanced at him, then crossed the narrow road and spoke to the two men he had set to guard the place. A Mr Churchill who owned the premises next door saw Francis standing there and approached, his shoulders drawn up to his ears, his chin almost on his chest. He stood by Francis's side and said nothing. The roof had collapsed and the floor that supported the attic rooms where Eliza kept her press for engravings had given way into the first floor, where she had lived. As he stared, Francis could hear again the bursting of the timbers above him and the hungry cackle of the fire. The window to the parlour had shattered and the plasterwork above it was thickly blackened by smoke. Francis thought of the wound to Eliza's eye and at once felt the tears running down his cheeks. He did not wipe them away. The door to the shop and the ground floor seemed intact; only the windows, usually showing a display of the prints and books and papers Eliza had sold to the ambitious matrons of the city, were smoke-stained and fogged.

For the most part the crowds passed without even noticing. Occasionally someone would pause, confused, and look up. They were shocked or sorry for a moment, then turned their backs and hurried on.

Mr Churchill spoke at last. 'I can lend you my clerk to help you sort through the stock, Mr Glass.' Francis thanked him without taking his eyes from the ruin. 'Fire is the greatest terror of any person in our profession,' Churchill continued. 'I have spent many a night fretting over it when I should have been sleeping. Why would God allow a woman like Mrs Smith to die? She was the kindest soul in the parish. But then it's questions like that which send the philosophers to our doors at all hours. I'll shake your hand, sir.'

Francis turned towards him and saw his hand outstretched. For a moment in the blankness of his grief he did not know what to do. He put out his own and felt Churchill's fingers around his own. 'It was murder, Mr Churchill.'

The other man inhaled sharply. 'Then I hope the guilty are found and hanged. For they have taken from us a prize of great worth.' He released Francis's hand. 'I shall send my clerk over at once.'

Francis was busy among the ashes all morning, fighting with his grief and his anger, and trying to find solace in protecting whatever Eliza had left behind her. The greatest part of the stock downstairs was ruined by smoke and water, though many volumes had escaped more lightly and there were a number of portfolios of prints only slightly damaged at their edges. There was still no sign of the cashbox.

Miller helped him hire a couple of trustworthy men to keep watch over what was left until a fire sale could be arranged, then an hour later brought him fresh news of the inquest. The constable looked uncomfortable. 'The coroner already seems to have decided it was an accident,' he said.

'Why?'

Miller gestured over towards St Paul's. 'Bit too much murder in the neighbourhood. Any more and they think trade will be getting nervous. They've got a lad for that crime though.' He bent down, picking up some twisted piece of metal, fallen through from upstairs, then not sure what to do with it, placed it carefully on the counter.

The cashbox should have been just behind there. When she closed on Saturday evening, Eliza would have removed the takings and locked them in her bureau upstairs, leaving only coppers behind her in the cashbox. Penny would know that. Did she kill Eliza, to steal the money from the bureau? But if she did that, why had the cashbox disappeared? And if her object had been the few coins in the cashbox, why had she not just taken them and walked out of the shop?

'I've been tasked with gathering the jury for the coroner,' Miller went on. 'Three o'clock this afternoon at the Black Swan. Took a little shuffling, but there it is. I'm thinking of gathering Mr Scudder in as foreman.'

Francis concentrated. 'Scudder, the butcher? Why would he listen to me? He always seems to clutch his cleaver a little more closely when I pass by.'

Miller shrugged. 'We are in need of some miserable suspicious old bastard on that jury, and he *will* listen to you. Mrs Smith was one of the few mortals on earth could ever get a smile out of him and more than that, I've never seen the bugger back away from a fight for the sake of a quiet life.'

'Thank you, Mr Miller.'

The constable touched his fingers to his forehead then stamped out of the shop again. Churchill's clerk appeared to be sorting through the stock calmly enough. Francis braced himself and climbed the stairs. If any of Eliza's personal possessions had escaped the fire, they must be collected and taken to Hinckley's so her brother George could see them there.

The private quarters were largely destroyed. The prints and paintings had all been eaten up by smoke and flame, the dainty items of porcelain smashed, her own private library fit for nothing but the waste merchant. He could close his eyes and remake it as it had been the previous afternoon, then he opened them again to devastation. There was nothing but the ruins of a life here now.

He could see the remains of the couch behind which she'd lain. The mess of wood, tile and board which had fallen on her poor body had been half-cleared in order to remove her and was still sodden with the water pumped up to douse the flames. It reflected the light of the spring sun. He stood in the doorway for a moment, wishing he had died there too. Her bureau, he saw, was still against the wall nearest to him, scorched beyond saving but protected to a degree by a beam which had come down from the roof and into the space where her usual armchair had sat. He edged towards it, testing each step and his shoes cracking the debris as he hung onto the wall. The top drawer was locked. He looked about him. The chisel-like handle which fitted into the screw of the plate press had fallen just behind him on the far side of the beam. He crouched down and reached for it, hissing with pain as he leaned on his left hand and stretched out. His fingers brushed its cold metal tip and he pulled it towards him, then stood and used it to force the lock on the drawer. He could probably have broken it with a sharp tug. It gave easily. He placed the handle on the floor again and pulled open the drawer to reveal Eliza's account books, damp but whole, and a soft leather wallet. He noticed it was marked with her father's initials. Inside were four Rose Guineas, and two half-sovereigns along with handfuls of crowns, florins and shillings. So her takings were there quite correctly. He tipped the coins back into the bag, placed it in his pocket and lifted out the account books to take downstairs.

The other drawers contained her private and business correspondence; the catalogues of her competitors; and the lowest drawer held a number of manuscripts. Each was bound into a parcel and had a note in her own handwriting on the front. Each note was a carefully phrased rejection and they were all dated on Saturday. He sighed. Churchill's clerk could take them to the parcel post. How like Eliza it was, to leave things in such order, though she could never persuade her hair to stay in its pins, while Francis, always so neat and clean, had a back office filled with towering piles of the hopes of numberless authors. He wiped his eyes. He must return to the shop soon and speak to Eustache Thornleigh. He would take the account books to see what, if anything, Eliza owed, and ask Churchill's clerk to gather up whatever other small treasures the bureau had saved.

He was about to make his cautious way back to the door when he saw a pale wooden case, its surface scarred but the fastening still apparently secure, lying on the floor by the bureau. He opened it. A set of engraving tools. He remembered them. She had insisted that even with the trouble and responsibility of her own printsellers to run, she would still use her skills as an engraver from time to time, and when she didn't she would have the tools of her trade on display so she might look at them and take a little pride in the fact that it was her skill with them that had allowed her to buy and stock her own shop.

It was strange. She had always kept the case open on the bureau. Given the destruction in the room, its survival was a minor miracle. It should have been thrown down when the roof gave way and the contents scattered. The tools were all there, her initials burned neatly into the underside of each mushroom-shaped wooden handle. Perhaps he would buy them from George himself and give them to Walter. It would offer him some ease, knowing her tools were still being used. Beloved tools were living things, and they carried some part of their users with them for ever after. And she had loved these tools. The lozenge or square ends of each well-tempered steel shaft were carefully sharpened on their cutting edges. The shafts themselves were pristine, polished. Apart from one. Only by looking closely could he see the spots and smears on the metal. He lifted the graver out of its velvet cradle and ran the shaft gently through the folds of his white handkerchief. It left a stain of dark red behind it.

III.7

HARRIET HAD THE BIT between her teeth, Crowther noted. There was always a peculiar sort of animation about her person when she set her mind on a problem. Her movements became quicker, and there was a brightness in them. He watched her as they drove in the direction of the Jamaica Coffee House. She stared out of the window and chewed her lip. Crowther had not realised how far Rachel had got with her matchmaking plans. The letter he had had from the young woman had amused him, but there was also a lurch of fear as he read the name Babington. Babington was not a bad man. Not uncultured. Not unhandsome. Crowther was not inclined to be introspective, but he did know that he was a man of very few pleasures and most of them would be lost if Mrs Westerman married. Their easy relationship would be stopped and fouled by a husband.

'What are you thinking on, Crowther? You look quite mournful.'

He cleared his throat. 'I feel my examination of Mr Trimnell's body has not left us with any fresh avenue of enquiry. This disappoints me. And the washing and redressing of the body were not helpful.'

'A point you have made forcefully and frequently.' The carriage drew to a halt while she was speaking and Philip opened the door for them.

The Jamaica Coffee House was a modest building in a modest side street, yet more men of wealth passed in and out of it each day than through those of some of the more exclusive clubs on The Mall. As Harriet entered, she expected the air to be sweet with sugar and rum.

The room was not uncomfortably crowded, but already there were enough men in the room for the waiters to be moving quickly and much occupied. Several of the patrons turned to look at them and run their eyes over Harriet with a frown of suspicion. A well-dressed woman was an unusual sight in such a place. She returned the observation calmly enough. There were some obvious sailors among them of various ranks. Others had the look of professional men. They leaned over the tables towards each other, their eyes bright with business.

The owner, Mr Sanden, must have felt the tremor in the air, for he emerged from a side room almost the moment they had entered. He greeted them politely enough and led the way into his private sitting room before Harriet's presence could disturb the customers any further. The talk started up again behind them, and they were swallowed into the place like stones into a pool.

'So the boy is locked away,' Sanden said with forced cheerfulness as soon as they were seated round his empty fireplace. 'Poor Mr Trimnell. But I am delighted such a dangerous boy has been removed from the streets.'

'Indeed,' Harriet said, looking about her. It was a comfortable room, with the wooden panelling painted olive green, polished pewter on the dresser and thick red rugs on the floor. 'Mr Sanden, we heard you had a disagreement with Mr Trimnell recently that ended with him being thrown out into the street.'

Sanden's tree-frog face went red at once. He pursed his lips and blew out his cheeks. He didn't speak but began to push with his palms on the thighs of his breeches.

'Mr Sanden?' she repeated. 'We understand he was ranting against the slave trade.'

'Thief!' he exploded at last. 'Thief and a liar! There. Said it.' He folded his arms and looked between them defiantly with his strange bulbous eyes.

Crowther put his head to one side. 'Mr Trimnell was a thief and a liar?'

Harriet watched Sanden. He looked like a concerned frog, trying to puff himself up to intimidate an attacker. She had often observed that the best method to make a man talk was Crowther's attentive silence. Very few could withstand the pressure.

'He borrowed money from me, and a fair amount of it, when he first came back. Sent his poor wife to do it too. Lovely girl. Deserved better. She said there'd been a delay in getting the final payments from his estate. They had expenses.'

'Did she come here?' Crowther asked.

Sanden shook his head. 'Oh, no! She's too fine a lady for this establishment.' He touched a finger to his collar. 'We happened to meet while walking in St James's Park.'

'Why did he not simply ask his father-in-law for money?' Harriet said. She had not noticed when they first came into the room, but there were engravings of various botanical samples framed around the wall. Mr Sanden had a taste for the beautiful and exotic then.

'Mr Sawbridge was already paying for the rooms in Cheapside, and much of his capital is sunk into this place. I was happy to oblige. Happy! But then!' He began rubbing at his knees again and his face changed from red to almost purple.

'Then what?' Crowther prompted.

'He came here and started preaching in my parlour against the trade, like you said. Against slavery itself. Here in my home and place of business!'

'I can see that would be most irritating,' Crowther said.

Sanden jutted his head towards Crowther. 'It was! I tell him to get out till I have my money back, and he denies ever having it. Liar! Thief!

Then he puts a paper in my hand. I think it's a banknote, but when I open it out . . .' He sprang to his feet and attacked the top drawer of the dresser with various mutterings and cursing until he produced triumphantly a crumpled handbill. He thrust it at Crowther, almost tripping over the carpet in his eagerness and indignation. 'Take a look at that!'

Crowther glanced at it then passed it to Harriet. It was a sheet informing the citizens of London that their salvation was at hand, and all true Christians would be warmly received at prayer meetings and discussions under the guidance of a Mr Willoughby on Wednesday and Friday evenings at six above the Tavern in Red Lion Court. It was rather well done. An angel with a trumpet headed the page and the text was engraved, the paper thick. Harriet understood, however, it would be disappointing if you were expecting a banknote.

Sanden flopped back onto his chair. 'I had the waiter, Bounder, show him the door, and told him not to be too gentle about it. Aye, there was a cheer when he went out the door. People don't come here to be called sinners. Slavery's in the Bible!'

Harriet put the handbill into her reticule. 'Did you get the money back, Mr Sanden?'

'What? Oh yes – after a manner of speaking. Sawbridge signed over a little of his share in this place to cover it.' The man had grown calmer now. He spoke into his chest, his shoulders hunched. 'Owes me money – and offers me a prayer sheet! You have no idea how I suffered to make my capital. Those years in the trade between here, Africa and the islands. God, the stench. I earned every penny – and he takes it and offers me only prayers in return.'

Francis made a careful parcel of the tool and told Miller. The constable was both delighted by the find and horrified, and offered to keep it for him. Francis was glad he did. He did not know if he would be able to stop himself throwing it in the fire or the river. Free of it, he went first to his lodgings to clean the soot from his hands and brush off his clothes, then returned to the shop and went in search of Eustache. He found the boy in the small office behind the counter hunched over a manuscript and reading hard, his fists pressed to the side of his head. Francis pulled up a stool beside him.

'Master Eustache, we need to speak about the book you stole.' The boy looked suspiciously up at him through his long dark eyelashes.

'You said if I worked hard, I might keep it.'

'I did. And I shall not go back on my word, but I think we should speak about what is written in it of your own history.'

Eustache turned back to the page in front of him. 'I knew some of it anyway. Both my parents were evil and they died. Mama meant me to die in the fire. I am not surprised that no one likes me. I will prob-ably be bad too. I wish she had just killed me.'

'*I* like you,' Francis said. The boy became still, attentive. 'I think Joshua likes you too. Why should we not?'

'I look like her,' he said very quietly.

'But you decide who you are going to *be* like, Eustache. No one else.'

'The things she did . . . the things in the book. It's all written down.'

Francis put his head in his hands. 'Eustache, I love books as you do, but they tell different truths. Do not think what you read is the whole truth about your father and mother, or about you.' The boy looked so small, surrounded by those great towers of words, their weight. 'When I was a little older than you I read *Robinson Crusoe*. It meant more to me than anything. Then, some years later, Mr James Smith, the father of the lady who was killed yesterday, gave me another book, called *Oronooko*. There was a black man in that book too, but he was not a slave like Friday. Oronooko was noble, and no slave. That book, and the kindness of the man who gave it to me, gave me hope. I decided the world was too complicated for one book to describe, and from that day on, I read everything I could find. I *decided* to be an educated man.

I even taught myself some Latin in order to read more. It has been written in books that men born in Africa like me are savages, liars, half-men who cannot learn. My mother and father never saw a book, yet here I am making and selling them, a free man in London. Do you understand me, Eustache? I decided to be the man I am. I decided to believe that what people said or wrote about my heritage was *not* what made me!'

'Yes, Mr Glass.' Eustache was still staring at the page in front of him. Francis stood, weary to his bones and not knowing if he had helped or not. 'Thank you.' The boy said it so quietly he could hardly hear him. A need for Eliza ran through his body so intense and complete that he was surprised he did not fall to the ground. She would have known what to say to the boy, what kindness could cure.

III.8

THE RED LION TAVERN showed signs that it had been a prosperous place in times gone by: the taproom was wide and high, but the city workshops had crowded in around it and the filth on the windows was so thick one would have thought it close to dusk. The landlord himself was also filmed in grime. He had the features of a drinker, and eyes set so far back in his head, he looked like a skull tightly wrapped and meanly padded. He gave the impression they were taking him from important business, though his only customers seemed to be half a dozen souls sunk into the places where the shadows were deepest. He admitted that he rented the upper parlour to a Mr Willoughby for his prayer meetings twice a week, but he could not, or would not, give them any indication of where that gentleman might be found at any other time.

Harriet was preparing to ask the shadow patrons when a young woman bustled in with a basket over her arm. The atmosphere of the room lightened immediately, as if she had brought the spring in with her.

Harriet asked the girl as she passed them if she knew where Willoughby lived. She nodded at once. 'Little Sheep Lane, madam. I remember it because I thought it funny. Shepherd and his flock, if you understand me.' Harriet smiled. 'You won't find him at home when it's light', the maid went on. 'Best look for him along The Strand.'

'Is there any place in particular he frequents?' Crowther asked. 'And can you describe him? I do not know the gentleman by sight.'

The girl laughed and with such lightness and good humour Harriet thought she could not have been in London long. 'Oh, you'll have no trouble finding him, sir. He'll be out there in the street preaching. Poor lamb! Most people only stop if they've something to throw at him for his trouble. State his coat is in sometimes when he comes in for his meetings would make you weep. As for his looks, well, he's as thin as you, sir, and dressed in black, so I'd look for an image of your younger self with a religious turn and there he'll be. Now if you'll forgive me, I put a soup on before I went out, and if I don't go and stir it quick, it'll stick.'

She turned to go, but Harriet put her hand on the girl's sleeve. 'Miss, did you ever see a gentleman called Trimnell at Mr Willoughby's meetings?'

'Lord, Mr Trimnell never misses a one. He's a little strange, ma'am. Said he wanted to save our souls, but he always looks to me as if he'd rather eat 'em.' Some of the listening shadows laughed. 'But it was Mr Trimnell paid for the room, ma'am. He came in with Mr Willoughby a month ago and paid up front, all the way through to Christmas.'

Harriet released her and she disappeared into the warren of dark and smoke-filled rooms.

Crowther handed Mrs Westerman down from the carriage opposite

Somerset House. The air was already cleaner than around St Paul's and there were more strolling macaronis and bored ladies of fashion moving along the streets here, but it was still a mixed and busy crowd. The self-conscious elegance of the town and the thrusting merchants of the city met here and mingled like hot water and cold.

The girl had been quite right: Mr Willoughby was not difficult to find. He stood on the corner of Catherine Street upon an upturned apple crate, his Bible in one hand, the other raised to the Heavens and his head thrown back. He had managed to gather a rather motley collection of listeners: a pair of women, arm-in-arm and giggling, and two men, labourers by the look of their clothes, who were watching the girls as much as the preacher. Others passed with a casual or contemptuous glance.

'Come to the Lord your saviour!' he called to them. 'There is room in His heart and in Heaven for every one of you, whatever your sins. How will you account before God? Have you been charitable? Have you been kind? The great and the poor, the mighty and the weak will burn together without the love of Jesus to save them!'

A gentleman in a tight-fitting coat glanced over his shoulder at the preacher as he passed Harriet and Crowther. 'Mixed company, how perfectly foul.' The man walking alongside him tittered.

'Save yourself from the flames! The everlasting torment of Hell!'

Harriet sighed. 'How long do you think this might go on for, Crowther? The man seems to have plenty of breath.'

'Even Methodists must exhaust themselves eventually,' Crowther said and continued to watch the preacher and the people that passed by, all caught in their own dramas and business. It was as if the character from every play in London, from the low farces of servants and shopkeepers and the comedies of the drawing room to the poetical works of the Classical Age, had all been thrown out of the theatres and into the street. He observed them with a professional eye, picking out specimens in the crowd. The young woman with her skirts hitched around her ankles, a swaying walk and showing the first hints of disease under her rouge; the man in good broadcloth with the blood vessels under his eyes bursting with brandy, his walk stiff and painful – gout probably; the child, pale and coughing with the last stages of lung disease.

He glanced at Mrs Westerman and the fine lines developing around her eyes, and wondered if Mr Palmer were married. The preacher was still exhorting the crowd at full voice but then a middle-aged man emerged from the shop behind where he had set up his pulpit among the refuse. Purple with anger, he kicked the crate under the preacher's feet so hard that he stumbled off it and onto the pavement.

'Enough! That's it! You're bloody ruining me, you crow!' He grabbed handfuls of the preacher's coat in his hands and brought him close to his face. 'Christ, I'd rather have a bagpiper on the street than you. Get out of it!'

The preacher's arms hung by his side. 'I will preach the word of God, brother. Listen to me or face the flames of Hell! I will not be moved.'

The shopkeeper slapped the preacher hard across the face. He flinched from the blow but made no move to defend himself. Harriet released Crowther's arm. He bowed to her and crossed the street.

'Come on then, you bugger! Where's your God-given strength now?' The shopkeeper slapped the preacher's face again, hard enough for the sound to crack the air. The preacher's arm spasmed and his black Bible dropped to the ground. London paused and turned to enjoy the entertainment. The preacher looked at the man who held him for a moment, then slowly turned his face, showing the other cheek. The crowd, for though they would not gather in numbers to hear preaching, a fight was another thing, called out in delight and there was a smattering of applause. Harriet could hear the suede gloves of a lily-white macaroni standing next to her clapping together.

'Fine then! If that's what you want, it's what you'll get!' The man lifted his hand once more to deliver the back blow but found himself interrupted by the firm pressure of Crowther's cane on his shoulder. He turned, not relinquishing his grasp on the collar of the priest. 'What?'

'I'll watch a fair fight as happily as any man,' Crowther said. 'But if the man will not fight back, it is not fair. Let him go.'

The crowd hooted with enthusiasm. A priest getting beaten and now a gentleman – and all for free.

'Very well,' the man said, shoving the priest away from him. 'You want the blow, you take it.' He swung rather wildly. Crowther rocked backwards and as the man's fist sailed by him, he bent slightly and swept his cane sharply against the back of the man's knees. His opponent stumbled and fell flat on his face in the filth of the street. The crowd roared; Harriet's neighbour laughed and applauded again. Crowther placed one foot on the man's lower back, holding him down.

'Stay there a moment, there's a good fellow.' He pressed a little harder with the edge of his black heel against the man's kidney to reinforce the point. The man stopped wriggling. The crowd had been cheated. It had been shaping up well, but now, just as they were getting comfortable, it seemed to be over with. London shifted its packages, looked at its pocket-watch, and began to drift away.

Crowther released the shopkeeper and bent down to pick up the preacher's Bible, knocking the muck off it with his handkerchief. Then he offered his hand to his fallen foe, whose rage had been knocked out of him, along with his breath. He looked sulky, but more sheepish than angry now. 'Next time, just hire the pipe-player,' Crowther said and left him.

Harriet had gathered the preacher up, taking his arm and leading him away from the corner. He looked back over his shoulder. 'They'll take my crate!'

'You will find another,' Harriet replied, then when they were at a sufficient distance, waited for Crowther to join them. He did so, and Harriet watched his thin face for any sign of pleasure or self-congratulation. She saw none. He could find cause for pride and vanity in many things but not, it seemed, in knocking a tradesman over into the filth. He handed the Bible to Mr Willoughby, who accepted it with a bobbing bow and a troubled expression. The slap had put some angry red into his cheek, but he was otherwise a pale fellow and seemed smaller now he was not up on a crate and in the full flight of speech.

He turned the Bible in his hands. 'I should thank you, and I do with all my heart, for picking up my Bible, but you should never strike another man, sir. No matter what the provocation. God Himself told us it is a sin to answer violence with violence.' There was a sweetness in his voice when he spoke of God. The skin on his bruising face seemed to glow, as when a girl mentions her sweetheart's name.

Crowther raised one eyebrow and was opening his mouth to speak, but Harriet intervened before the conversation could become theological. 'Mr Willoughby, we would have some speech with you. It touches upon Mr Trimnell.'

The passion left his face and was replaced with warm concern. 'Oh, has he sent you to speak to me? I had worries for his health on Friday and hoped he might take the air and help me distribute notices for my prayer meetings. People will not take them from me, but when he stares at them, they take them like lambs. I sent a note to his lodgings.' He produced from his pocket a bundle of the handbills matching the one that had led them to him in the first instance.

Harriet put his hand on Willoughby's arm. 'I am sorry to tell you of it, but Mr Trimnell is dead.'

The man's face fell and the bills were returned to his pocket. 'He is? I had not heard. No, I had not. I am sorry to lose a friend, but thanks be to God, he is with Jesus now. I hoped God might spare him a little while longer. I shall pray for him. Thank you for bringing me word.'

'He was attacked, and died as a result, Mr Willoughby.'

'Oh!' The preacher looked down at the Bible in his hands. 'Oh, poor Mr Trimnell. Oh, that is very bad, I thought perhaps a recurrence of his sickness. He was become so thin. Some robbery, I suppose. The luxury of these late times has dragged many a poor soul into sin. We are none of us free from the guilt of it.'

His distress seemed genuine and Harriet pitied him too much in that moment to tell him the exact circumstances of Trimnell's death. He would find out soon enough.

'Mr Willoughby, did you see Mr Trimnell then on Friday evening?'

He folded his arms, holding his Bible across his chest. 'Oh yes, I saw him almost every day, and he would never fail to come to one of our regular meetings. It was after midnight when he left me.'

No visit to the Jamaica Coffee House then, Harriet thought, and Trimnell would have to pass by the Cathedral on his way home. She had a sudden vision of a man, or men waiting in the darkness by the Cathedral, their whip and ropes at the ready. 'Are we right in believing it was you who brought Mr Trimnell to the Lord?'

Willoughby said solemnly, 'It is Jesus Himself who calls, madam, and He alone, but I was there to guide him as best I could. I was preaching in the city and he happened to pass by in the days that followed his return from Jamaica. I could see that God had called him, and after that day we had many conversations. Poor man. He was much tormented by his past. What he told me of his life on those islands . . .'

'When did he repent of his part in the slave trade, Dr Willoughby?' Harriet asked. 'Was it on hearing you preach?'

The man blushed like a schoolgirl. 'No, no. He began to think on his sins during his illness in Jamaica and told me he spent his time on board ship reading a Bible he had borrowed from the ship's captain. When he arrived here, he went at once to speak to a priest he knew, but did not find the assistance he craved. Then, while walking the streets in a great confusion of mind, he heard me speak.' He looked at the ground in front of him as if he expected them to join him in a moment of prayer. 'He was distraught at what he had done, the sufferings he had inflicted on his African brothers and sisters.' Willoughby looked a little grey. 'He had worked as a trader of slaves on the coast before inheriting his estate.' To Harriet it seemed that the sounds of the street had dulled. She thought of the sunken face she had seen, whatever expression it had, hidden by death. She thought of the creeping dawn finding his body staked out in the churchyard and found at last a small tremor of pity for Trimnell.

'You are no friend of slavery then, sir?' Crowther asked.

Willoughby shook his head violently. 'A man can be under no necessity of degrading himself into a wolf, as Mr Wesley said himself. It is an evil. An absolute evil.'

'And Mr Trimnell was persuaded of this?'

'Absolutely. He was sick with horror at his past sins and determined to do penance. He was terrified at facing Judgement before he had done all he could to appease God's anger.' There was a tremor of doubt in his face and Harriet saw it.

'Asking God's forgiveness was not enough?'

A sedan chair was being carried past them at a great pace. They had to step close to the window of a goldsmith's shop to avoid being knocked aside. Harriet had the flash of a female face inside the chair. An impression of powder, silk, ostrich plumes.

'My God is the God of love Who rejoices when a sinner returns to Him. He asks for our repentance, not our pain. Though I applauded Mr Trimnell's attempts to make amends.'

'He paid for the room at the Red Lion?' Harriet said gently.

Willoughby nodded. 'Oh yes. And he arranged and paid for the printing of my handbills, but he did more. He meant to do more. I rejoiced with Mr Trimnell when he found that a runaway slave of his was in London, so that he might assure the man that he was free. It must have been a great relief for the poor fellow. He also believed that he had a mulatto daughter in the city. He told me he was planning to acknowledge her and bring her up in his home. He even found another boy whom he had sold to a merchant, working in a grocer's shop in Charles Street, and gave him all the money he had about him.'

No wonder he was poor then, Harriet thought. 'And Mrs Trimnell?' she asked.

'I do not know. She never came with him to pray with me. But she lost four children during their years in Jamaica. Whatever her sins, surely God punished her enough by taking her children from her.'

His hands were shaking now and the fire of his preaching had grown cold.

'When you saw him on Friday evening,' Crowther said, 'was Mr Trimnell carrying a metal mask with him?'

Willoughby shuddered. 'No – that is to say, I have no recollection of his having it. He had once brought it to a meeting. He wished to show another member of the congregation that such things did in truth exist. I asked him not to bring it again. Such an evil object.' His voice had become distressed. 'Forgive me. If you wish to speak more to me, you may find me here or in my lodgings. I must pray. I *must* pray. Good day to you both.'

He hurried off along the street and Harriet looked back to the corner where he had been preaching. 'Did you see what happened when he dropped his Bible, Crowther? How he took the blow and his body wished to defend itself, but he would not allow it?'

'I did. You believe it might explain why Trimnell did not defend himself from his attackers?'

'Perhaps.' The glimmer of the goldsmith's wares caught her eye. The shopkeeper was removing something from the window. She could just see him passing it with a bow to a gentleman waiting inside. 'I think I shall call on Mrs Trimnell.' She looked down at her dress. 'Though I should probably wear something a great deal less muddy to do so.'

III.9

CONSTABLE MILLER HAD BEEN right about the proceedings of the Coroner's Court. The coroner seemed to be attending only under duress and was expecting to close the proceedings before his beer had even settled in his tankard. He noted carefully that there was ready money in the house which had not been taken, so dismissed the idea of a robbery and seemed not to note the disappearance of the maid at all.

Francis recognised the look the man gave him when he stated that he had seen a wound to Eliza's eye and that her body was cold. It was a twitch in the lip that indicated he was being troublesome. The jury paid attention, however. Constable Miller had gathered together a group of men who had got used to these sorts of proceedings over the years and were not intimidated by Barthlomew's stares. The constable produced the graver, and it was passed between them. They handled it as carefully as a relic, though Bartholomew only frowned at it and waved it back into the constable's possession. The jury asked to speak to the surgeon again, a man as dismissive as the coroner. Under the foreman's careful questioning, however, he conceded that the condition of the body when pulled from the ruin meant he could not say there was no injury to the eye. He equally could not say whether 'the woman' had died in the fire or not. If he had called her by her name, the coroner might have got the answer he wanted, but the foreman was Scudder indeed, and was justifying the faith that Miller had shown in him.

'It needs adjourning,' the butcher said, and crossed his fat arms over his chest. The coroner began to argue but Scudder shook his great head. 'Now, Mr Bartholomew. You know I served on a dozen juries like this and for the Aldermen too. Happy to do my duty, as are we all.' He looked around him and the rest of the jurors, local tradesmen all and a bookseller or two among them, Francis noted, bobbed their heads in agreement. 'If this fella can't say how good Mrs Smith died, get someone who can. And bills. You can print up bills asking if anyone saw anything dubious. Tell 'em to take the cost out of my rates.'

The coroner was irritated. 'It is likely no one could tell, Mr Scudder, from the condition of the body. And we cannot go to the expense of printing bills just because of the impressions of one confused man.'

One of the younger jurors tapped Scudder on the shoulder and leaned forward to him, whispering. Scudder bent his neck slightly to listen. 'Two things, Mr Bartholomew. Thing one, Mr Glass here don't seem confused to us. Thing two, young Jarvis here has just mentioned you had a smart fella in for that slave-monger this morning. Let him have a look at her.'

Mr Bartholomew said severely, 'Mr Trimnell was a landowner in Jamaica, not a trader, and Mr Crowther is an authority who happened to be on hand. I cannot order him to come again.'

Scudder was a stubborn man. He seemed to settle himself even more firmly into his seat. 'What would be the harm in sending this authority a little note with our compliments. Seeing as this other bloke don't seem to know his arse from his elbow,' he added in slightly lower, but still perfectly audible tones. It was too much for the surgeon. He stood up and stalked out of the room. Scudder watched him go with no sign of either discomfort or regret.

Mr Bartholomew stared at Scudder, who met his gaze with calm assurance. Bartholomew blinked first. 'Very well. I shall adjourn for a week and write to Mr Crowther – though I doubt he will come. But this is most irregular, Mr Scudder. And a waste of our time.'

The younger juror murmured something and Scudder laughed. Bartholomew did not ask the reason and gathered his papers with obvious irritation. Scudder did not move until the coroner was gone, then he stood with a deep sigh and approached Francis.

'Take an ale with me, Mr Glass?' he said. Normally Francis would have refused him, but he couldn't say no today.

When they had their beer in front of them, Scudder offered a toast to Mrs Smith and Glass drank with him.

'Not that she'd approve of us taking a drink, even in her name,' Scudder said.

'She wouldn't. Thank you, Mr Scudder, for insisting.'

'Didn't do it for you, Pompey,' he said. Francis managed to conceal his flinch. 'He's getting above himself, Bartholomew, ever since he started dreaming of becoming an Alderman some day. It's good to remind him, once in a while, that he serves us. I'll not be asked to sit on a jury for a while either, which suits me fine.' Glass said nothing. 'You know I don't have any great fondness for you black fellows, but Mrs Smith liked you and I've never heard it said you are dishonest.'

'Her apprentice says he heard nothing, saw nothing out of the ordinary,' Glass said.

'Some mornings I have to wake my apprentice by throwing the frying pan at the little bugger.' The butcher stood up. 'They won't print bills though. I'll ask about and you'd best do the same. Miller's asking all the ladies for word of Penny. We've got a week and the hopes this Crowther fella will come along and be useful – leastways say a murder is a murder. Where's Mrs Smith's brother?'

'Travelling in the north. I've been asked to manage the business until he returns.'

Scudder rolled his massive shoulders. 'Poor sod. He'll take it hard.'

Glass finished his beer and stood as well. 'I need to get back to the shop. Thank you for the drink.'

Scudder hesitated then put out his hand. 'Do right by her, Mr Glass.'

Francis shook it and left Scudder still staring thoughtfully after him.

Crowther waited in the tiled hallway of 24, Berkeley Square while Harriet changed. As he did so, the kitchen boy from his own home brought a note to the house, and in it he found Mr Bartholomew's tightly worded request for a consultation on the body of another unfortunate. Crowther had refused the housekeeper's offer of refreshment, but William appeared with bread and cheese anyway, and he ate it without noticing he did so. When Harriet came back down the stairs looking a great deal less muddied and windblown, he handed the note to her.

'You must go, Crowther. I think perhaps it would be better for me to visit Mrs Trimnell alone, in any case. What bounty London bestows on you! Another body. I hope the clergy of St Paul's have not been at this one too, redressing and washing it.'

William was removing Crowther's plate from the side table as they spoke.

'Excuse me, Mrs Westerman.'

'Yes, William?'

'When slaves are bound down for a whipping, their shirts are removed. Not their britches,' he said. 'Your mention of the clothing brought it to mind, ma'am.'

'Thank you, William.' She handed the note back to Crowther and he folded it into his pocket. 'African or English, I thought whoever did this had intimate knowledge of slavery. Could someone have paid for the attack?' She sighed. 'You do not wish me to examine the body with you this time? Has your faith in my powers wavered?'

Crowther stood. 'Not in the least, but fire does almost as much damage as the clergy of St Paul's. You are better occupied visiting the widow before word reaches her that we have been asking about her husband. How shall you explain your visit?'

Harriet smiled. 'I shall take her an improving book. James was hardly cold before someone thrust Marcus Aurelius into my hands with their earnest good wishes.'

The maid who opened the street door in Cheapside informed Harriet quite sharply that Mrs Trimnell was not at home.

'Then I shall go and leave my gift for her in her rooms. Stand aside, if you please.' And when the maid hesitated: 'Good God, girl. Do you think I am going to rob the place?' Harriet moved just enough so the maid could see the Earl of Sussex's carriage and Philip, gorgeous in his blue and gold livery, beside it. The maid gave her a wary look, then stood aside.

'First floor, first on your right, ma'am. The door is open.'

The rooms that Mr and Mrs Trimnell occupied were large but shabby. There was a good-sized parlour with armchairs by the fire and a lady's desk under the window, but the whole room had an air of exhaustion. The furniture was scuffed, the cheap prints on the walls had worked loose in their frames, and the carpet that lay in front of the fire was bald in patches. No wonder Mrs Trimnell fled as often as she might. There were two doors leading out of the room. Harriet pushed one open. It made the main room look cheerful by comparison. A desk, a bed, a dresser and a wash-stand, all in poor repair, but it was the atmosphere of the room that Harriet felt like a cold rain. Misery seemed to have soaked into the walls. For a moment she believed she could hear weeping, then she heard a movement next door and realised the weeping was real. Her heart froze. Perhaps Mrs Trimnell was at home and grieving. She went quickly back into the main chamber then lifted her hand to knock gently at the second door, her volume of Marcus Aurelius held in her other hand feeling like a poor excuse. There was a flurry of movement and the door opened, but instead of Mrs Trimnell, Harriet found herself facing a young woman dressed in black. She looked at Harriet, astonished and afraid.

'I am sorry to disturb you, my dear,' Harriet said. 'Are you Mrs Trimnell's maid?'

The girl covered her face with her hands and began to cry again. Deep, terrified sobs. Harriet put her arm around the girl's shoulders and led her to one of the armchairs, then crouched beside her.

'My dear, please do not cry so. What is your name?'

'Martha, madam,' the girl said, and tried to control herself.

'And are you Mrs Trimnell's maid?'

'I *was*. Ten years and now she means to turn me off. Master says I am to go free, but he left no paper for me! Now *she* will send me back, I know it. She says she must have a French maid now, and I've kept her so fine all these years with nothing but my own needle to do it with. French!'

Harriet patted her arm. 'I am grieved to hear that. Was the dress Mrs Trimnell wore on Saturday your work?' A nod. 'It was very fine. No Frenchwoman could do half so well, I'm certain.'

Martha pulled out a handkerchief and wiped her eyes. 'She did look fine, didn't she? I bought the silk for it only last week. The ribbons came from an old dress of hers, but I know how to hide the worn parts.'

'I thought it very beautiful. And such lovely jewels. A present from Randolph Jennings, I believe?'

The maid nodded, all innocence. Harriet pulled up the other chair so she could sit close to her. 'I came to see your mistress. She is not at home?'

'Sir Charles bade her to stay at Portman Square, while I'm sent to pack up the last of her things. Oh, I don't want to go back to Jamaica! But she'll get good money for me. Oh, after all these years . . .'

'She cannot send you back,' Harriet said stoutly. 'It is against English law to send you back against your will.'

Martha looked up at her, confused. Harriet began to search through her reticule until she found Mr Christopher's card. 'Pack up her things and send them to Portman Square, then go and see this gentleman. He will help you. You shall not go back, Martha. And a woman as clever as you are with a needle can earn good money in this town. Better than a Frenchwoman.'

The girl said dully, 'She'll give me no reference, and I have no friends here. I was born under Mr Trimnell's roof.' Harriet did not know what to say. 'Though Mr Willoughby was kind to me.'

'You went to the prayer meetings?'

'Sometimes. When Mrs Lucy didn't need me. They all speak very nicely to me there.' She began to weep again, though quietly this time. 'What shall happen to me?'

Harriet felt a bubble of rage burst in her chest. 'Nothing that you do not wish to happen, Martha! You must only be brave.' Martha looked up at her, on her face an expression of such disgust that Harriet's blood went from hot to cold in a heartbeat.

'*You* don't know!' She stood up and threw Mr Christopher's card into the grate. 'You don't *know*!' Then she turned on her heel and went back into the second chamber, slamming the door behind her.

Harriet found she was shaking. She picked up the card and set it on the mantelpiece in case Martha changed her mind. It was becoming clear to her that she didn't know very much at all. With that uncomfortable thought in mind, she left the room.

III.10

THE HOME OF SIR Charles Jennings looked elegant rather than magnificent from the Square, but when the footman bowed her into the hallway and then retreated with her card, Harriet had the chance to look about her and was astonished. The lobby was twice the size of the one in Berkeley Square, and painted canary yellow. She saw marble stairs, wrought-iron and polished railings, a white plaster ceiling decorated in geometric patterns with Greek key borders. Around the walls hung an array of Italian landscapes in curling gilded frames, so that it seemed on every side vistas opened into antique harbours scattered with butter-coloured ruins.

The footman returned and bowed again, then invited Harriet to follow him up the marble staircase to the first floor. At the end of its first flight, and below an enormous oil of some tropical view, the staircase folded back on itself in tight but gracious curves. Above her, the spring sun fell through a domed skylight patterned with iron tracery, and on each side the steady progression of paintings continued, each showing some new view of tropical shores. She felt as if she were climbing some tower set magically on the earth in such a way that all the great sights of the globe could be enjoyed at once.

Mrs Trimnell was in the Green Salon with Mrs Jennings, the footman explained in low tones, as they reached the landing on the first floor. He pushed open a set of double doors, announced her name and left her to walk in.

It was a room that would make most of the crowned heads of Europe ashamed of their palaces. Much of the south wall was taken up with huge windows, dressed with swathes of green and gold fabric. The room was so large that Harriet would have struggled to see her hosts, except that an elderly lady on the eastern side of the room got to her feet and approached. Harriet recognised her from church and from the Coroner's Court. In the distance behind her Harriet could make out the black shadow of Mrs Trimnell, also rising to curtsey, and in the south-eastern corner stood the tall, white-headed figure of her father, Mr Sawbridge. The contrast between these surroundings and those of the shabby little rooms in Cheapside was dizzying. Mrs Jennings put her hand out to Harriet with a warm smile.

'My dear Mrs Westerman, I am delighted to meet you! I shall not stand on ceremony. We saw each other in church yesterday, after all – and was not Fischer in good voice? I am such an admirer of yours, I feel I know you already. Indeed, if I had known you were in town I would have sent you cards for our little party last week.'

Her face was deeply lined, and Harriet thought she could not be under eighty, but her expression was lively and her step firm and easy. She was a small woman, dressed in stiff green silks that gossiped as she moved, and her hair was dressed very high. Harriet could do no more than murmur her thanks before Mrs Jennings leaned her narrow body closer to her and spoke in a lower tone. 'If you manage to get that designing trollop and her goat of a father out of my house as soon as possible, I shall be *most* grateful. Sir Charles is far too good to them. To invite *her* here! But of course, one's children can do no wrong, can they? The best of us turn blind and deaf. If they are here a whole week together, I shall have to burn down the house, which would be a great shame, as the paint is only just dry.'

She put her arm through Harriet's and began leading her towards the others. Her voice became louder. 'I know Mr Graves may not feel he would find many friends here, but he is quite wrong. So much more unites us than drives us apart. Music, for instance.' Then in her lower tone. 'Sir Charles is foolishly generous. She has been sniffing after Randolph for weeks – it's barely decent – and now she seems to think she is part of the family. I dare not let any acquaintance of mine into the house while she is here — dear God, I'd rather expect them to take tea with my footman. I know people mix more freely in the Indies, but this is beyond endurance.'

As soon as this last was out, her face was transformed by a charming smile and the parties were joined. The ladies shook hands.

'Mrs Westerman, you have met my father, Mr Sawbridge,' Mrs Trimnell said, and the gentleman bowed. Even at his age he was an imposing presence, broad without being fat, with large hands, the strong lines of his chin and forehead unsoftened by age. Mrs Jennings did not sit down again.

'Well, I must leave you, my *dear* friends. The cook is threatening to leave again and Sir Charles cannot possibly be in London without him.' Under the guise of an affectionate farewell, she murmured to Harriet: 'Do try and make sure they don't steal anything.'

Harriet was given a place beside Mrs Trimnell. Black suited her, emphasising her slender figure and the whiteness of her skin. She looked very lovely. Her father, after making a slightly awkward bow, remained by the window. He was sipping his tea rather noisily. The saucer balanced on his right hand, he carried the cup to his mouth with his left.

'The black boy is in Bridewell until the next sessions at the Old Bailey,' Mrs Trimnell said as soon as Harriet had her own tea-cup in her hand. 'I am greatly indebted to the constables that they managed to find him so quickly. Everyone has been so kind.'

'I wished to come and offer you my sympathies again. You must have been looking forward to your husband's retirement to England. What a cruel blow, to have it cut short so quickly.'

'My homecoming was not as I expected,' she said. 'That is certainly true.' As she offered Harriet a plate of dainties, her movements were stiff, very unlike the grace she had shown when Harriet first saw her. The sleeves of her jacket were long and tight, fringed with black lace, but as she moved, Harriet thought she saw a garnet bracelet just hidden under it. She looked more carefully out of the corner of her eye. It *was* a bracelet – but then Harriet saw something else: yellow bruising on the soft white underside of Mrs Trimnell's wrist.

'Your husband was ill?' Harriet said. Mrs Trimnell looked up at her sharply. 'The weakness of his heart . . .'

'Oh yes, before we came home. He was out on the estate and was overcome by the heat. Such reverses we had out there in recent years. He wore himself out trying to make the land profitable again.'

Mr Sawbridge had been staring out of the window at the mature trees in Sir Charles's garden, the horse chestnuts' white candles of blossom. He turned back into the room. 'He was addle-brained when he came home,' he said. 'Should have been locked up weeks ago.'

Harriet was surprised. Mrs Trimnell blushed. 'He was not quite recovered from his illness,' she said. 'But he was a most excellent man, Father.' The older man did not seem in any way abashed, but rather let out a bark of contemptuous laughter.

'I heard that he had become very religious in his final weeks,' Harriet said.

Mrs Trimnell put down her cup. 'You heard that, Mrs Westerman? Well, it is true. I do not think my husband had picked up a Bible any day in our married life until after his illness. I am afraid he then fell in with people who took advantage of him.'

'You shouldn't have protected him, Lucy. Saying he was working at his papers when he was off trying to ingratiate himself with Negroes. He was never good enough for you. Never.'

Mrs Trimnell closed her eyes briefly, but if she was trying to conceal grief or rage, Harriet could not tell. 'It was my duty.'

'Duty be damned. You were ashamed of him, and rightly so, while you were trying to make friends here and begging for a shilling to put in your pocket.'

Harriet had thought that some years sailing the world with her husband, and the various adventures she had survived with Crowther at her side had made her difficult to shock, but to hear Mr Sawbridge speak so among the beauties of the house in Portman Square rendered her speechless.

'Father! If you cannot conduct yourself like a gentleman, please leave.'

'Gentleman? I'd rather be a plain man than a gentleman like your husband! Still, you're where you should be now. The rest is just words.'

'Go Father.'

He put down his cup and saucer and stalked from the room without taking his leave. Mrs Trimnell did not try to speak at once, but stared hard at the polished veneer of the table in front of her.

'My husband tried to sell our home for the price of a horse a few weeks before he died,' Harriet said at last. 'He was injured – a blow to his head that almost killed him – and though he seemed to recover, he was not the man he had been. More like a child in some ways. A child with a violent temper.'

Mrs Trimnell lifted a handkerchief to her eyes. 'What happened to him?'

Harriet could see James in front of her again. He had been such a handsome man. 'My friends feared for my safety and that of our children. He lived his last months in the care of a doctor in Hampstead.'

'My father has the manners of a butcher, but I think he is only sorry. He should have sent me back to England to find a husband, but he wished to keep me with him. There are not many eligible men in Jamaica.' She sighed. 'I did try to be a good wife to Jacob.'

'You have no brother or sister, Mrs Trimnell? My sister was a great comfort after my husband died.'

The young woman shook her head. 'I was my mother's only surviving child. She died when I was six, finally exhausted by the climate of the islands. There is no rivalry then, between your sister and yourself? Your money comes from your husband, does it not? Does your sister not mind that you have so much while she has less through no fault of her own?'

Harriet wondered if Mrs Trimnell was thinking of the relative fortunes of her husband and her current hosts. 'My sister is married to a man she loves. I am certain she would rather have his love, than my money.'

'Ah, love,' Mrs Trimnell said. 'It can work miracles, can it not?'

'Did you know Mr Randolph Jennings before you returned to these shores, Mrs Trimnell?'

Even after the indiscretions of her father, it was a dangerous question, but Mrs Trimnell gave no sign of offence. 'We knew each other in Jamaica as little children. Then after his mother died he was sent to school in England. We saw each other next when he was seventeen, and I a year or two older. We thought he was going to settle among us and learn the business of the estate from his father.' She sighed. 'But Sir Charles changed his mind. Randolph was sent back to England and later went to university. I married my husband. When Sir Charles came back to London permanently and my father retired, Sir Charles sent out another man to manage his plantation. Oh, those last years I spent in Jamaica were difficult. My husband working so hard, nothing to listen to but the savage music of the slaves in their huts. No one to speak to, and the fear of being murdered in our beds every night. Our home was isolated. Almost a prison in those years.'

'So Mr Randolph Jennings takes no part in running his father's business concerns?' Harriet said, hoping that Mrs Trimnell could not see the expression in her eyes.

Mrs Trimnell sipped at her tea again. 'He is a gentleman. He plans to go into Parliament in due course.' Her eyes misted over slightly. 'Naturally Randolph and I met in London, given the close connection between our families. It was as if those last terrible years simply disappeared. Some people do not understand the true sympathy that can arise between friends. But I know *you* understand it, Mrs Westerman. You and Mr Crowther have had many adventures together, have you not?'

Harriet could almost feel the blade sliding clean in between her ribs. 'Such sympathy *can* indeed be misunderstood,' she said coolly. 'And can occasionally lead to unpleasantness from the ignorant or cruel. Did anything of that nature occur on Thursday evening, at Sir Charles's musical party here?'

Mrs Trimnell flushed; the counterblow had struck home. 'It was a charming evening. Mrs Westerman, you ask a great many strange questions. The boy who killed my husband is in custody. Mr Trimnell took some strange fancies before he died, but he was always a respectable man before that. My relations with the Jennings family are intimate, born of deep friendship – and no concern of yours. Your curiosity verges on the indecent.'

The fiction of good behaviour between them weakened to such thinness Harriet felt even the slightest breath could tear it. She thought of William, of what Trimnell had been when he was respectable. 'I am sure the last few days must have been very tiring for you, Mrs Trimnell, and to show you I mean you no ill, perhaps I can give you a friendly word of advice. Go carefully. Mrs Jennings seems to dislike you intensely.'

She gasped. 'Mrs Jennings took me to Astley's Ampitheatre on Friday evening! We saw the Dancing Dogs.'

'Perhaps she had instructions to keep you away from Randolph for an evening,' Harriet said, standing and picking up her gloves.

'I am certain Randolph cares for me very much. You are very wrong to speak to me in this way. I have the protection of this family!'

'I'm not so sure of that,' Harriet said. 'It seems to me that whatever Randolph Jennings wanted from you he has already got,' her eyes drifted to the bracelets on her wrists, 'and paid for. Your husband was a monster, and you are wearing your lover's tokens with your widow's weeds. Take this warning from a sympathetic friend then: you can have nothing that will make Sir Charles tolerate you for long, so do not talk to me of indecency.'

The satisfaction of having spoken her mind carried Harriet on her walk back to the double doors, while Mrs Trimnell remained seated, white-faced and silent. She pushed the doors open to find a footman standing to attention outside. Harriet was not aware of having raised her voice, but there was a glint in the servant's eye which suggested that she may have done so, and perhaps also that the servants thought of Mrs Trimnell much as Mrs Jennings did. The footman made his bow and closed the doors behind her while she stood horrified at herself, on the landing. It was inexcusable that she had said such things, and worse that they had come to her lips with such fluency and pleasure. If the footman had not been at her side, ready to escort her back down to the hallway, she would have groaned aloud.

As they descended the stairs, the main door was being opened by another man in livery. Randolph Jennings and a younger man tumbled into the hallway, their arms round each other's shoulders, and unless Jennings owned two waistcoats with a mauve stripe, he was wearing the same clothes he had had on, on Saturday morning. The pair shrieked with laughter as they staggered in, and Harriet could swear the stink of sour spirits reached her even halfway up the marble stairs. The footman in front of her hesitated. Below them, a door opened and Sir Charles, calm and controlled as ever, came to meet the new arrivals. Randolph tugged on his rumpled waistcoat.

'Randolph, wait for me in my study. Oxford, a word with you, please.'

Randolph did not make any farewell to his friend, only lowered his head and went off into one of the rooms on the ground floor. His eyes flickered up to Harriet as he passed her, but he gave no sign that he marked her any more than the surrounding servants. The other young man approached Sir Charles and the latter spoke to him briefly. It could not have been more than a sentence or two, but the effect on Oxford was considerable. He turned on his heel and the footman only just managed to open the door before he flung himself out into the street. As soon as he was gone, Harriet's guide continued down the stairs in front of her, and by the time they reached the hallway, Sir Charles had disappeared.

III.11

OXFORD WAS NOT DIFFICULT to overtake. Harriet's coachman, David, slowed to a walk and she leaned out of the carriage just far enough to introduce herself and ask the young man if he needed driving anywhere. He looked at her with deep distrust, then admitted he was making his way to Brooke Street.

She nodded and he opened the door and had jumped inside before Philip could get down from the back of the carriage to assist him. David clucked to the horses and they were on their way once more.

He was slouching opposite her, his ankles crossed and biting his nails.

'Were you part of the party who saw the balloon on Saturday?' Harriet asked politely.

'I was.'

'And you have been playing cards ever since.'

His smile became cunning, and curious. 'How did you know?'

'You still have your coat on inside out.'

He looked at his cuffs, aghast, then burst into peals of laughter. 'Oh, that is famous!' He pulled off and turned it rightways again. 'I always do that for luck.'

'And does it work?' Harriet asked, raising her eyebrows.

'Most of the time. It worked last night, anyhow. If I could have kept Jennings at table another hour, *I* would be inheriting the estates in Jamaica, not him.'

'Perhaps next time.'

His face fell again. 'Not if Sir Charles has anything to do with it. There is to be no more gaming for us, or I will suffer the wrath of the sugar baronet himself. I find that rich, when it was Sir Charles himself who told me to keep Randolph out of the way for a while. He sent a note to my club. I found it when we got back from chasing the balloon. It's not my fault, is it, if the only way to keep Randolph from women is cards and drink.'

'Can they stop you gaming? You are both grown men, after all.'

He sank still further into his seat. 'Oh, Sir Charles is not a stupid man. Don't let all that virtue fool you. He knows how to apply pressure when he wishes to, and he is not one for half-measures. If I stay away he'll pay off my tailor or something of the kind. If I defy him, I'll be thrown out of my club, or all the mamas of this year's heiresses will hear all kinds of terrible stories about me. And it is time I married. Not that he said that, of course, but I know what he means. He won't even do it himself. Drax will go to a ball or two and have his monkey do tricks for the old crones and drop a little poison at the same time.' He yawned.

'Have you known Randolph Jennings long?'

'Since he came back to England to go up to Cambridge. He's not bad fun and he has deep pockets. We lived together in Rome for a year or two afterwards until his temper got us thrown out of the city.' He frowned over her name. 'Westerman . . . You know that slave-lover Graves, don't you? That man is a disgrace. He should have stuck with scribbling for newspapers like a good boy.'

Harriet pulled the cord and the carriage came to a stop.

Oxford sat up a little. 'We are nowhere close to Brooke Street as yet.'

She glanced out of the window. 'No, we are not. It seems you will have to walk home in those filthy clothes, after all.' The footman, Philip, opened the door and stood by it. 'Goodbye.' Oxford did not move, but stared at her as if still suspecting some joke. Harriet leaned forward. 'You stink, Oxford,' she said clearly. 'You are also drunk, and I am bored. *Goodbye*.'

He clambered out onto the roadway. 'Bitch,' he muttered, She half-turned towards him, and drew in her breath to reply when there was a stifled exclamation and Oxford disappeared from view.

'Oh dear, sir,' Philip's voice said very kindly. 'Took a tumble in the muck there, did we?' Harriet held her tongue and instead watched Oxford struggle to his feet and stumble into the shelter of the houses away from the road. He had obviously fallen into something unpleasant. 'Berkeley Square, Mrs Westerman?'

'Thank you, Philip.'

When Francis returned to the booksellers after the inquest, he found an African man in livery leaning against the spiral staircase to the upper gallery and reading one of the histories of London that were kept on the shelves. The man straightened when Francis entered and bowed slightly from the waist. 'I am William Geddings,' he said, 'come from Berkeley Square to gather up Master Eustache.' He added something else in Yoruba.

Francis put out his hand and smiled briefly, but said: 'I know nothing of the language of my fathers.'

William shook his proffered fingers carefully, avoiding the bandages. 'You are Yoruba though, I think,' he said. 'It is a beautiful language – you should try and remember it.'

Francis nodded, but said nothing. William looked confused then went on: 'Master Eustache would not leave without wishing you good evening and finding out what hour you require him to return in the morning. He is still bent over your papers in the back office. I was sent out to wait for you here. The young man did not wish to be disturbed.' There was the twitch of a laugh at the corner of his mouth.

'Shall I say eight o'clock?' Francis asked. William pursed his lips and examined the rafters. 'Nine, then,' Francis amended.

'Good. I have left a parcel of cures for you with the compliments of Mr Graves. The lady who makes them knows her business and puts her good soul into them. You should make use of them.'

'I shall, Mr Geddings. Will you send Mr Graves my thanks?'

Eustache had heard them speaking. He came into the shop with a confident step, his face very earnest. 'You are here, sir! Good evening. I have read such a lot today – and written out what I thought.'

William grinned at him. 'You are a regular ink-drinker, Master Eustache. Why Mr Graves thought it would be a punishment to put you to work in a booksellers, I have no notion.'

Eustache looked wary. 'You shan't tell him, shall you, William?'

'No, no, Master Eustache.' The footman put his finger to his lips. 'Not a word, on my honour.'

Eustache gave a quick smile, looking relieved, and Francis was touched to see he took his teasing from William with a lot more grace than he had the gibes of Susan Thornleigh.

Francis bowed them both out of the shop and examined the parcel that had been left for him. There was a cordial for his throat and a lotion for his hands. He poured a draught of the first and drank it. It had a bitter taste to it, but felt like silk in his throat. Then he sat down behind the counter and slowly unwound the bandages from his hands. They stung as he pulled them free. It was growing darker now and the shop was nothing but a cluster of tobacco-stained shadows. The lamp beside him caught some of the gold on the bindings of the most expensive sets of volumes and sent them glimmering like eyes in the undergrowth. For a moment he felt the heat of an African evening, and the laughter of a pair of women on the street outside became the voices of his aunts gossiping as they prepared the evening meal. He felt the low sweet pain of the memory. The noises of his childhood retreated again into the dark. He opened the jar of ointment and scooped some out with his fingers. It was pale and viscous and smelled of Mr Hinckley's flower garden after the rain. He smoothed it over the dozen or so cuts on each palm and it felt as if he were dressing his wounds in cold air. It seemed to suck the anger from them. She must be a good soul indeed, whoever made this. As Eliza had been a good soul. He let this pain too flower in his heart for a moment, then returned the stopper to the jar, took his rags and threw them into the fire in the back parlour then went in search of Joshua.

He found Eliza's apprentice upstairs and alone, just finishing up the dampening of the sheets required for the next day's printing. Mr Ferguson and the others had shrugged into their coats and left for the night. Their day's work – great sheets of printed words – hung up and down the length of the room, drying and shifting in the air, a low conversation. Joshua looked tired, and Francis noticed the shake in his limbs as he set the weights down on top of the piles of dampened paper. He had not heard Francis climbing the stairs towards him.

'Heavy work, Joshua?'

The boy started. 'No, no, Mr Glass! That is to say – yes, a little. But I can do it, sir!'

Glass smiled and leaned against the bannister at the top of the staircase.

'Don't fret, Joshua. I know you have the heart for the work.' He looked about him. 'Have you done all that was asked of you?' The boy nodded. 'Then I shall buy you some supper from the bakehouse and we may watch the boats on the river while you eat it, if you wish. As to your lodging, will you be scared to sleep here alone? The girl who comes to clean lives out. You'll have a bedroll in the back kitchen. The shop itself will be locked and the back door, but you may unlock the window from the inside if you need to get out to the necessary house. Will that suit?'

The apprentice looked relieved and took a step towards him. 'Yes, sir. I would like that. We used to be so many to a room at the Hospital. I feel like a king when I'm on my own.'

'Come along then. Mrs James makes a pastry that is the only cure for sore limbs.'

The examination of the remains of Mrs Smith took some considerable time. Crowther was working in a section of the stables behind the Black Swan. He could hear the horses moving uneasily in their stalls some yards from him.

Crowther treated every corpse he encountered with a detached respect. He had no faith in those men of his profession who behaved and acted like butchers. Their bravado, he thought, concealed a lack of learning at best, and was frequently an attempt to hide their own fear of mortality. He went about his work then in as measured and considered a way as he knew how. The surgeon who had had sight of the body before him had not even opened up the woman's chest. He had seen the external injuries and made the same guess a child would have done, then sought no evidence to support it. There was no sign of soot in the lungs or throat. The tissue was that of a healthy young woman whose last breath had been of air, not smoke. The front of the skull had been broken with extreme force: a great weight falling from some height while the woman lay on her back – a roof beam in all probability. He thought at first that he would not be able to give Bartholomew's jury the definitive answer they wished from him, since any injury to the head would have been hidden by that later damage, and there was no evidence of any piercing injuries on her internal organs. Nor indications of throttling – the hyoid bone was intact.

Bartholomew mentioned that a witness had spoken of a wound in the eye. Crowther carefully cleaned the skull fragments until he found what he was looking for: a v-shaped mark on the delicate inner curve of the bone, at the back of the skull.

It was growing dark while he wrote and drew up his notes with only the body and the horses for company. Then he washed away the signs of his work, cleaned himself, covered the body, put his notes in his pocket and prepared to leave. As he closed the door behind him, some noise made him turn around. The figure of a man, broad and heavy, reared up out of the darkness of the yard. Crowther dropped his bag and swung his lamp at the man, but his attacker was too close for him to connect with much force. Then a second pair of hands grabbed him and forced his arms behind him. The man in front of him swung at his stomach, fierce punches which drove the air out of his lungs. Crowther collapsed – then swung his head back as hard as he could. He felt the back of his skull connect and the grip on him slackened, but the man in front was too quick; he struck a blow under Crowther's jaw that sent him sprawling. He felt his body hit the ground, then darkness and silence.

III.12

EVEN AS THE LIGHT began to fade there was still sound and activity on the river, but the evening seemed to dull the sound. Sunset turned the river red and gold, barges sailed goods further upstream towards the last of the light, and the wherries and rowboats crossed back and forth across the tide. Some had already lit lamps in their prow. To the east, the masts of the great sailing ships loading and unloading the wealth of nations became a black and bare forest, swinging gently as the waters tugged on them.

'You all think it was Penny,' Joshua said suddenly. 'I hear the others talking when they think I can't hear them.'

Francis looked at him sideways. The boy had a narrow pinched little face, high cheekbones and a thin nose that could have been rat-like, but his eyelashes were long and dark, which made him oddly pretty. He was frowning now as he took a mouthful of Mrs James's pie.

'She has disappeared, Joshua. Don't you think that strange? Constable Miller has been asking in her old haunts, and there is no sign of her. Why would she hide herself so completely if she is not guilty?' Francis spoke wearily. He hated the idea that someone Eliza had trusted had hurt her, but it was what he believed had happened.

'I don't know,' Joshua said. 'But Penny would never lay a finger on her. If you'd found *me* dead and stuffed up a chimney, or half the shopkeepers on Paternoster Row poisoned, and you said "Penny did this", I might believe you, sure. But not Mrs Smith. Penny loved her – thought she was a saint come to bless us. She only gave you hard looks because she worried you were trifling with Mrs Smith's "pure and charitable heart".'

Francis turned and looked at him squarely, at his small hands wrapped round the pastry. The boy ate in the same way Francis used to eat, caught between a hunger that made you want to consume whatever you were given in a crazed rush, and a desire to make the delicious process of eating last. Even so, he radiated absolute conviction.

'Penny had led a bad life, Joshua.'

The boy looked at him as if he were stupid. 'She had to eat, didn't she? She was at the Foundling, you know, years ago, but they 'prenticed her out to an evil old cow in Hampstead who beat her with a strap and whose son liked to catch her alone. She ran away. Then she had to eat. And she didn't steal even then.'

He tore off a lump of the pie with his teeth and chewed vigorously.

'Very well, Joshua,' Francis said. 'Tell me what happened. I know you had your own duties, but who came and went during the afternoon of the fire?'

'I don't know, sir. I was cleaning upstairs in the print room.'

'Did you go through Mrs Smith's parlour to get back to the kitchen then?'

The boy wiped some of the crumbs from his face. 'No, Mr Glass. I used the back staircase. I was all inky, see.'

'Still, Joshua, what did you hear? After I left.'

He put the last of the pastry in his mouth, then when it was swallowed, he stood up and brushed the crumbs off his front. 'We were in the kitchen at the back. Someone knocked on the front door, and Penny went to let them in, but she didn't say who it was. I heard the front door close again a while later, so I reckoned whoever it was had shown themselves out. Most people do. Then we had our supper. Penny took a tray up to Mrs Smith, then I got ready for bed and she sat up with her sewing.' He settled his elbows on the wall in front of them, and Francis did the same as they watched the water together. 'She used to sing while she worked. I liked that. I think she knew I liked it too, though she'd never want it known she was doing anything for my benefit.'

Francis remembered his stumbling fall on the landing, at the door to the parlour, the glass on his hands. The glass that had cut him had been full. 'Did Penny always take the supper in to Mrs Smith?'

The child shook his head. 'No. Mrs S. prayed. A lot. Specially Sunday evenings. She'd close the door so as not to be bothered, and Penny would leave the tray outside for her to have when she and God had talked things out.'

'And no one else came that evening?'

'Maybe,' he shrugged. 'I was bone weary, Mr Glass. Penny knew you were meant to call, so I suppose she was listening out for a knock. Perhaps I heard her move off again. Next thing I remember, right after Penny singing, is that constable shaking me – and the smoke.'

Francis studied the waters below them for a few moments longer,

175

thinking of the tray, the locked door. 'Come along then. Let's settle you for the night.'

They turned together and walked back up Puddle Dock Hill.

On her return from Portman Square, Harriet had made her way to the top of the house to visit the children. Anne was making a model of the balloon with her nurse and was as joyfully filthy and proud of it as a five year old can be. Eustache was helping her, which meant that Anne was in a state of near ecstasy. Harriet watched the boy. He was being kind to her daughter and seemed to take pleasure in her enjoyment.

Susan received Harriet with icy politeness then retreated to a corner with a book, though Harriet noticed, as she admired the model and advised on its decoration, that she never turned a page. Jonathan and Stephen lay on the floor, playing at Fox and Geese. Jonathan asked his sister for help, which she ignored until he had made too many loud and obvious tactical mistakes for it to be borne, and she took a place on the floor next to them. Harriet joined in with the model-building and asked Eustache about his day, but he gave only short answers in return and did not look at her.

Once Anne was taken off for her very necessary bath, Harriet retreated to the library and stared at the paintings of ships, most of which wore too much sail for the apparent weather conditions. She realised she was preparing a narrative for Crowther of her visits to Cheapside and Portman Square, hoping that he would laugh at her for losing her temper and expecting to feel better when he did. Hearing the clang of the bell in the hall, followed by the door to the library opening, she looked up with a smile, expecting to see him on the threshold. Instead of Crowther though, she saw William.

'Ma'am, Mr Crowther's been attacked.'

She flew from her chair and pushed past him. Crowther was in the hallway and standing, but dead white. He was being supported by Graves on his left and Mr Bartholomew on his right. She ran across the tiles towards him. 'Gabriel! Oh, Gabriel. Good God, what happened?'

'The sofa in my study, I think,' Graves said. 'William, the door.' They half-carried, half-dragged him in while Harriet could only watch, her hand over her mouth and tears already running down her face.

As soon as they lowered his weight onto the settee and let him sink onto his side, the men stepped away. Mrs Martin came in at once with ice and towels. William followed with brandy. They gently removed his coat and then Harriet dropped to her knees beside him and began to undo the buttons on his waistcoat while Mrs Martin pulled off his shoes.

'Mr Crowther said he'd meet me in the taproom to give me his conclusions,' Bartholomew was saying to the room in general. 'He hadn't come, so I went to look for him and found him outside the stables, knocked cold.'

Harriet was pushing through the buttons on his waistcoat when she sensed a change in him. Crowther had opened his eyes slightly and was looking at her.

'Mrs Westerman?'

She blushed in spite of herself. 'I must see how badly you are injured, Crowther, and let you breathe at least.'

She undid the last. There was no sign of blood other than the grazes on the side of his face. His eyes fluttered shut again. Harriet felt a touch on her shoulder. Graves was standing over her, a glass of brandy in his hand. She took it from him and put it to Crowther's mouth. He swallowed some and then winced. His jaw was an angry red. Harriet set the glass down and touched the place with her hand. It was beginning to swell, but seemed whole. Then she began to feel round the back of his head. He hissed. Harriet drew back her hand: her fingertips were bloody.

'Mrs Martin, can you make an ice pack, please – no, two – and hand me the cloth.' She wiped very gently the wound at the back of his head. It was at least not bleeding badly. 'Crowther? How should I know if you are injured internally?'

He did not open his eyes again. 'I can breathe, so I have hope for my lungs. If I piss blood or develop a fever you may despair of me.'

She wiped her eyes with the back of her hand. Then she turned to Graves and Bartholomew. 'Gentlemen, if you would leave us, I shall care for him now. Mrs Martin, please would you make up the fire in here, and William – I wish you to fetch some blankets and pillows, please. Crowther, are you likely to be sick?'

'Very likely.' Harriet glanced at William and he nodded. Bartholomew and Graves tactfully followed the servants out of the room. For a moment they were alone. Harriet bent over Crowther and kissed his forehead very lightly. He opened his eyes again and managed to smile at her.

'Who did this, Gabriel?'

'A man who struck me in the stomach like a fighter, while his friend held me.' He spoke quietly, moving his jaw as little as possible.

'Oh Lord! You think you were attacked by the same men who set on Trimnell?' She sat back a little.

'I am certain of it, but there *will* be bruising on my upper arms.' He went pale again and clenched his teeth as the pain washed over him. She lifted the brandy to his mouth again and he drank.

'What can I do for you? Should I send for a physician?'

'Not unless you want me dead.' He sighed. 'Ice. Your sister's lotions . . .'

The door opened and Mrs Martin came in with pillows and blankets and an enamel basin which she passed to Harriet. She held it for him while he vomited then wiped his mouth. He panted for a few moments then seemed to relax a little. Harriet put her hand over his.

'You have green paint on your face,' he said at last. 'Go and wash it off, my dear, and then tell Bartholomew that Mrs Smith was certainly murdered. My notes are in my coat pocket.'

She would not go until William had set the fire ablaze and taken a seat beside it where he could hand Crowther his brandy and make sure the ice packs for his head and jaw were kept in place. Then she stood reluctantly and went out into the hallway. The light of the candles shone off the tiles and pale plasterwork, giving a dusk-like glow to the air. She looked up. A row of small frightened faces were peering through the upper bannisters. She noticed that Eustache had his arm around Anne and felt a stab of affection for him. She smiled and climbed the stairs to tell them that Crowther was not mortally wounded, and to wash her face.

Once Harriet was tidy she went in search of Bartholomew and found him with Graves and Mrs Service in the Salon on the first floor. Harriet took her seat among them and told Mrs Service she had spoken with the children. Graves frowned and turned away as she said it, and she remembered with a pang her promise only hours ago not to bring violence into the house. She then handed Crowther's notes to Mr Bartholomew and reported his conclusions.

Bartholomew read over the notes and tutted. 'It was the maid then. I hope she will be found, though London is full of places to hide.'

Harriet took the glass of wine Philip offered to her. 'The maid?' she repeated.

Bartholomew nodded. 'A former prostitute whom Mrs Smith took in out of charity.'

Mrs Service covered her mouth. 'And to think I spoke with them both on Saturday. Mrs Smith was such a kind woman. Such goodness, but a merry heart with it.'

Graves finished his wine and held the glass out for more. The crystal shimmered as Philip took it from him. 'The man at Hinckley's, Mr

Glass, seemed broken by the loss, poor fellow. He was injured trying to save her and the shop.'

Bartholomew grunted over the notes. 'Oh, him. Yes, well. It seems he was right that the fire did not kill her, though we would all rather not have another murder within a stone's throw of St Paul's so soon.'

'I'm sure Mrs Smith and her friends would agree with you,' Mrs Service said a little tartly. Bartholomew had the grace to look embarrassed.

The slight lull in the conversation that followed this was broken by Harriet. 'Who knew Crowther was there this evening?' she asked.

Bartholomew looked confused. 'Footpads, surely? Mere bad luck.'

'No one ran away as you approached. You said you found Crowther senseless on the ground, so if it were footpads, they had time to rob him and escape. Crowther has his money about him. I found his purse while I was fetching those notes. We have been making enquiries today about how Mr Trimnell spent his last weeks. Crowther told me he was attacked in the same manner as Mr Trimnell was. So I ask you again, Mr Bartholomew, whom did you tell that Crowther would be examining the body of that unfortunate lady at the Black Swan?'

He looked offended. 'Are you suggesting that the same person who beat Trimnell, also beat Mr Crowther? Nonsense!'

Mrs Service sipped her wine. 'I think Mrs Westerman is not just suggesting it, but asserting it. And quite reasonably in the circumstances.'

'We have the boy in custody who attacked Trimnell!' Bartholomew said.

'You have a boy who found a watch,' Graves replied. Harriet glanced at him. She had not realised he had been paying such close attention. 'He did not admit the crime, did he?'

'No, but—'

'Mr Bartholomew, whom did you tell?' Graves asked again. For the first time in the years since she had known him, Graves looked to Harriet like a man she would entrust with the fortune and safety of an Earl. By now, the coroner had grown a little red in the face.

'I . . . I wrote to Mr Crowther from the Jamaica Coffee House. I was out of temper with the jury. I thought their insistence on an adjourn-ment unnecessary. I said as much to Mr Sanden, and any number of people might have overheard me. And of course I sent a note to Sir Charles at Portman Square. As Alderman, he likes to be kept informed of such matters as this.' He lapsed into a miserable silence. 'There must be some mistake.'

'Thank you for the assistance you gave to Mr Crowther,' Harriet said, 'but I do not think there is a mistake.'

It was with some difficulty that Harriet was persuaded she was not the person to sit with Crowther overnight. Only when he told her sharply that he would be a great deal more comfortable with William's assistance when he needed to check his urine for blood did she withdraw.

Crowther slept at least part of the night. At one point he awoke and groaned.

'Do you need anything, Mr Crowther?'

He let the world steady itself before he answered. 'No, William. Thank you. I was not quite awake.' Nevertheless, William took the chance to apply more of one of Rachel's salves to his jaw and to the back of his skull.

'May I ask, Mr Crowther, why you seem to trust Miss Rachel's – pardon, Mrs Clode's – remedies rather than those of professional physicians?'

Crowther leaned forward so William could adjust the pillows under his head. 'She and those who have taught her learn by trial and observa-tion, Mr Geddings. The physicians in the capital learn by reading Latin and Greek philosophy.' There was a candle lit on the table behind them and in its glow, Crowther saw him smile.

'I am sorry I ever mentioned the body, Mr Crowther.'

'At this moment, so am I.' Crowther shifted his position. He thought one at least of his ribs was cracked, and his stomach ached from the blows it had taken, but the pain in his head was lessening and his memory was clear. 'William, why do you go and listen to the African music?'

'It reminds me that I come from somewhere, Mr Crowther. That I had people there.'

'Do you wish to return?'

'No. That is, I know some do and I understand it, but I have been away too long, Mr Crowther. If I went back now, my people would say I have become a white man. You do not wish to return to the place you were born, do you?'

'Keswick? No, certainly not. They would accuse me of having become a southerner.' He heard William's low laugh behind him and he slept again.

PART IV

IV.1

WHEN CROWTHER AWOKE, WILLIAM had gone and Philip had taken his place. He helped Crowther with his morning ablutions and then told him with a discreet cough that Mrs Westerman was asking if he was awake. He gave his permission for her to be fetched. Without even wishing him good morning she checked his various wounds and asked a long series of questions. She seemed angry with him, which Crowther understood to mean she had been very worried, so he suffered it all with as much patience as he could muster.

'No, there is no sign at all of internal bleeding and yes, I would have expected it by now if serious damage had been done', he told her. 'Have you breakfasted? When will you leave to see Tobias Christopher?'

She looked annoyed. 'I am going nowhere at all while you are like this, Crowther. I am staying with you.'

'Harriet, there are by my count at least twelve servants in this house, as well as Mrs Service and Graves. I have a further half-dozen of my own available at a moment's notice. What exactly do you think you can do for me that they cannot?'

She sat down firmly on the armchair by the fire and her skirts puffed around her. 'Nonsense. I cannot leave you.'

He leaned over and grabbed the handbell placed there for him and rang it, grunting slightly as his bruises complained. Philip appeared at once.

'Philip, my clothes and my shoes, if you please.'

The young man looked confused. 'They are filthy, sir.'

'Nevertheless, Mrs Westerman will not visit Mr Christopher without me, and I wish to know what he has discovered. My clothes, if you please.'

'Oh, Crowther stop, I beg you!' Harriet said. 'Philip, you shall fetch nothing.'

'Oh Philip, you shall. Unless Mrs Westerman orders the carriage at once.'

And when Harriet hesitated: 'Come, I am well looked after and I am sure you are as curious as I am to know how Guadeloupe came by that watch.'

She capitulated. 'Very well. If you could ask for the carriage to be sent round, Philip.'

The senior footman bowed and retreated, hardly smiling at all.

'You are in truth not seriously hurt, Crowther?' Harriet asked.

'I will survive, I believe. Now I would be glad if you could do something to find whoever put me into this condition.'

Harriet put her chin in her hand. 'You saw nothing useful of your attackers?'

He settled himself again. 'No, apart from the fact that the man who struck me was somewhat shorter than I am, and was solidly built.'

'Mr Sanden, perhaps?' she said hopefully.

'I do not remember Mr Sanden's breath stinking so foully.' Crowther yawned. He was more tired than he had realised. The older he became, the deeper these injuries seemed to go. 'I am sorry that I do not recall more, but it was dark, and it all happened so damnably fast.'

She smiled at him. 'Just don't die, Crowther. You know I couldn't bear it.'

'I will do my best. Now tell me what happened yesterday after we parted. And try not to make me laugh, my jaw hurts like the devil.'

She had just finished with an account of Oxford's 'accident', and Crowther's jaw was sore, when Philip returned to announce that the carriage was ready. Mr Crowther would not let him leave the room until he had shaken his hand.

Mr Christopher's Academy was housed in a considerable building on Soho Square. Even this early in the day, figures could be seen through the high windows on the ground floor taking instruction on the use of the short sword.

Harriet was shown into what must at one time have been the ballroom. A number of gentlemen, their coats removed, stood in a wide semi-circle while in front of them Mr Christopher was trading strikes with another young man. As they fought, Mr Christopher maintained a commentary on his actions. He moved with such grace and economy it seemed he was hardly exerting himself at all. His opponent, by contrast, was red in the face and sweating. Harriet looked around her. There was a large portrait of the Prince of Wales prominently displayed, but otherwise the walls were decorated solely with crossed swords and foils. In each of the alcoves were racks holding what seemed to her a great variety of weaponry.

Her attention was drawn back to the fight by the sound of a sword clattering to the scuffed wooden floor. Mr Christopher had disarmed his opponent and was now explaining how he had done so. The gentlemen all nodded and stroked their chins, and Christopher bowed to them, and having given them liberty to continue their practice alone as long as they saw fit, he wished them good morning and picked up his coat. He carried it over his arm as he came towards Harriet, then at once took her arm and bent towards her.

'Mrs Westerman, I was not certain to see you this morning. How is Mr Crowther?'

'You have heard? He is badly bruised and in more pain than he is willing to admit, but he assures me he will live. How did you hear?'

'I had a note at daybreak from Palmer. Will you come upstairs and take a dish of tea with me and my wife, and you may reassure me further. I am sorry I was not there last night.'

Behind her, the irregular clashes of metal on metal rang through the high chamber. 'How did Palmer know? No matter. I should be delighted. Crowther thinks he broke the nose of the man who was holding him.'

'Good,' Christopher said firmly. 'This way, please.'

He led her out of the ballroom and up a wide oak staircase. As they climbed, it seemed the house became less martial and more feminine. On the landing hung a pretty landscape in oils over a table with a red ceramic vase placed on it. Christopher took her into a sunny parlour on the first floor. A lady who Harriet presumed was Mrs Christopher was sitting at a round, high table with three small children. One, a boy of about Eustache's age, seemed to be at his studies judging by the scattered papers and his look of fierce confusion. The two girls and their mother were at their sewing. The youngest, who could not be more than six, was working with great concentration and limited success on a scrap of material. Her sister, perhaps not much older than the boy, was neatly embroidering initials on a blue square of linen. The scene would have made an excellent subject for a print extolling domestic harmony. The children were all tawny-skinned, pitched halfway it seemed between their parents.

Mrs Christopher and her children all stood at once and the introductions were made. When the children had shaken hands with their guest they were ushered out and Harriet was seated and tea placed at her side. She liked the look of Mrs Christopher; the woman was cheerful and composed, seemed concerned for Crowther and interested in the lotions used to treat him. 'You can imagine, given my husband's profession, that I have had to treat a great many bruises in my time. Have I not, Tobias?'

'You have healing hands, my dear.'

She grinned. 'And I make liberal use of the brandy bottle. I find that cures most men under forty admirably. But Mrs Westerman has not come here only to discuss ointments.'

At this, Christopher heaved a sigh. 'I am ashamed to speak to you after all my fervour yesterday, my friend. Guadeloupe refuses to tell me where he "found" the watch, despite all my threats and promises. I am disgraced.' He sat down heavily in his chair. 'I begin to fear perhaps he did have some hand in Trimnell's death. Bystander, accomplice, perhaps? The tool in the hand of some other fiend. God knows, the boy never thinks for himself.'

'I think you are too hard on him, Tobias,' his wife said. 'There is more good in him than he will himself admit.' She turned towards Harriet. 'Do you think Guadeloupe had any part in it, Mrs Westerman?'

Harriet considered, then replied: 'No. Crowther was beaten as a warning. I am sure of that. That suggests that someone has heard about us asking questions yesterday and is afraid we will find something out about Trimnell's death. Therefore Guadeloupe must be innocent. Though perhaps the attack was meant to punish me. Still, Crowther is sure that the men who assaulted him were the same who assaulted Trimnell, so perhaps Guadeloupe found the watch, after all.'

'What did you do, Mrs Westerman, that deserves punishment?' Christopher asked.

Harriet told them about her encounters with Mrs Trimnell and young Oxford the day before. Mrs Christopher stifled a giggle when she spoke of the young man being tumbled into the muck. Her husband looked at her disapprovingly.

'Well,' she grinned, 'I'm sorry, Tobias, but I am glad to hear of it. He sounds like just the sort of man who loves to hurl abuse at us from the other side of the street.'

Harriet looked between them, more hurt than she knew how to show. 'You are insulted in London?'

Tobias shrugged his massive shoulders. 'If we go to the Pleasure Gardens or the fair in a modest sort of way, Mrs Westerman, our reception is friendly enough. But I found in the first days of my prosperity that those who had a mind to dislike us – a black man with a white woman and tawny children – were provoked beyond endurance when we dressed finely and went abroad in a carriage. An African walking with a white woman is one thing. A rich African walking with a fashionably dressed white woman is too much for them. My wife has money in her purse to dress in high fashion should she wish, but she does not. Modest gentility is as high as we can style ourselves in safety. It goes against my nature, for I would dress my wife in gold and think it only a fraction of her worth.'

Mrs Christopher patted her husband's arm. 'As if I would have the time to dress in silk while managing your home.' She looked back to Harriet. 'I am very glad you think Guadeloupe innocent of the charge against him.'

As she was saying this, the door was flung open and an attractive girl of about sixteen years of age flew into the room. 'Papa, Mama! I am home! I had such a fine visit. Mrs Green was quite charming and Cecelia and I drove all around the lanes in a gig.' She suddenly noticed Harriet and faltered. 'Oh, forgive me, I did not know we had a guest.' She dropped a neat little curtsey and Harriet stood to shake her hand.

'My eldest daughter, Sally,' Christopher said by way of explanation. 'Sally, Mrs Westerman. Believe it or not, madam, Sally is usually quite a sensible girl. My wife runs the house while my daughter manages the accounts and bills my pupils, but she has been spending a few days with a schoolfriend in the country and the fresh air has obviously turned her brain.'

Sally still looked a little flustered. 'Papa, you are unfair.' She smiled very sweetly at Harriet. 'Papa would not charge anyone if he could avoid it, Mrs Westerman. He is far too soft-hearted.' She looked at her mother. 'Were you speaking of Guadeloupe? Of what is he innocent?'

The girl took a low seat at her father's side and her mother fetched a cup of tea for her while she removed her bonnet. Her hair was a shock of dark copper curls that matched her complexion; her eyes were hazel. She was, Harriet thought, quite beautiful.

'Trimnell was discovered killed on Saturday morning, Sally,' her father said. The girl opened her lips. 'Guadeloupe was found to have pawned his watch and is confined in Bridewell. Did you not read of it in the newspaper yesterday?'

'Oh Papa, no,' Sally said. 'No, Guadeloupe never met him!'

Christopher spoke more quietly. 'Sally?'

She swallowed and managed to say, '*I* gave Guadeloupe the watch, sir. I told him it was Trimnell's and I didn't want it.'

'You!' Christopher looked far more fearsome now than he had done with a sword in his hand. '*You?* And how did you, my daughter, come to have that man's watch?'

'He gave it to me, Papa. I did not want to take it, but he put it in my basket. I did not know what to do, so I gave it to Guadeloupe. I just wanted to get rid of it. I was afraid to tell you, because Trimnell stopped me in the street and I thought you'd be terribly angry, and it seemed better just to get rid of it.' Her voice trailed away as she said this last, then she looked up at her father again, her eyes open and pleading. 'Oh, sir! I would have told you, but then I went down to Kent with Cecelia and her family, and the ladies do not read the newspaper at her home and I was having such a nice time, I simply forgot all about him.' She shuddered as if the memory of the man revolted her.

'Trimnell stopped you in the street?' Christopher spat out each word as if he was throwing a stone. Harriet thought she could see the blood swelling in his veins and recognised the rage and fear of a parent.

'I wanted to get away, but he would not let go of my basket.'

Christopher clenched his hands. 'If he were not dead already . . . Why did you not tell me at once?'

His wife sighed. 'Why indeed, Tobias?'

Christopher sank back in his chair, fiercely silent. Harriet put down her cup. 'Miss Christopher, *why* did he give you the watch?'

Sally looked at her father and mother. Mrs Christopher smiled encouragingly at her. Harriet thought for a few moments. 'Had you ever seen Mr Trimnell before he gave you the watch?'

The girl spoke very quietly. 'I saw him here. That is, he came to speak to Papa and I heard a little of their conversation as I passed the door.'

'You were listening at key-holes,' her father said, though the heat had gone out of his voice. He reached out and brushed her cheek with his knuckles. She pulled a handkerchief from her pocket and wiped her eyes.

'Yes, perhaps a little, Papa. I heard some of what was said and realised he was your old master, and I waited upstairs at the window so I might see him as he went. I didn't have any thought of speaking to him. I just wanted to see him.'

Harriet felt her heart sink in her chest. Willoughby's remark about Mr Trimnell finding a mulatto daughter alive in London came back to her as clearly as if it had just been spoken in her ear.

'Miss Christopher, your father said he arrived in London some fourteen years ago. I think you are a little older than that.'

'I am sixteen, ma'am,' The girl murmured. She lowered her head so her curls fell over her face.

'So you were born in Jamaica?'

'Yes,' she whispered.

'Sally was born to my first wife,' Christopher said slowly. 'She was a fellow slave, Ebele Ngozi, Igbo like myself. We married on the plantation according to our own rites. She died a little more than a year after Sally was born.' He reached out and pulled at one of the girl's ringlets. 'She wished to return to Africa and her people. Her exile had been too long, and too painful. She took the shorter route home.'

'Mr Christopher, were there other white men on Mr Trimnell's estate while you and your wife were enslaved there?' Harriet looked only at the delicately painted patterns on the tea-cup as she spoke.

'No.' She heard him sigh and move in his chair. 'Ebele was attacked by Trimnell. She, and many other of the women he owned. Do you think that makes me less Sally's father? I married Grace eleven years ago and she has raised Sally since. Is she not Sally's mother as much as Ebele?'

'Yes, Mr Christopher,' Harriet said, still staring at her cup. 'I believe that absolutely. But would Mr Trimnell agree with us?'

Mr Christopher did not reply.

'I knew he was my father,' Sally said at last. 'I have known since I was five years old.'

Harriet looked up at that. 'Mr Christopher told you?'

She shook her head quickly. 'There was no need to tell. Papa told me of my mother, told me enough of the estate. The rest I could work out in my own mind, and after Papa married again and my sister was born . . . We are just alike.'

Christopher laughed softly. 'Not so alike. Your sister is far more obedient than you are, and not so wilful. You have your Mama Ebele's fire. Your sister has never stormed at me to raise my fees, or to refuse some fine gentleman teaching until his bill is paid.'

His daughter smiled.

'What did Trimnell know about Sally, Mr Christopher?' Harriet asked.

'He knew I took her with me when I ran, and when Trimnell came to me last week, he brought Sally's manumission as well as mine, and asked, if she had lived. Then if he might see her. The manumission I took, but I would not let him look on my child.' He was still looking at his daughter. 'I always meant to tell him you were dead, but when the moment came, I could not say the words, even if they might protect you. I could not say them.'

Sally wiped at her eyes with the sort of vigour Harriet used herself when she wished to stop crying immediately. 'Trimnell saw me looking from the window upstairs as he left,' she confessed. 'I stepped away as soon as he turned round, but it was too late.'

Harriet got to her feet and went to the window. Soho Square lay below them in the sunshine. A pair of young men who had just left the Academy were talking excitedly as they crossed towards Greek Street, still miming the thrusts and parries Christopher had been teaching them. 'Did you wish to see him again, Miss Christopher?'

'No. To see him that once was enough. He walked like a beggar.' Harriet looked back into the room. Mrs Christopher had changed her seat so she might sit on Sally's other side, not touching her, but as determined a guardian as her husband. 'He must have been watching for me. He stopped me on Thursday afternoon as I came back from the butcher's and held onto my basket: I could not run away for fear of losing it.'

'Did he try and claim you?' Harriet said. 'Not as his property, but as his daughter?'

'He said he wanted to *acknowledge* me.' She said it with utter scorn.

'He said he would take me into his home and his wife would be a mother to me. I told him I had a home, a father and a mother already – but it was as if he couldn't understand. He was so thin and dirty, and he seemed to think that I should be *pleased* at the idea of leaving my home to live with him.' Scorn became a baffled contempt.

Harriet put her hand on the glass pane and imagined it. Trimnell twisted with guilt, with hopes of redeeming himself but still unable to understand that a girl might prefer the black father who had raised her to the white man who had raped her mother. 'Was he angry with you?'

The girl shook her head. 'He just kept speaking more loudly and slowly as if he thought I was soft-brained. Why would he think I wanted *him* as a father when I have Papa? When I have this? He said he wanted to give me a present and put his silly watch into my basket. I did not want it! Cornforth the grocer came out of his shop and asked him what he was about and he let me go. I ran back home.'

So Trimnell had caused enough of a scene to make the grocer come out of his shop.

'Miss Christopher, was anyone watching you while Trimnell spoke to you? Might someone have overheard?'

She thought for a moment. 'I do not know. He was so close to me I could hardly see anything. And he talked and shouted so.'

Harriet left the window. 'Thank you, Miss Christopher. And thank you for the tea, Mrs Christopher.'

The family stood. 'My pleasure, Mrs Westerman,' said her hostess.

Sally leaned against her father. 'May we fetch Guadeloupe from Bridewell, Papa?'

'At once, though you should never have given him the watch, Sally. You knew he would pawn it and drink the money away.' She apologised quietly. 'I am sure that explaining your actions to the city magistrate will be punishment enough. Now, Mrs Westerman, I shall see you out.'

IV.2

FRANCIS WOKE SLOWLY AND later than he had intended, and rang for hot water. His landlady had complained in the first weeks after he'd taken this room that he called for more hot water than the rest of her tenants put together. They had agreed a little extra for the work, and went on now in a friendly fashion, though she called him eccentric for it. Particularly as his skin didn't show the dirt, she said. It was one of the many mysteries of the English, how they decorated themselves, their homes and their palaces with such extravagance, yet were so careless in keeping clean. The maid brought up the can and his shirts clean and mended over her arm. He lifted the fabric to his face and breathed in the smell of starch and felt it comfort him. The girl grinned at him and asked after his wounds. He had almost forgotten them. The lotion from Berkeley Square must have done its work well.

Francis washed and dressed himself with care, took his breakfast of bread and cheese and small beer at the chandler's on the corner, and made his way to the shop.

He found Constable Miller on the doorstep. The man was shifting from foot to foot and occasionally glancing over his shoulder at the books set out in the window, as if they might be planning a surprise attack. Francis smiled at him. 'You may always wait for me inside, Mr Miller,' he said as he opened the door. 'Ferguson is always here at dawn.'

Miller took off his hat as he came in. 'Books make me nervy, Mr Glass. I'm happy to sit in by the fire with you but I feel, standing in here, like they are all talking about me behind my back.' Francis laughed softly. 'I've had word from Bartholomew,' Miller went on. 'It was murder proved. Still no sight nor sound of Penny though.'

'Thank you.'

'And, there's a lawyer in your parlour. Says he has Mrs Smith's will. The fellows at her place told him you were charged with the business.'

Francis glanced over his shoulder towards the parlour. 'Again, my thanks, Mr Miller. You are very kind.'

The constable scratched the back of his neck. 'You're making up for not thanking me the night I pulled you from the fire now, Mr Glass. No thanks needed. Just wish I had something more useful to do than flounder about in the stews asking for Penny. Half of them answer they'll be Penny if I want 'em to be.' He tutted. 'Not one in three of them over fifteen neither.'

The lawyer was indeed waiting in the parlour. A small man who talked in a whisper, he explained the will and its terms to Francis with great care, as if instructing a small child. Francis was courteous and minded less than he would have done on other days. The loss of Elizabeth had made everything else in the world dull. What harm could be done to him now? The will was like her. Clear, loving, well thought out and showing great devotion to her church. All her personal effects she left to her brother to keep, sell or distribute as he thought fit – with one exception: a ring of her father's that she wished to go to Francis. What wealth she left was, after her bills were paid, to be inherited by her brother with one sizeable bequest to St Mary Woolnoth.

The lawyer turned the page and pointed out an addition on the last page. Ten pounds each to her apprentice Joshua Stevenson and her maid Penny Rendell in thanks for their service. It hurt Francis to read it. The executors were named as George Smith, Eliza's brother, and Dr Thomas Fischer of St Mary Woolnoth. 'Perhaps you might consult with Dr Fischer,' the lawyer murmured. 'And one or other of you should present yourselves at Mrs Smith's banking house with the relevant documents.

Have you kept the letter giving you the right to act for Mr Smith in this matter?' Francis only nodded. The lawyer beamed. 'Well *done*, Mr Glass.'

The church was a fine one, part of the generation conjured into the air by Hawksmoor as the city scrambled to rebuild itself after the Great Fire. It had a barrel-vaulted ceiling and pale stone walls. Dr Fischer was not there, the verger told Francis, looking the bookseller up and down with a sneer, but could be found in his house a little further along the same street. It must be a good living, or Dr Fischer was earning very well from his pamphlets, collections of hymn tunes and bundles of sermons, Francis decided, for although the house was not large, it was big enough to entertain and impress.

A maid opened the door to him, and after asking him his business in an aggressive tone of voice, told him to wait in the hallway while she saw if her master could receive him. When she returned, she confessed rather reluctantly that Dr Fischer was willing, and guided him up to a good-sized room on the first floor.

The Reverend Fischer sat at his desk, dressed in the clothes of a prosperous gentleman rather than clerical garb. He was a tall man, vigorous-looking, and his cluttered desk suggested a prodigious workload. He was surrounded by papers and books in untidy piles, and was engaged in filling more sheets at a steady pace. He stood when Francis entered the room and put out his hand, apparently overjoyed to be called away from his work.

'Mr Glass! I am delighted to meet you. I have been told of your heroism. Are you recovered as yet, sir?'

Francis offered his hand and the Reverend took it, though he rather cradled it than shook it. He frowned over the healing wounds. 'Not quite, not quite! What can I do for you? When may we receive dear Mrs Smith's body for burial?'

He was warm, genial. Francis could understand why Eliza had admired him.

'I have brought you Mrs Smith's will to examine, sir,' he said. 'You are named as an executor and Eliza left a bequest to your church. Her brother is away; I act for him in his absence.' He passed the papers from the lawyer to Fischer, who sat sideways in his chair to read them, waving Francis to an armchair as he did so. The armchair was already occupied with a number of books – some left open with their spines cracking, Francis noticed with discomfort. He perched on its edge as well as he could while Fischer read. 'As to the burial,' he added, 'I am afraid I cannot tell you when that will be. The inquest was adjourned, sir. Yesterday afternoon.'

The Reverend looked up and made a sweeping gesture towards the piles of paper on his desk. 'Adjourned? How so?'

'Mrs Smith was murdered before the fire began, sir.'

Fischer stared at him. 'Good God.'

Francis was afraid he had been clumsy. 'Forgive me, I have thought of nothing else and I forget this is still grave news to her friends.'

Dr Fischer's face seemed to sag. 'She had been a parishioner of mine for many years, Mr Glass. A better and more charitable woman never lived. Murdered? How cruel. Was there any sign of robbery?'

'Her maid is missing, though there was some money left behind. We are making enquiries.'

'Good, good. Oh, poor Mrs Smith. I fear her honour and her innocence were her undoing.' He handed the will back to Francis. 'As to the winding up of her estate, you must do whatever you think right, Mr Glass.'

'I wish to sell the remaining stock as soon as I might – tomorrow, if possible. We have done what we can to protect what remains from the elements, but a thunderstorm would destroy all their worth.'

'I thought the fire had destroyed everything.'

Francis shifted his position slightly. The movement almost caused an avalanche of papers. He steadied the stacks with his hand.

'The fire consumed the upper part of the building, but the floor of the first storey held. The majority of Mrs Smith's stock was held on the ground floor. Much has been damaged by water and smoke, but there will still be a market for what is whole if the items are not damaged any further. My hope is that one of the wholesale traders by London Bridge might take a gamble and buy the whole stock. Her private papers, those that survived, jewellery and so on, I have removed to Mr Hinckley's shop to wait for her brother there, but most of her possessions were destroyed, being as they were kept in the upper rooms.'

'She has been most generous to the church,' Fischer said. 'You think there will be money enough to cover the bequest?'

'Her bankers must be visited, naturally. But judging from her account books, and after the sale, I imagine that not only can the bequests be covered, but she will leave a generous sum to her brother's family.'

Fischer stood. 'You are much pressed,' he said. 'I shall delay you no longer with my questions. My thanks, Mr Glass.'

Francis stood also, carefully nudging the books behind him into more stable piles. 'Would you like to speak to her bankers yourself, Dr Fischer? As executor of the will . . .'

Fischer cut him off with a sad smile. 'No, no. I place the same confidence in you as do the rest of the family, Mr Glass.' He paused. 'You are certain she died *before* the fire?'

'I am. And the surgeon called in by the jury confirms it.' Francis paused in turn. 'Dr Fischer, you knew Mrs Smith well, I think?'

'Indeed. We were good friends, I hope. Good enough friends for me to know she thought very highly of you, Mr Glass.'

'May I ask you then, sir, did she confide any trouble to you? I cannot think of anyone who might wish to do her harm and her apprentice, Joshua, is convinced we suspect Penny unjustly.'

Dr Fischer appeared to consider. 'No, no. She said nothing to me, and as you said, she was a good woman. A very good woman. Joshua's faith is touching, but . . .' He lifted his palms and shrugged sadly.

There was little else left to say. They made their farewells with careful politeness on both sides and Francis left the man to his piles of papers. Having walked halfway down the street, however, he found himself growing irritated. He had much to do and worry over, yet Fischer had made no offer or effort to take any part of the burden from him. His church was due to receive a good sum of money, yet he shuffled the entire work of dealing with the estate over to Francis. He stopped in the street and thought. Then he turned back. He would simply, and with the greatest courtesy, tell Dr Fischer he had enough to do organising the sale of the stock, and ask him to undertake the necessary visit to her bankers. No doubt they would much prefer to deal with Fischer than with an African barely mentioned on the official documents. It would take but an hour of Fischer's time.

Rehearsing his speech, Francis began to walk back along the road, but was surprised to see as he approached the house the Reverend himself leaving it, marching along the pavement with every appearance of great haste. Francis cursed him and himself. It was bad enough to force all the work on him, but then not even to stay at his desk afterwards! He followed the Reverend at a steady pace, meaning to catch him up and make his speech on the pavement if necessary. Dr Fischer was not going far, however. Before Francis had quite managed to close the distance between them, Fischer turned in off the street – straight into the Jamaica Coffee House. Francis stopped. There were not many places in London he disliked more, and a civilised conversation with Dr Fischer there would be impossible. The idea of an African trying to teach a white Reverend his business and responsibilities on those premises . . . He would be thrown out bodily at best and he did not wish to be humiliated.

The boy sweeping the street next to him was following the direction of his eyes and seemed happy to take the chance of conversation.

'You don't want to go in there, Pompey,' he said with deep emphasis.

199

'I know,' Francis said, still so intent on watching the door, he hardly noticed the 'Pompey'. He told himself he was a British man now. A man of responsibilities. If they assaulted him, he would prosecute. Though half the magistrates in the city were planters or bankers whose wealth had been born and swelled in the West Indies. He would be mocked.

'Honestly, fella. Don't do it!' The sweeper sounded alarmed. Francis stared at him – an undernourished and grubby-looking boy just reaching his teens, he guessed.

'Rest easy, I will not. Do you work here every day?'

'I do. Anything goes on here, I see it. What do you want to know?'

'Does Reverend Fischer go to that place often?'

The boy nodded happily. 'Course he does! He worked the slave trade for *years* before he got religious and started writing his hymns, so he comes here to chat over the good old days with his pals. Surgeon on one of the boats, he was. Have you never noticed how his preaching is full of "on the night of the hurricane", and "as the great seas swelled below me" . . . ?'

Francis frowned. 'I do not go to his church.'

'You should! Good preaching, but not so heavy on the hellfire as the Methodists. And he gets the crowds in now. Yup, he's an up and coming.'

The boy leaned on the handle of his broom while he spoke, a weary and wise observer of the world before he had even reached fourteen. Francis was feeling for a shilling to give to the lad when the Reverend Fischer re-emerged onto the street, in the company of another man. 'Watch out, cock,' the boy hissed. 'Step back if you don't want to be seen gawking.'

Francis found he did not and retreated into the shadow of a neighbouring building. 'All clear,' the boy said a minute or two later.

Francis handed him his shilling with his thanks and the boy looked very pleased with the exchange.

'Who was he talking to?' Francis asked.

'Sir Charles Jennings. Lovely gentleman. Civil to everyone and a big tipper. If the world were full of men like him it'd be cake every day for us all.' The boy scratched his nose.

'Did you hear what was said?'

'Do I look like a rabbit to you, with ears to hear that far off? Dr Fischer looked sad and Sir Charles put a hand on his arm, as if he were comforting him. Then they both went their ways.'

'Sir Charles Jennings?' Francis tasted something bitter in his mouth. The clerk from Humphrey's had left a pamphlet by Sir Charles on his counter last year and Francis had picked it up before Cutter could throw it on the fire. The tone was one of sorry sympathy, of reason and forgiveness. It pointed out that though slavery could be abused, it was a far gentler state than that which the African enjoyed in his own country. Slavery was a mercy. He should not have read past the first line, but he had been unable to resist that soft reasonable tone. He read the recommendations on how to better care for the slaves on their journey between Africa and the West Indies. Regulation, moderation and Christian instruction for the captured savages. He had wondered what Sir Charles Jennings looked like. Now he knew. The man was as smooth and polished as his prose.

IV.3

WHEN HARRIET LEFT THE Christophers' house she told David to walk the horses in the Square for a while and found her own way to Canford's grocery shop on Carlisle Street. The business of the day was in hand. The shopkeepers had set out their goods on trays in front of their windows and chalked up the prices. Maids scrubbed at the stone steps of the better houses, and the boot-menders had carried their tools and their chairs from the basements to work in the open air and enjoy what spring breezes managed to waft between the high houses. A boy no older than Jonathan was setting down a basket of spinning tops on the pavement and beginning to demonstrate the whipping of them to a little girl whose mother lingered too long at the fishmonger's, and so her daughter was hooked.

Harriet crossed the road as coin and top were exchanged and approached the boy. She asked him if he had been selling here the previous Thursday. As she spoke, he began to whip up his top again: it was a strange-looking thing attached to a long string, and as he listened he jerked it upwards so it span on the palm of his hand. 'You got little ones, my lady? Only fivepence to make them happy all afternoon.'

'There was a young girl. A man stopped her on the street just there. The shopkeeper had to come out and speak to him. Did you see it?' she said.

'What, Miss Sally? The black lass with a pa who looks like he could pull your head off with two fingers?' Harriet nodded. The boy span his top again. 'Well, I *was* here, right enough, but my recollection gets a bit cloudy when I haven't had any breakfast. How many little ones you got? Three for tenpence, then I won't get cloudy with worry as for how I'm to eat.'

Harriet sighed. 'You will get enough for your breakfast. Did you see anything?'

He pursed his lips. 'There was a mangy old fella grabbing on her arm. And there might have been another bloke standing here and watching. Here, look at this.' He whipped the cord again and sprang the top up so it landed on his shoulder.

Harriet fished for a shilling in her bag. 'I'll take four.' The boy made a grab for the coin but she lifted it out of his reach.

'Own hair, darkish coat,' he said. 'Came out the wine merchant's two doors down.'

The shop was empty when she entered. It was a dark room which smelled deeply of coffee and spice. Harriet paused for a moment as her eyes adjusted to the gloom and pretended to admire the displays of various snuffs and tobaccos in small polished barrels, the selection of coffees and teas. There were a number of sets of scales on the counter and behind it a great variety of dull green bottles. It was obviously an establishment of some standing; every surface glowed with a sort of superior ease. The shopkeeper emerged and made her a deep bow. He was a short, broadish man of considerable personal dignity. A shilling would not be enough. Harriet decided to aim high and placed a half-sovereign on the shining counter. It made a satisfyingly heavy click.

'Thursday morning. You had a customer. A gentleman in a darkish coat who wore his own hair. I should like very much to know his name.'

The shopkeeper hardly moved his mouth when he spoke. 'We have many customers, naturally. But we prefer gentlemen to keep an account.' Very smoothly, he pushed a large leather-bound volume towards her. 'If you'll excuse me, there is something I must attend to, briefly, to the rear of the building.' He bowed again and turned away. The fat gold coin had somehow disappeared.

Harriet turned the pages back to Thursday. It was the first entry on the list. *Dr Drax. For delivery to Portman Square. One dozen Port Wine 1776 vintage.*

She nodded to herself and left the shop, the brass bell above the door ringing as it closed behind her like dignified applause.

Francis was in thoughtful mood when he returned to Hinckley's, but the necessities of the day pushed Fischer and the Jamaica Coffee House from his mind. He scribbled down a few words then went upstairs to the lair of Mr Ferguson. A handbill needed printing for the sale, to take place at the Chapter Coffee House at 4 p.m. Viewing allowed at Mrs Smith's establishment between noon and 3 p.m.

Ferguson made his recommendations; a mention of the religious prints available was added.

'How many do you want?' he asked, once he had made his neat pencil notes on Francis's scrawl.

'Say a hundred, that should be more than enough. I want Joshua to take them down Paternoster Row, then along to London Bridge.' Ferguson nodded and set to work without complaint. Francis had reached the head of the stairs before he turned back.

'What if we added a line, asking for information into her killing? Say, "Any persons who have knowledge of the unlawful killing of Mrs Smith or the whereabouts of her maid, Penny, should apply to Francis Glass at Hinckley's Booksellers, Ivy Yard. All useful information rewarded".'

'I think we can fit that into the page. Particularly if we squeeze up a little on the sale details.' Ferguson sniffed. 'Add "good" – "killing of *good* Mrs Smith", and after your name say "or his clerk Cutter". That way, they'll leave their names and thoughts if you're out.'

'Just as you say. Thank you, Mr Ferguson.'

When Harriet returned to Berkeley Square she found Crowther sitting upright on the sofa, wrapped in a long linen dressing gown and supported by a great many pillows. His jaw was much inflamed and his skin was pale. There were grazes on his forehead. Someone had provided him with paper and ink.

She sat in the armchair opposite him and took off her hat, a little careless with the arrangement of her hair, and told him the sum of her adventures that morning.

'I think I shall pay a visit to Dr Drax this afternoon and ask who he told about what he saw,' she said as she finished, and pulled at one of her red ringlets. She stood up again and tried to see what Crowther had been writing. 'They are a violent group of men, I think. Mrs

Trimnell had bruising on her wrists yesterday. I think someone has struck her.'

He moved the papers so she could not see them.

'What are you thinking on, Crowther? You always write when you think.'

He sighed. 'I have not had as much time to think as I would have liked. I had a visit from Mr Palmer while you were gone.'

'I hope he apologised for putting you in harm's way.'

Crowther smiled. 'He did. He also offered me the services of an agent of his who has been listening in at the Jamaica Coffee House since Mr Trimnell's death. Mr Molloy.'

Harriet turned back towards him. 'Molloy? No! He is working for Palmer?'

'Palmer has found him a very useful person since he first made his acquaintance through ourselves, it seems. From what Palmer said, I suspect Molloy is finding money-lending a little dull and enjoys spicing up his days with assisting our friend from the Admiralty. He is no doubt well rewarded for it.'

Harriet abandoned her attempt to read over his shoulder. 'I would imagine his skill with a lock-pick might serve Mr Palmer's purposes well from time to time.'

'All for King and Country, I am certain,' Crowther said mildly. 'Though Molloy did apparently say he was afraid his skills in that area were in danger of becoming rusty.'

There was a knock at the door and William entered with a folded piece of paper in his gloved hand. 'The address of Dr Drax, Mrs Westerman.'

'Thank you, William. I shall leave you to your thinking, Crowther.'

'Hat,' he said, pointing and without looking up. She grabbed it up and swept out of the room, closing the door behind her. Crowther returned to his papers. 'Why thank you, Mrs Westerman. I am feeling much improved,' he murmured.

Francis was giving Joshua detailed instructions as to where the finished handbills should be delivered and glancing at his watch to see if he still had time to visit Mrs Smith's bankers when Eustache interrupted them.

'Mr Glass, are you going out again today?'

Eustache was so quiet in the back office among the manuscripts that Francis hardly remembered he was there. 'I am sorry for it, Eustache, but I must. I hope you have not found the work too wearisome. Remember, you must ask Cutter if you are hungry or need any other thing, and I am sure he would be glad to talk to you when the shop is quiet.'

Eustache shook his head. 'I am not bored at all, only I was wondering: I've just started reading a new manuscript, and I was hoping I might take it home with me if William comes to fetch me before I have finished it.'

A regular ink-drinker indeed. 'If you promise me you will take good care of it, Eustache, you may.'

Eustache thanked him with great solemnity then returned to his cubbyhole in the back office, and Francis gave his final instructions to Joshua.

Crowther's attempts to think were cut short by the arrival of Mr Christopher. They shook hands.

'I know I sent my best wishes with Mrs Westerman,' Tobias said, making himself comfortable in the armchair, 'but I am glad to see you myself.'

'Guadeloupe is free?'

'He is. Sally did well and looked the magistrate in the eye.'

'From what Mrs Westerman told me, you and your daughter would have convinced any reasonable man.'

'Ah, reasonable! A pure English word, I think. And now I have come here in all my courtroom finery to act as a messenger boy. Guadeloupe wishes you and Mrs Westerman to know, should you require his services, he can be found at my house.' He smiled. 'I hope you are grateful; to my knowledge it is the first time that boy has offered to be of help to anyone.'

Christopher's hand brushed the snow-white of his cravat as he spoke and Crowther frowned. 'Did you wear the mask frequently?' he asked.

Christopher's eyes widened in surprise. 'I did.' His hand lifted to his neck and Crowther's eyes followed the movement.

'You are scarred? Do I have your permission to examine your throat?'

Christopher was still for one moment, his eyes on Crowther. Finally he said: 'Very well.'

'Forgive me, Mr Christopher, my movements are still somewhat restricted. Might you come to me?'

Christopher stood and approached the sofa then crouched down in front of him. Crowther reached out and ran his finger over his skin just above the Adam's apple. The African stayed absolutely still. Crowther nodded, and Christopher got to his feet and turned away.

'Thank you, Mr Christopher. Will you take a glass of wine with me? There is a decanter and glasses on the sideboard there.'

Christopher did so in silence, and drained off his glass in a single swallow. 'So what did my throat teach you, Mr Crowther?'

Crowther's head had begun to ache again and there was a somewhat nauseous feeling in the pit of his stomach. 'You have a little scarring there. I imagine that however much you tried not to move when the mask was fastened, even the action of swallowing your own spit must have pressed your throat against the jagged edge of the plate which held the jaw shut. Many of Trimnell's slaves must have had this mark, somewhere between a callus and a scar. Am I correct?'

'You are.'

'There is a similar marking on Trimnell's own throat in much the same place. It had been puzzling me. Now it is explained. Do take another glass.'

Christopher returned to the decanter. 'I shall.' He poured his wine and sat down in the armchair again. 'I do not wish to teach you your business, Mr Crowther, but such a mark would not appear in the time it takes to strike a man a few blows in the belly and deliver one whiplash across the back.'

His feeling of nausea was stronger. 'No, it would not.'

'You believe then that Trimnell wore that mask more than once?' Tobias said slowly.

Crowther stared at the papers in front of him. 'Yes – many times in all likelihood. And for extended periods.'

'Good God. The man was mad,' Christopher said and drained his glass again.

IV.4

DR DRAX GREETED HARRIET with all proper civility and showed her into his consulting room. His monkey was chained to a stand behind his desk, designed so the little beast could have a fair amount of freedom to scamper, but in a carefully prescribed area. It clambered back onto its perch as Harriet came in, and stared at her.

'Cleopatra, where are your manners?' Drax said. The monkey stood up on its hind legs, sketched a bow, then hunkered back down again.

Harriet took the chair offered to her. 'Your monkey does not like me, and has not been in town long enough to learn how to conceal the fact.'

The corner of Drax's mouth twitched. 'How may I serve you, Mrs Westerman? You appear to be in good health. Is it my medical opinion you seek?'

She looked up at him from under her eyelashes. 'How did you make your money in Jamaica, Dr Drax? Did you trade sugar or people?'

He said nothing for some time, then opened his drawer and produced a walnut. The monkey uncurled itself and stared at it. Drax closed his fist over it and crushed it so the shell cracked, then lifted up his palm so the monkey could pick out the meat of the nut. Harriet did not flinch or look away, but kept the same polite smile on her face.

'People, Mrs Westerman.' He dusted the fragments of shell from his hands. 'Many of the slaves arrive on the islands in a deplorable state. I bought all of those for whom I thought there was some hope, did my best to help them regain their health, and sold them.'

'At great profit?'

'At a reasonable profit. It seems you have become very curious about such matters of late, Mrs Westerman. I would advise you to listen to your friends and leave matters alone. The boy is in custody.'

'No, Guadeloupe is to be released,' she said gently. Drax turned and put up his hand. The monkey leaped onto his palm, then up onto his shoulder, its chain jingling. 'Mr Crowther was set upon by a pair of thugs last night. We neither of us like bullies, Dr Drax, so we are all the more determined to find who ordered these assaults.'

She could not have sworn to it, but Harriet had the impression that both of these pieces of information were new to Drax. 'Who did you tell about seeing Mr Trimnell trying to claim a mulatto girl as his daughter on Thursday?'

The man was rattled now. His shoulders tensed and the monkey scrabbled away from him back onto its perch. 'Mrs Trimnell. Then Sawbridge and Sir Charles.' He pointed his finger at her. 'And *because* of what I saw, Sir Charles and I spent much of Friday night discussing how Trimnell might be safely and quietly put away in some home for the mentally incapable. The man was a danger to himself and others, borrowing money and giving it away. Preaching on street corners. We wished to help him, for his own good. Yes, even for the good of his bastard slave.'

Harriet stood very gracefully. 'I am sure Miss Christopher would be grateful.' Then with the scarcest nod, she left him.

Francis found the ring meant for him in Eliza's jewel box when he returned from the bank. He remembered very clearly seeing her father wear it. A plain gold signet ring, with his initials *JS* marked on the metal. It had been too big for Eliza's finger, but he would see her wear it from time to time on a chain around her neck. She liked to have it about her as she worked, she said. It felt then as if her father were there to advise her and guide her hand. He kissed it and slipped it onto his finger. It fitted perfectly, as if it had been made for him. From now on, he knew it would displace that battered volume of *Robinson Crusoe* as his own personal talisman. He was grateful for how much comfort it gave him, bringing Eliza close to him. He closed the box and set it aside, thinking.

Crowther listened to Harriet's recital and told her about the scar on Mr Christopher's neck. She felt her skin grow cold as he continued, thinking of that miserable room in Trimnell's lodgings.

'They were right to think of confining him, Mrs Westerman. I suspect he had contracted some sort of brain fever when he was ill. It would not be unlikely, given the condition his heart was in. The effects of an attack could give rise to the same manner of symptoms your husband suffered after he was knocked unconscious.' Harriet thought of her husband as he had been when he came home. Full of strange passions and rages. She thought of Mrs Trimnell and the rooms on Cheapside. No wonder the woman had tried to escape, by whatever means she had open to her. Harriet began to feel she had been unjust.

'She was trapped in a marriage to that man,' she said. 'It must have been hell.'

The weeks before and after her husband's death had been the most difficult in Harriet's life. She thought of that time again and of her life now. For a moment she could not even recall why she had been irritated by Rachel's match-making attempts, or hurt at the criticisms made of the way she managed the estate James had left her. Remembering what had passed, her present seemed suddenly so easy and pleasant she could not understand why she had ever felt anything other than profound gratitude.

She decided at that moment that she would politely refuse Mr Babington, engage a steward and then live as she wished. Remembering that clinging and complete darkness of those tragic months in her life made the present light by comparison. She thought of William and Mr Christopher.

'What are you thinking of, Harriet? You seemed dangerously miser-able and now I think you are smiling.'

She turned towards him. 'You know I will never marry again, don't you, Gabriel? I cannot be subject to others. I cannot be bound. I loved James, but I cannot belong to someone else again. The risk is too great now I have had a little freedom. Does that make me an unnatural female?'

'Possibly,' he said after a long silence. 'I do not think I have known enough females to be able to judge, my dear.'

She stood, the urge to move too great again. 'It seems to me there are a great number of people who might wish to see Trimnell punished, but I cannot choose between them. What should we do, Crowther? Retreat? Return to Sussex and learn to be humble?'

'That might be wise. But I was thinking of sending for Molloy.'

'An excellent idea. How are your injuries, Crowther?'

'Tolerably painful. Mrs Westerman, a package arrived for you from Caveley. It is waiting for you in your sitting room.'

The package was on Harriet's desk as promised, neatly tied. She took her seat in front of it with a heavy heart before she noticed there was a folded sheet placed on top of the parcel, but not tied up with it. She lifted it carefully, for the paper seemed worn, and unfolded it. Her eyes stung. The form of words was familiar from the manumission certificate Tobias Christopher had shown them.

Know ye, that I, Captain James Frederick Westerman, for and in consideration of the sum of sixty pounds current money of this island to me paid in hand and to the intent that a negro man-slave, William Geddings, shall and may become free, have manumitted, emancipated, enfranchised, and set free, and by these presents do manumit, emancipate, enfranchise, and set free the aforesaid negro man-slave William Geddings forever; hereby giving, granting and releasing unto him, the said William Geddings, all right, title, dominion, sovereignty and property which as lord and master over the aforesaid William Geddings I have had, or which I now have.

And there at the end was the familiar and loved signature followed by the seal of the registrar in Kingston. She held the paper with great delicacy, then set it down as she started to feel the tears running down her face. She had so hoped that she would prove James innocent of ever having had a hand in the trade, but here was his own signature to condemn him.

After a few minutes she rang the bell, and it was answered by William himself. She handed the paper back to him and noted the particular care with which he took it from her and tucked it back into his coat pocket.

'I do not think I have to open the package from Caveley, after all,' she said. 'Why did you not show it to me at once?'

He hesitated. 'It costs me some pain to put it into the hands of any other person, Mrs Westerman. I was not sure at first what you might do on seeing it.'

She smiled very sadly. 'Did you fear I might rip it up, have you kidnapped and sent back to Jamaica, William?'

'No, madam. I cannot say quite what I thought. On reflection, I was sure Dido would prevent you from sending me away in chains.' Harriet tried to smile, but did not quite manage it. 'Mrs Westerman, I saw that the news came hard to you. I know it troubles you still, but let me say this. For all the Captain bought me, he was the nearest thing I knew to a friend among white men at that time. He was a good commander, and he had my loyalty and friendship before and after he returned me my freedom.'

'You are generous,' she said, almost too quietly for him to hear.

'And I like my place,' he added robustly. 'I have grown used to Caveley and the people about me.'

'I hope I shall never give you reason to leave us, William,' Harriet said as she stood up and put out her hand. He shook it, then as if to make clear the moment was done with, bowed and withdrew from the room. Harriet wrapped her arms around her middle and tried to picture her husband buying William. Agreeing a price. The image was so foreign and sore to her it was like picturing him in the arms of another woman. She went in search of Mrs Service and found her with her mending basket by the fire in the Blue Salon.

'Mrs Service, did Jonathan inherit any slaves with his grandfather's fortune?'

She continued her sewing at an even pace. 'Yes, dear. Quite a number and an estate on St Isaac's.'

Harriet watched her as she worked; there was something soothing about the motion of her needle. 'And what did you do?'

Mrs Service sighed and cut her thread. 'It was a terrible fuss. Graves was worried that he could not in conscience sell, but keeping the place

213

ate at him. In the end they managed to set free the slaves and make proper provision for them, then sell the land. His father-in-law, dear Mr Chase, was most helpful. He has some contacts in the West Indies but there was a great deal of unpleasantness, nevertheless. Letters mostly, and a number of paragraphs in the newspapers saying Graves was proving beyond doubt he was unfit to run the estate.' She held her work up to the light and gave a small nod of satisfaction. 'Some of the second cousins got terribly worked up, but Clode was able to prove that Graves was handling the business quite responsibly. Then the Duke of Devonshire took him riding in the park once or twice. That helped, though Graves felt an idiot being stared at. It also helped us that Jonathan's father had often told his friends and neighbours about how he hated slavery. He held a little dance at the shop when Somersett was released in seventy-two.' She looked into the distance. 'Such a pleasant evening that was. Susan just born and her poor parents so happy. Joseph Codrington played a horn concerto. A fine player.'

Harriet cleared her throat. 'How can I have known nothing about this, Mrs Service? The sale and all the unpleasantness?'

The old lady put out her hand and patted Harriet's knee. 'Dear Mrs Westerman, this was all the winter poor Captain Westerman died. You had grief and concerns enough of your own. By the time you were yourself again, the matter was dealt with and we were all only too pleased to forget about it.'

Harriet fidgeted with her ringlets. 'I am glad you set them free.'

'It was the right thing to do. And we received a number of very dear letters from former slaves, or letters written on their behalf. Some African gentlemen also wrote to the newspapers in support of Graves, which was very kind of them. Yet I know Graves frets still over selling the land.'

'Why is that, Mrs Service?'

'Because now it is worked by another man's slaves. Part of him wishes he could have kept it, worked it with free labour to demonstrate the lie of slavery, but there was so much to be done and no one who could be trusted to go there and manage the place. He said he felt he was merely washing his hands of old blood rather than doing any active good, though judging by the letters I think the men and women whom he freed were glad he did so much.'

Harriet remembered Oxford's sneers and the hints of Mrs Jennings. 'So that is why the West Indians dislike him so particularly.'

'Oh yes, and they've made things very difficult at times. Papers going astray at the bank, things forgotten or letters "accidentally" misdirected.' She sighed. 'They have great power, these people, Harriet. And I believe they are growing afraid that slavery will no longer be tolerated by the British people. That makes them rather dangerous. When rats are cornered, they tend to show their true nature.'

IV.5

FRANCIS TOOK A LANTERN with him. He should have thought earlier and harder about the maid, Penny. Francis had always viewed the whores of London with particular distaste. Now he tried to remember the girl without that distaste clouding his vision. Neither plain nor pretty, she was a little hard around the eyes and not one for smiling much, but she had always been civil. She had done her duty for all those weeks when it had been sworn up and down that she would be off with everything of value in the house before she'd slept more than two nights in the place. Did she kill her mistress? Francis tried to imagine it. Perhaps too much God and sin from Eliza and the woman had broken under it and picked up that tool. Perhaps it had happened when she took up the supper tray. It was possible, but the supper tray had been left outside. Would she have replaced the tool in its case, taken the tray away again and left it at the head of the stairs and locked the door behind her, waited till the boy was asleep and set fire to the place? All that without taking the money waiting in the bureau drawer behind a weak lock? No, it didn't make sense.

Perhaps in the smoke and noise the girl had been afraid, then simply run back to her old way of living and her friends – innocent of the murder, but unwilling to return now her mistress was dead. He had almost convinced himself of this when he reached the sorry ashy ruin on Paternoster Row. Even if she were innocent, she still must know who had visited Eliza after he himself had left. Penny knew, so Penny must be found. Perhaps the handbills would do their work.

He nodded to the men guarding the house and they stood aside to let him enter. He went into the kitchen, sodden with shadows and smeared with smoke, and lifted his light. Here was Joshua's place, near the stove. His bedroll was still laid out and rumpled. A little further away was a wooden rocker, high-backed like a nursing chair, a work-basket next to it. He looked about the room for the place where Penny had slept. There was a cubbyhole under the back stairs with a door to it; inside, just enough room for a woman to lie – and there was her mat on the ground with a good blanket over it, not disturbed by a sleeper.

She might have run, he said to himself again. She might have run on smelling smoke, then ashamed that she had not tried to save Joshua or her mistress, slunk away to the Rookeries and left everything behind her. There was very little in the hole apart from the bedding; a print, tacked to the wall, too smudged to sell but still one could make out the bearded Jesus, lights beaming from His forehead and before Him on the ground a woman asking for mercy. If Miss Eliza had put it there, it would have been a clean copy and framed. This had been saved from the waste and taken, therefore it was a private shrine, and more likely sincere. A small bundle of clothes lay in the corner, he noticed. What poor girl would leave those behind, even in a panic? Francis crouched on his heels and considered. The light from his lamp seemed to make everything golden; it gave even this tight neat corner the air of a refuge. He remembered what it was like to be poor, rejected and alone only too well. He himself had slept in a space like this with his one possession, the copy of *Robinson Crusoe* that he tried to puzzle more out of each day, tucked under his pillow. Everyone has a treasure they keep close. It could be nothing more than a polished stone, a shell, a ribbon – but something you could look at from time to time to remind yourself there was beauty in the world somewhere, a talisman like the ring which glinted on his finger. He felt under the place where the girl's head rested, touched something metal and drew it out. It was a simple token of a tin heart on a cheap chain. He turned it over between his fingers. The back was engraved with the letter M, but it had been touched and stroked so often it was almost worn away. Francis put it into his pocket, then stood out of the cubbyhole, his heart heavy. Penny had kept and loved that trinket for years. Not unless it were on fire itself would she leave it.

He returned to the body of the shop and tried to think. A visitor had come in the early evening and left again. Then after supper, with the apprentice Joshua already dreaming, someone else had arrived. Penny had opened the door to this visitor and turned to lead him upstairs to her mistress. What had the visitor done then? Francis looked to his left on the counter; just as in his own shop, the ink-bottle stood next to the stand. He picked it up. Full and heavy. He moved it into the light. There was blood on its edge.

Within half an hour Francis had raised Constable Miller and dragged him, sleepy and fire-warm, from his house to the butcher Scudder's place. The men took Walter Sharp the engraver out of the tavern on their way. Only when they were all seated round Scudder's table in his comfortable kitchen was Francis ready to explain, and then he did it so fast they did not get the sense of it at first.

'Hold, hold, Francis,' Walter said. His eyes were pink with gin, but he was trying to fight the fog of it. 'Someone killed Mrs Smith.'

'Yes, they locked her door and left her there. Now the fire may only have been burning for a few minutes when I got there . . .'

'Not more than half an hour, I'd say,' Miller put in.

'. . . but her flesh was cold. She must have died some time before, so I believe it was that first caller who killed her.' Francis leaned across the table towards them, his palms open and reaching in the air, as if gathering them in. The men nodded, following him so far. 'Then Penny took up her mistress's supper and left it at the door, thinking her at prayer – but it was falling on that tray cut up my hands, and the glass of lemonade was full. That is my second reason for thinking it was the earlier caller who killed her: the tray untouched outside the door.'

'Say on,' Scudder said, folding his arms.

'So whoever killed Eliza leaves, knowing she must eventually be discovered, Penny having seen him into the house. Perhaps he did not mean to kill Eliza and it was just some moment of rage. He ran at first, but then he had time to consider his situation. He thinks of fire. So he comes back, Penny lets him in again – and he strikes her down, using the ink-bottle. Then he goes upstairs, puts the graver that went through Eliza's eye back in its place, and sets the fire to hide the all. Bundles Penny out of the place and is gone.'

'Why not just leave Penny for the flames?' Miller asked. 'It would be a risk to carry her from the house.'

'More of a risk to leave her there,' Scudder said. 'This way we all thought in our black and jaded hearts she'd done the thing.'

'The lad Joshua did not,' Francis reminded them, and the other men nodded.

'He must have had a carriage – no, a wagon maybe,' Walter said. 'Couldn't just walk through London with her.'

Constable Miller had sunk his chin on his chest. 'Left her clothing and treasures behind and blood on the bottle. I see it clear. Wish I didn't, Mr Glass, but I do.'

Francis felt a wave of tiredness sweeping through his bones. His mind was sore with thinking, and he was glad to hear them take their turn at the problem.

Miller continued: 'He'd want to get her away, but he needs to move fast. Got to be somewhere just far enough. Got to head north, somewhere quiet between here and Islington.' He paused and looked steadily at Francis. 'We're looking for a grave, ain't we?'

Francis nodded. He put the blanket from Penny's sleeping place on the table. 'Mr Miller, do you know anyone with dogs that can follow a trail?'

'I do,' the constable said. 'I know a fellow in Hackney. He'll lend a hand.'

Scudder rasped his fingers over the stubble on his chin. 'You running the fire sale tomorrow, Mr Glass?'

'That is my intention,' Francis replied. 'I've taken Eliza's private things away, what could be saved. I want everything ready for her brother George when he arrives, so he need do nothing but grieve.' He passed the back of his hands over his eyes. 'But Penny must be looked for.'

Scudder studied him a moment. 'It's not all on your shoulders, Mr Glass. You do as needs doing in town and leave the search to us.' The butcher then turned to Walter. 'As for you, you're staying here where the gin can't find you.'

Walter shrugged, but seemed compliant. 'Dogs, eh?' he said, and whistled.

'Trust me,' Francis told him. 'A good dog can find anyone.'

PART V

V.1

Wednesday, 11 May 1785

M RS MARTIN STARTED HER days early. The earlier the better. She would wash in her room then be in the kitchen as soon as the fires were lit and sit at the head of the table with her tea and her pocketbook as the other servants gathered. It gave her the chance to observe discreetly those under her authority; their tempers and manners in those first hours of the morning when the night was still clinging to the streets told her a great deal.

Today, when she had glanced in on the store cupboards and meat lockers, the pantry and the linen cupboards, and walked through the family rooms putting back the shutters, she made her tea, took her place at the table and licked the end of her pencil. This morning she was considering what should be sent up to Mr Crowther for breakfast. Mrs Service had persuaded him to give Graves back his office and take the Yellow Bedroom. She would ask William to take him his tray. Cow'sfoot jelly and toast. But then his jaw was so inflamed perhaps more soup would be better. She had just decided on this when she heard someone cough in the shadows and almost leaped out of her skin. From the shadows extended a pair of legs in black riding boots. They shone.

'Morning, Bessie.'

She watied until the pace of her heart had decreased a little. 'Good morning, Lucretius. You startled me.' She turned back to her pocketbook. 'And it'll be "Mrs Martin" please, in my place of employment.' She heard him chuckle, heard the hiss of a taper in the fire and smelled tobacco. 'I would ask how you got in, but I'm not sure I wish to know.'

'No damage done.' There was a pause as he got his pipe glowing as he wanted it. 'How are them upstairs?'

Mrs Martin put down her pencil and turned round so she could look at him properly. Molloy sat close to the fire. His face was deeply lined, cracked all over like cheap china, a tricorn, worn and greasy, pulled low over his forehead, and his green black cape as always wrapped around him, summer or winter as if he distrusted the sun itself. He probably did.

'Aside from Mr Crowther being beaten and Mrs Westerman chasing all over town making new enemies?' she said tartly.

He leaned back and crossed his ankles. Mrs Martin wondered why he always wore riding boots. She'd never seen him anywhere near a horse. 'Aye, aside from that.'

'Lady Susan has been thrown out of her school in Golden Square and Master Eustache was caught stealing.'

He laughed, a full-throated laugh that ended in a cough. Mrs Martin almost smiled. She knew Molloy had a wife and children of his own living respectably in Stoke Newington on the proceeds of his rather dubious activities. She also knew he never slept there, but moved through the shadows of London obeying some obscure morality of his own. At some stage he had developed a grudging fondness for the family Mrs Martin served, and they a liking for him.

'It's not to be laughed at, Lucretius. Mr Graves is tearing his hair out over them, and Mrs Graves is expecting, and resting in Sussex, so he has that to worry over too, even though she writes him a line every day to tell him she is happy and well.'

'She's a good girl, his lady. Has sense enough for both of them, thank the Lord. His fretting won't do her any favours. What of young Westerman and his sister?'

'Stephen's tutor is taking Holy Orders, so I think he is to go to school. Anne is a good child when she has her way, and has a fond-ness for Master Eustache. He's at his best when he's taking care of that little girl.'

He nodded and stretched like a cat. Mrs Martin could hear the bones in his knees crack. 'Why are you here, Mr Molloy?'

'Mr Crowther sent for me.'

'He won't be awake for hours yet. Why did you come so early?'

Molloy knocked his pipe out on the fender, blew down it and tucked it back somewhere in the depths of his coat. 'It's not early, you daft female. It's late.' He stretched out his legs again, pulled down the brim of his hat and wrapped his cloak around him. 'Wake me up when His Lordiness is ready to receive.'

Francis spent the morning at Eliza's shop watching as any number of wholesalers and those sellers who sold to the poor of the city inspected what was left of her business. A few men who sold furniture secondhand had also taken the time to come and sniff at what remained.

The clerk whom Mr Churchill next door had sent to help had made a good job of gathering the majority of the stock together and laying it out in piles according to the damage done. There were a good few volumes of children's verses with engraved plates, a little swollen with water, but still whole. Eliza had done the illustrations herself. Francis saw a flash of her lying cold on the floor upstairs again and put down the copy he was holding. There were portfolios full of Walter's work too. It was true, Francis thought, looking at the sketches: the more noble the child, the more they developed a slight squint. Several mysterious bundles of assorted prints and hymnsheets were piled in hopeless confusion, however, by the staircase. The clerk had not had time to organise everything.

The auctioneer Francis had hired to run the sale appeared just then at his shoulder. Churchill had recommended him and Francis was glad of it. 'I think two lots, Mr Glass,' he said without preamble. His reputation was of a solid, no-nonsense man who knew the trade. 'The furniture and fittings for a start. Ten pounds the lot, I'd say. Then all the paper goods. It's good stock for the pedlars, and that crowd from London Bridge know it. Don't let all that tutting and shaking of heads fool you. I'll see you at Chapter's, four o'clock sharp.' He looked about him for a moment. 'Damn shame,' he said, then disappeared back into the crowd before Francis could reply.

'Mr Glass?' It was the clerk from Churchill's. Francis thanked him for his work and he shrugged. 'Sad business, but there we are. There's a girl asking for you outside. She's come over from Hinckley's, asking about a reward.'

Crowther was sitting up in bed contemplating the soup when Molloy was shown in.

'Have you breakfasted, Molloy?'

'Bacon and sausages downstairs.'

Crowther put down his spoon with a sigh. Molloy picked up a chair from the edge of the room and swung it over to the bed so he could sit at Crowther's side. He frowned disapprovingly. 'Good people put in time and thought making that for you,' he growled. 'I can wait till you're done.'

Crowther picked up the spoon again. 'How are your children, Molloy?'

'Idiots, the lot of them.'

Crowther laughed. The door opened again and Harriet came in. Her hair was loosely dressed and the cut of her green silk dress showed off her figure rather well. Crowther did not think he had seen her wear it before, and approved.

'There's a sight to make the dogs bark,' Molloy said. Crowther gave him a warning look and Molloy shrugged.

Harriet tried not to smile. 'Molloy, you are an evil influence, and I have no idea why we receive you.'

A not entirely convincing look of offence rearranged the cracks on Molloy's face. 'There's thankful, and just when I got My Lord High Whatsit to eat his soup.'

'It's Keswick,' Crowther said, wiping his mouth. 'As you well know, though you may call me Crowther as usual. There, the soup is eaten.'

Molloy yawned. 'And you don't "receive me", my girl. I came up the backstairs. Now where do you want me to go where you can't?'

Harriet handed him a folded paper, then went and sat at the dressing table. 'We need the names of the men who beat Crowther and Mr Trimnell,' she said. 'Crowther thinks they pawned his clothes and shoes, but there's been no sign of them, in spite of the handbills.'

Molloy scraped at his stubble with his yellow nails and unfolded the paper she had given him, read it and put it into one of his pockets. 'They're sharper than they look, the city marshals. Most of the pop shops near there are well under their eye now. Seems the brokers are never more joyful than when informing on a poor fella just picked up a hanky by chance.'

'A boy I spoke to mentioned a Mother Brown,' Crowther said. 'As someone who asks no questions.'

Molloy's eyebrows shot up. 'Mother Brown? She's back, is she, and before her time, I reckon. I thank you, Mr Crowther. You've told me something I didn't know.'

'I should imagine you'll still want paying, however.'

'Well, that's a matter of principle, son. And necessary expenses.'

Harriet leaned on the back of the chair. 'Molloy, what have you learned at the coffee house? Mr Palmer said you'd been spending some time there.'

225

'That they like to hear themselves complain while they count their money, like most men of business. Wolves that like to pretend they're patriots. It's all business – what's good for it, what's bad for it.' He stood and brushed down his cloak. 'And they've gone through a quantity of ink in there, these last days. I wouldn't read the paper till yer breakfast is settled, Mrs W.'

Harriet groaned. 'The paper? Oh Lord, that will mean another letter from Rachel.'

'What about you, Molloy, and your work with Mr Palmer?' Crowther asked.

Molloy gave a surprisingly elegant bow. 'I'm thinking I can be wolf *and* patriot both – when there's money in it.'

'Of course. There's my purse by the door. Take what you think is right. And there's a boy of apparently rather dubious morality named Guadeloupe staying at Christopher's Academy on Soho Square. Should you need assistance, you may find him helpful.'

Molloy picked up the purse and counted a number of coins into his hand. There was a chink as he set it back down. 'I'll send when I have news. Enjoy your healing, Mr Crowther. My best to you, Mrs W.' He let himself out. Crowther looked at the purse he'd left behind him.

'Good Lord, we might make an honest subject of him yet.'

Harriet yawned. 'I doubt it. He chinked the coins in his pocket, your purse he emptied. "A matter of principle", I'm sure.'

V.2

THE GIRL WHO WAITED for him outside was not someone Francis would have chosen to be seen with in a public place. She was not more than twenty, but looked far older. Her eyes had the slightly lost stare of a gin drinker. She looked him up and down.

'You the one asking about Penny?'

'I am. Do you know something of use?'

She tutted. 'Nice manners on you! I was told there was a reward.' She slurred her words a little.

Francis thought of Eliza, her unfailing charity, and had the grace to feel a little ashamed. God alone knew there were enough Africans in London who had escaped from their memories with a gin bottle in their hand. 'My apologies, miss. I *am* asking after Penny. I was a friend of her mistress, Mrs Smith who was murdered, and now I worry Penny might have been hurt too. Did you know her?'

Her expression softened, and Francis caught a glimpse of the girl she might have been. 'I did. I thought it wouldn't take, her coming here. And when I saw her come out and get lifted into a carriage by some fellow, I was sorry. Thought, Oh it was all a play, after all; she'd just got some rich fella.'

'When was this?'

'Couple of nights past. He was sort of carrying her. Thought she was flustered. She never could take her drink.'

'You did not speak to her?'

The girl laughed, dark as tar. 'I was entertaining a gentleman. Not really the moment for conversation with a old friend now, is it?'

He could only look at the ground beneath his feet. 'Did you recognise the man, or the driver? It was a carriage, you say.'

'The driver I know. Miserable bastard named Hodges, works off the stand on Cornhill. The fella, thought I'd seen him looking for company round here from time to time. That was why I thought . . .' She scratched the back of her neck.

'Thank you, thank you indeed.' Francis took her hand and shook it briefly before searching in his pockets for a coin or two. 'If I need to speak to you again, where might I find you?'

She seemed surprised, staring at her fingers for a second where he had touched them, then she waved his tribute away. 'Find a place nearby that stinks of gin, lift the lid and holler for Mary-Anne. You'll find me. And keep your coin, handsome. I'm drunk already.' She turned away and headed off, unsteadily, in the direction of St Martin le Grand. Francis watched her go, then put the coins back in his pocket and set off for the stand on Cheapside.

Molloy should have realised that having spent the last few hours fast asleep and snoring in the servants' hall, his visit would be widely reported in the house. He had made it almost to the kitchen though before Lady Susan found him, threw her arms around his shoulders and kissed him hard on his unlovely cheek.

'Mr Molloy! Oh, I haven't seen you for an age! You weren't going to sneak away without seeing me, were you?' Her eyes were glimmering and large, her skin the delicate pink of some expensive cream in a shop window down Piccadilly.

'I was. And I would have sneaked faster if I knew you were going to cover me in scent and rouge.'

She grabbed his hand and pulled him into the library. 'Don't be silly. I don't wear rouge or scent. I'm too young. Tell me how everyone is in Tichfield Street. I so long for news.'

He looked down at her and spoke sharp. 'Long for news, do you? Then go and visit. Your boy Graves still owns the shop there, doesn't he? And if you wish to greet me, Lady Susan, a civil nod is enough. Fine thing it is for a man of my reputation to be handled like a lapdog by a member of the peerage. And what would people think of you? Have some sense.'

Her face fell, all the life wiped out of it, and she looked as small as a beaten dog. 'You've never called me Lady Susan before.' Her lip trembled.

'And that's something to snivel over, is it?' He produced a

handkerchief and handed it to her – clean and hemmed by his own wife who, bless her, had learned long ago that tears made no miles with him. 'I hear you're at odds with young Graves. Time was, you offered me your mother's own ring to keep him out of debtor's prison. Why you so peevish with him now?'

'He wants me to be a lady.'

Molloy had never read a novel. He avoided them because he had always suspected they were full of foolish women with full bellies saying things of this sort. 'You *are* a lady, you daft child. That's not his fault, so you'd better learn how to act like one.' He lifted his finger and narrowed his eyes. 'Like not kissing men like me in front of your servants. Or kissing any man, for that matter – Graves and your brother excepted. You're not a child. What are you thinking of?'

'There was no one there.' Her voice shook.

'And would it have stopped you if there had been? Christ, give me patience. And no more crying, or I'll forget my station enough to show you the back of my hand. Don't think I won't.'

She managed to control herself and looked up at him carefully, as if perhaps she'd managed to crawl out of her own head for a second and look around. 'You wouldn't.'

He folded his arms across his chest and studied her. So she had some sense yet. 'No, like as not. Graves would have me in the stocks for it. What's your gripe at a few dancing lessons and learning your manners? Want to disgrace your friends and sundry, do you?'

She was still managing not to cry, but began twisting his handkerchief in her hands. 'They are never going to let me do anything interesting, and then they shall force me to marry some monster with money and a title.'

He whistled up at the ceilings. 'What *troubles* you do have! Force? Your brain's gone soft. Talk to me about force when Graves walks you to the altar with a knife at your throat, or locks you in a dungeon to starve. Force!'

'Well, what am I to do?'

'Lord above us, Sue. You're in this house and you come hammering on me for guidance? I've eaten creatures with more sense. Come to an arrangement, girl. Tell Graves the "interesting things" you want to do and see what he says. Graves is a soft-hearted bloke, but he's not a fool. He'll negotiate. Now, if he's telling you you need to know the rules before you go blundering about in the world, he's right, and all your sniffing and maundering shan't change it. For the rest show some sense and some backbone. You hear? And give me back my handkerchief.'

She did, though reluctantly. 'I hear. I miss Mother and Father. And Soho and the shop, Molloy.'

He remembered her there. Full of mischief as a monkey and a hero with all the gutter urchins in the street for her jokes and mocks. 'It's only right you should miss them, sunbeam, but my bet is if you'd stayed in Soho you'd be itching to be out of it by now.' She did not say anything but continued to look at the carpet under her silk slippers. 'Will you think on?'

'I will try.'

'That's a good brat. You've got a fine heart. Listen to it and stop picking fights where none need to be had.' He put a hand on her arm and squeezed. She straightened her back, and squared her shoulders like a trooper. Then looked him in the eye. Better.

'If Graves does lock me in a dungeon, will you break me out?'

'More like I'll throw one of my kids in there with you.' She giggled and he at once scowled until his eyes became almost invisible under the brim of his hat.

'Enough. I've got a duty to make some folks curse the day I was born, and another minute in this house will turn me soft as a milkmaid. Off with you, girl. And my best to boy Sussex.'

Francis walked the length of Cheapside with his head down. He would find the cabman, then the fare, and then the reason why Eliza had been killed. The streets were dry and the rattle and crunch of iron wheels on the dirt seemed to push him on. He was hardly aware of the people around him, their various conditions and complaints filling the pavements, peering in at the shop windows, their hands in their pockets feeling at their purses for the measure of their worth. He passed the Mansion House and the Royal Exchange, the embodiment in stone of British Pride, and instead watched only for the cab-stand, the fine heavy horses and dull yellow carriages, the cabmen in their long blue coats.

He stepped up to the man at the back of the line. 'I'm looking for a driver named Hodges.'

The driver yawned and peered up at the carriages in front of him. 'Best hurry then, son. Looks like he's got himself a fare.'

Francis sprinted up to the carriage at the front of the stand. A gentleman in a long red coat with sleeves wide enough to hide a rabbit in was settling into his seat with a look of vague disgust. The driver was already clicking his horses into a walk.

'Hold! Hold there! Are you Hodges?' The driver turned and grunted at the name, but showed no sign of waiting. Francis put his hand to the horse's bridle.

'Get off out of it!' the driver yelled, half-standing in his seat.

'Just one moment, sir,' Francis said, holding on tight. He could feel the horse's breath on his neck, its confused thick animal smell bundled together with the scent of leather from its trappings and blinders. 'A fare, on Sunday night. A man and a woman who seemed drunk from Paternoster Row. Who was he and where did you take them?'

The man sitting in the cab leaned forward. 'If you need to speak to the Negro, driver, I can find another man to take me.'

'Not at all, sir. One moment.' The driver turned back to Francis, his face puce. 'Get away from my horse.' The animal whinnied, trying to pull its great head away.

'It's a matter of murder.'

'It will be, if I ever see your face again.' He lifted his arm and the movement was so quick Francis had no time to prepare. The thin whip caught him across the cheek and he staggered backwards, covering the place where it had struck with his hands. The cab drove away at a quick trot.

'You hurt, son?' Francis's eyes were stinging and the pain was like a cold brand on his skin. He felt a hand on his arm and looked up. And old, square white man. 'Let me see, now.' Francis took his hand away and the man hissed. 'An inch higher and he'd have had your eye out. It's bleeding, but put your handkerchief to it and you'll not stain your collar.' Francis did as he was told and found he was trembling. The old man smiled. 'Don't fret. Ladies all love a scar, don't they?'

Francis tried to breathe. 'Thank you.'

'Mustn't hold a man's horse, son. Enrage any fellow, and Hodges is a mean-hearted son of a bitch. Always has been.'

The first shock of the pain had lessened. Francis saw the man was standing by a yoke, wide wooden buckets tied with rope onto each end. He was the waterman for the horses on the stand then. 'Did you notice anything Sunday night, uncle?'

'I'll remember it till my last breath. That vicious bastard what struck you tipped me sixpence. Sundays are normally quiet here by evening. He had a fare kept him busy a couple of hours. Didn't see him pick the fella up, but he came back saying he'd been all the way up Islington Road and home again. Got tipped five shillings, which went on punch judging by his temper Monday morning.'

'He said nothing more? Nothing about a woman?'

'No, son, though he was in ribald humour, if you understand me. Now go and get some ice for your face before you lose your good looks.'

V.3

GRAVES AND MRS SERVICE both made efforts to prevent Mrs Westerman reading the newspapers, even claiming they had not been fetched in. Harriet was perversely determined to read what had been written. They were for the most part sneering in their tone, and she flinched when she saw one writer's amusement that Mrs W— had fled her home to pursue Mr C— to London. What distressed her the most was seeing the lightly disguised names of her hosts in the same paragraphs. Someone had taken the trouble to discover that Susan had been removed from her school in Golden Square.

Having finished reading, she left the house without speaking to anyone but the servants, and walked in the gardens of Berkeley Square until her temper had cooled. Deciding to return to the house, apologise to Graves and Susan for exposing them to the gibes and insinuations of the ink-stained monsters, and wait for Molloy, she turned north and began to make her way along the gravel pathways, only to see a carriage coming to a halt at the house and Sir Charles walking up the steps to the front door. By the time she had taken off her cloak and hurried up to the Blue Salon, Sir Charles and Crowther were seated in the cluster of striped settees in the middle of the room. Mrs Service was pouring tea, William handing out the cups and Graves, looking ill at ease, watching from his post by the mantelpiece.

The gentlemen stood as she entered, but she waved them back to their places and took a seat between Mrs Service and Crowther, from where she could watch Sir Charles. He smiled at her with a warmth and sympathy that lifted the corners of his eyes.

'I came as soon as I saw the news-sheets, Mrs Westerman. I am sorry that you have been subject to these attacks. I wished to say the same to Mr Graves here.'

It was possible Harriet had not entirely succeeded in walking off her temper. 'Did you, Sir Charles? How kind. I rather thought you were behind them.'

Graves coughed into his tea. Sir Charles's expression, however, did not change. 'No, no. I am sorry you ever considered such a possibility. You over-estimate my influence. I fear your interference in the matter of Mr Trimnell may have been misconstrued in some quarters as an attack on the city itself. I am certain, however, that your motives are pure.'

'Your confidence is a great compliment,' Harriet said. 'Have you heard that Crowther thinks the men who attacked him on Monday evening were the same who were responsible for Mr Trimnell's death?'

Sir Charles turned towards Crowther who was sitting back among the cushions. The bruise on his jaw had developed all the colours of sunset. Crowther, Harriet noticed out of the corner of her eye, appeared to be enjoying himself. 'Indeed, Mr Crowther, is that so? I understood from Bartholomew that you saw very little.'

'I did not need to do so, Sir Charles. Their pattern of attack was distinctive enough.'

Sir Charles nodded very slowly. 'How interesting. Could you see, Mr Crowther, if they were white men or Negroes?'

Crowther's expression tightened. 'I could not.'

Sir Charles put down his cup. 'I see. Well, I am sorry indeed, and I make this apology in my role as Alderman and on behalf of the city, that you were injured while doing our coroner a service. I wished to tell you also that no effort is being spared in searching for Mrs Smith's maid. She is suspected of the killing.'

Harriet extended her arm across the back of the settee. 'When did you conclude that Mr Trimnell needed to be locked in a madhouse, Sir Charles?'

He hesitated, upon which Mrs Service lifted her hand. 'William, would you offer Sir Charles one of those delightful lemon cakes?' William did so. 'They are so sweet without being overwhelming, I think. Do take one.' Sir Charles gave her his most grateful smile, and for a moment Harriet's rage increased to the point where it swallowed Mrs Service too and all her rules of hospitality. Then the frail-looking widow continued in the same voice: 'Opponents of slavery are to be locked up as mad now? Why, Graves, we should make arrangements to have ourselves committed at once.' Harriet loved her again.

Sir Charles set down his plate. 'Mrs Service, a reasoned debate with a lady such as yourself must always be a pleasure . . .'

Graves had recovered from his cough. 'Perhaps you might like to debate the trade with Mrs Westerman's senior footman.' He nodded towards William, who without a flicker of expression bowed very slightly from the waist. Harriet felt almost giddy.

'I would debate the trade with any reasonable man or woman,' Sir Charles said, irritation cracking his words into flint-edged syllables. 'But Mr Trimnell was not reasonable. I know you have heard, Mrs Westerman, that he was seen trying to grab his mulatto by-blow off the street. He ranted and raved on the public highway and spread about him the most toxic mixture of half-truths and wild fantasy. He was trying to do active harm to the reputations of honourable men, men who have served this country and her interests quite as loyally as anyone in this room.'

'William,' Harriet said lazily, 'remind me when you received the injury to your leg.'

'I fell from the rigging when Captain Westerman's ship was demasted. It was during the holding of Admiral Barrington's line at Barbados, December 'seventy-eight, madam.'

'Oh, of course, I remember now,' Harriet said.

'Honourable men,' Sir Charles repeated fiercely. He controlled his breathing. 'William, I thank you for your service.'

Crowther's voice was dry and clear. 'What did Mr Sawbridge say to your plan, Sir Charles? Was Mrs Trimnell happy to have her husband declared mad?'

Sir Charles looked at him, frowning. 'The conversation was between myself, Dr Drax and the Reverend Fischer. Fischer was well acquainted with Trimnell in their younger days, Drax is a medical man and Trimnell was a neighbour of mine for a long time. Before we had the opportunity to speak to Sawbridge or Mrs Trimnell, Mrs Westerman had arrived at the balloon-launch with news of Trimnell's death.' He got to his feet and the company did also. 'Those cakes are delicious, Mrs Service. West Indian sugar, I'd know the taste anywhere.'

'Is it indeed?' Mrs Service said, offering him her fingertips. 'I must speak to the housekeeper.'

Harriet let Sir Charles bend over her hand. 'I have not had the opportunity to ask after Mrs Trimnell. Is she comfortably settled in your family?'

He let her hand fall. 'Mrs Trimnell's stay with us was only ever to have been of short duration while Sawbridge arranged rooms where they might live together.'

'Indeed?' Harriet answered. 'She seemed so comfortable there. Will she not be a great loss to the family circle?'

'Her place is with her father,' Sir Charles said shortly. 'Good day.'

William showed him out of the room and Crowther settled again into his place among the cushions. 'Mrs Service, I believe you have cured me. So, Mrs Westerman?'

'I trust Molloy will track down those thugs. And when they do, I am sure we shall find in their pockets the gold of Mr Sawbridge or of Randolph Jennings. They care for Mrs Trimnell and could not bear her humiliation any longer. The others only wished him to be shut away where he could not tell the world about their crimes.'

'Chivalry then?' Graves said, curling his lip.

The Chapter Coffee House was as full as Francis could have hoped. The large open room, split with booths like box pews in a church, was loud with male voices, laughing, jeering and jostling. The half-dozen waiters dashed about the place with the dented coffee pots, and tobacco smoke hung around the brass chandeliers in slowly shifting clouds. The back wall showed a map of the Americas and, what was looked at more, a clock like a full moon tapping out the seconds. The daylight found its way in cautiously through the high windows and a glass door that opened and closed a dozen times each minute.

Auctions of this type seemed always to be exclusively masculine preserves. There were several women in the book and print trade, often daughters or windows of sellers, all called 'Mrs', like Eliza, whether married or not. They were treated with avuncular respect by the men, and given credit for their good sense when they showed it, but they would not jostle in an auction with them. The only woman present this afternoon was the well-preserved matron of the coffee house who sat behind the bar keeping a tally of pipes and pots and saying little, only nodding to her regular customers like a queen at a review of her troops.

The business of the furniture and fittings was swiftly dealt with, the price of ten pounds reached exactly as predicted. The dealers then melted from the crowd, leaving the room the province of print. The auctioneer called them to order. 'We all know what we're about, gentlemen,' he shouted out when the noise had been reduced to a rumble. His voice was professionally loud and came from his belly. He could shake the glass in the windows with it. 'The remaining contents of good Mrs Smith's place of business with whatever stock on site as seen today. Mr Glass stands for the family. One price for the lot. You've had your chance to view, so there'll be no carping afterwards, thank you. All present stand witness to that. Before we start, however, you'll bow your heads a minute by the clock in memory of the lady herself and in hopes she'll help us into Heaven with her, for the Lord knows you're a miserable bunch of scoundrels, slanderers, back-biters and ink-stained reprobates, and each soul here present will need all the help it can get when it reaches the Gates.'

There was a low rumble of laughter at that as the men nodded and shoved at each other, then a silence, broken only by the soft footsteps of the waiters and a settling sigh or two from Mrs Smith's more sentimental colleagues. When the minute was up, the auctioneer said, 'Now then, gentlemen, I'm opening at twenty pounds. Up and at 'em for a bargain. Speak up and speak fast.'

The bidding was brisk and soon Francis was able to release the breath held in his lungs. The price would be fair at least, and he'd be able to look Master George in the eye. It climbed to somewhere near the limit of his hopes and slowed. Looked like the winning bid would come from one of the warehouses which sold stock to the pedlars. There was a longish silence and the auctioneer raised his eyebrows and his arm, ready to call it, when a small voice to his left piped up and added an extra five pounds to the bid. The gentlemen all turned to stare and a whisper began between them. Several men half-stood in their seats to look at the one who'd bid, then sat again, shrugging to their neighbours and shaking their heads.

The auctioneer frowned. 'Sir, you're a stranger in the room. It's ready money only, and all costs of clearing and carriage fall to you.'

'Agreed,' the voice said. Francis too craned to look at him but could see only the side of his face.

'No more bids? Sold then, to the gentleman on my left for fifty pounds.' He struck the hammer on the bargain, but before the puzzled crowd could fall back into conversation, he held up his hand again. 'One more word, gentlemen! A vote of thanks to Mr Glass, who risked his neck to try and save Mrs Smith – and all strength to his arm as he tries to find the bastard what did for her. So say we all.'

Loud and full the crowd cried, 'Hear, hear!' to it and Francis looked at the ground, his throat rather tight. The conversation became general, and when Francis had recovered himself he tried to see the stranger again. One of the unsuccessful bidders arrived at his elbow. 'That's an oddity, Mr Glass.'

'It is,' he said.

The under-bidder took off his glasses and polished them, and Francis was treated to the sight of the dirt in his wig as the man bent. He looked as if he had walked the roads between here and Newcastle a dozen times, worn down his fat legs in the process and brought the mud of it home with him each time. 'Heard Mrs Smith was leaving money to St Mary's. She didn't change the will then?'

'What? Change her will?'

The man winked up myopically. His blue eyes were watery from the smoke of his neighbours' clay pipes. 'I go to that church – when I can get in and see anything for all the fancy bonnets in the front row. Well, I'm shamed to say it but I'd been up late and . . . the long and short of it is, I was there last Sunday and fell asleep before the service was done. By the time I woke up, everyone else was going, but Fischer and Mrs Smith were there in the shadows of the west aisle talking, and it looked like no pleasant conversation.'

'Could you hear what was said, Winslow?' Francis said, bowing closer to the man in spite of the filth of him.

'No, no. Just to say it didn't look comfortable. Then someone else came in and Mrs Smith went away looking troubled.'

Francis thanked him, then hurried out of the room to try and follow the successful bidder. He managed to weave through the crowd, but the man he sought was in the street before he could reach him.

'Hold there!' he called. 'A word?'

The man turned towards him. 'What do you want?'

'I wish to know who you are.'

The stranger hardly looked at him. 'You have been paid, boy. That is all you need to know.' Francis had not been called 'boy' in that manner for some years. The word seemed to suck his will out of him for a moment – and in that moment the man was gone. The wound on Francis's face began to throb again. Slowly, he went back to collect the money from the auctioneer.

V.4

EUSTACHE WAS DISAPPOINTED THAT Mr Glass had not returned before William came to collect him. Once the footman had entered the shop and he had tidied away his pen and ink, he placed his report on the manuscript he had read last night carefully in the centre of his writing space. After a moment, he shifted the stacks of other manuscripts a little further away to make his report stand out more clearly. He then examined the manuscript itself. He did not want to leave it behind. Mr Glass had said that booksellers only occasionally caught fire, but he knew that sometimes they did. It had become precious to him, this manuscript, as he read and wrote out what he had thought. Even as he spent his day reading other novels, he had kept his hand on this one.

Mr Glass had given him permission to take it home and had told him to keep it safe, so he would take it with him. He put the bundle of papers into one of the leather folders Glass kept about the place, then tied the leather ties around it and tucked it under his arm. He climbed the back stairs to say goodnight to Joshua and Mr Ferguson, and was surprised to see they smiled at him; Cutter too winked at him as he left the shop. They must know who he was, must have read those stories about his mother and father, but it didn't seem to colour how they treated him. The thought made Eustache nervous suddenly, as if he were exposed to cold air after being swaddled in the warmth and dark for a long while.

As the afternoon wore on and no word came from Molloy, Harriet found she had some use for the account books from Caveley, after all. She usually asked William for help when the numbers began to swim in front of her eyes, but this time she asked her son. It felt a little strange to find herself being patiently instructed by a boy of ten years, and she felt it that he was already better schooled in the mysteries of numbers than she. His tutor, who had recently left the household to take Holy Orders, had been an even better bargain than she had imagined. In the course of their calculations Stephen began to look serious, and after he asked a question which suggested he understood more than she had thought, Harriet felt she had to explain to him what they were about. He became very quiet. He loved William, and had always worshipped his father and his memory.

'It is stealing, isn't it, Mama?' he said at last. 'It's stealing a person's right to be a person, their life.'

She put out her arms and he clambered onto her lap as he had used to do when he was much younger. 'I believe you are right, Stephen. I do not know what your father was thinking of. I can only suppose there were so many others who traded in human lives around him, it ceased to shock him as it does us.'

The boy leaned against her. 'He would have seen it was wrong when we explained it to him. Sometimes people don't know things until they are explained. But we shall pay William back, shan't we?'

She kissed the top of his head and wished she could keep him with her like this for all days. 'We can try.'

Still no news from Molloy. She thought of the thousand alleyways and doss-houses in London, the drinking dens and cellars with damp straw on the ground. The world had grown dark outside her window. No doubt the lights were burning in Portman Place, adding an extra burnish to that sweet splendour. Even if they could prove it was one of that community of planters and traders who had arranged a beating for Mr Trimnell to punish him for his repentance, would the papers even print the news? Even if it were proven, who was to say if the papers would print the news? Just because they had been so eager to fill their pages with the story on Monday did not mean they would be willing to say they had been entirely wrong about the threat posed by the 'flood of Africans'. Would they speak of Trimnell's wish to make amends, or would they shut their mouths and look away? She consulted her pocket-watch. There was still time, and she felt in great need of spiritual comfort.

Walter came to find Francis at the shop just as Francis was shutting up for the night. The engraver plodded in with a weary slump to his shoulders and no good news. Francis fetched a bottle and glasses from the back parlour and poured a drink for them both. The dogs had found nothing but rabbits all day, and Walter confessed that he and Scudder and Miller were all beginning to lose hope. 'You got us all fired up, Francis,' he said, leaning his arms on the counter and his chin on his arms. 'But once you've gone out there and looked at all those fields and barns and tracks in front of you, seems like there's a lot of room to hide a girl. In fact, you could hide a hundred girls out there.' He stopped abruptly. 'What happened to your face?'

Francis told him, ending with: 'Perhaps Constable Miller can frighten something more out of the cabman.' Walter looked hopeful again and was about to reply when the door handle rattled.

Francis looked up to see a white face surrounded by a shock of red hair peering in at the window. He was about to pull Walter back into the shadows in the hope they had not been seen when the face smiled broadly at him. He accepted his fate, went to the door and let the man in. He entered more hesitantly this time. Francis realised he had forgotten his name, but not the fact that he was writing an essay for the Cambridge Latin Prize.

'Clarkson!' The young man supplied, seeing his confusion, and shook hands with both of them. 'I am sorry to disturb you so late, but I saw a light and hoped . . .

'I am afraid I am still not much inclined to discuss my experience as a slave,' Francis said at once.

'No, no,' Clarkson said hastily. 'That is, should you ever feel able to, I would of course be eager, but no, I came to thank you for those verses you recommended, of Miss Phillis Wheatley.'

'Mr Clarkson is writing an essay on slavery,' Francis said over his shoulder to Walter and picked up his glass from the counter. 'He is against it.'

'More than ever,' Clarkson said. 'I wished also . . . I have been reading a great deal, sir, and it occurs to me that my manner when I came to speak to you . . . I offer you my sincere apologies.'

Francis was surprised into a smile. 'Not at all, Mr Clarkson.'

'Still, I am shocked by the way members of your race are described in the literature.'

Walter set his glass on the table again. 'You're shocked, are you? They have to justify the fact that they kill men like Francis by the boatload then work to death the ones that survive.'

Clarkson nodded. 'Yes, that must be true, but their evidence—'

'Evidence?' Walter slung what was in his glass down his throat and refilled it. 'They call Africans thieves and rebels, for not obeying them. What right do they have to touch the hair on another man's head without his consent, let alone kidnap him from liberty and work him to death without trial or process?' He drank again.

Clarkson's expression became animated and he turned towards Walter with a light in his eyes. Francis had worked too long in the book trade not to recognise the signs of a man warming to a debate.

'Enough,' he said. 'Gentlemen, please. Mr Clarkson, it was good of you to come, and I wish you every success with your work, but slavery is a topic I have no pleasure in hearing discussed.'

Clarkson blushed again, so furiously Francis thought his skin must burn. 'Of course. I shall be on my way, but may I shake your hand, sir?'

He put out his hand to Francis – and Francis realised that the young man feared he might be refused. The shock was like cold water in his throat. He took Clarkson's hand and shook it. 'Good night, Mr Clarkson.'

The man sketched a little bow then retreated outside, back into the darkness.

Walter filled up Francis's glass and Francis told him what Winslow, the under-bidder at the auction, had said about the argument at St Mary Woolnoth between Eliza and Dr Fischer.

'Can't have been the doctor who took the cab though,' Walter concluded. 'The stand is right near his church, so they'd all know him. They probably all go to hear him preach. He's good. You should take a turn at printing up some of his sermons.'

'No,' Francis said, simply and finally. He told his friend of having seen Fischer at the Jamaica Coffee House and finding out he had been a surgeon on a number of slave voyages. 'I remember the man who deemed me fit for purchase off the slave coast,' he said, suddenly seeing it as he spoke. 'His breath stank of rum, and we poor African souls meant no more to him than sheep. When they chained us in the hold I was glad for a moment that my brother had died before we reached the ships.'

Walter was half-hidden in the shadows now, his arms folded and leaning against the various volumes kept behind the counter. 'I thought you didn't remember anything about Africa.'

'I lied,' Francis said, and finished what was in his glass.

'You should write a book, Francis. Tell the truth of it. Don't just leave it to fellows like Clarkson and his ilk.'

Francis shook his head. 'Why? Believe me, no one would want to read such horrors – and what good would it do me? I have some friends here, I am treated with a measure of respect by my neighbours. Why antagonise every white man in this city by railing against what cannot be changed?'

Walter rolled his shoulders. 'Well, it's your story and your neck, my friend. So I won't try to persuade you. Just, I know you found the Smith family and they were kind to you and fed you pie, but it was English people who bought you and sold you, stole your brother and years of your life, whipped you and branded you — and now tell you to your face you're not a whole human being.'

Francis clenched his jaw. 'Do you have a point to make, Walter?'

'I do. Stop being so damned polite about it. No man of sense would respect you any less.'

V.5

THE UPPER PARLOUR, LIKE the rest of the Red Lion, had seen better days, but it was a fair-sized room and Willoughby had managed to gather a respectable congregation. Harriet slipped into the rear of the room and studied the backs of the heads in front of her. A mix of men and women; none in comfortable circumstances by the look of the worn collars of their coats, though there were a couple in slightly better cloth whom she took to be servants. Willoughby was speaking to them, not in the high rhetoric he had used on the Strand but quietly, in a conversational tone. He was speaking of honesty. Of those who were dishonest in their manners and how such hypocrisy hid their hearts from the light until they withered. He spoke of the powder and paint of women, of the silks worn by men of fashion with horsehair stuffed into their shoulders. Then he spoke of honesty in the heart, of how we must learn to understand the truth of our own characters, our own weaknesses so we can come to God, not pretending, not blaming anyone else, but with humility. Then, and only then, would we be worthy of God's grace, and might receive it.

Harriet was moved and rather impressed by his sermon. She thought her own father would have been proud to preach it. Willoughby finished his homily and then invited his company to divide into small groups to discuss what they had heard among themselves. Two men and two women, each with a Bible in their hand and holding the pages open at the verses they might discuss, began to draw the others into groups.

It was then, as the men and women scraped their chairs across the floor that Harriet noticed Martha, Mrs Trimnell's maid, among them. One of the women with a Bible was settling by her side, and as the others in the group found their places, Harriet could see her showing Martha the passage they were studying and reading it to her. As Harriet watched, Willoughby noticed her and joined her at the back of the room.

'I have heard of how Mr Trimnell died,' he said, shaking her hand, 'and learned also that you are Mrs Westerman. Do you know yet who attacked him, madam?'

'I am sorry to say, I do not,' Harriet replied. 'I came hoping to speak to any friends he might have had in your congregation. I see Mrs Trimnell's maid is here.'

He nodded. 'Yes. Martha is a good girl. I think she is afraid she offended you on Monday and you mean to make sure Mrs Trimnell casts her out. May I reassure her that is not the case?'

Harriet was surprised. 'Please do, Mr Willoughby.'

He made her a slight bow and then went to fetch Martha from the group and brought her over, a hand on her arm.

'See, Sister Martha? Mrs Westerman is here to shake hands with you.'

Harriet put out her hand at once and Martha brushed her fingertips with her own. 'I am sorry if you were uneasy, Martha. I am often told I speak my mind too quickly for most. I am no friend of Mrs Trimnell,

I fear, but if I can assist you in any way, you must let me know.' The girl gave her a shy smile. 'May I ask you a question? I am sorry if it seems strange, but did you ever see Mr Trimnell wearing the mask he designed for his slaves?'

She heard Mr Willoughby next to her sigh. It was not shock perhaps, but more a weary acceptance that one's suspicions might be true, just when one had persuaded oneself they were fancy.

Martha looked up at her and nodded. Her face was very round and her nose snub and small, but she was saved from plainness by her large eyes. 'He did, ma'am. All the time. Since we first came home he would shut himself in his room when not coming here or getting the leaflets made. He would wear it then. Once Miss Lucinda went quite mad with him, tried to pull it off him, but he only went back to his room and left her crying on the floor.'

'Did he ever strike her?' Harriet asked.

'No, ma'am. Not in London. Before he would, from time to time, when she railed at him for the life she led. She was lonely when we were in Jamaica, his plantation being tucked away, tucked under the wing of Sir Charles's, but no, I never saw him lift a hand to her since we came to England.'

Harriet considered. 'Was he at prayer when he wore the mask, Martha?'

'Yes, and at study. And writing. For hours and hours he wrote.' She looked over her shoulder at her empty chair. 'May I go back now?' she asked. 'I like the talking part of the evening almost more than the listening.' She grinned at Mr Willoughby as she said this last.

'Of course,' Harriet said. 'And thank you for shaking my hand.'

As she left, Willoughby sank down onto a chair. Harriet perched next to him and waited. He wiped his eyes. 'When I said I was concerned for his health . . . I meant that I was worried he had been starving himself deliberately. When he was thrown out of the coffee house, the way he described the violence used against him, I could see he revelled in it. I told him Jesus wants our love, not our pain — but I could not convince him. He had chosen his own path.' The man passed his hand in front of his eyes, then blurted out suddenly: 'I had to ask him not to tell me any more of his sins.'

'Mr Willoughby?'

'That is *my* sin — that I could not hear him any more, but the scenes he described . . . those poor children. Hearing him was like watching a man tear off his own skin. I know Hell now, from his words.' The preacher had begun to weep and Harriet did not know how to comfort him. 'Oh, Mrs Westerman, and I have the arrogance to lecture these people about honesty. I should have had the strength to hear him, but I could not. My faith was not strong enough.'

Harriet could think of nothing to do for him but sit by his side.

Molloy had spent a fair portion of the day asleep in the private chamber of an inn in Soho which he kept for his exclusive use. When he awoke there was a hot meal waiting for him and a pickpocket who owed him a number of favours. When the meal was eaten and the pickpocket had slipped off into the shadows, Molloy paid a visit to Mr Christopher's Academy and left with Guadeloupe at his elbow.

They were making for an alley off Little Trinity Street within sniffing distance of the river. As they walked, Molloy took another long look at the boy by his side.

'You know how to fight, lad?' And when he only nodded: 'How then?'

'Whoever cares less what comes, he wins.'

Molloy was satisfied. 'Mother Brown's no fool. She'll have a man with her, the sort that looks hard and fights slow.' Again, no response but a nod. 'When we go in, don't wait for him to square up. Just drop him.'

'You want him dead?'

Molloy considered. 'Not unless you have to. Just put him down.' They walked the rest of the way in silence.

The doorway was low, Molloy had to bend down to find his way inside. There was a woman seated at a rough wooden table in the centre of the room, sewing buttons onto a blue coat by the light of a cheap candle. Her white cap and black dress, with a black heavy shawl over her shoulders, made it feel as if there was no colour in the room at all, apart from the coat in front of her: broadcloth and with bone buttons she was slowly replacing with brass ones. A simple disguise for goods of doubtful provenance, but Molloy had seen it work time and time again. The back wall of the place was lined with half a dozen trunks bound with leather straps. Around her neck she wore a ribbon with a number of small keys hanging from it. They caught the light of the candle as she worked, and chinked as she lifted her head. She looked a hundred years old, her face as wrinkled and worn as Molloy's own.

'Mother Brown,' he said.

She gave a tiny nod of her head and out of the shadows in the corner a great figure of a man stood. He had the look of a fairytale giant about him. Before he had got to his full height, Guadeloupe had spun out of the doorway behind Molloy. Molloy caught the glimmer of a blade, and as the giant turned towards it, Guadeloupe's arm came out in a wide arc. The giant fell, clutching at his throat, and Guadeloupe stepped back, watching him until he was still.

The old woman turned back to her sewing. 'Whatever Molloy is paying you, I'll double it, boy.'

He bent down and wiped his blade on the giant's coat. 'Too big not to kill,' he said. 'I'll do no work for a witch,' he added, then stepped back.

'That's a shame, boy. I could use you. Use you more than Molloy here who spends his time kissing the hands of the gentry and helping them across the street.' She laughed.

Molloy grabbed the edge of the table and turned it over, knocking the coat and candle to the ground, then he gripped the woman and shoved her hard against the wall, his own knife out now, one arm across her chest, the blade in his other hand tickling just below her ear. The only light now came from the feeble fire. He brought his face against hers.

'You think I've lost my teeth, Mother Brown? Think I've softened, do you? Is that what they're saying up north? I told you ten years ago not to come back to London breathing. I meant it.'

She looked at him. No fear on her, just a slow reassessment of her situation. Then she dropped her eyes.

'What's the fine?' she asked.

He released her and folded his knife. 'Clear up here. Then get back to Newcastle and tell them you were misinformed about me.'

She looked down at the body in disgust. 'It was a bad day for me when I conned you, Molloy. I'll say that.'

'And you'll keep saying it while you have breath in your lungs, woman.' He picked up the chair on which she had been sitting and set it down straight. 'But first I want information on some clients of yours. Sit down and tell me where you got that handsome coat from. And remember, I can smell a lie like a dog smells blood.'

PART VI

VI.1

F RANCIS ARRIVED AT HINCKLEY'S booksellers in a dark mood after a largely sleepless night. When he did sleep he dreamed of the fire and his early childhood, the two memories bundled together so he was once again in his village, but then he saw his father's compound in flames and realised his brother and Eliza were both inside. Or he dreamed he was sitting drinking tea with Eliza, but his brother was there too and Francis was terribly afraid he would ruin the portfolio of prints he was looking at, although Eliza kept telling him not to worry and that the wound in her eye did not hurt at all.

He was trying to forget the fragments of these dreams which had clung to him by calculating when George Smith might receive the news of his sister's death, and how quickly he might make his way back to London. Wishing for him, Francis kept his eyes down until he was almost on the doorstep. When he looked up, what he saw came as a shock – clean and sudden as a knife wound. The front door of the shop had been forced open. Cutter was on the steps, looking out for him. He hurried down and took his arm.

'It's mess and bother for the most part, Mr Glass,' he said in a rush, while all Francis could do was stare. 'The office, back parlour and

251

everything under the counter has been torn up and gone through, and some bugger has pulled down all the volumes on the street side.'

Francis was still too shocked to speak. He was aware of a little crowd of neighbours gathering at his back. 'Joshua?' he said at last.

'Scared, is all. He heard the noise in the shop, nipped out the back window, sneaked out of the yard then ran to the watch-house. By the time he dragged a constable back here the place was empty again.'

'Why was I not called?' Francis said. He pushed Cutter away from him and went into the body of the shop.

'Mr Ferguson lodges just over the way,' Cutter said, following him. 'He came over, hearing the noise, and he and Josuha slept on the shop floor to make sure no one came back. But what was the point in calling you when there was no light to see by, and no one to tell us who had been here or what they had done? We all wanted you to get a night's rest and a good breakfast before you looked this in the face. We all thought it and said it, so if you want to tear a strip off us, you may. But we were all of one mind, and that's that.'

'I should have been called,' Francis said, but weary rather than angry.

The shop looked as if it had been hit by a hurricane. Volumes torn from the polished shelves and thrown to the floor. Cracked spines and crumpled pages, they looked like so many corpses of birds smashed down by the wind. The ink-bottle had been knocked off the counter and bled darkly into the floorboards. The books which had fallen near it had gathered its staining into their pages. The neatly kept volumes where Cutter and Francis recorded each book purchased had been opened, thrown down, then stamped flat.

Francis could not speak so instead picked his way across the wreckage and into the office. Paper everywhere. All the loose manuscripts awaiting his attention in the cubby-hole where Eustache had been working had been taken out and cast about. The comfortable-looking room was buried under a storm of words. All the cupboards had been opened and the contents swept out in armfuls. Each piece of furniture was on its side, as if knocked over by the stories that now gabbled incoherent and confused around them.

Francis swayed on his feet. Cutter saw him and with one arm caught hold of him, while with the other he snatched up a low stool, shook the pages off it and set it down so Francis could sit before he fell. 'It's not as bad as it seems, Mr Glass.'

'It is bad enough,' Francis said thickly. 'Where is Joshua?'

'Ferguson's taken him off for his breakfast. They'll be back in a moment, sure. He was in a state, poor little fella. Seems he's decided he's a curse to anyone who takes him on.'

'He's a good boy. I'm glad that Ferguson is kind to him.'

Cutter grinned. 'Aye, they've taken to each other, no doubting it.'

'Jesus save us!' Francis looked up to see Walter Sharp standing in the door, his eyes as wide as saucers. 'I came as soon as I heard! What in God's name . . . Do you think it was a critic? Or an author displeased you wouldn't print him?' Francis almost laughed, but he didn't have it in him quite. 'Anything taken, Cutter?'

Cutter shook his head. 'Not that I can tell. Whoever that bastard was, he had no use for the sort of books we sell, it seems. Mr Francis keeps the monies with him, and they didn't even take the leaving of the bottle of aquavite you gentlemen opened last evening. It had been knocked over and had soaked three copies of *Evelina* through.'

'A warning, perhaps,' Francis said slowly. 'Someone who does not like our asking questions about Eliza's death?'

Walter looked about him. 'I think we must be asking the right questions then. God, I hope we find that girl. I swear between them, Scudder and Miller have asked every soul who ever bought a shilling print off Mrs Smith if they knew of any enemies she had. They've had nothing but good words from them all and tales of what a righteous and helpful woman she was.' Walter shifted his weight. 'A couple of 'em thought it worth mentioning there was a black fella kept calling round, pointing their finger at you, Francis. Though both gentlemen were fairly free in telling them what they could do with talk like that. Miller's going to go and growl at your cabman when he's broken his fast, by the way.'

Francis remained crouched on the stool in the middle of the room where Cutter had set him down, his head in his hands. Walter was used to seeing him go through life with a straight back and a quick smile. Always glad to help his neighbours and friends, stepping over any insults thrown at his feet as if he hadn't noticed them and grateful for the small kindnesses of friends. Walter had borrowed money from him a dozen times and never paid it back, relied on him as a friend he could stay with when he was thrown out of his lodgings, and the shop he regarded as a sort of free club where he could find refuge and company when it suited him. He wondered what Hinckley paid him, and felt certain it was not as much as he deserved. Walter had always thought Hinckley more sharp than kindly. Perhaps having a manager who was an African served him particularly well. It made him seem liberal, almost revolutionary, and it meant he got loyal service from an intelligent man for less than he would otherwise have paid.

Walter found himself wondering too what *he* had done for Francis over the years they had known each other. He had perhaps thought the charm of his company was enough, even that he was conferring a favour on Francis. He was as bad as Hinckley. No – the thought came up from his heart, uncomfortable and sore, he was worse.

'Francis, leave this to us,' he said, and Francis looked up in surprise. 'Clearing up this mess will break your heart and it will do us good. Let me and Cutter and little Lord Whatever he's called, and Ferguson and the rest go to work.'

'You are kind, Walter, but I cannot—'

'I am *not* kind!' Then more calmly: 'I am not, Francis. But let me try to be so, this once at least. We can put the manuscripts back together easily enough. These writers have appalling handwriting, but at least it is appalling in different ways. We shall replace what is undamaged on the shelves and stack what is hurt for your inspection. What say you, Cutter?'

Cutter planted his feet sturdily and tucked his thumbs into his waistcoat. 'Most sensible thing I've ever heard you say, Mr Sharp. And I've heard you say a lot.'

'And what am *I* to do with my time?' Francis asked.

'I would tell you to go home and rest your bones, but I shouldn't think you will. I am supposed to take the dogs out today. Will you take my place?' He scratched the back of his head. 'A day's walking in the spring air will do you good and you'll know you're doing something that needs to be done in the same moment.' He picked his way carefully across the room, treading as lightly on the broken stories as he could, and pulled a map from his coat pocket. It was already a little soft with being folded and refolded. 'We've marked on where we've been. The dogs are at Scudder's. Go, and don't come back till dusk is coming on. And when you come back, go to your supper, your lodgings and your bed. We'll have the place back and looking like your kingdom by the morning.'

Francis took the map and turned it in his fingers, his expression doubtful. 'You'll take care of Eustache? He's been bent double over these . . .' His gesture took in the pages around him and he felt his throat close.

'He'll be of help putting them in order again,' Walter said stoutly.

'And you'll explain to Joshua that I don't think him a curse and he did well running to fetch the Watch?'

'I shall, Francis. Now please, get away with yourself and let me be of assistance for once in my life.'

It had been decided – and Francis was too tired in his head and heart to resist them.

When Eustache arrived at the bookshop with William and his leather folder clutched in his arms, he had a great deal of trouble fighting the urge to burst into tears. He felt personally harmed by the attack on the books, and a swelling of pity for them lifted in his chest. He wanted to scratch someone's eyes out. Cutter was on his knees in one corner of the room examining each volume and deciding what harm had come to it. He looked up and saw Eustache and William in the door.

'Ah, there you are, Master Eustache, Mr Geddings! We have work a-plenty for you today, young man!'

William looked concerned. 'I am certain Mr Graves would not want Master Eustache in the way. Equally, if you need another hand to help, I am just as sure he'd want me to stay.'

Cutter got to his feet and dusted his hands off on his jacket. 'No, we have want of Master Eustache indeed, but with him we have all the hands we need, Mr Geddings.'

'Was there a robbery?' William asked.

'No, it seems not. Just some evil spite. We've sent Mr Glass away until we can get cleaned up. The poor lad felt it hard.'

'And Joshua?' Eustache asked.

'A little snivelly still, but fine in himself. He's in the back room ready to help you make sense of all them piles of manuscript, Mr Eustache. You'll be brave now, won't you? You had it lovely neat in there, better than Mr Glass does and he's a stickler for order in the general run of things. You got the stomach to put it all back together for him?'

Eustache hesitated, then nodded and headed for the back office. William watched him go, and having exchanged final civilities with Cutter, headed back out into the street.

VI.2

HARRIET ASKED TO SEE William as soon as he returned to the house. She had written out the results of her calculations from the previous evening on a sheet of paper and kept nervously picking it up and putting it down. She had snapped at Dido that morning and been able to take nothing but coffee at breakfast. William seemed to take a very long time getting back from the city.

He came in at last and she stood at once and put the note in his hand. He unfolded it and looked at the numbers, then back at her again. 'I do not understand, Mrs Westerman.'

She found it easier to pace while she spoke. 'As an ordinary seaman, you were due a certain share in each prize. I have been checking exactly what prizes were taken while you were . . . before you were free. I am afraid my husband was not entirely scrupulous even in putting aside the quarter of what you were actually due while taking the rest.'

'Mrs Westerman . . .'

'Please let me finish, William. I worked out what you were due from each prize, actually due. Then there was the matter of your wages for those years. It all came to a rather neat sum, but then I calculated the compound interest, given, you should have had it in 'seventy-nine at the latest, and that,' she pointed to the note, 'is what you are owed.' He had raised his eyebrows when she mentioned compound interest and she saw it. 'Stephen helped me.'

'Mrs Westerman . . .'

'Please do not try and persuade me you should not have it, nor that it is not necessary. It is *entirely* necessary to me, and to Stephen. You shall have it, William.'

He looked down at the note. It was a large sum indeed. He hesitated. 'Very well. May I keep this?'

She nodded, a little unsure, and watched him fold it up with his certificate of manumission. 'William, the money is yours to do with as you will, of course. But I wondered what you might think of building a house just on the edge of Hartswood? It would be convenient if you were willing to take on the role of steward of the estate. I was thinking a salary of perhaps forty pounds per annum? And I would buy you a horse.'

He smiled suddenly, fully, and Harriet felt some of the tension leave her. 'Yes, that would indeed be acceptable, Mrs Westerman. I shall put off my livery when we leave town and buy a coat with buttons large enough to terrify your tenants.'

'Oh, thank goodness for that,' Harriet said, putting her hand on her chest and William laughed.

Eustache and Joshua worked steadily in the back room gathering the papers into piles and then beginning to sort them. It was not as difficult as they had feared. Only a very few of the pages were damaged at all, beyond a few creases, and most had fallen in clumps as if they had struggled to huddle together when attacked. Eustache even began to find his own reports on the various manuscripts he had read for Mr Glass in the last few days. It was not until late in the afternoon that he began to suspect that the most recent one, the important one, was missing.

A message from Molloy arrived in Berkeley Square at midday. It gave a place and a time. The household breathed a deep sigh of relief. Mrs Westerman would still be pacing, but now the message was come, at least she would be pacing the Square rather than the confines of the house itself.

VI.3

F RANCIS HAD NEVER BEEN fond of dogs and was ready by mid-
afternoon to throttle both brown and white spaniels and throw their
useless carcases in the New River. They had found nothing but rabbits
in the woods and so, believing his quest failed and that all now rested
on Miller's ability to intimidate the cabman, Francis turned back down
Hornsey Lane and then down Devil's Lane footsore and frustrated.

It had been meant as a kindness, getting him out of the city, but with
nothing but the fields to look at, and nothing to occupy his mind but
memories of Eliza, he did not feel improved for it. The sun was settling
lower in the sky. The horizon was normally hidden from him by the
buildings of London, but now there was a sky so much greater than
what he was used to. The hedgerows were thick with the stars of Queen
Anne's Lace, and the hawthorn bushes heavy with blossom – and the
quiet cut through him. He wished that Eliza were there. It was a wish
deeper than words. He closed his eyes and rested for a moment against
the fence-post, tried to fight his grief, then surrendered to it. Great sobs
shook his whole body and he turned away from the sunset as if he was
ashamed. He had no idea how long he spent there. The world – his
life – had ceased to be a thing that could be measured in time; there
was nothing but an awareness of hope stolen away. When finally he
returned to himself he stood up slowly and tasted dusk in the air. The
sky had become a riot of reds and pinks, long clouds of dusty purple
and a solid gold blaze of the sinking sun.

He looked around him, but the dogs were out of sight, barking at
something where the road bent down into a narrow valley. He pulled
out his handkerchief and wiped his face then set off in pursuit of the
noise, his mind still blank and his limbs carrying him without his will

taking any part in it. The dogs were some hundred yards down the track, snuffling and yapping self-importantly not at a verge or ditch, but rather at the gateway set back from the road and half-hidden by the shadows of the ash trees planted alongside it.

He put the dogs back on their leashes and tried to pull them away, but the dogs were stubborn and insistent. He saw something in the long grass under the wall and bent down to look. A cashbox. He bent down and picked it up, and it carried him like a charm back into Eliza's shop. He could see her closing the lid and tucking it under the counter. She smiled at him. He opened his eyes and looked about him. Could Penny have been buried here, on this verge? But there was no sign of disturbed earth, and there was no doubt the dogs wished to go through the gates. He set the cashbox down tenderly in the grass again and pushed at them. They swung back without a sound and he went through them, the dogs pulling hard at him. At the end of a short driveway, and completely screened from the road by the trees, he saw a very elegant villa. There were lights showing on the ground floor. The sight seemed almost a mirage, especially coming upon it like this when daylight was changing subtly into the bronzed shades of evening. It was a beautiful house, unusual to be built so far away from fashion and on such a lonely and inconvenient road, but the square garden was full of new spring blooms surrounding green lawns.

The dogs tugged him up the path and began scrabbling at the door. Francis was shaken by the excited certainty of the animals. If they had led him to an outhouse perhaps, or to some side garden, he might have believed them, but it seemed incredible that Penny might have been carried or dragged through this front door. The dogs looked up at him, large-eyed and whining. He knocked. After a minute or so the door was opened by a maid. She was older than most of the girls Francis saw opening doors and scrubbing steps. The dogs strained forward. Now that the door was open Francis could hear music playing and a male voice singing — a light tenor and clear, rounded. The woman looked him up and down.

'Go away,' she said at last and began to shut the door again.

Francis put his hand out to stop it closing and his weight behind it. 'One moment, madam,' he said. The music stopped and a man's voice called out: 'Who is it, Mrs Rogers?'

'No one,' the woman said, and tried to push the door to. Francis pushed harder till it sprang back and the woman was forced into the hallway.

He stepped over the threshold and saw: a wide-open vestibule, a shining marble floor with the occasional white and pink Turkish carpet; ironwork on the staircase — and such a feel of light and air about the place it seemed to have been made from thistledown. The maid looked at him and he saw himself through her eyes: African, grubby and red-eyed, his cravat none too clean and a fresh whip-strike on his cheek.

'Forgive me, I mean you no harm. My name is Francis Glass. I have come in search of a girl named Penny,' he said. She did not reply. 'The dogs seem to think they have followed her scent here. I am a friend of Mrs Smith — Penny's mistress. She was killed and we are worried about Penny's safety. Please, miss, I know I look a fool but have you seen a girl? She is nineteen or so, with dark hair. We fear she may be injured or have been taken against her will.'

There was a footstep from inside the house and a tall young man emerged from a door on the left of the hall. Francis stared at him in amazement. He wore no wig, just his own hair, close-cropped, and his skin was a dark gold. He hesitated as he saw Francis, then lifted his chin.

'Ridiculous,' he said. 'There is no Penny here, just myself and Mrs Rogers. Leave at once.'

Francis bent down and released the dogs. They yelped in happy amazement and went dashing into the hall, then barking loudly, they ran straight up to the first floor, their white feathered tails wagging furiously and their claws tapping on the uncarpeted marble stairs.

Francis bowed. 'I shall leave, but not before I have seen what trail these dogs are following.' He walked past them.

The young man was astonished. 'I shall call the footman and have him throw you out.'

Francis was too tired to care. 'Then call him.'

He climbed the stairs two at a time and found the dogs snuffling and scratching at one of the doors which led off the landing. He tried the handle but found it locked. The young man had hastened up the stairs behind him.

'Open the door for me,' Francis said. 'If you do not, I shall break it down.'

The other man sighed very deeply, produced a fat key from his waistcoat and handed it over with a slight bow.

Francis unlocked the door and the dogs tumbled in. It was a bedroom, on the south-east corner of the house, with windows on two sides. The dogs dashed up to the bed and sat on their haunches in front of it, panting and proud. Francis walked quickly over. There was a body lying under the covers. He pulled the sheet down until he could see the face. *Penny*. There was a bandage wrapped around the side of her head and her breathing was loud and laboured, but she was breathing. Francis closed his eyes and thanked God. The young man was still standing in the doorway. Francis took in the elegance of his clothing, and the beauty of his face.

'How came she here?'

The man shrugged. Francis looked around him. There was a table in front of the fireplace with armchairs on either side. He took one facing the bed and slung his bag onto the floor beside him. The young man crossed the room with a slightly swaying walk, and took the other, then crossed his legs and put his chin in his hands.

'I must make a confession. I am afraid I have no footman.'

Francis almost smiled. He had not had the heart to open the pack that Scudder had handed him when he left the house that morning. Now he did so, he found two bottles of beer, bread and cheese, and a pair of pistols complete with powder and ball. That explained the weight of the pack at least.

'Are you going to shoot me and Mrs Rogers? *We* didn't hit the girl, you know.'

'Then I shan't shoot you unless you make any move to harm her.'

'Do you wish to know my name?'

'I do.'

'My name is Dauda. Do you like it?'

Francis cleared his throat. 'I do. I was born Yoruba.'

Dauda opened his hazel eyes very wide. 'And so what are you now?'

Francis folded the bag and placed it on the ground. The dogs seemed to take this as some sort of signal and came to flop, glowing with achievement, at his feet. He reached down to rub their heads. Time was, he had found the British attitude to their animals incomprehensible. Perhaps he had become English, after all.

Dauda was still looking at him. 'Even if I don't have a footman, I might send Mrs Rogers to fetch help.'

'Unless she can find someone and bring them here before I load these guns, Dauda, then I will shoot the first one who comes into this room.'

Dauda considered this, then shrugged. 'She cannot be moved, you know, Mr Glass. She is a sick little girl. So perhaps we cannot get you out, but then you cannot leave to get help either, can you?'

Francis had already realised this. The risk that some harm would come to Penny while he went looking for assistance was too great. 'My friends have some idea where I am. I shall wait for them.'

Dauda frowned and put his head on one side. 'What if I send for the man who brought her here?'

'I think the man who brought Penny here murdered the woman I loved, so please, Dauda, send for him. Then I may shoot him myself.'

The other looked at him through half-shut eyes and long lashes. 'You are a difficult boy to argue with! What is your real name?'

'I have told it to you.'

'That's not the one you were given when you were born, dearest. That is a slave name.'

'It was. Now it is the name of a free man. The girl is here – she lives. Do not try and shake me, Dauda, with talk of slaves. What are you?'

He stretched his legs out and yawned, though Francis thought he was neither bored, nor tired. 'I'm a musician.'

Francis raised his eyebrows. 'Are you?'

'Yes, that is what I am.' His voice suddenly pettish. 'Though I will admit I have an audience of only one.' There was the sign of real pain in his eyes at that and Francis felt for him. 'Oh, put away that foul-looking cheese before it stinks up my lovely cage. I shall give you and your mutts a proper supper. Lord knows if any of us will live much longer. We may as well live in comfort while we can.'

VI.4

D R FISCHER CALLED IN the late afternoon. Cutter told him that they were closed to business and Francis was away, but nevertheless the Reverend was disposed to linger. He made some mention of papers belonging to Mrs Smith that he needed to consult and went into the office without waiting for permission. There he found Eustache and Joshua still at work. He smiled at both boys, then gave Joshua a shilling and asked him to fetch him a pie from the bake house, and something for himself if there was change. Joshua looked a bit baffled and glanced at Eustache. Eustache nodded to him and off he went. Fischer beamed at him as he went, then shut the office door behind him and turned to Eustache.

'Eustache,' he said gently, 'where is it? It is very important you give it to me. The man who wrote it was quite mad, and everything he says in those pages is a lie. I am sure of that. It is fit only for the fire.'

'You stole my report. You ruined the shop.'

Fischer smiled his bright, handsome, confident smile. 'I have a temper, I admit that it is a sin, I know, and one I struggle with every day. I was frustrated, Eustache, finding that the manuscript was not here and your rather detailed description of it was. But that does not matter. Give it to me.'

Fischer towered over him, but Eustache was surprised to find he was not afraid. He looked into the square-jawed face of the Reverend, and thinking of what he had read, felt instead a pure white blossom of hate. 'It is safe in Berkeley Square,' he said. 'Everyone will read it. And everyone will know you had Mr Hinckley's bookshop broken into to try and get it. Then no one will come to listen to you talk. When they have read what I have read, they will throw stones at you in the street rather than hear you preach.'

Fischer's lips went thin and pale and his anger felt like sunshine on Eustache's skin. 'You are a child, you understand nothing of these things! I have made no secret of my time at sea or how I was employed.'

'I understand this,' Eustache said clearly and carefully. 'You say you were a slaver as if it is being a real sailor, and we never thought about it. But you never said you were sorry. You said you were sorry for swearing, or drinking or thinking about women, you talk about spending the nights praying or reading your wife's letters from home and writing to her every day and how you saw God's face in a thunderstorm. Why didn't you see God on the faces of the people you had dying in the hold? Why? You talked to us about spending weeks in Jamaica walking the hills and feeling yourself called to God, but I know that was not all you did there! You are a dog. And soon everyone will know it.'

Fischer's chest rose and fell and his hands clenched into fists at his side.

'When Mr Glass comes back, I shall tell him everything,' Eustache said, every word tasting delicious to him. 'Then Mr Ferguson will set it all in type and you'll be done, dog. Graves will see it is read everywhere.'

Fischer took three steps towards him and grabbed hold of his wrist, twisting his grip so it stung and pulled the boy close to him. His voice came in a hiss. 'Graves will hate you for this.' It was such a surprise to him, Eustache felt his skin go suddenly cold. Fischer shifted his grip, making the bones in Eustache's wrist ache. 'Think of those names in your little report, Eustache. Bankers, politicians, Sir Charles and his son. And they all have friends, all very good friends, and slavery is *their* money, *their* trade. It is England's money, England's trade – and every right-thinking Englishman agrees. You make trouble for us and we shall make Graves's life hell. God, he must want rid of you already. Poor modest, obliging Mr Graves, all he ever wanted was his wife and a chance to live his own life, but your murderous parents ruined that for him, didn't they? He must loathe you, though he tries to be good, him and poor old Mrs Service, they do *try* so to like you, don't they? And now you're going to make it all a thousand times worse. Give me that manuscript, or for ever after, every time Graves looks at you, he's going to wish you were dead. *Every time.*' His voice had become a snarl. 'Your family will be mocked in the papers till even your servants don't want to look you in the face. Every scandal attached to your name will be repeated every morning in the press. None of the traders in London will deal with anyone who crosses the threshold. The little troupe of freaks and misfits from Thornleigh Hall have pushed the city too far, boy.'

Eustache could not speak. He could only think of Graves, his weary kindness. His rage began to turn inwards and eat at his bones.

'Or,' Fischer's voice became kinder, 'or everyone could make Graves's life a little easier. His unfortunate decisions of the past will be forgotten. The family will be praised, loved, invited everywhere. Even Mrs Westerman will be spoken of admiringly in society. Should her son wish to join the Navy, he will find a thousand friends there. You are a clever boy. Perhaps you will go into the Church. You may pick your appointments. Imagine how having good friends in every banking house, every newspaper, in every corner of government, will make your lives *so* much easier. Then Graves will find all his kindness and sacrifice rewarded at last. All you have to do is give me that manuscript – those ravings of a madman about the fate of some poor ignorant slaves you have never met. Give it to me and earn the love that has been wasted on you so long.'

Dr Fischer released his grip on Eustache's wrist and smiled. 'Bring the manuscript to me tomorrow morning, Eustache, there's a good lad.' Then he simply walked away and left the boy staring after him.

Joshua was very surprised to find Fischer gone when he returned a few minutes later. He offered to share the pie with Eustache, but he was not hungry so Joshua ate it himself and enjoyed the novelty of feeling too full to eat another bite. He wiped the grease off his fingers very carefully before touching any of the papers again.

The supper Dauda returned with on a tray was delicious. The dogs ate chicken breast from china bowls and fell happily asleep on the luxurious carpet in front of the fire. Francis was careful not to eat too much. He would not sleep until Penny was safe.

'She is still unwell,' Dauda said, patting his lips with a napkin. 'She has woken once or twice, enough for us to give her water, but mostly she sleeps.'

'Where does she think she is?'

'Heaven. At least, she asked if she were in Heaven when she woke last.'

Francis felt only a soft wave of sorrow. Penny had been snatched back from death; Eliza had not.

'This woman whom you loved, this Mrs Smith,' Dauda went on. 'Was she a white woman?'

'She was.'

'Tell me how you knew her.' But Francis felt his throat close up and said nothing. 'We have the time, Mr Glass. Indulge me, and who knows, perhaps we will be friends. I have never had a friend – it would be interesting for me.'

The fading light that still lit the room made Dauda's face look as if it were cast from bronze. Francis found himself thinking it would be like confessing to an idol.

'When I came to England first, my master lodged with her family in Norfolk Street. That was in 'sixty-six and I was ten years old, two years a slave and very frightened. I could speak little English. My master, Allear, was a trader in Bridgetown and I was one of his warehouse brats, though he would sell my labour to whomever was willing to pay.' The window was open slightly so the evening air could stir through the sick-room from time to time, and the plain little English birds were singing out the last of the light. 'I think he meant to give me to someone as a present when we came to England, but found that the rich women whom he sought to be his patrons wanted blacks who could sing or recite, not just some weakling child who could hardly speak. Eliza and her brother made a friend of me and tried to teach me English. When I did well, they would reward me with slices of their mother's apple pie.'

'And so won your loyalty forever,' Dauda said gently.

Francis nodded. 'Their kindness was the first I'd met with since I was taken. And the pie was delicious.' Dauda's musical laugh rippled among shadows. 'I was sold to another man and taken back to Jamaica, though I learned to read a little on the journey. Then I was sold again and brought back to London by another man some months later.'

'Why did no one wish to keep you, Francis?'

'I cannot say. But I was a gangling child with no strength and the appetite of a grenadier.'

Dauda laughed again. 'Poor Francis. Was your last master a better man?'

'No better or worse than the one before, but my English had improved by then and I had taught myself to read well, and to write a little so I was more use to him. Still, he whipped me every day and I was so frightened of him I began to piss my bed. Then he would whip me more. Once I woke up in the night with the sheets damp and I was so frightened I ran away. I found Norfolk Street, broke in through the kitchen window and stole an apple pie.'

'You did not! Why, Mr Glass, you poor miserable infant. You come in here with your mud and your dogs and your threats, and now I fear you will break my heart. Did they know it was you?'

'They guessed. I went up for theft in front of the Old Bailey, sure they would hang me, but Mr Smith, Eliza's father, told the judge how I had not stolen the silver spoons from the larder and that he forgave me the pie. I was found not guilty and released. I was sure I was dead, but the man I had stolen from put his hand on my shoulder and called me his friend. I would have crossed the earth for him after that.'

'That does not surprise me, Mr Glass. Now tell me the rest. What happened between your release at the Old Bailey and the hour you appeared on my doorstep with your silly dogs?'

So Francis told him, as the light continued to fade and the dogs chased rabbits in their sleep, how Mr Smith had bought him, and told him he was free the same day. How he was christened and Mr Smith stood his godfather, how he had fed his love of books and learning, and had eventually got him work with his old friend Mr Hinckley. How one of the proudest days of his life had been when he had paid back his purchase price to Mr Smith from his wages; Mr Smith had held a party to celebrate and they had cleared the front parlour of the house in Norfolk Street so that they could dance, and dance they had.

At some point in the story Dauda had rung for the candles to be lit and Mrs Rogers had come upstairs with a taper in her hand. The dogs were woken and taken to sleep outside. Now Dauda listened to the story of Francis's work, his constant love for Eliza, and her death – the hopes taken from him.

'Tell me who did this, Dauda. I must learn some time. Why should I not hear it from you? Why protect him?'

'I cannot tell you, Francis. I simply cannot. I wish I had been loved, as you have been loved, but only my mother cared for me that way. After she was gone I had to take what forms of love I could find, and imperfect as they are, I still must honour them tonight.'

Dauda smiled at him then stood and turned his back. Before Francis understood what he was doing, he had taken off his beautiful coat and waistcoat and lifted his undershirt so Francis could see his naked back. The light drifted over his skin as if it wanted to caress it. He was perfect, unmarked. He let the shirt fall again and sat down. 'I have always been too beautiful for the whip. It has been a blessing and a curse.' He stretched out his legs, crossing them at the ankles, and rested his chin in his hand.

'I shall tell you what I can, Francis dear. I was born in Jamaica. My mother was the favourite slave of an overseer on a good plantation. After his wife died she lived in the house like a white woman and ate with him when there were no visitors. I was brought up there and treated like a little pet by the household. Only my father's white daughter ever beat me. Slapping and pinching and delighting that the bruises hardly showed on my skin. Then sometimes she would hold me and tell me stories, and I would love her so much for those moments.' Francis remembered the devotion George and Eliza had inspired when he had learned he need not fear them. 'I think my mother believed she and the overseer were married, that I was safe as a pure white boy. Then when I was thirteen a man offered a great deal of money to buy me, and my father accepted. My mother begged him not to, but it did no good.'

'What happened?' Francis said, and the candles flickered a little in the night breeze.

'The day I was taken away, my mother killed herself. It was not done out of despair, not out of misery. It was punishment to my father for selling me, her jewel, made out of all her suffering. She knew he loved her above all things, so she drank poison just so he was forced to watch her die.'

VI.5

A S NIGHT THICKENED IN London, Harriet and Crowther were sitting in a tiny room overlooking a court near Smithfield Market. They had met under the great medieval mass of St John's Gate, in between the shadows cast by the smoking lamps. Molloy gathered them away with him at once. It was a corner of London where you might expect a gentleman to exercise a little caution whilst walking the dirt ways between the sagging and slipping wrecks of houses, and where a lady would never dare to venture. Every third building held a cellar where the gin was cheap and the voices loud. An occasional fiddler could be heard, screeching out folk tunes in the bowels. Crowther was not nervous, however, partly because he had faith in his ability to scare off most rogues who might make a try for his purse, or for Mrs Westerman's, and partly because he walked alongside the familiar silhouette of Molloy – and no one would dare trouble *him*. Any number of legends clustered about him and hung in the folds of his long black and slightly greasy cloak. It may have been that most were lies, but he denied nothing, explained nothing, and so was immortal.

The air stank of blood from the meat market. The room's usual occupants had been paid to find somewhere else to spend their evening, and all Harriet could know about them was what they left behind. It seemed the room was home to a family. One side was flagged with washing hung out to dry. Two shirts, much darned, stockings and half a dozen items of baby clothing dripped quietly onto the wooden floors. Harriet's walking dress had never felt so magnificent. The room was cleanly swept and neatly arranged. She did not know what fee Molloy had promised to give the inhabitants for use of the place, but she knew he was proud of his reputation as a hard bargainer. Pulling a guinea from her purse, she hid it under a battered pint pot that sat next to her elbow. She tried to do it without Molloy noticing, but suspected she failed. The day of inactivity had weighed heavily on her.

'Their names are Bounder and Creech, Mrs W.,' he said.

'How did you find them, Molloy?'

The old man was wrapped in his usual dark cloak and hunched over his pipe with his back to the wall. 'Once I got the names from Mother Brown, it was that boy Guadeloupe. He's only been in the country five minutes, but he's found his way round most of the rat-holes of London.' He sounded impressed.

'You like him?' Harriet said, faintly amused by the idea of Molloy liking anyone very much.

'He knows how to shut up and listen. People think he's simple or can't talk English, him not being much of a conversationalist. He circled in on these two here while I slept, then sent me word he was close.'

'He did not want to be here when we confronted them?' she asked.

'No. He wanted his coin, which was well earned, and then the leisure to spend it. Then I came here and picked up a rock, saw them foundering below it and sent you my little note.'

Crowther smiled. 'You are sure they have not been warned we are here?'

Molloy went so far as to look up at Crowther from under the brim of his black hat. 'You think anyone here would carry a tale I don't want telling? Sorry indeed I'd be if my charm and kindness were so abused.'

'You have our thanks. I think you are grown too rich to want any more of our gold.'

Molloy grinned and even in the semi-darkness Crowther could see the deep lines in his face rearranging themselves. 'I'll take it, Mr Crowther, don't you worry about that. What do you reckon they'll do on seeing you?'

'They set on a man like Trimnell and then myself in the dark. One holds while the other punches. I think that they'll run away,' Crowther said after a pause.

Molloy gave a low and smoke-cracked laugh. 'Their room's off the yard and only one door to it. I'll take your words into consideration.' He removed his pipe and spat on the ground.

'What is your opinion on slavery, Molloy?' Harriet asked, after staring into the darkness a few minutes more.

He looked at her sideways. 'Who says I have one, Mrs?'

Harriet realised she had amused him. 'Everyone must.'

'Oh, must they? Law is it now?' He got his pipe glowing again and sent a great cloud into the air. 'Wouldn't want to be one of those darkies in their hands. Might go so far as to lend a fellow my knife if he wants to fight his way out. What's your opinion on kiddies selling themselves for pennies? On men trying to feed their little ones on grass? Misery enough on these shores to occupy most.'

Harriet was silent for a moment. 'We have built some almshouses in Hartswood,' she said at last and Molloy laughed again. He laughed like old buildings would laugh.

Then: 'Hold hard, gentry. I think our birds are come home. Bounder and Creech, it is.' They looked out of the window where two shadows were making their way across the yard, one tall and narrow, the other rounded as a ball. 'Let 'em settle,' murmured Molloy, 'then we shall pay those gentlemen a visit.'

Crowther and Harriet followed Molloy downstairs and into the shadows. It was a narrow yard, containing a rubbish pile and necessary house, and the stench made even the yards off Covent Garden smell like country air. Molloy pointed to a door and Crowther knocked on it, then pushed it open, revealing a bare room hardly larger than a shed. There was a fire going though, and by its light huddled the two men. The fat one was holding a pan in the coals with some grey mess in it. The thin one was watching it and him intently, like a dog watches his master cooking bacon.

They turned as the door opened, and on the instant the fat man leaped to his feet, almost spilling his pottage in his haste and tried to run, barging past Crowther's thin shadow in the doorway. He ran straight into Molloy's fist, however, and fell backwards into the room, ending up flat on his back on the dirt floor.

The other man stood up too. He was at least six feet and hardly had room to straighten. 'You've killed Bounder!' he said in a wail. The fat man on the ground groaned and the giant's face relaxed into a smile. 'Ah, no, you didn't.' Reassured on that point, he crouched back down again and tenderly lifted the pot off the fire. 'Bounder?' he said. 'I think it's done now.'

The fat man slowly pulled himself up on his elbows. 'Then eat it.' He looked steadily from Crowther to Molloy. Then, rubbing his jaw, he snapped at Harriet: 'What?'

It was Molloy, rubbing his knuckles, who replied. 'You pawned Trimnell's coat and shoes to an old acquaintance of mine.'

Harriet was frowning. 'Bounder . . . Sanden mentioned you. You are a waiter at the Jamaica Coffee House – you threw Trimnell out of there when he tried to preach Abolition.'

Bounder's heavy face assumed an expression of studied blankness. 'I was and I did. What of it? I know nothing of anyone's coat.' He said it with all the huffing dignity available to a man laid out on a dirty floor with a bruise blossoming on his jaw.

Crowther crouched down, resting his weight on his silver-headed cane and looked him in the eye. 'Now then, Bounder, you're stupid, but you are not as stupid as that. You didn't mean to kill Trimnell. He was a sick man. You assaulted him, and you may be fined some shillings for it. If you tell the truth, then so shall I, and explain that to the court.'

'It would be a different matter if it came out that you had taken his coat with you and pawned it, however,' Harriet said, her clear voice like a bell in the squalor. 'That would be Highway Robbery with Violence – and for that you would hang.'

Bounder began to look distinctly upset.

Creech had settled himself on a low stool by the fire; his long legs were bent almost double. He was eating whatever was in the pot with a wooden spoon and apparent relish. He spoke with his mouth full and his lips smacking. 'He just fell down. Thought he'd fainted but he was that floppy when I put the ropes on him. "Bounder," I said, "this bloke's only gone and died."'

Crowther stayed gazing at Bounder. The fat man sighed deeply and lay back down on the floor. 'Creech . . .' he said wearily.

'What? They know it all already. And I don't want my neck stretched.'

'Who paid you?' Crowther said.

Bounder sighed again. 'No one, in the end.'

'We *did* run off, Bounder,' Creech said gently. 'Trimnell bloke was supposed get a whipping. When he died that meant trouble and no money for us.' He pointed his spoon at Crowther. 'We got paid when we gave that man there a beating and did it right. Mr Sawbridge was fair then.'

Creech pouted a little. 'My nose still hurts, you know.'

The father, then, not the lover. Crowther stood up. It took an effort not to kick Bounder where he lay and pay him back for the vicious blows received. He glanced at Creech as he bent over the fire and was glad to see the bruising round his eyes and the swelling on his long nose. The fat man made no attempt to move from the ground.

'Tell us exactly what happened, Bounder,' Harriet said.

The man crossed his ankles and folded his hands together on his chest. 'Sawbridge came to see me Friday morning. Asked if I had a friend would help me deliver a lesson to a dog that deserved it and was shaming his daughter. I thought he meant young Jennings for a moment, but it seems it was Mr Trimnell, his own son-in-law, he had in mind so I said yes and went and found Creech. Sawbridge was the colour of raw meat, that angry he was.'

'I like meat,' Creech said, staring sadly into his pot.

Bounder went on as if he had not heard.

'The staking out and the whipping was Sawbridge's plan. He gathered the necessary gear and gave it to us with a word on where to wait for him. He promised to give us a whole guinea because of the elaboration.'

'We never got the guinea.' Creech's voice was almost tearful. 'And I hurt my hand.'

He held it up and Harriet saw the pink slice of the infected wound across his fingers. The idea that it was Creech's blood she had smeared on her skin from the mask was repulsive.

'He brought you the mask too?'

'He did,' Bounder said quickly while Creech poked at his wound.

Crowther pulled the last details from them. Bounder had silenced Trimnell with the blows to the belly, while Creech held him then fitted the mask. The darkness in the room seemed to thicken when Bounder told them that Trimnell had been forced to climb over the churchyard railings himself, the mask already on. Harriet wondered what he had been thinking: whether he had expected to survive; whether he had seen his suffering as an offering to God with the great white Cathedral looking down on them? The whip they had kept and sold to a cab driver the following day. Bounder admitted that he had struck the blow while Trimnell was still standing.

'My blood was up,' he explained with a shrug. 'I almost caught Creech here with the tail of it as he was still fitting the loops of rope to the rat's wrists. My apologies for that, Mr Creech.'

'Apology accepted, Mr Bounder.'

'Rat?' Harriet repeated, a slight break in her voice. 'Why do you call him a rat?'

Bounder sniffed and raised his eyebrows. 'I heard him at the Jamaica, didn't I? We may be down on our luck at the moment, but we are Englishmen enough to see he needed a lesson. Then he falls to the ground, and we starts the pegging out.'

'But Mr Trimnell is loose,' Creech added helpfully.

'So he is. I try and shake him, but he flops right back down. At which point I thought it wise to absent ourselves.'

'So we absented,' Creech said. 'And didn't get our guinea. Bounder, is there no more to eat?'

'No,' Bounder said, and Creech began to pick his teeth but protested no further.

'Molloy, can you keep them here till morning?' Crowther said. 'We will collect them on the way to the Magistrate.'

Bounder looked suspicious. 'We ain't done with the talking yet?'

'No,' Crowther replied, looking down on him with distaste. 'You'll have to swear to what you've just said in front of the authorities. Remember to stay friendly with me, Bounder. What I say in court will save you or hang you.'

'For you I'll keep an eye on them,' Molloy said. 'Though I doubt they've wit or will to run.'

'Thank you, Molloy, and good evening.'

The two men touched their hats to each other and Crowther offered Harriet his arm. Bounder still made no move to shift from where Molloy's punch had landed him, while Creech hopefully licked the spoon one last time.

VI.6

WHEN EUSTACHE ARRIVED HOME he went straight to the rooms set aside for the children on the upper storeys of the house, into his own chamber, and let himself cry. He had not realised that he loved Graves until Dr Fischer had threatened him. The nursemaid knocked on the door and told him supper was ready in the nursery, then she went back to the servants hall and reported to her fellows there that a few days' proper work had left Master Eustache exhausted.

Upstairs, Jonathan and Stephen and Susan bickered happily among themselves as they ate, and as usual Eustache paid them no attention, other than looking up from time to time and hating them. Stephen, with his hero father and his exciting mother who obviously loved him more than such an ordinary noisy boy deserved. Susan, always so pleased with herself for being the eldest and complaining about their wealth. And Jonathan. Biddable and kind, always happy to give you whatever he had, if you said you wanted it. Everyone thought he was wonderful.

Eustache had very little appetite. He sat as long as he could, then when Jonathan was laughing so hard at something Stephen had said it looked as if he would fall from his place, Eustache could bear it no longer. He pushed back his chair and slammed his way back to his own room and sat on his bed, his knees drawn up to his chest. The manuscript lay in front of him, and already it seemed as if it was on fire. He felt a misery deeper than any he had ever known. All those names. All those lives stolen, then destroyed: all details carefully noted and dated in neat cramped hand-writing, and he was going to give it to Fischer to burn. He knew he could do nothing else because he did not want Graves to hate him. He had felt alone his entire life, but he knew there was worse in front of him – and in front of the others – if he did not do what the man ordered. Eustache traced his hands over the writing on the page in front of him. It was wrong. They would take it away and burn it, and all those names would be lost. People like that fraud Fischer whom everyone liked so very much would carry on lying. It was wrong that all those people had died and no one would remember them, or ask after them. The pages under his hand were the one thread of words which stated they had existed and suffered in the world. It mattered. He thought about what Mr Glass had said about making decisions.

Eustache went into the nursery and without looking at the others opened the bureau drawer and pulled out a stack of paper. Then he picked up the ink-well and pen, and stormed back into his own room. There, he laid the paper and manuscript out on the floor and began to write.

A few minutes later there was a knock at the door, and without waiting for him to answer, Susan came in. She had a slice of lemon cake on a plate with her.

'Here, Eustache. Mrs Martin's been baking – you missed cake.'

He looked up, surprised. It was usually Jonathan who brought him things when he was in a foul temper. Susan was normally too busy making the servants laugh or playing the harpsichord and being told by everyone how clever she was. Her expression changed and he realised he had been crying again and rubbed at his face with his sleeve.

'What's the matter?' she asked. 'Is it as horrid as that, working in Hinckley's?'

He shook his head and took the cake from her.

'What is it then?' She seemed so comfortable, settling on the floor beside him and kicking off her shoes, even though she got into trouble for ruining them like that. 'Do tell, Eustache. What are you doing anyway?' She picked up one of the sheets and he snatched it away from her. 'Are you writing a book? Can I be in it?'

'I am not writing a book. Just go away, Susan.' He was only halfway down the first page. Should he copy it all out? Or just pick the worst parts? He was surprised by how hurt she looked, and surprised again when she didn't leave but just took a deep breath and stayed where she was.

'I might be able to help. I'm good at stories, everyone says so. My mother used to make up stories for us before we went to sleep. That's what Graves says anyway, I was too young to remember.'

'You're always talking about your mother!' Eustache said, suddenly enraged. 'I hate your mother! Everyone is always saying how good she was and how kind; even when you get scolded, everyone always says, "Susan, be more like your mother". No one ever says that to me, but I can see them thinking. I can see them wondering if I'm going to be a murderer like her. No one tells me stories about *my* mother. You all want rid of me. And now I have to give this away to be burned and they are all murderers too, much worse than my mother was, and everyone here will still hate me anyway, even though I helped.'

'I brought you cake,' Susan said reasonably after a long pause. Then after a minute longer she gave Eustache her handkerchief. 'Can you remember your mother?'

'What, you mean before she ordered your father to be killed?' It didn't work, Susan just nodded and waited. Eustache blew his nose and said sulkily, 'I think she was very beautiful. I sort of remember that. And I saw a picture of her in that book I stole. It has the story too, of how evil she was.'

Susan put her chin on her knee. 'You should ask Harriet about her. She knew her. And you have us now, Eustache. We don't hate you, you know. I don't think it's your fault I have to pretend to be an idiot and sew all the time. It's not Graves's fault, really either, I suppose.' Eustache did not look at her, but he did not say anything cutting to her either. 'Now eat the cake, and tell me what has happened.'

He sat up and crossed his legs, then began very slowly. 'Mr Glass at the shop said I could read the manuscripts in his office, and I found this one near the top of one of the piles . . .'

After listening to him for a minute, Susan got up and went to fetch Jonathan and Stephen and more cake. She sat them down, threatening terrible punishment if they interrupted, and made Eustache start all over from the beginning again.

It was agreed that the manuscript would have to be given to Dr Fischer in the morning. The idea of making Graves hate them ran like ice through each of them. Stephen had some more suggestions as to how they could take revenge on Fischer, but Susan supported Eustache's plan without hesitation. The important thing was to save the names that were written in the manuscript. Save the stories.

'But then what will you do with them, Eustache?' Jonathan asked.

'I don't know. But it is important. If we don't do this then they'll just disappear, and it feels wrong. It feels wrong in my stomach, and if you can't see that, then you're just being stupid.' Susan kicked him. He thought about kicking her back, but caught the look in her eye and changed his mind. 'Will you help me?'

Jonathan glanced at Stephen, who was lying on the hearthrug pushing the pile back and forward. 'It's like a special secret mission,' he said with considerable emphasis.

Jonathan nodded and pushed his hands into his pockets. 'When I'm twenty-five, Graves won't need to look after us any more. Then we can get it printed and you can tell everyone about it.' Eustache looked away comforted and hopeful for the first time. 'But first we're going to need lots of paper.'

VI.7

A T ONE POINT IN the night, Francis thought that Penny had woken. He put down his book and carried his lamp over to her so the light fell on her face, but her eyes remained closed. She was murmuring to herself in her sleep though – half-words and phrases he could not quite hear. He crouched beside her, thinking that if he waited he would make sense of it and the knowledge he wanted would shake itself free in the darkness. After a few minutes he realised he could understand the words, but they were not what he wished to know. Penny was dreaming of her life before she was taken in by Eliza. Obscenities slipped out from between her pale pink lips, negotiations and curses. They seemed to fall from her mouth and crawl into the dark corners of the room, laughing at him, toads in the shadows.

Harriet came back from the city feeling dirty to her bones. William told her that Graves would like a moment with her before she retired, and so she went to find him, in his office as usual. He asked after her progress, and when she was a little vague about when she had last eaten, he rang the bell to let the cook know that an opportunity for feeding Mrs Westerman was at hand.

'What will be the charge against Sawbridge?' he asked.

'I do not know,' she said. 'Conspiracy, I would imagine. Murder for Bounder and Creech, but that will become manslaughter on Crowther's evidence and they'll be given a fine. Crowther has gone back to his own house. He claims he has had enough of our fussing.'

As soon as the food was brought to her, she realised how hungry she was. There was a ragout of veal, rich and heavy, with white fritters. Then she thought of Creech bent over his pot and her appetite slackened. She pushed the plate away after a little while and Graves rang the bell. When they were alone again he asked her if she had spoken to Susan that day.

Harriet shook her head and Graves frowned. 'This evening after they had had their supper in the nursery, she came down and offered me a complete apology for her behaviour at Miss Eliot's, and thanked me, on her behalf and on Jonathan's, for all I have done for them since their father was killed.'

'Good Lord!' Harriet exclaimed. 'You thought it was due to my influence?'

He laughed. 'I admit I did not know what to think.'

'I had said nothing, Graves. Not since I made such a mess of things on Sunday.'

He looked down at the papers on his desk, but without seeing them. 'I believe you, Harriet. She also asked me if I loved Eustache.'

'And do you?'

He swallowed. 'I said I did, but I do not know, Harriet. I see their parents in Susan and Jonathan, and love them for it. When I see Eustache, I think of his parents too, and it makes me afraid of him. That is not fair and it is not kind.' He ran his hands through his hair. 'It is appalling of Susan to offer me her thanks, then make me feel like an inhuman monster in the next moment – but I do wonder what sort of man Eustache will become.'

Harriet considered carefully. 'To some degree we each have a choice.'

'Susan asked me if there is a portrait of Eustache's mother at Thornleigh Hall. I had to tell her there is not: the one painted by Gainsborough when she married was destroyed in the fire.'

Harriet was thinking of Tobias Christopher and his family, of Molloy, of Crowther and their various histories. 'I can speak to Eustache about his mother, Graves. I was frightened of her, you know, long before I found out quite what she was capable of, but she was a clever woman. These things should be spoken of; we avoid them because they make us uncomfortable,' the image of the mouthless mask was before her, 'but we pay a great price for avoiding the truth in the end.'

He still looked concerned, but nodded. 'Susan's reformation, however, remains a mystery.'

'I'm afraid it does. Have the children gone to bed?'

He smiled. 'Long ago, Harriet, and like lambs – and you should do the same.'

She stifled a yawn. 'I must first write to Mr Palmer and Mr Christopher and tell them what we are about. Crowther suggests Mr Christopher accompanies myself and Bounder and Creech to the magistrates, while he keeps a watch on Mr Sawbridge until I receive a warrant for his arrest. Then let justice and the newspapers make of it what they will. I shall be free again.'

PART VII

VII.1

Friday, 13 May 1785

MOLLOY HANDED OVER HIS charges to them a little after seven o'clock in the morning. If Bounder and Creech had thought of making a run for their liberty, the seriousness of Mr Christopher's presence was enough to make them think again. They got into the carriage like lambs and Molloy tipped his hat to them before making his way off into the crooked streets of the capital.

The Quaker magistrate who was taking his turn that morning peered at them meaningfully over his glasses when they arrived. The hall was still being swept and the clerk was only just unpacking his inkwell. Once he had their names and they had stated their business, he sighed.

'Very well. I had hopes that this business would pass me by, probably for the same reasons that you have come and sought me out at this terrible hour.' The high doors opened and shut behind them – a constable with a pair of young women looking frowsty and bad-tempered after spending half the night in the watch-house.

He explained to Bounder and Creech, with great patience, what indulgence their cooperation might secure, and then with his clerk making careful notes beside him, he coaxed an account out of them of Mr Sawbridge and the taking of Mr Trimnell.

'I suppose we require a warrant for Mr Sawbridge's arrest.'

'Yes, sir,' said Harriet meekly.

He looked heavenwards. 'No need to play the wide-eyed innocent with me, Mrs Westerman. I am glad to meet you, though I am sure my fellow Aldermen will find a way to blame all of this farrago on me. I am grateful the black called Guadeloupe is gone from our custody already, rather than obliging me to release him and issue a warrant for a planter at the same moment.' There was an interesting mix of regret and satisfaction in his voice. 'Why we style women the gentler sex, I do not know.'

Creech had been following proceedings with a lively interest, though Harriet could not say how much he understood. This last made him beam more widely than Harriet thought his narrow face could have accommodated. 'Sawbridge would never have thought of staking him out without her.'

VII.2

CROWTHER ARRIVED AT THE Jamaica Coffee House a little before eight in the morning. The shutters were down and the door bolted. He dismissed the chair that had brought him and made himself comfortable leaning against a wall on the opposite side of the alley. He had only turned a few pages of his book, however, when the door sprang open and a girl in a maid's uniform staggered out and vomited into the gutter.

Crowther closed his book. Within less than a minute, Mr Sanden too stumbled into the street, only half-dressed. 'Murder,' he croaked. 'Murder!' He made a dash in the direction of Cornhill without seeing Crowther. He put his book away, crossed the alley and went in through the open door.

It appeared that the maid had found Sawbridge as she came to bring him his hot water. His rooms were on the first floor, and the door to his parlour was still ajar. Crowther stepped over the fallen water kettle, pushing the door wide with the head of his cane. Blood. A great spraying arc of it across the wall facing him as he entered the room. There was a high-backed armchair in front of the grate with its back to him. A man's arms were visible, hanging down either side. To the right-hand side, as if half-flung, half-fallen, was a razor, open and bloody. Crowther walked across the bare boards, and, keeping clear of the blood, looked at the man in the chair.

The head hung down and the front of the body's waistcoat was solid with blood. He lifted the head slightly. It was Sawbridge, certainly, and his carotid artery had been cut through. The blow had been fierce enough to slit his windpipe. Crowther tried to think if there was any way that Sawbridge could have known the authorities were coming for him, but could not imagine one.

He straightened his back and examined the spray of blood across the wall. He could still hear the maid crying downstairs, but the room itself seemed very quiet.

Creech seemed at first unsure why everyone was staring at him.

'Who is "her"?' Harriet asked carefully.

Creech looked instead at Bounder, his eyes wide with appeal. Bounder smoothed his lank black hair over his ears with the palm of his hand. 'Ah, well. Indeed. There was a lady present, but it seemed unnecessary to involve her. I had a wife once. I had a mother. I thought if we told you what you already knew about Sawbridge, then, out of respect for the fairer sex, we might stay quiet about the lady as she hadn't come up in conversation in the normal way of things. Only Mr Creech does get carried away.'

Creech sucked in his thin cheeks. His head looked like a blunt hatchet. 'I do, Mr Bounder. I do.'

'Respect?' Christopher said. 'You thought to blackmail the woman.'

Bounder coughed. 'That is a terrible accusation from a fellow unaware of the finer feelings of a white man.' Mr Christopher took a half-step forward and Bounder flinched away, almost tripping over Creech. 'Just my little joke, sir! A poor one, no doubt, but no offence meant.'

'Who was she?' Harriet interrupted.

'No idea,' Bounder said. 'Haven't had sight of her since. Thought we might scout about for her after the testifying was done.'

'Or might see her at the trial. Then we could go and have a talk with her,' Creech added, pleased to be helpful again.

Bounder lifted his hand. 'Purely to put the lady's mind at rest, naturally.'

'A description please, gentlemen,' Harriet said sharply. She glanced at the magistrate, suddenly conscious that she was usurping his role as questioner. He did not seem to mind, but sat back in his chair and winked at her. 'Was she old or young?'

When Francis awoke, the room was already light. It took him some moments to remember where he was. Dauda was in the room, bending over Penny, and Francis started to his feet.

'Peace, Francis', said the other man. 'I have no ill intent.'

Nevertheless Francis went over to join him. Dauda was washing the girl's face, sitting beside her on the bed with a brass bowl in one hand, a soft cloth in the other.

'You have been tending to her yourself?'

'Yes. Mrs Rogers is a devoted servant, but I thought it best if, when the girl wakes, it is I who hears whatever she has to say.' He rinsed the cloth, squeezed it out again and gently wiped the girl's mouth.

'What did you intend to do with her before I came?' Francis said quietly.

'I hoped she'd die. She still may. If she lived . . . I thought I might see what bribery could do.'

'Why did he not kill her, the man who brought her here?' Francis asked. It was a question that had formed in his dreams.

Dauda examined the bandage on Penny's head and seemed content. 'You know what she was before she became a maid, this girl?' Francis nodded. 'The man who brought her here knew her in that life, and could not bring himself to throttle her while she lay helpless. He can be sentimental about women, and many men confuse lust and affection.'

Francis let this sink into his tired brain. 'And what do you intend to do now?'

Dauda smiled. 'I don't know, Francis. I *have* thought about sending a message to the man who brought her here, but that could bring nothing but blood into my house. I have decided to wait and see how events unfold.'

Francis watched as he finished washing the girl's face and set the bowl aside. 'Has a doctor seen her, Dauda?'

He shook his head. 'There would have been too many questions. But I have some skills in healing. My mother used to take care of the other slaves, and I went at her side.'

Francis was about to ask him something more when there was a frantic knocking at the front door. Dauda went onto the landing then after a few moments returned. They heard the front door open and close, then the soft step of the maid approaching.

Mrs Rogers pushed open the door and Dauda lifted his hand. 'I know who it is, dear. Take her into the garden and then you may go out for a while.' She looked suspicious and unsure. 'Hawthorn blossom, my dear. Go and gather great bunches of it. I shall have it in every room in the house.' Then, when the woman still hesitated, he added: 'Mrs Rogers, you have treated me well. Leave for a few hours for your own sake and with my thanks, please.' Mrs Rogers curtseyed and left, then Dauda went to the window at the back of the room and pushed it open. 'I would ask you to stay here, Francis.'

'What is happening, Dauda?'

'I am not exactly sure, dear heart. But I suspect I am about to be the unwilling host of another lost soul.'

He left the room and Francis went to the window he had just opened. The scents of the spring garden were carried in on a light breeze and Francis could hear the loud trillings of blackbirds claiming their property for another day. The dogs were tied up towards the rear of the garden, lolling in the spring sunshine. He pulled back the curtain a little way. There was a woman dressed in black walking swiftly up and down the small terrace. As Dauda emerged from the back of the house she turned and took his hands.

'You have to help me!' she cried. 'Please, darling, they are going to kill me. He had a knife and . . . oh Brother, our father is dead. Oh, he threatened – he said your name! But I would not! I'll do whatever they say, but don't let them take me. Oh, they won't listen, I know they will not! Is it true the girl is still alive? If she were dead, perhaps they would not desert me. There would be no witness then. I would never threaten the way Father did. Dauda, you have to save me!'

Francis could not see the expression on Dauda's face. Only it seemed to him that the young man's back stiffened. The woman in black began to sob. 'I was alone all night in London. I had to wait until I could pawn my bracelet, and the man didn't give me half what he should have done for it. You're my last hope, Dauda.'

'Lucinda, what have you done?' Dauda said at last.

VII.3

IT WAS NOT LONG before Harriet joined him. He heard her familiar step on the stairs and turned as she entered. The brightness in her eyes faded as she saw the great arc of blood. She put out her hand to steady herself on the doorframe.

'Is it Sawbridge?'

'It is. His throat is sliced through.'

She lifted her right hand. 'I have a warrant here for his arrest.'

He left the body and went to stand at her side. She leaned forward so her forehead rested against his chest and he felt her take a slow, shuddering breath. 'And another warrant for his daughter.' He stood back slightly and she looked up at him. 'She was there. Creech let it drop during the questioning. It was Mrs Trimnell who suggested the mask and whip and delivered the mask to them on the corner as she returned from the theatre. She must have sat through the performances with it under her chair. Sawbridge hired them, but the plan and performance were all hers.'

Crowther did not know what to say. It should not surprise him that a wife could be so vicious with her husband, but he realised he had accepted Mrs Trimnell as what she appeared to be: a young, selfish, unfaithful wife – and considered her no further. There was a dining chair just by the door. Harriet sat down in it. 'Why?' she cried. 'Why would Sawbridge kill himself? To protect his daughter? But even so, what good does *this* do her?'

Crowther knew he lacked the ability to comfort her, so he did what he always had done, and told her what he knew.

'He died at some point during the night – the body has not yet stiffened – from a single blow delivered with a great deal of power.'

'He was at the inquest,' Harriet said, almost to herself. 'Even if he *knew* we were coming with a warrant – and I cannot see how he could have known – he knew the charge would not be murder. He was not escaping the noose. God, I would have thought us lucky if he were even fined. Why then?'

'Harriet, I do not think he was alone when he died.'

She looked up at him. 'Tell me.'

Crowther pointed his cane towards the spray of blood. 'Look at the pattern here across the mantel.'

Her eyes focused and she frowned. 'There is a gap,' she said slowly.

'Indeed. Someone was standing directly in front of Sawbridge when his throat was cut.'

'Good God.' She was silent for a few moments, examining the blood. It was not a tragedy now, but a puzzle. 'And someone else was sitting there,' she added, pointing at an armchair to the left of the fireplace. Crowther had not noticed that before, but she was correct. There were droplets of blood on the back and arm, but there should have been others between them. 'Who commits suicide with an audience?' She shuddered. 'Though a man such as he was . . . the sort who would want to humiliate his son-in-law so cruelly, perhaps he would enjoy seeing their expressions. He loved to shock, but then? Then the audience leaves quietly and abandons him for the maid to find? No one calls out or attempts to save him?'

'If it *was* suicide.'

She looked up at Crowther. 'Who on earth would want to murder him?'

'Mrs Westerman, I cannot possibly say. All I do say is that the wound to his throat is very deep. Also, the wound curves upwards on the right-hand side. That suggests to me it was someone standing behind him who delivered the blow. It is not conclusive, but . . .'

She squeezed her eyes shut. 'Crowther, I think he was left-handed. Certainly he used his left hand to drink his tea, but I thought at the time that it meant perhaps his right was injured.'

'If we can find someone to swear he favoured his left hand in the general run of things, then I can suggest this is murder, not suicide.'

'Might a woman have done this?'

'Possible, but improbable. It would take a great deal of strength to cut so deep.'

He was waiting for her to speak again, but instead she lowered her head and folded her cloak around her as if she wanted to hide from the world entire.

'I thought standing in that hovel listening to Bounder and Creech would be the worst of it, Crowther,' she said at last.

'What can I do to be of help to you?' He took the warrant for Sawbridge's arrest out of her hand and saw the other for Mrs Trimnell. 'Is it facing Mrs Trimnell that distresses you? I shall go and root her out of Portman Square and give her the news of her father.'

'Oh Gabriel, there is no need to tell Mrs Trimnell,' she said. She nodded over towards the side table, on which lay forgotten a pair of black gloves with pearl fastenings. 'If she did not kill him herself, then she certainly watched while someone else did.' She looked up at Crowther, her green eyes slightly dulled. 'Then she did not fetch help. She did not fight whoever attacked him, or try to stop the bleeding. She just ran.'

'You don't understand, Dauda!' The voice of the woman's pleading swept up and down with the urgency and drama of a swallow's flight, reaching Francis as he watched and listened from his hiding place. 'He had become a monster! He only spoke to me to rant about God. He was humiliating me, running around London begging for forgiveness from slaves. Dear God, he wanted to *adopt* some mulatto bastard of his! And I did not mean to kill him, only give him the punishment he deserved – that he craved. I swear I was so sorry to hear of his death, I fainted away the moment I was told.'

Dauda had folded his arms across his chest while the girl still marched up and down the terrace as she spoke, her arms always in movement so she became a whirl of words and hands.

'I know you would not want another "mulatto bastard" in the family, Lucinda. Humiliating you? How many hours had you been in London before you managed to get Randolph Jennings into your bed for bangles and beads. Don't think I was not told. *I* have only ever been a whore out of necessity. With you, it was a choice.' The obscenity shocked Francis, like a blow across the face, but it did not check the woman in black.

She span round and put out her arms. Francis could see her thin white wrists, her long fingers. 'I loved Randolph, always! I believed he loved me. I was destroyed when he said he would not marry me.'

'You love yourself and money in that order, Lucinda. You have always believed yourself better than you are, and Father encouraged you in that. It cost him his life.'

'Brother, I was good to you,' the woman whined.

Dauda stared at her. 'Good to me? Do you remember the day I was sold, *Sister*? Do you remember how I ran to you and begged for your help? How I hid in your room and sobbed and asked you to hide me? You called for him. Our father. Do you think I'll ever forget the look of satisfaction on your face when they tied my hands and carried me out of the house?'

She was breathing hard, her hands held together in front of her now, concentrating. 'I was jealous, Dauda. Father loved your mother more than mine. She was not even buried when Father moved your mother out of the slave huts and into our home.' She dropped to her knees. The black silk of her dress spread out around her on the pale polished marble of the terrace. 'We are still brother and sister. And I did not know about the manuscript he wrote describing all his "sins" until he was already dead. Dr Fischer told us about it. Please, Dauda, I am begging you for my life.'

Francis heard the name Fischer and his mind went white. The man who had paid over the odds for all the paper in Eliza's shop – it was the sneering verger who had directed him from St Mary Woolnoth to Fischer's home.

It could not be long now before Mr Sanden returned with a constable. Harriet had got to her feet and gone into Sawbridge's bedchamber. Crowther let her go without comment, unsure if she wanted to look through the dead man's possessions, or wished only for privacy. Until she returned or summoned him, he gave his attention again to the patterns of blood on the wall and floor. Whoever was seated in the chair could have easily left the room without smearing the blood. The person who was standing in front of Trimnell would certainly have disturbed the traces if he had not moved from that position with great care. Whoever it was, had nerve. To remain still in such circumstances and wait suggested a great deal of control.

So Sawbridge, his daughter and two other men had been in the room. One standing in front of the fireplace, and one standing behind the murdered man, poised to cut his throat. Sawbridge cannot have feared them. He was seated, defenceless and unsuspecting, while his guests were standing. He had obviously made some miscalculation about who held the balance of power in the room.

Crowther's first thought was of Randolph Jennings. But why would he want Sawbridge dead? Was Sawbridge pushing him to protect Mrs Trimnell if the scandal of her husband's death became public? He thought over the motives for murder he had ever seen or heard discussed. Madness? Certainly there was a little madness in every killing, a failure of reason. Money or power? Sawbridge was a moderately successful man in moderate circumstances, judging by the room and its furnishings, so it was unlikely he had enough of either to serve as a motive. Knowledge? What better way to silence a man than cut his throat? He thought of the mouthless mask again. There was another act of silencing.

'The razor is part of a matching set.' He heard Harriet's voice and turned to see her in the doorway. 'Whoever did this was calm and clever after the fact. They killed him, fetched the razor and dropped it where it would have fallen, had he done the deed himself.'

'Yes,' he said. 'Which causes me to believe they had good reason to kill Sawbridge.'

She nodded. 'He must have known something that would bring great shame on them – but why would Sawbridge overplay his hand so badly? Suppose the truth of Mr Trimnell's death had been made public. There would have been a scandal, but also sympathy for the widow of a mad man in some quarters. She and Sawbridge would have been able to expect some quiet assistance. If he and his daughter had been accused of murdering someone by their own hands on *these* shores, then of course even the West Indian community would have cast them off. They might try to blackmail the wrong person for protection or help in escaping the country . . .' The expression on her face changed. 'Crowther, I think we may have been investigating the wrong killing.'

'Mrs Westerman?'

She left her post in the doorway, reached into her reticule and produced the handbill for Willoughby's prayer meetings, then lifted it close to her face so she could read the fine print at the bottom of the page. She then passed it to Crowther to read. At the bottom of the page where the copperplate had sunk into the paper, he read *Engraved by Mrs Eliza Smith, Paternoster Row.* At once he was back in the chill stables again, bending over her fire-blackened corpse in the candlelight.

'I remember that Willoughby said that Trimnell arranged and paid for the printing,' he said slowly. 'So they knew each other. A strange coincidence, but why would that lead to the murder of Mrs Smith?'

'She was a bookseller, Crowther. And Martha said that Trimnell spent his time while he was wearing that mask, writing. Remember, no one would listen to him. He was crazed with the wish to confess his sins, but no one listened! They threw him out of the coffee house, Mr Christopher could not stand to hear him repeat his crimes, and even Willoughby had not the strength to listen!'

'He wrote out the confession,' Crowther said at last. 'And gave it to the bookseller and engraver whom he had met, in hopes of a wider audience. But how would anyone but Trimnell and Mrs Smith know that?'

Harriet's eyes were glowing again as she followed the thought down. 'I saw her, Crowther! I saw her speak to Dr Fischer on the morning she was killed. Fischer was a trader. He'd known Trimnell for years. What if *his* sins were in there alongside Trimnell's? Oh, do remember! Sir Charles said Fischer and Trimnell had known each other well in their youth. And Mrs Smith liked Dr Fischer, just as Mrs Service does. Tell me, if someone gave you a manuscript, claiming that I was guilty of all manner of monstrous crimes, you would tell me of it, would you not?'

He smiled. 'Not before I had burned it and beaten the man who gave it to me in the street, but I understand you. So you think Mrs Smith told Dr Fischer and he alerted his friends to the existence of the manuscript?'

'Yes, and who better to go and ask for its return than the grieving widow and her father? What reasonable person would refuse to give it back to her?'

'A woman of strong convictions.'

Harriet groaned. 'The bruises on her wrists. The stiffness of her movements when I saw her on Monday. I thought that her father or lover had beaten her, and thought all the viciousness theirs. What if Mrs Trimnell received those bruises fighting with Mrs Smith and then killed her?'

'It was her fault, not mine!'

Francis heard the words and felt the strength leave his body. The woman in black was still on her knees.

'I came, I came as a widow, as one woman to another, to beg that she give me back his manuscript. I thought if I could bring it back, put it in Randolph's hands, he would see that I loved him, and his father. They would welcome me. But she would not give it to me! She wanted to *pray* with me! Then I saw my husband's writing on a sheet on the desk, but the manuscript was not there.'

Dauda had covered his eyes as if the sight of his half-sister on her knees was no longer to be borne.

'She began it – she tried to pull me away as I was looking, but I needed it, Dauda – I *needed* it – but she would not be still and let me look. I swear to you I did not mean to kill her. The first I knew of it, she was dead at my feet. I did not even know I had picked up the tool until I saw it in her eye.'

VII.4

CROWTHER WAS TRYING TO recall the name of the young man who had found the engraving tool. 'He is a bookseller, as I remember, near St Paul's. Francis Glass.'

'We must go to him, but I want to find Mrs Trimnell first, Crowther. Either she is hand in hand with whoever killed her father, or she is in danger from them. I will see what news they might have of her at Portman Square. Will you wait for the coroner here? Then I will come and search you out at the bookshop.'

They heard a step on the stairs and Mr Christopher appeared in the doorway. He paused for a moment, taking in the sight. 'I can get no sense from the maid. The door to these rooms opens from the same lobby as the door to the coffee house itself. Half of London was in and out last night.'

Harriet turned to him. 'We must find Mrs Trimnell – she was here when it happened. Crowther will wait for the coroner here and then join us . . .'

'At Hinckley's Bookshop,' Crowther supplied.

'So her lodgings, or Portman Square,' Christopher said. 'I shall try her lodgings then, while you take the carriage to Portman Square, Mrs Westerman. I shall join you at Hinckley's.' He touched his hat to them and was gone.

'They must have destroyed the manuscript,' Harriet said as she put up her hood. 'I wonder what horrors were in it?'

'Enough to ruin a fashionable preacher, I imagine.' Crowther sighed. 'Go then, and good luck to you. I shall wait for the proper officials and put matters into their hands. If they will be willing to hear the suggestion that this is murder and not suicide though, I cannot say.'

Eustache was led into Dr Fischer's study by a friendly-looking maid who winked at him before announcing his title with great ceremony. He had walked from Ivy Lane as quickly as he could and his hands were sweating where they held the leather portfolio. There was a fire already burning in the grate in spite of the warmth of the day.

Fischer turned in his chair, but did not get up. 'Thank you, Mary. No, we require no refreshment.' He smiled at her with great warmth until she had closed the door again. Then his face became a blank. 'Give it to me.'

Eustache handed over the portfolio and watched as the man undid the straps with his long fingers and began to look through the pages. Apparently content there was no trick, he stood, dragged his chair to the fire and began to feed the pages into the flames one by one, checking as he did so that each page followed on from the last. Eustache watched him and a tight white rage began to build again in his bones.

'You have read these pages, Master Eustache,' Fischer said, 'and I am sure you feel for the slaves mentioned in them, but you cannot understand the complexity of the trade from this nonsense. There are occasional abuses, deeply regrettable, but they are the exception, not the rule. You must trust those of us with direct experience. The slaves are happy! Often fond of their masters and deeply grateful to have been saved from the savagery of their native lands.' Eustache made no reply, and when Fischer looked up at him and saw the fierce concentration on the boy's pale face, he spoke on very calmly. 'The country needs the slave trade. Requires it absolutely. You will forget what you have read in time, and I am sure when you are grown into a man you will thank me for doing this. The incident that led to young Jennings being sent home to England, for instance. He did not know his own strength and the wife of the slave in question had been deeply disrespectful. It is wrong that the son of so great a family should be ruined by a youthful indiscretion.'

'I will *not* forget,' Eustache said. 'I will not forget because I aim to be a good man – and no good man could forget this once he has read it.'

Fischer snorted.' A good man? With your parentage? A bold ambition indeed. When did you decide this?'

'Last night.'

Fischer laughed again, more comfortable now the flames were being fed and no pages were missing. 'How charming.'

'Titus,' Eustache said.

'What?'

'Titus is the name of the slave Randolph Jennings beat to death because he would not whip his wife as ordered. You told everyone he had died of a fever.'

'Was it? Well, Randolph Jennings, his prospects and career were more important than the truth. Even a child might see that. In any case, Titus is dead now. No more harm can come to him.'

'Punch and Quacoo.'

'What do you say, boy?' Fischer was sweating a little from leaning so close to the fire. Eustache pictured him in Hell already and felt the satisfaction of it in his bones.

'Punch and Quacoo. It was after you and Mr Trimnell had dined together and discussed the best treatments to put on a slave's skin after a whipping. When Punch and Quacoo were whipped, he had bird pepper, lime and salt rubbed into their wounds.' Fischer began feeding the pages into the fire a little more quickly. 'Stompe and Polly. You and Trimnell went to see them hanged. They had tried to run away.'

'Enough. Be quiet, boy.'

'Damsel. You were staying with Trimnell between voyages out to the Guinea Coast. You dressed her leg after she was bitten by a dog. She'd hidden the wound from Trimnell and he waited for you to tell her she was fit enough to be whipped and put in the stocks for wishing to die. It was punishment for wanting to rob Trimnell of his property.'

Fischer shoved the last pages into the flames as if touching them might poison him. 'I told you to be quiet, boy, or I shall make you shut your mouth.'

'Phoebe! When she died, you told Trimnell he had "worn her through". She kept trying to run but they kept finding her and bringing her back – and he'd rape her again and again – and you knew that – and *you* tell us to pray! You stand there every Sunday and *you* dare tell *us* to pray!'

Fischer stood up, red in the face and his fists tight closed. 'I told you to be quiet.'

Eustache was lost in the delicious passion of his own rage. He stood firm where he was and shouted it, shouted it so he thought the panes in the windows might break. 'Titus! Punch! Quacoo! Stompe! Polly! Damsel! Phoebe!' The fear and rage on Fischer's face made him drunk. 'Titus! Punch! Quacoo! Stompe! Polly! Damsel! Phoebe!' He did not stop even as Fischer drew back his arm. 'Titus! Punch! Quacoo! Stompe! Polly! Damsel! Phoebe!' The blow came across the side of his head, knocked him across the floor.

VII.5

MRS SERVICE WAS A stronger supporter of Harriet's against charges of unnatural or unwomanly behaviour than perhaps Harriet had ever realised. She felt Harriet did what was necessary, but she still was worried and upset by the effect these alarms seemed to have on the children. They were all listless and red about the eyes but full of a sort of nervous energy that made her extremely suspicious. Only little Anne went about her morning as usual, drawing a great many pictures of cats and seeing how much of the house she could cover with strawberry jam. Despite all of the hopeful signs the previous evening, Susan was rude to her maid and would not settle to her sewing, but neither would she play the harpsichord or work on her music. She jumped every time the door to the street opened, and every other minute ran upstairs on some unlikely errand. The gentleman who came to teach the boys short sword found them so distracted and careless that he left early. Before ten Mrs Service, in desperation, suggested taking them all to one of the parks for some exercise, and they all shook their heads in unison. Susan glanced at the boys then looked up at her.

'Might we visit Eustache?' she said. 'You are always saying Jonathan and Stephen should read more. He might show us some new books we might like.' Mrs Service waited for the boys to treat this suggestion with masculine scorn. No protest came.

Jonathan thrust his hands in his pockets. 'Eustache did say they had some quite *exciting* books there.'

Mrs Service wondered if the boy was ill. 'We have already caused Mr Glass quite enough trouble. It would go against my conscience to bother him any further.'

'But Mrs Service, it's a *shop*,' Jonathan said, then noticing the looks he got from the others added, 'I only mean we wish to buy some books, so that would not be bothering him at all, would it? I mean, rather the opposite.'

She had to concede that point. 'Is this really what you wish to do this morning?'

They all assured her that it was, and so, rather warily, she rang the bell and asked Philip to order the carriage round. She sent the children off to get themselves ready and a few moments later was in the hallway herself, tying the ribbons of her cloak, when William came into the hall and bowed.

'Ma'am, I hear you are going to Hinckley's and I was wondering whether I might ride along with you, unless you particularly wish for Philip or Gregory.'

Mrs Service smoothed down her ribbons. 'You are very welcome to join us, but what is happening, William? I see no reason why those three little monkeys should not visit Eustache, but they are in such an odd humour today and I am afraid I am suspicious. If you know anything, I do hope you will tell me.'

William's hands were clasped behind his back. 'I am not sure, ma'am. Only Eustache has been in a strange mood for the last day or so, and he looked unwell this morning when I took him to Ivy Lane. I asked if he wished to come home, but he would not. I noticed the other children looked much the same when I came back. I do not know what they are about, and I hope you don't think I am speaking where I should stay silent, but I am a little concerned.'

Mrs Service considered. She had seen a great deal since she had met Mr Crowther and Mrs Westerman, and much of it had disturbed her. The children were behaving strangely and Harriet and Gabriel were chasing round the capital after slavers. 'I hear the bookshop was broken into the evening before last, William.'

'It was.'

'Mr Glass was a particular friend of Mrs Smith, was he not?'

William nodded. 'It is my understanding he has been trying to find the person or persons who killed her.'

Mrs Service sniffed. 'Perhaps you had better come along then. I assume David will have his pistols about him?'

'Yes, ma'am.'

'I think I shall have a word with Mr Graves before we leave. You may put the children into the carriage when they come down.'

The children were very surprised to find that Graves was coming with them, and not a little perturbed. Mrs Service did ask once more for some explanation of their behaviour in the carriage, but the children avoided her gaze and Stephen lifted his chin in a way that reminded her painfully of his mother. 'We just wish to visit Eustache,' he said stoutly. Susan was more nervous of her disapproval. She put her hand into Mrs Service's as they rode through the avenues of the west of the city and into the narrower and more crowded streets of the east. 'It is nothing bad,' she said, and there was an element of pleading in her voice which meant that Mrs Service could not help squeezing her hand.

The atmosphere in the shop was strange from the moment Mr Graves opened the door for her and Mrs Service entered with the children following round her skirts like goslings. At the ring of the bell the clerk's head snapped up, but as soon as he saw them, his expression became one of deep disappointment and distress. Mrs Service politely asked after Eustache, and the clerk, looking distracted, disappeared into the back of the shop, only to reappear a moment later to say Eustache wasn't there and must have stepped out to the bakehouse with Joshua, the apprentice. Mrs Service said they would wait and the children huddled into the far corner of the shop floor, pretending to look at the books but obviously in close debate.

Graves was silent and serious, watching the children. Mrs Service smiled at the clerk. 'Mr Glass is not here today? We met very briefly a few days ago at the house of the late Mrs Smith. I am Mrs Service.'

'Cutter, ma'am,' he said, glancing towards the door again and tapping his fingers on the counter top. 'I remember you from the fetching of Master Eustache and the young lady there. No, Mr Glass hasn't shown his face here this morning, and to tell you the truth, ma'am,' he leaned towards her over the desk and lowered his voice, 'we are beginning to worry ourselves a little. Mr Sharp and Constable Miller have gone to his lodgings just this minute to see if perhaps he's slept on this morning, such times we've had of it of late, and so that's my hope. He's been sleeping and is this moment buttoning up his coat. But I have a fear, a presentiment. My mother used to have them, and now I feel it too. Just here.' He stabbed at a spot in his chest just under the breastbone. 'Our shop was broken into the night before last, and we drove Mr Glass off so we could clean it up for him. We thought he'd be back yesterday evening, were *sure* he'd be here creeping in with the light this morning, but he's not here and now I have a presentiment.'

'That is uncomfortable,' Mrs Service said mildly. She was about to ask something more when a boy came tripping out of the back room and looked about him. His face showed the same pattern of hope and then dismay that Cutter's had when they first came in. 'He's not here,' he said.

Cutter looked mournful. 'Joshua, where's Master Eustache? I thought he was with you.'

The boy shook his head slowly. 'No . . . he said he had an errand and slipped out. But that was a while ago.'

Graves had run through his stock of patience, and now he turned on the children. 'Enough of this! I am happy for you to have your secrets, but Eustache is missing, as is Mr Glass, and I think it is time for you to be open with me.'

Susan took a half-step forward, but it was Jonathan who spoke first. 'It's all right, Suzy, I'll do it.' He looked steadily up at his guardian. 'Mr Glass had Eustache read the manuscripts in his office . . .'

The door to the house of the private palace of Sir Charles was opened not by one of the immaculate footmen whom Harriet had seen on her previous visit, but by Mrs Jennings herself. Harriet was astonished; Mrs Jennings apparently very disappointed.

'I thought you were the hackney carriage,' she said by way of explanation. 'I am very sorry for it, Mrs Westerman, but no one here is receiving today.'

She was beginning to close the door on her, but Harriet put her hand against it to prevent her.

'I must speak to Mrs Trimnell, and at once.'

'That trollop isn't here,' Mrs Jennings said and tried to close the door again. Harriet's patience snapped.

'Mrs Jennings, you shall let me in and we shall discuss this inside. I have just come from Mr Sawbridge's rooms where he sits dead and drenched in his own blood, and unless you will have me scream out the news to your neighbours, you will let me in.'

The old woman hesitated, then opened the door fully and made a somewhat ironic curtsey. Harriet moved past her into the hallway. The impression of luxury and taste with which the hall was designed to overawe its visitors was somewhat marred by the pair of trunks in the hall. One was open and a footman was apparently repacking it. It was surrounded by a number of clothes and some smaller cases that Harriet expected to have been stowed inside the larger ones. Mrs Jennings picked up one of these smaller cases and opened it. As far as Harriet could see from where she stood, it contained a number of trinkets, those small items of jewellery every woman collects and may be worth nothing, but from which no female could separate herself.

'Where is Mrs Trimnell?'

'In one of the Covent Garden stews, if she has finally learned her place. I found her yesterday afternoon pawing at Randolph on the settee in the Blue Salon and told her what I thought of her.'

'And then?'

'She had a short discussion with Randolph and left the house rather quickly. She did not come home yesterday evening. The air in Portman Square is purer already.' She removed a piece of lace from the box and handed it to a footman standing behind her. 'Put that back in my room, Parker, if you'd be so kind. So her father is dead? I never liked him. I was going to send her luggage to his rooms, but they may as well go to her old place on Cheapside, I suppose.'

'Mrs Jennings, it is of the greatest importance that I find her. Can you really tell me nothing that might be of use? Is Sir Charles at home?'

She clicked the box shut. 'No, Mrs Westerman, I cannot. And no, Sir Charles is not here. He is gone up to the Surrey house. I must ask you to leave now. Once I have made sure that woman has not stuffed her trunks with our silverware, I have to arrange for his luggage to be sent on.'

'Randolph Jennings perhaps?'

'He is still asleep.'

'No, I'm not.' They looked up to see him walking down the stairs. 'What? Is that Lucinda's baggage? I ordered it to be packed in her rooms.'

Mrs Jennings pursed her lips. 'Go away, Randolph, I'm out of patience with you. I would not let this luggage leave until I have checked it. Mrs Trimnell and her oafish father are not to be received here any more and you are to go up to Paradise this afternoon.'

The young man seemed remarkably unconcerned. 'I knew Father intended to cut ties with them since Tuesday. Dr Fischer dragged him out of the coffee house to tell him he should do so, but I did not think he intended you to make it into a spectacle for the servants and our visitor.'

Mrs Jennings was unabashed. 'The visitor was uninvited and unluckily timed. And I will not have that woman steal from us.'

'I think we can spare anything she can carry,' Randolph said, and with such a sharpness to his voice that Mrs Jennings started. She put down the case she was rifling through.

'Geoffrey, you may repack,' she said and left them, walking up the stairs with her back straight and not looking at Randolph as she passed him.

Once she had gone a sufficient distance, Randolph finished his elegant saunter down the stairway and put his hand out to Harriet. 'Good morning, Mrs Westerman. Tell me, is it true your footman knocked

Oxford over in the muck the other day? I heard the story in the club, but thought it too good to be true.'

'It is.'

'Capital. No wonder he is off sulking somewhere or other. Can I be of any help to you?'

'I am looking for Mrs Trimnell. Her father is dead.'

'Is he?' Jennings looked surprised. 'How so?'

'His throat was cut.'

'I had no idea he would take being exiled from our family so much to heart.' He snorted. Harriet looked at him with distaste. The gilded youth in his gaudy setting.

'There was an attachment between you and Mrs Trimnell. How can you take this news so carelessly?' she said.

He looked down on her. 'Lucinda was entertaining company, and I was kind enough to her, Mrs Westerman. But she has been behaving a little strangely since her husband died. She seemed to think she had greater claims on me than she did. Silly girl. She never really did understand her place in the world. Some women are like that.'

Harriet resisted the temptation to slap his face. 'So you have not seen her or her father since Mrs Jennings found you together yesterday afternoon.'

'No, I have not. She went running off to her father, but I think she expected me to follow her. Of course, I did not. My own father went to them to make certain they understood that connections between us were at an end.'

'Your father went to see Mr Sawbridge last night?'

Jennings nodded and stifled a yawn. 'Yes. As I said, he told me on Tuesday he'd heard rumours that father and daughter had been involved in something unpleasant. He meant to do it all very gently, but then Aunt Maria found Mrs Trimnell and me together and it all came rather to a head. Lucinda ran off to Daddy, and Drax and Pa went over there later in the evening to say we were going to have no more to do with them. I am quite sure Pa would have made a generous contribution to the family fortune; he always seemed to be giving Sawbridge money, but the man must have taken the separation hard.'

VII.6

EUSTACHE OPENED HIS EYES, and the pain in the side of his head tore into white light. He squeezed his eyes shut again until it dulled to a throb; meanwhile, a heavy nausea had seized him. He was lying on a couch in a small room, divided from another by folding panels. There were voices coming from the far side. One belonged to Fischer, but the other he did not recognise.

'If you let a child goad you in that way, Fischer, I am afraid the problem is yours. I sympathise, but there is somewhere else I simply must be.'

'But I burned the manuscript! Do you not owe me something for that? The stories that were in there about you, Drax, almost turned my stomach. Please, you must tell me what to do.'

'Fischer, you *know* what you have to do! Get rid of the boy and do it quickly and quietly. Good God, you're almost as bad as that Trimnell woman. Letting your temper run away with you and then whining to other people to clear up after you.' There was a weary anger in the man's voice. 'You could have sent the boy home and denied everything if he ever told Graves about the manuscript, but oh no. Now Graves will have you on charges of assault. So stop snivelling into your brandy and do what needs to be done – or face the fact that your flourishing career as the handsome shepherd of the city sheep is over.'

'Not everyone finds killing as easy as you do, Drax.'

There was a pause followed by a theatrical sigh. 'Very well, I shall show you.'

The panels were thrown back and a man in a plum-coloured coat with a monkey perched on his shoulder came into the room. Eustache tried to push himself upwards – shout, strike out – but he could hardly control his limbs.

'Now then, my boy.' Drax gathered him up almost carelessly, sat beside him on the couch and held him in place with his left hand while with his right he shut Eustache's mouth and clamped his nose. Eustache tried to struggle and kick, but Drax simply adjusted his hold slightly. Lights exploded behind his eyes. After a few moments Drax released him and Eustache took in a shuddering breath.

'There – you see, Fischer? Quite simple.'

Fischer was peering at them from the doorway. 'Won't you . . . ?'

'No. It's time to get *your* hands dirty, man.'

'I'll pay you?' Fischer was hopeful and pleading.

'Pay me?' Drax still had hold of Eustache's arms and the pressure on them suddenly increased. 'I have enough money, thank you, Fischer. What, do you think I am Sawbridge? And don't pretend there was anything about me in those pages that came as a revelation to you. I have heard you and Jennings both joking over your wine about how I know when to cut my losses. The ones that were too sick to be worth saving, I got rid of. You knew that.'

'There's nothing . . .' Eustache's voice was slurred.

'What, lad?' Drax grinned down at him. The monkey had its head on one side, and was listening with its master.

'In the manuscript. There's nothing about what you did. It only says you purchased the sick ones off the ship . . . tried to make them healthy and sell them on.'

'Really? Oh, that's famous! So in comparison to the rest I must seem a saint?'

Eustache managed to nod and Drax laughed out loud again before wagging a finger at Fischer. 'And you said . . . oh, what a naughty man you are.' He turned back to Eustache. 'Well, my dear. Now you know what happened with those whom I judged in the end to be too sick for my skills. Though if they fought me off I might keep them a while longer just to see.' He smiled and the monkey stood straight and pirou‹ etted. 'Well, I certainly won't kill you *now*. Not even as a favour to an old friend. Goodbye, Fischer. I doubt we will be seeing each other for a while. I feel a sudden urge to travel.'

Eustache watched him go then looked at Fischer, trying to think. Fischer still looked nervous. He could be kicked, bitten. Fischer turned away and filled his brandy glass, his hands trembling so hard he spilled some of it. Drax had taken Eustache by surprise. This man would not. If he could just carry on being scared and drinking his brandy for a few minutes longer, then Eustache could get his breath and perhaps the sick pain in his head might lessen a little. He was not afraid though. His anger came back to him like a friend. Even as he was gathering it to himself, trying to force it through his body to make do until his own strength might return, Fischer downed his drink in great shaking gulps then strode over to the door and turned the key.

As soon as the name of Fischer was out of Jonathan's mouth, Graves began to run. He was not even aware that William Geddings was following close behind him. He bellowed at the crowds in front of him and even the chairmen understood it was better not to block his path. He cut through the mass of people, leaving them confused and staring in his wake. William ran hard behind him, the old ache in his leg flaring with each step, but not slowing for it, and the great white Cathedral with its apostles and worthies lined along its pediments looked down on them in weary compassion as their shouts bounced off its white flanks.

As Fischer began to lower himself onto the sofa, Eustache lashed out, aiming his fingers at Fischer's eyes. The Reverend swung away and

Eustache sprang down and scrambled for the door, falling onto his knees from weakness. He heard Fischer grunt but did not look back, crawling towards the door in a crouch, his vision blurred. The sickness in his head threatened to drag him under, but he could still see the door. He reached for the handle, then felt Fischer's hard grip on his ankle. He tried to kick with his other foot, but Fischer dodged it and hauled him towards him. Eustache could smell the sweat on him, the brandy on his breath. He jabbed at Fischer's eyes again, but the priest caught hold of his wrist and held him.

The front door opened and Graves burst into the hallway before the maid could speak. He heard a crash upstairs. The maid was holding onto his arm. He shoved her away and dashed up the staircase in front of him, roaring, 'Eustache!'

He heard the maid shriek and begin to shout for a constable. On the first landing he paused, faced with doors to the right and left – then there was another muffled shout. William tried the handle. Locked. The two men put their shoulders to it together.

Fischer was lying across him, panting and wheezing. He had managed to trap Eustache's arms under him. The boy tried to bite but Fischer was too strong for him; his hand forced his mouth closed and pinched his nose tight, the weight of him pressing down his head against the floor so he was unable to shake himself free. He could not fight the panic any further: it crashed over him as he tried to draw breath, found nothing.

William came falling into the room first. Through a haze Eustache saw him hook his arms round Fischer and try to drag him off; at the same moment he heard Graves calling his name in a cracked voice and felt his guardian's arms round him, pulling him back, but Fischer was full of some desperate fever. Eustache thought he must faint, his panicked heart must burst – then he saw William's fist bunch and drive with all its strength into the side of Fischer's head. The blow stunned the man and he fell back; Eustache found himself panting and choking in his guardian's arms.

'Eustache, my boy. Eustache!' He felt Graves's cheek pressed against the top of his head, his hands checking him over for wounds or hurt.

'I'm whole, Papa, I'm whole,' he gasped out, and drank in great gulps of air. Fischer was on his knees, cowering in the corner while William stood over him, his fists balled.

Graves got up, took two strides across the room and hauled Fischer to his feet.

'That is my child!' He drew back his hand and slapped Fischer hard across the face, releasing his grip on the priest's collar at the same time, so he slumped back down to the ground and began to cry. Graves stared down and said quietly, 'God help me, William, I may be about to kill a man.'

William was still breathing hard. 'I'll swear it was in defence of our lives if you do.'

Eustache did not mean to make a sound, but he must have done so, as both men turned back towards him. Graves hesitated then bent down and picked up the boy, holding him so he could rest his cheek on his guardian's chest. 'Expect the constables, Fischer. I'll see you prosecuted for the attempted murder of my boy and I will see you hang for it.'

William looked at the priest a moment longer, noticed the empty portfolio and the ashes piled deep in the grate, then spat on the floor just in front of where the man crouched and cowered. Eustache saw it and rejoiced. Graves walked out first, Eustache still in his arms, his hands around Graves's neck, and William followed. They went down the stairs past the hysterical maid. A verger, his expression confused and angry, prepared to block their way. William moved forward slightly and, slow and controlled, simply swept the man aside so Graves could pass. They did not even notice the crates and boxes torn open and spilling papers into the hall, the strange tang of smoke that rose from them. The Thornleigh coach was already in sight, with David yelling and cursing at every other vehicle in the road until he could get close enough to them.

'The boy?' he said, his face white.

Eustache looked up from his guardian's shoulder and managed a small wave. The coachman's expression collapsed with relief. A constable of the city was puffing up to them as William opened the carriage door and Graves carried the child inside, cradling his head.

'Hold hard! What's the meaning of all this?' the constable managed to say between gasps.

Graves looked at him as if from very far away and made no reply. Instead, he settled himself in the plush interior of the carriage, Eustache still held on his knee, then addressed his servants. 'David, Berkeley Square as quick as you might. William, would you be able to go back to the bookshop and tell them?' William nodded, and Graves put out his hand through the window. 'Thank you, Mr Geddings.'

William shook it and as they released each other the coach pulled smartly away. The constable put his hand on William's arm. 'What's happening?'

William spoke loudly enough for the curious slowing their steps to hear him. 'Dr Fischer tried to murder a child. You may look for us in Berkeley Square if you have need of us.' Then he turned and walked back in the direction of the Cathedral.

VII.7

HARRIET, TOBIAS CHRISTOPHER AND Crowther all arrived at Hinckley's Booksellers shortly after William had returned. Instead of enjoying a quiet conversation with Mr Glass, they found themselves surrounded by the family from Berkeley Square. The children had been badly frightened by what William had told them of Fischer's attack on

Eustache. Stephen ran to his mother when he came in and clung to her hand with an urgency she recalled from his early childhood. Lord Sussex had found a seat next to William, and looked as if he would hide under the footman's livery if he could. Susan was sitting very straight, but she was pale to her lips and held Mrs Service's hand in her own. They looked all, absurdly young.

William and Mrs Service explained to the rest what had happened. The employees of the bookshop had been joined by three other gentlemen Harriet had never met: a rather bedraggled young man called Walter Sharp, a butcher whom Crowther called Scudder and a miserable-looking constable by the name of Miller. They explained that Glass could still not be found, and that they feared for him.

Into the terrible quiet, Mrs Service said at last: 'Harriet, Mr Crowther, I shall take the children home if William will fetch us a cab. I must help Graves with Eustache.' Her voice broke slightly. 'Lord, that I took them to his church! The world is too wicked.'

'Harriet,' Susan said, 'did Dr Fischer kill the bookshop lady? Mrs Smith?'

Mrs Westerman shook her head. 'I think not, my darling. Mrs Trimnell did so, I believe, when she tried to recover the manuscript. Fischer burned it only this morning? Oh, Lord.'

Crowther put out his hand and smoothed Stephen's hair. 'We discovered Sawbridge paid for the attack on Mr Trimnell, but we found him dead this morning. We know Sir Charles went with Drax to tell Mrs Trimnell and Sawbridge that he was severing his ties with them yesterday evening. Some news of what had happened in the bookshop must have reached them. Mrs Westerman suspects that Sawbridge was desperate for their protection for himself and his daughter, and so threatened Drax or Sir Charles in some way and that threat got him killed. Now Mrs Trimnell is missing. She was not at Sir Charles Jennings's home, nor at her lodgings.'

Christopher rolled his shoulders. 'Perhaps we should go and pay a visit to Drax. I have heard rumours of how he made his money. Let me go and I shall take the ghosts of some of my murdered brothers with me. He will tell you quickly enough what happened in that room yesterday evening.'

'I have no doubt of that, Mr Christopher,' Harriet said, 'but would we find him at home? If he or Sir Charles killed Sawbridge, they will be hunting Mrs Trimnell now.'

Walter was leaning on the counter, his hands in his hair. 'Drax? Sawbridge? Mrs Trimnell? I have never heard of these people! If they did for Eliza Smith, then I hope their wicked carcasses rot in hell. Where will you look for this woman?'

Harriet sighed. 'We do not know where to begin. I think Mrs Trimnell is in fear of her life, but I do not know where she would go for sanctuary.'

It was Scudder who noticed the looks passing between the children. 'There is some knowledge here we do not have. What do you know, young ones?'

'It's a secret,' Susan said so quietly they could hardly hear her. 'Eustache's secret, and there will be terrible trouble if we say—'

Harriet rounded on her. 'Susan, for God's sake, enough! The time for secrets is long gone.' Susan was shocked into silence. It was Lord Sussex who spoke, indistinctly, from William's lapels.

'Dauda,' he said. 'Dauda has a house to the north.'

William put a finger under Jonathan's chin and lifted it gently till they were looking each other in the eye. 'What do you say, My Lord?'

'Sawbridge had a daughter with one of his slaves. She was very pretty and Sir Charles fell in love with her.'

Stephen tugged on his mother's hand. 'When he came back to England he could not leave her, so he bought her a house near London.'

'He made it all very beautiful and she lives there by herself and Sir Charles visits her,' Susan said. 'She has one maid and a blind cook and when the local girls come in to do the rough work she has to stay in her room because she is such a secret. Mr Sawbridge used to write and tell his other daughter Mrs Trimnell about it, and she'd get very jealous. Mr Trimnell read the letters and wrote it down.' Susan wiped her eyes. 'Might she go there? They are sisters, after all.'

'How do you know these things?' Harriet asked.

'The manuscript. Eustache was trying to copy it out last night and we helped him,' she said.

Stephen let out an exhausted sigh. 'We didn't manage to finish it all. We left out all the God business.'

'You copied it?' Harriet said. 'The four of you?' She took a tighter hold of her son. 'Dear God, what have you read?'

'It was horrible,' Susan said. 'And everyone knows it happens really, and we wander around pretending we don't. Eustache didn't want the names to be lost and we thought he was right.'

Harriet looked round at them all; she felt horrified and diminished by what they might have learned, and sore at the thought of Eustache hurt in Berkeley Square. All to save those names. She wished they didn't know. They had already seen too much, this odd collection of children, while so many others in their privileged position glided from golden cage to golden cage, knowing neither that the cages existed, nor the blood cost of their building.

'Mr Glass is there too,' Miller said with sudden conviction into the silence.

Crowther looked at him with interest. 'Constable Miller?'

The man puffed out his cheeks as he collected his thoughts. 'I got some conversation out of a certain cabman. He took a fare, who I'm thinking was this Sawbridge, up to a place near Devil's Lane. That's north. Now you say Mrs Trimnell killed Eliza Smith, and I'll take that on your say-so – but she didn't carry a fit young lass like Penny out of the shop over her shoulder. I think Mr Sawbridge went to clear up after his daughter. He hits Penny over the head with a bottle and then needs to get rid of her. Now I spent half a day walking round up there, and it's lonely true enough, but not such a great place to bury a girl on an evening. There's not enough by way of cover when you're doing your digging. Hornsey Wood, then, you might think. True, it's quieter, but there are always folks up at Copt Hall and they'd notice something going on. But if I knew a friendly house out there with a bit of garden, it'd make sense to go there and borrow a shovel. Especially if I knew there were no servants to speak of in the place. I reckon Sawbridge went and covered up the murder done by one daughter by burying Penny in the garden of his other girl. I'd swear to it.' The constable thought a moment then looked disappointed again. 'Though if Mr Glass and the dogs *had* found a grave there, I don't know why he'd still be standing over it weeping. He's no fighting man, but I doubt a maid and her mistress could prevent him coming back to tell us what he'd discovered.'

'Perhaps your Penny is still alive,' Tobias said. He had been standing listening to them all, his arms crossed over his chest. 'Alive but hurt, so Mr Glass can't just take her away over his shoulder.'

Walter brightened. 'Yes – he'd have to stay and guard her, hope that Constable Miller here had forced the address from the driver and that we'd come after him.'

'Go and find out,' Harriet said immediately.

'Too bloody right we will! Come on, those that will,' Scudder said. 'I know a fella will give us good horses off Smithfields.' He reached for his coat, then he paused. 'Any of you fighting men? I've got a good bit of strength in my arm, but it seems like there's a parcel of murdering dogs on the loose and I'd as lief have a fellow with us who knows how to handle a gun.' Tobias stood up to his full height. Scudder looked him up and down. 'You'll do.'

318

'Mr Crowther?' Christopher said, turning towards him. Crowther reluctantly shook his head. 'I will not be able to keep pace with you until my ribs heal.'

'You must finish it, Mr Christopher, please,' Harriet said, still holding her son's hand tightly.

He bowed. 'But there is something wrong here, my friends. Dauda is not a woman's name. It is a man's.'

Susan looked confused. 'Trimnell says "she", and "daughter", and "girl" in the papers he wrote. He calls her "Sir Charles's creature".'

William was firm. 'Mr Christopher is right. It is a man's name, never a woman's.'

Harriet and Crowther looked at each other over the children's heads, and Harriet suddenly understood why Sawbridge's throat was cut with such a violent blow.

VII.8

'DAUDA! ONLY GIVE ME enough money to get away and I shall leave at once, I swear it, and I shall never say your name or Sir Charles's ever again!'

Francis was sitting under the window with his back to the wall and wiping his face clean with his handkerchief. He felt as if he would never run out of tears. The woman in black on the terrace below had said enough. Eliza had been killed because she thought the English should know what slavery was, and some madman had put a manuscript in her hands that told the truth of it. He could not help wondering whether, if she had not known him, loved him, even, perhaps she would have cared less about the sufferings of the Africans. Perhaps if he had never insinuated himself into the life of the family on Norfolk Street, she would have handed back the manuscript and gone on with her life, her useful, good life that had always seemed to him so surrounded in blessings. Even as he thought it, he told himself he was wrong. It did not need him to make Eliza feel for those slaves. She would have fought for that manuscript even if she had never had a conversation with a man or woman of his colour. She had been a brave heart, a kind heart.

'I have no money, Lucinda!' Dauda's voice had a harsh edge to it. 'What do you think my life is? If I had been given ready money, do you think I would have *stayed* here?'

From the bed there came a groan. Francis approached and Penny's eyes fluttered open. He took the glass from the table and gave her water. She drank a little then groaned again. 'Mr Glass? Oh, I feel so ill. Where are we, sir?'

He put his hand to her forehead and she closed her eyes again. 'Do not worry, Penny', he murmured. 'Sleep on a little. And if you hear anything strange, stay quiet. Help is coming.' She would live, surely now she would live. Suddenly he heard the sound of a carriage approaching. Penny's breathing slowed to an even pace again. He ran to the window on the landing and looked out. It was not Walter, nor Miller, nor any other friend arriving. He went to the table between the armchairs and began loading the guns.

They had heard the carriage downstairs as well. There was a scream and the sound of footsteps on the stairs. Francis picked up one of the pistols. The door flew open and the woman in black collapsed into the room.

She was out of her mind with fear. With a lurch Francis remembered the face of a runaway slave he had seen paraded through the town square in the moments after he had been recaptured, the way his eyes seemed to roll in his head. The woman flung herself into the corner of the room, breathing hard.

'Don't let him kill me. Please.' Francis did not answer her but rested the barrel of the gun on his left forearm, his right hand on the trigger, and turned towards the door. It opened again only a moment later and Sir Charles Jennings appeared on the threshold. He looked just as he had outside the Jamaica Coffee House, a man of quiet good taste and confidence. Mrs Trimnell screamed and covered her face. Dauda came in calmly behind Sir Charles and crossed the room to sit on the edge of Penny's bed. Francis noticed him put one hand on the girl's flank as if to calm her and keep her quiet.

Sir Charles saw Lucinda panting in the corner of the room and nodded as if pleased. Then he looked at Francis and smiled pleasantly enough.

'Good morning, young man. And who might you be?'

Francis kept the gun raised. 'My name is Adisa Enitan. This woman killed Miss Eliza Smith, who was the person I loved best in the world.' He heard a whimper of fear from the corner, but did not look round.

'No need to point that pistol at me then, Adisa, my friend,' Sir Charles said with a smile. He sat down in the armchair nearest to him and crossed his legs. Francis moved away slightly, keeping the gun pointed in his direction. Behind him he heard Dauda move from the bed to the other armchair.

'Let me go, Sir Charles,' the woman whispered from the corner. 'I swear I will say nothing. You will never hear from me again. I swear it.'

Sir Charles did not look at her. 'Ah, Lucinda. I intend never to hear from you again. But why should I risk my peace, the peace that exists between Dauda and myself, even for a moment?' He smiled at the young man and kissed his fingertips towards him. 'I trust my knife a great deal more than I trust you, dear, jealous whore that you are. Now, Adisa, the woman cowering in the corner does not deserve to live. On this we agree. So she shall die. She will be punished properly for her sins and be forgotten. You may return to your life with my gratitude, knowing that your Eliza Smith is revenged.'

Francis shifted his grip. 'It is not your right to judge and punish in *this* country, Jennings. That woman will be tried and judged according to the law.'

Sir Charles's smile tightened. 'Come now, my boy. You must realise that is not going to happen.'

'Leave, Jennings.'

The man frowned and got up slowly from his chair. 'Dauda, you are very quiet. Will you not help me persuade your visitor?'

'He killed our father, Dauda!' Mrs Trimnell burst out. 'I watched him slit our father's throat because he asked for his help. After all the years our family have served him!'

Sir Charles looked at her. 'You scheming, vile little whore. If you weren't so destructive, you'd be amusing. You have a feeble prettiness and a feeble mind, and you could never understand why Dauda should have all this while you deserved nothing more than Trimnell and Cheapside.'

He looked back towards Francis and stood up, took a step forward.

Francis edged away slightly. 'Leave here, Jennings.'

'Come, Adisa, enough of this. Give me the gun, boy.' He took a straight-edged razor from his pocket and opened it, never taking his eyes off Francis.

Mrs Trimnell made a run for the door behind him. Sir Charles span round and grabbed at her arm with one hand, the other holding the knife raised in the air. Francis pulled the trigger. The gun clicked but there was no explosion. He stepped forward, thinking he might at least strike Jennings before he managed to use his blade on the woman and there was an explosion behind him. The sound was deafening in the small room. Francis felt as if his head would burst. He clapped his hands to his ears and choked on the smoke of the gunpowder. He heard Mrs Trimnell scream, but if it was from pain or fear he could not say. His own gun fell to the floor and he rubbed his streaming eyes. Mrs Trimnell was gone, the door to the stairs open. In front of him, Sir

Charles was lying against the wall, his hand pressed to his side. A red bloom was beginning to show, seeping through the pale fabric of his waistcoat. His face was dead white, and he was staring past Francis at where Dauda was standing, the smoking gun still in his hand. While Francis watched, Dauda lowered the gun and placed it gently on the table. 'Now I have peace,' he said.

They arrived while the smoke was still clearing. Walter was sent to fetch a surgeon, while Constable Miller went in pursuit of Mrs Trimnell. Scudder took Francis's place guarding Penny, and Tobias Christopher stood in an elegant drawing room on the ground floor, his shoulders hunched and a glass of excellent brandy in his hand. He had not yet emptied it when Francis joined him. His shirt and waistcoat were badly stained with blood from when he had tried to staunch the bleeding in Sir Charles's side while waiting for his rescuers, and Dauda had watched without moving from the armchair, immaculate as ever.

'Well?'

'The surgeon is hopeful Sir Charles will live. Walter assists him.' Francis threw himself into one of the chairs, not caring how he spread the blood spilled around the place. Tobias filled a second glass and gave it to him.

'My name is Tobias Christopher. Your name and business here I know.'

Francis nodded and drank. 'I'm glad to meet you, Mr Christopher. Dauda is packing a bag. I have given him what ready money I have, but how far it will get him I do not know. He makes for France.'

Tobias frowned. 'For his sake I hope he gets there. If they do not hang him for shooting Jennings, they will find a way to kill him for . . .' He gestured around the room.

'Sodomy?' Francis said. 'Yes, well, this is England. Sir Charles could be Lord Mayor with everyone knowing he was complicit in the deaths of thousands of men, women and children, but that he might be thought

323

a sodomite? Of course, he had to murder one of his oldest servants to keep that a secret.'

The corner of Tobias's mouth twitched. 'You have a fine turn of phrase, Mr Glass. I think perhaps you have a touch of Igbo blood.' He refilled his glass and offered the decanter to Francis, and on getting his nod refilled his as well. 'So what does little Dauda plan to do if he reaches France?'

Francis nodded towards the harpsichord. 'He is a musician and had nothing to do here but practise. I think that is how he means to earn his money.'

Tobias took out his wallet and from it drew an impressive number of banknotes. He handed them to Francis. 'Give the boy that. It should carry him to Paris and on a bit if he is careful.' Francis took them, amazed, and Tobias caught his look. 'Ever since I could afford to do so I have carried my purchase price with me at all times. It has been one of my several precautions against being retaken. As well as lawyers. And learning to fight well enough to take on a shipload of traders.' Francis laughed into his drink. 'I only received my manu-mission a week ago, Mr Glass. I am still not used to being a free British man.'

'Were you baptised also?' Francis said with a grin.

Tobias opened his eyes wide. 'Yes – a week after I arrived, may my fathers forgive me! I handed that crow priest money I needed for bread for his trouble, and it was a year before I was told it was no help before the law.' Francis had begun to laugh again, and this time he could not stop. Christopher did not seem to mind; he spread his arms open wide. 'The Christians have some fine poetry, I shall give them that. I make great use of it when I am talking to the whites. When I am too old to fight I shall become a preacher and roar them into righteousness. I was born to be evangelical!'

He began to laugh himself and the two men were both still in the throes of it when Miller came in. The constable looked between them with a nervous smile.

'Miller, my friend!' Tobias said, pointing at the decanter. 'Come have a drink with us. Justice and liberty! You found the wench?'

The man took the drink that was offered. 'I did. She hadn't got far. I could almost have pitied her and there's the truth said.' He drained his glass then looked at the empty vessel with sudden appreciation. 'She's in the watch-house in Islington, and the constable there will take her to the Guildhall in the morning.' He looked suddenly confused. 'Do you think I should arrest Sir Charles?'

For some reason this made them all laugh again. They could not stop, even when Walter and Scudder came to complain. The newcomers were given their share of the brandy, and were soon adding to the noise.

VII.9

MRS WESTERMAN AND MR Crowther arrived at the house of Dr Drax too late. His housekeeper opened the door to them in tears. She had woken that morning a contented woman whose greatest problem in life was the fact that her master's pet monkey had a dislike of her and a talent for finding ways of showing it. Now, before she had even had her bit of dinner, she was without a position, and her only remaining duties were packing up the rest of her master's goods. Harriet was sympathetic and within a few minutes they were seated in Drax's office.

'I woke up this morning to find him packing his things,' she said wetly. 'And all day there have been his patients coming to see him, some of them important personages too, and they become angry with me when I say he's not here! Means more to me than it does to them.' She wiped her nose. 'He left me wages for the quarter and said he'd write and tell me what to do with all his books, but after three years' service to say no more – and I swear that bloody little monkey was laughing at me all the while. Forgive my language, but it is upsetting.'

'Naturally it is,' Harriet said, and patted the woman's knee. 'And he really said nothing else, left nothing else behind him?'

She sniffed again. 'Only one thing, but it made no sense to me. He said if a red-headed female and a man who looked like a priest were to come calling, I was to show them the waistcoat he went out wearing last night.' She frowned and looked between them. 'I shall just fetch it.'

She was back in a moment, walking into the study and holding the garment high. 'I don't understand. It's very dirty.' She turned it so they could see the front of it: a pattern of yellow and pale blue stripes, and across in, from left to right, a falling spray of blood. Crowther stood up and took it from her.

'A confession that he was there at Sawbridge's murder – and a declaration of innocence all at once,' Harriet said.

'Indeed, Mrs Westerman.'

The surgeon insisted on keeping both Penny and Sir Charles where they were until he was sure they were out of danger. Mr Christopher and Scudder both chose to remain on the premises while Francis, Walter and Miller were sent back to London. Francis was given notes for both the Scudder and Christopher households and an address in Berkeley Square. The notes he trusted to Cutter for delivery, who flung his arms around him when he finally entered the shop in the late afternoon like a father greeting a lost child. Joshua too clung to him, and as he told them what had happened, and in turn heard about Eustache and the manuscript, Ferguson the compositor was sufficiently moved to reach over and shake his hand several times.

When they had all convinced themselves that their friends had survived without serious harm, Francis returned to his lodgings to wash and change his clothes. His landlady shrieked when she saw him, but at least he knew, having told her the story, that everyone else within a mile would have heard it by the morning. He then went to the address in Berkeley Square he had been given to tell his story once more. When he was done, he could hardly find the energy to move, and Graves insisted that he would return to his lodgings in the family coach. Francis accepted the offer, thinking it was somehow fitting that he had spent one evening of that week sleeping on the floor of a grocer's kitchen and another having the hospitality of an Earl pressed upon him. Before the carriage was ordered, however, he asked if he might make another visit in the house.

William took him upstairs to visit Eustache. The boy was looking pale, but he grinned when he saw Francis arrive. The girl who had come to the shop with him that first morning was sitting by his bed, a book in her hand.

'It makes me a bit sick to read, Mr Glass,' Eustache said. 'So Susan is reading to me. She's the best at doing voices. Did you find the maid?'

'Yes, and I think she might recover yet. Mr Scudder, the butcher, and Mr Christopher are guarding her as if she was one of their own. Sir Charles was shot, though he lives, but please ask me no more. My tongue is thick with the tale and I am sure Mrs Westerman and Mr Crowther will explain the rest in the morning.'

'But Mrs Trimnell, sir?' Susan asked.

'Constable Miller took her up and saw her secured in the watch-house.'

Eustache sighed. 'You sound as if you were sorry for her.'

'I cannot help but pity anyone who is hunted, Eustache. No matter what they have done.'

'I do not pity Dr Fischer. I wish he would hang.'

Francis shook his head slightly, but said nothing.

Susan marked her place in the book and set it down. 'Would you like to see our copy of the manuscript, Mr Glass?' She looked down at the counterpane and spoke sadly. 'Graves has explained to us that it cannot be published or used in evidence or anything, because there is nothing to say we did not make it up, but you know we didn't.'

'I would like to see it very much.'

She went into the next room to fetch it, and when she returned there were two other boys with her of about Eustache's age. Francis guessed who they were, but it did not seem an occasion for formal introductions. Susan put the pages into his hands and he began to look through them while the children watched him. There was something unbearable about seeing the horrors recorded in the handwriting of children of their age.

The darker of the two boys said sadly, 'And it was all a waste of time.'

'You knew about Dauda and where he lived,' Francis said mildly. 'The help you sent was very gratefully received, I assure you.'

Trimnell's confession was very thorough. Francis began to feel his mouth go dry as he read. The corruption of it, the hours worked and the punishments handed out.

'And saving this is not wasted, children,' he told them. 'I do not care what the law says. I don't think any person living could read this and not recognise it as the truth. You have saved it. If you do nothing good for the rest of your lives, you can always be proud of this, and you have my deepest gratitude.'

The boys looked both pleased and embarrassed. The girl actually leaned over Eustache and kissed Francis on the cheek before blushing and sitting back down again.

'But how can they know it's the truth if they don't read it?' the dark boy said. He had a definite look of Mrs Westerman about him. 'Everyone should know. Then people can't pretend any more.'

Francis found himself frowning. The thought of Mrs Westerman's red hair had reminded him of something.

'There might be a way. Would you trust me with this, my friends?'
It seemed they trusted him completely.

There was a knock at the door and Graves looked up to see Jonathan hesitating on the threshold. He pushed the papers away from him.

'You should be in bed, Jonathan. But I suppose we can be a little lax this evening.'

His ward nodded then walked stiffly over to the settee and sat on its edge so his feet would touch the ground. Graves watched him, not knowing if he should be concerned or amused. 'What can I do for you, Jon?'

'My grandfather had slaves, didn't he? You freed them and sold the estate.'

'That's right. In the winter of 'eighty-one.'

'It's not enough.'

Graves felt the old ache of it. 'I could not arrange to farm the land with free labour, Jon, my dear. I tried . . .'

But the boy was shaking his head. 'No, not that – I know that. I mean we kept the money, didn't we? The money from the sale and all the profit made from the place for years and years and years. We kept that, didn't we?' Graves nodded. 'Stephen was doing calculations with his mother about William – what he should have got and what was owed to him. Really owed to him from when Captain Westerman owned him.'

Graves ran a hand through his hair. 'Jonathan, I'm not sure it would be possible to find those former slaves again. We did make provision for them when they were freed, I assure you, but to trace them . . .'

'I know you did all that, Graves, and I'm glad. But we've been talking about it since Mr Glass left. Not Anne because she only cares about balloons, but the rest of us. We could work out the profit we got from the plantation while my grandfather was alive, couldn't we? And the interest earned. And then we could give the money to people who hate slavery so they can print pamphlets and books and write petitions tell *everyone*. Mr Christopher could tell us what to do, whom to give it to.'

Graves considered. Certainly a national campaign against slavery would need funds from somewhere. 'I'm sure he could. Jonathan, you do understand it is likely to be quite a large sum of money? Lord knows, you have enough – but I must know you understand what you are asking, and that this is truly what you want. And there will be questions asked: if you have been unduly influenced by myself. You might have to explain to any number of lawyers your reasons and beliefs.'

'But it can be done?'

'Certainly it can, if it is your wish.'

'It is what I want done. I can tell any lawyer what I think.'

'Then we shall speak of it again in the morning and I shall set some of your bankers to work.'

'Thank you.' The boy got to his feet and walked to the door, his hands still deep in his pockets.

'Good night, Sussex,' Graves said as he went. He did not realise what he was saying until it was spoken, and then he looked up at the boy a little amazed. Jonathan was smiling at him shyly.

'Good night, Graves.'

The taproom at the White Rose was densely crowded. It took some time before Francis could find someone who would show him where Mr Clarkson's room was. Eventually a sulking waiter in a torn apron showed him to the upper storey and a rather cramped room under the eaves. The immensely tall, red-headed young man was folded over his small desk writing. Around him, a dozen volumes lay open and there were a number of sheets of paper drifting round the bare floorboards.

'Mr Clarkson?'

The redhead almost jumped out of his skin. He turned and for a moment Francis was afraid that he was not recognised. 'Francis Glass, from Hinckley's Bookshop,' he said.

The redhead wiped his face with slightly shaking hands. 'Of course, forgive me. I have hardly slept this week.' He struggled to his feet. 'I am so glad you have come. What I have learned even in these past days, every hour some fresh horror . . . Might you be willing to tell me of your experiences?'

Francis shook his head. 'No, Mr Clarkson. I would rather tell my own story. But take this.' He handed him the trade card of Christopher's Academy. 'Tobias Christopher has a story to tell you that you should hear before you leave London. And there are other Africans in London he knows who will be willing to talk to you, with his blessing. I will write to him and tell him you come at my suggestion and with my approval.'

'Thank you,' Clarkson said, staring at the card as if it were a winning ticket in the lottery. 'Thank you indeed!'

'That is not all I have for you.' He put the portfolio into his hands and took a seat on the end of Mr Clarkson's rather rickety bed. Clarkson looked at him, surprised. Then he sat back down at the table and began to read. After a few minutes he looked up. 'Did a child write this?'

'A man wrote it; four children copied it out to save it from the fire.' He told him as briefly as he could, the story of Mrs Smith and the manuscript. Clarkson offered his condolences sincerely, but Francis noticed even as he did so that he continued to read the pages in front of him. His eyes were wide and he was already looking a little sick. Francis watched him read, feeling himself at a great distance from the shadowed room. At last Clarkson looked up.

'*Can* such things indeed be true?' There were tears in his eyes.

Francis stood, shrugged off his coat, unbuttoned his waistcoat and then lifted it and his shirt over his head and set them down on the bed and waited. Clarkson was staring at the brand on his chest just below his collarbone.

'They say,' he swallowed. 'They say the branding does not hurt and the Africans do the same to their own people with hot knives.'

'It does hurt, Mr Clarkson. A great deal. And yes, there are villages where the headmen are scarred on the face. It is a sign of standing among our people. Not the same, I think you'll agree.'

'I do.'

Then Francis turned his back to the young man and heard Clarkson's gasp. He stared deep into the shadows clustering in the corners of the modest room. He knew the picture of suffering his back showed, the scar tissue from a hundred beatings crossed into an ugly mass in the middle of his spine. The pale snaking twitching ghosts of pain and humiliation that he would carry with him always. He counted to fifty under his breath, trying not to rush the count, then picked up his clothing from the bed and covered himself again with his clean shirt, his pressed waistcoat, shrugged on his broadcloth coat with pewter buttons and smoothed down the wide sleeves before turning back. Clarkson's face was drawn and paler than mist on the river. He did not speak for a while, but Francis saw his lips were moving and realised the man was praying.

Clarkson was in a pool of candlelight, the children's manuscript held tightly in his hands, his eyes fixed on the floor.

'Forgive us,' he said at last. His voice a whisper.

'Earn our forgiveness,' Francis replied, and picked up his hat and cloak. Clarkson only nodded and Francis left him there, going down the stairs into the throng and the jostle of the coaching yard. Into the noise and stench of London, its comings and goings, its sharp laughter and clink of coins.

EPILOGUE

T HE ADJOURNED CORONER'S INQUEST into Mrs Smith's death
found she had been murdered by Mrs Lucinda Trimnell; the
papers were passed to the quarterly sessions at the Old Bailey. George
Smith arrived in London on the same day and buried his sister two days
later. Her funeral was attended by a large crowd, and most of the book-
and print-sellers in that part of town lowered their shutters early so that
the owners, the authors, the printers, the artists and engravers, the appren-
tices, book-binders and ink-makers could follow her coffin. Francis
walked behind George with Penny, pale but determined, leaning on his
arm and Scudder, Walter and Miller just behind them.

Sir Charles Jennings disappeared from the house near Hornsey the
same day. Rumours that he had killed his old overseer and had kept a
young mulatto boy as a lover flew around the city and were repeated in
whispers at every fashionable party for the rest of the season.

The coroner's inquest into Sawbridge's death was held late one
evening in an out-of-the-way tavern in one of the smaller yards of the
city. Mrs Trimnell was not called as a witness, since the fact that
she was awaiting trial for murder herself rendered any evidence she
gave as highly suspect. The servants at the Jamaica Coffee House had
all developed holes in their memory, and Mr Crowther was not called to
attend. In fact, the first he knew of the hearing was that it had taken
place and found that Sawbridge had committed suicide. Crowther

protested – and his protests were met with silence. In revenge, he wrote an additional chapter for his book about the possibility of corruption in the Coroner's Courts. His book was well-received, and the evening he spent watching Harriet read it was one of the happiest he had spent in many years.

After negotiating very politely with Graves and Mrs Service, Susan agreed to go to a school that had been recommended by Mrs Smith. There was still an amount of what Susan thought of as nonsense to be learned, but the ladies were also taught geography, some mathematics and languages. When Susan learned the amount that had been written on music in German, she took to it with some enthusiasm. She also, at her request, received private lessons in composition with M. Pieltain, and took her compositions with her when she visited her musical friends in Soho and elsewhere. They were admired, and she took increasing pains with her work. Harriet and Graves decided on Westminster for Jonathan and Stephen. Eustache said he preferred to be educated at home, and Graves remarked that finding tutors clever enough for him would drain Jonathan's fortune entirely. Eustache laughed. Harriet took the time to speak to him at length about his mother and all she knew about her. Mrs Graves's pregnancy continued well, and Harriet wrote a firm but loving letter to her sister. Mr Babington's sister did not call again.

George Smith stayed in London for some days after his sister's funeral. There was business he had to do both with Eliza's estate and his own. He made a careful tour of all the newspaper proprietors and gave them to understand that while he understood the need for some discretion, any man who wrote slightingly of his sister, of Mr Francis Glass, or of any members of, or friends of a certain family in Berkeley Square, would find the costs of their paper rise considerably. Mostly, however, he remained in London to be with his friend Francis, and they talked to their hearts' content of Eliza, of their childhood and the house on Norfolk Street, and both took comfort in their conversation.

Shortly before George was due to return home, the two men came back to the shop from their dinner to find a print laid out in the middle of the counter. It showed a number of cartoonish Negroes dressed in satirical exaggerations of the current fashions. Francis looked out of his door in time to see the clerk from Humphrey's gallery peering in from the street and grinning. George clenched his fists but Francis shook his head.

'This is mine, George,' he said, picked up the print and walked out of the door. Alarmed, the clerk scuttled back into his own workplace. Francis followed him inside and round the counter, then grabbed the man's collar, almost lifting him off his feet. With his free hand he crumpled the print into a ball and forced it in between the man's lips.

'Never again, boy,' he said while the man struggled, then dropped him, dusted his hands and left the shop. The clerk waited till he was gone and then spat out the damp paper and whined a complaint to his employer, who had been calmly watching the whole episode from the door to the back office.

Mrs Humphrey sniffed and rubbed at an ink-stain on her fingers until the clerk had worked himself to a pitch of indignation that made him sound like a kettle boiling. 'Oh, shut your bone box,' she said at last. 'Glass should have done that years ago.' Then she turned her back on him.

The Reverend Dr Fischer's prosecution for assault was almost missed. He was fined five pounds. After consulting with the Bishop of London he found he no longer wished for the responsibilities of a large parish in the city and retired to the country. A month later he wrote to Eustache, apologising with apparent sincerity for his moment of madness and fear. He declared his intention of making a full confession of his own role in the slave trade and closed with a request that he might live in hopes of Eustache's forgiveness. Gritting his teeth, Eustache said he would wait until he had read the damned book. Graves did not scold him for swearing and sent Fischer a tightly worded note saying approximately the same thing.

Bounder and Creech were both found guilty of the manslaughter of Mr Trimnell, fined a pound each and discharged. The trial of Mrs Trimnell for murder was reported in the newspapers, but the references to it were brief and factual. She confessed to the crime of killing Mrs Smith and stated that she had at once gone to the Jamaica Coffee House and told her father what she had done. He had returned to Mrs Smith's premises, set the fire and carried off the maid. Penny gave her evidence clearly and calmly and left the court between Mr and Mrs Scudder. Mrs Trimnell's claims that Sir Charles Jennings had murdered her father by cutting his throat and made an attempt on her own life were not reported by the gentlemen of the press, nor did they appear in any of the official records. Her hanging was the usual London carnival.

Neither Mrs Westerman nor Crowther attended, but at about the hour it was due to take place they found themselves together with Mr Palmer in Christopher's Academy in Soho Square. They drank tea with Mrs Christopher and the children. Harriet discussed female education with Sally and Mrs Christopher, and took a note of the school Miss Christopher was attending, thinking of Anne's future. The gentlemen discussed different philosophies of fighting with a short sword, and Trimnell's name was not spoken. Mr Palmer did say, however, that he had heard from a reliable source that Sir Charles was living under an assumed name in Rome, and Drax had taken a position as Court Physician to the Margrave of Baden. He had also heard from the same source that a young mulatto singer and harpsichord player had made an impressive debut in Paris.

Theft of Life

On the same day that Mrs Trimnell was hanged, Thomas Clarkson read his prize-winning essay to an audience of dignitaries in the Senate House of Cambridge University. His future in the Church assured, he rode back to London, but on the way his mind could not cease turning over the essay in his mind – what he had read, heard and written. He got off his horse and began to walk, trying to persuade himself that it could not really be true, or even if it was, it was not really his concern. Coming in sight of Wades Mill in Hertfordshire, he sat disconsolate on the turf by the roadside, holding his horse's reins. The thought came into his mind that, if the contents of the essay *were* true, it was time some person put an end to these horrors. There by the roadside, and with only his horse for witness, he decided it might as well be him.

Francis also found he had no wish to see the hanging. Instead, he spent the morning finishing a project he had begun the day he had forced the clerk at Humphrey's to eat the print. He wrote *finis* with a feeling of relief more than happiness, then carried the pages upstairs to where Mr Ferguson was waiting. The older man examined the first few sheets and nodded. 'All that singing black folks do – means something then, does it?'

'It's how we record our history, Mr Ferguson.'

'Is it now? *Is* it now? Well, how many are you thinking?' he said.

'Two hundred?' Francis replied.

Ferguson shook his heavy head. 'No, lad. Five hundred for something new like this, and if we don't sell them all in two months, you can dock the paper costs from my wages.'

'Perhaps I will.'

Ferguson held the page up. '*The Life of Adisa Enitan, the African, also known as Francis Glass, by himself. Including the story of his kidnapping from his native land, his sufferings as a slave and trial as a child at the Old Bailey, with an account of the many cruelties and kindnesses he met with in Christian lands leading to his freedom, with his thoughts on slavery and an appeal to all good English men and women for its immediate abolition.* Oh, those are good words. Five hundred, no doubt.' He turned away from the page. 'Joshua! Up here, my lad! There's work to be done.'

'Thank you, Mr Ferguson.'

'My pleasure, Mr Glass.'

As he walked away, Francis could already hear the type rattling into place.

HISTORICAL NOTE

The history of British involvement in slavery and the slave trade is complex, contradictory, evolving and unsettling. Much of the prosperity this country has enjoyed over the last two hundred years was built on human misery and suffering on an almost unimaginable scale. Our institutions, our monuments and our culture are all stained and coloured by slavery, and it's not talked about enough.

The transatlantic slave trade was outlawed in 1807 after massive public pressure, and slavery was finally abolished in 1833. At that point, £20 million in compensation was paid out by the British Government – not to the slaves but to the slave-owners. You can see where this money went and find a great deal more information at the Legacies of British Slave-ownership site at *http://www.ucl.ac.uk/lbs/* which was launched during the writing of this book.

For a general history of the Abolition movement in Britain I'd recommend *Bury the Chains: the British Struggle to Abolish Slavery* by Adam Hochschild, and for an account of the British in the West Indies *The Sugar Barons* by Matthew Parker. For more about the lives of black people in Britain, as well as Peter Fryer's book *Staying Power*, I'd recommend Florian Shyllon's *Black People in Britain 1555–1833*. The book I would most like everyone to read though is *The Interesting Narrative of the Life of Olaudah Equiano*, also known as Gustavus Vassa. It was published in 1789. The Penguin Classics edition has an excellent introduction and notes from Vincent Carretta.

Thomas Clarkson (1760–1846) did indeed write an essay against slavery for the Cambridge Latin Prize in 1785 and included in it testimony from unpublished manuscripts and extracts of the poetry of Phillis Wheatley. After winning the prize, he dedicated the rest of his life to fighting slavery, and records the moment of his revelation on the road in Hertfordshire in his memoirs. I've drawn very heavily on his account of that moment in my description of it. His essay was published in English in 1786 and was instrumental in turning the public mood against slavery. You can read it online. The story of a slave beaten to death on the quayside and thrown to the sharks comes from the English version of his essay, quoting from unpublished papers. In 1787 he formed the Society for the Abolition of the Slave Trade with the lawyer Granville Sharp, who is also mentioned in the novel, and a number of prominent Quakers. He met William Wilberforce in the same year.

Stephen Paxton and Dieudonné-Pascal Pieltain were both real composers and performers working in London in May 1785. Paxton has a cameo in *Instruments of Darkness*, the first novel in this series.

All of the other characters who appear in the book are fictional, but some are more fictional than others. Students of the period might notice some similarities between the careers of Dr Fischer and that of John Newton (1725–1807), who wrote 'Amazing Grace', among other famous hymns. Newton was a slave trader for some years then, after taking Holy Orders and preaching very successfully in Olney, he was invited to become Rector of St Mary Woolnoth in 1779. He was an evangelical, obviously a charismatic preacher, and attracted a large congregation. He did not speak out against slavery until 1788, but when he did, it was with considerable effect. I do not think he ever attacked small children to cover up his past, nor is there any evidence I have seen of active sadism on his part during his time as a trader.

The manuscript is also, like Trimnell himself, a fiction, but deeply influenced by the diary left by Thomas Thistlewood of his time in

Jamaica. The names Eustache yells at Fischer come from this document, and the stories Eustache quotes are loosely adapted from the same source. I left out the worst of it. Professor James Walvin's *The Trader, The Owner, The Slave: Parallel Lives in the Age of Slavery* is a gripping account of the lives of Newton, Thistlewood and Equiano.

Tobias Christopher owes much of his rhetoric to Quobna Ottobah Cugoano and his *Thoughts and Sentiments on the Evil of Slavery* published in 1787.

Francis Glass as he appears in this book is my own creation, though much of his story is deeply influenced by, and draws on, that of Olaudah Equiano and his *Interesting Narrative*. There is an historical Francis Glass behind the fictional one, however. Below is the complete text of a record I found on www.oldbaileyonline.org (*Old Bailey Online: The Proceedings of the Old Bailey, 1674–1913*) during my research for this novel:

Francis Glass, Theft > burglary, 7th September 1768
573. (M.) Francis Glass was indicted for that he, on the 5th of September, about the hour of two in the night, the dwelling-house of James Smith did break and enter, and stealing a silk handker-chief, value 10 d. the property of the said James.*

James Smith. I live in Norfolk-street in the Strand; the boy at the bar was servant to a gentleman named Allear, who lodged at my house. (Note, the prisoner was a Black.) It is about 12 months since the prisoner was sent to Jamaica, and he has been returned about six weeks; my servant came up to me this day se'nnight in the morning, about eight o'clock, and told me my house was broke open; I came down and found the kitchen window broke open; there was a little place where I kept some brandy and wine, that had been pulled all about the parlour, and particularly an apple-pie which the young man at the bar was very fond of; I believe he had filled his belly, but the silver spoon in the pie was there safe; I immediately called my servants, and asked them if they had seen any thing of the prisoner he having served me so some time before; I said, I fancy it is my friend Glass come again; I being about going out of town, desired them to see if they could see him; accordingly one of them found him; he was brought to me; I said to him, how came you here again; he told me a gentleman had bought him in Jamaica, and that he lived with one Dr Fisher in Cecil-street; I could not find such a gentleman; at last he confessed he lived with Dr Fisher; I wrote the doctor a letter, he came to me; the prisoner told me the doctor had threatened to whip him for pissing his bed, and that was the occasion of his running away from him; he left the silver spoon and several things of value, he only took a hand-kerchief which our people found upon him; I cannot tell where it was taken from.

Acquitted.

Old Bailey Proceedings Online (version 7.0, 20 September 2013), September 1768, trial of Francis Glass (*t17680907-69*)

I've not been able to find any further record of the real Francis Glass and I wish very much there was a way to find out what happened to him. However, in fiction – possibly in crime fiction in particular – we are allowed to make occasional attempts to save some of the innocent, and punish at least some of the guilty.

Have you read them all?

Also by Imogen Robertson,
featuring Gabriel Crowther and Harriet Westerman.

In the year 1780, Harriet Westerman, the unconventional mistress of a country house in Sussex, finds a dead man on her grounds with a ring bearing the crest of the nearby Thornleigh Hall in his pocket. With the help of a reclusive local anatomist, Gabriel Crowther, Harriet resolves to find the murderer.

London, 1781. Harriet Westerman anxiously awaits news of her husband, a ship's captain who has been gravely injured in the King's naval battles with France. As London's streets seethe with rumour, a body is dragged form the murky waters of the Thames.

Cumbria, 1783. The tomb of the first Earl of Greta should have lain undisturbed on its island of bones for three hundred years. When idle curiosity opens the stone lid, however, inside is one body too many.

Circle of Shadows

Shrove Tuesday, 1783. Beautiful Lady Martesen is murdered at a masked ball. Daniel Clode is found by her body, his wrists slit and his memories nightmarish. What has he done? Harriet Westerman and Gabriel Crowther race to the Duchy of Maulberg to save Daniel from the executioner's axe.

To find out more about Imogen Robertson
visit www.imogenrobertson.com

IMOGEN ROBERTSON

The Paris Winter

Maud Heighton came to Lafond's famous Academy to paint, and to flee the constraints of her small English town. It took all her courage to escape, but Paris eats money. While her fellow students enjoy the dazzling joys of the Belle Époque, Maud slips into poverty. Quietly starving, and dreading another cold Paris winter, Maud takes a job as companion to young, beautiful Sylvie Morel. But Sylvie has a secret: an addiction to opium. As Maud is drawn into the Morels' world of elegant luxury, their secrets become hers. Before the New Year arrives, a greater deception will plunge her into the darkness that waits beneath this glittering city of light.

Praise for *The Paris Winter* and Imogen Robertson's novels:

'*The Paris Winter* is another class altogether ... The vivid description of life in the Belle Époque ... the plausible plot, and a sensitive understanding of art and artists make this a fascinating novel that I read in a sitting and admired greatly' *Literary Review*

'Matchless storytelling, gripping and moving in equal measure. Addictive' Nicci French

'Imogen Robertson's fourth novel is a breakaway from her much-acclaimed Harriet Westerman books, and fully confirms her as a true force in historical fiction' *Daily Mail*

978 0 7553 9013 7

headline
review